Titles by K S Ferguson

River Madden series:

Touching Madness

Undercover Madness

Rafe & Kama series:

Calculated Risk

Hostile Takeover

Family Owned

The Hellhound series:

No Place Like Hell

Novella:

Puncher's Chance
(with James Grayson)

Undercover Madness

Contact the publisher: http://www.ksferguson.net

ISBN: 1-938179-21-8
ISBN-13: 978-1938179-21-1

Undercover Madness

River Madden
Book 2

K S Ferguson

Published by

K S FERGUSON

Acknowledgments

I would like to thank the many people who assisted with this novel. First, thanks to my beta readers, Winnie, Michael, Chotley, and Luke without whom it would have been a very different story. Thanks also to Luke for his sharp eyes on the copyedit pass.

I'd also like to thank my readers, without whom there'd be little point in writing. If you've enjoyed this book please consider leaving a review at the retailer or library site of your choice. Reviews are an enormous help to authors.

If you would like to be notified when the next book in the Madness series becomes available, please sign up at http://www.ksferguson.net/sign-up-for-news.html. I won't sell your contact information to anyone for any reason.

1

~~~~~

"River Madden!"

I jerked in my seat and glanced at my classmates, all five of whom stifled laughter while keeping their eyes on their electronic tablets. They'd been sniggering ever since we'd handed in our assignments, and I wasn't sure why.

It wasn't one of them shouting my name.

Professor Higgins glowered behind his monstrous wooden desk. Our desk/chair thingys sat in a semi-circle eight feet from him, all the distance the overheated cubby hole of a classroom allowed. Late afternoon autumn sun filtered through the tall windows to my right. The row of overhead fluorescent lights switched from humming a lullaby to belting out *Bad Boys*—off-key.

I ignored them. Paying attention to hallucinations was never a good idea.

Higgins' narrowed eyes stared at me from his purpled face, and his plump hands clenched a stack of papers. *Uh-oh.* My essay topped the pile. I recognized it by the bright pink stationery.

It's not a color I would have chosen for a dissertation on the Neanderthal religion, especially with the colorful dancing-flowers border at the bottom, but I didn't know who to ask for paper. So I'd used what I'd found in my desk, left by the previous occupant of my dorm room. It sucked being the new guy at Dimensional Protective Service.

From the tone of his voice and use of my full name, Higgins had called more than once. *Hell.* My schizophrenic brain had tuned him out to listen for patterns in the clicking of the heat ducts.

"Um, yes, sir?"

The digital clock on Higgins' desk chimed. *Saved by the bell.*

"Come here, Mr. Madden," Higgins rumbled.

Not saved by the bell. While my fellow talent recruits filed out, I shuffled up to Higgins' desk, feeling more like a first-grader who'd been sent to the principal's office than a twenty-five year old super-talent who'd saved the multiverse just three days earlier.

"You may think, Mr. Madden, that because you're a hero, you can be disrespectful to a lowly anthropology professor. Someday, when you're in the middle of a multi-dimensional political incident because you made some cultural faux pas, you'll wish you'd paid attention. Having a talent for fracturing dimensional barriers won't prepare you for inter-species communication."

His hand shook as he thrust my paper at me. With dawning horror, the source of my classmates' amusement became clear.

I'd used my best semi-script calligraphy to write my fifteen hundred words with a pencil stump I'd found in a drawer. I'd made sure each letter was perfect, each line arrow straight. No smears or smudges blotted the pages. Not bad for someone who'd never completed fourth grade.

I hadn't realized that while I'd perfected the writing, I'd also darkened a stroke here, a letter there, until I'd created a caricature of Higgins—complete with exaggerated fleshy jowls, bulbous nose, and little devil horns—in the text of the first page. *Aw, hell.* My stomach dropped into my shoes.

Sweat popped out on my forehead, and I cursed my schizophrenia. Sammie, the light of my life, deserved better than an unemployed homeless bum, which is what I'd been when we met. She'd changed my life, changed my goals and expectations for myself.

I wanted to be worthy of Sammie's love, wanted to be someone she'd be proud to associate with. A steady job was my first step toward a respectable future shared with her. The job offer from DPS was my salvation.

Sammie'd been so certain I'd fit in at DPS. But I had doubts, big hungry doubts that ate through any confidence I managed to muster. *Please don't let me be fired.*

"Allowing miscreants like you to represent humanity in our joint ventures with the Raptors and Neanderthals is a disgrace. You're nothing more than a jumped-up class clown. You're on report. Now get out."

I grabbed my backpack and hurried away, face burning. Better to be thought of as a deliberate troublemaker than crazy. How could I ask Sammie to share a life with me if I was the target of slurs about my mental illness and the butt of jokes caused by my unusual behavior? Sammie deserved better than to be whispered about because she dated a freak.

I jogged down the worn linoleum of the corridor to the exit, sure everyone I passed could see my shame. Outside, the chill air cooled my cheeks. Across the quad, a three-story stone building mirrored the one

I'd just left. Beyond it, the mountains rose into the twilight of the North Idaho sky.

That's where I belonged, out there in the world, not locked up here in a super-secret government facility dedicated to protecting dimensional travel from exploitation. I smothered my desire to run away and considered other options.

Dinner in the mess hall was out; I couldn't face the laughter of my fellow talent recruits. I'd head back to my room and start again on my reading assignments. I was woefully behind compared to the others, who'd been here a month or more.

As I walked, I pondered what *on report* meant. Was I confined to quarters? Was there detention? Extra chores? Not that I had any now, which seemed odd. We all had them at the orphanage.

Would DPS make me scrub bathrooms with a toothbrush? I'd heard the Army did that if you messed up. If they did, I hoped it wasn't my toothbrush. *Eww.*

As I contemplated potential punishments, the tattooed symbols that ringed both my wrists flared into intense itching. I spun around to face an eight-foot tall demon and gasped.

Smoke whispered from the creature's bovine nostrils to wreathe his big bull head and impressive curling horns. His glassy black eyes stared down at me.

Standing only five foot eight myself, I had to crane my neck back uncomfortably to address him, or else speak to the bulging muscles of his chest, which he scratched absently with the six-inch talons on the ends of his fingers. I hadn't heard the clop of his cloven hooves as he'd approached, but maybe he'd come across the grass instead of along the walkway. Or maybe I only hallucinated the clopping when I knew he was coming.

"Hey, Smokey," I said, uncertain whether I should mention his renewed height. Wasn't a person's size one of those taboo social topics? Did demons count as people?

The last time I'd seen him, he'd shrunken to a seven-foot tall spindly creature, and it had kind of been my fault. But I hadn't done it intentionally. Destroyed a dimension, that is. Well, I had, but in a good cause.

"Traveler, I have come to claim my favor," the demon said.

I gulped. I would never, ever bargain with Smokey again. No, no, no. Very bad idea, even if it did get my baby nightmare a foster dad cum bodyguard. No nasty D-space demons munching my soot-ball as a snack.

"What did you have in mind?" I wasn't sure I wanted to know.

"A soul has fallen from one of your conveyances while Between, and it must be retrieved."

I frowned and rubbed at my watch cap. In demon-speak, were Neans and Raps considered souls? Or only humans? And if someone had fallen off a trans-dimensional platform in D-space, why did Smokey need me to retrieve them? DPS should already be mounting a rescue mission, one that wouldn't include a green recruit.

On the other hand, I was in hot water with Higgins. Maybe if I proved myself useful, he'd forgive my essay screw-up. Maybe DPS wouldn't fire me for insubordination. Or maybe I was hallucinating this meeting with Smokey.

Who would I ask? I didn't know anyone here except Sammie, and she'd gone to California with her father to bury her brother. I couldn't think of her without feeling a twinge of loneliness.

"You must go now," Smokey urged. "Before consequences evolve."

Before consequences evolve? What the heck did that mean? A chill passed over me, and it wasn't from the cool breeze blowing between the buildings.

"How do I find this lost soul?"

"The Council will guide you," he replied.

"The Council?" My voice climbed. "Not you?"

The last thing I wanted was an all-powerful council of demons guiding me through D-space. After the commotion I'd caused there while saving the multiverse, I didn't think they'd be too glad to see me again. Smokey said they were still on the fence about destroying the E-Prime dimension to get rid of all talents. Was this a plan to start thinning the herd?

His big bull brows drew down. "Will you break your bargain, Traveler?"

I wiped my sweaty hands on my pants. I couldn't see any options. Then I brightened. I'd ask Doc for help.

My previous experiences with psychiatrists notwithstanding, Doc was a decent guy. I hadn't seen much of him since my arrival. He'd been busy trying to save the super-talents Sammie and I rescued.

"I'll meet you at the fracture," I said.

"Be quick." With that, the big demon clopped away.

I found Doc at a desk in the infirmary. He wiped a hand over his thinning gray hair and watched me with those calm brown eyes of his. His face was etched with laugh lines, but he wasn't laughing now. Despite his best efforts to save the sick, mad super-talents we'd brought him, he'd lost one already, and the remaining three were in grave condition.

"You're sure this demon isn't a hallucination caused by your schizophrenia?" he asked.

What could I do to verify I'd seen Smokey? Demons were visible only to talents and Nean priests. And maybe Raps. Doc was a garden-variety human with no ability to create dimensional fractures or see beings from D-space.

"Bring a talent to the fracture. If the talent can see Smokey, then the request is real."

Doc put in a call to Colonel Juarez, the head of DPS. A minute later, we crossed the quad and trotted down the three flights to the underground fracture chamber. We could have used the elevator but didn't. Elevators are death traps. You won't catch me in one. *Ever.*

"What's DPS doing in the way of a rescue?" I asked.

Doc's mouth pulled into a hard line. "The scientist who fell isn't a super-talent whose fracture would register on Rap instruments. He's an ordinary human. We have no way to track him. Our response has been to mount an investigation into how it happened so we can prevent it in the future."

Most talents didn't have the oomph to create a fracture unless they partnered with another talent. Super-talents like me generated enough negative energy to fracture all alone, and did—without warning.

Our fractures caused power changes in the D-space energy currents. The Raps used those changes to track a super-talent's final destination. That's how DPS found me at E-4, where I'd first met Sammie.

Unlike other super-talents, I didn't go mad if I fell through a fracture, possibly because I'd become adept at ignoring my psychotic symptoms. Most days, clinging to the tiny island of sanity in my brain took every bit of thinking power I possessed. That same skill got me through D-space.

We passed through the steel double-doors into the main fracture room. It was the size of a football field, with a twenty-foot high ceiling. In another life, the facility had been a silver mine, and then it became a monastery that used the old shafts to age wine.

Mercury-vapor lamps strung along overhead conduit lit the space and hummed Beethoven's Fifth. The room had a modern concrete floor, but the walls and ceiling were still gray-brown stone. Locked storage cupboards stood against one wall.

At the far end, a wide dimensional fracture glittered, all sparkly and jagged and threatening. Its tidal pull urged me forward. The Rap-made cuff doohickies on my wrists were all that prevented me from being dragged through.

Three of the trans-dimensional platforms lined one wall. Their mushroom-shaped control panels rose from the center of their seven-foot diameter, six-inch thick stone bases. The runes around their edges were dark.

Close to the door, two men and a woman dressed in the black shirts, pants, and berets of the talent uniform chatted, their eyes tracking Doc and me. Soldiers with traditional military uniforms and weapons stood guard around the walls.

When Smokey stepped through the fracture, the talents drew their little wizard-wand stunners and shouted at the guards to lock down the facility. An alarm echoed through the space. The guards, unable to see the demon, waved their rifles back and forth.

"What the hell's going on?" Doc shouted over the racket.

"Demon." I gestured at Smokey.

"Okay, River, I believe you."

The demon clopped over to me. The talents backed away. Their faces were white and grim, but their wands held steady.

"Are you prepared, Traveler?"

I turned to Doc. "I need my robe back. And a spare."

Doc crossed to the storage cupboard, withdrew two bundles, and returned to me.

"Be careful with these." He handed me both bundles. "The Raps don't know we still have them, and Col. Juarez would prefer to keep it that way."

I tied one bundle to my belt. I strapped a metal-studded nylon harness from the second bundle around my own black uniform shirt. Even on its smallest adjustment, the harness threatened to slide off my shoulders. I hated being a runt.

I double-tapped the plastic plate centered on my chest, and it glowed to life. After a bit of fumbling, I switched to the shield screen. The shields didn't actually shield me from the horrors of D-space. Something about me caused them to fail, whether they were Rap tech shields or Nean priest magic shields. But at least when I used them, I arrived wearing my clothes, which I saw as a big plus.

I pulled on the long black robe and flipped up the hood. Forgetting my previous experience, I started for the fracture, promptly tripped on the robe hem, and fell to hands and knees.

Doc helped me up and slipped me a black plastic box the size of a cell phone with a single button in the middle of it and two metal nubs at the end.

"What's this for?" I took the taser from him. I was a Luddite when it came to technology, but cops used these, and I had more than a passing acquaintance with Johnny Law's methods to discourage the homeless from hanging around.

"In case he's uncooperative. He'll be mentally disturbed, remember, and he's a big guy. Press the contacts against him and push the button. It'll quiet him."

"I don't get a stunner wand?"

Doc chuckled. "They have to be tuned to the user's DNA. You won't get one until you graduate."

Doc lost the smile. "You don't know what you'll find when you get there. Shouldn't you take some backup?"

I didn't know if the demons could guide anyone else. And I didn't want to look like a wimp. Besides, I'd fallen through fractures lots of times, and except for ending up naked or in the middle of a deadly sonic banana gun fight, nothing bad happened.

"I'll be fine," I assured Doc. "Traveling D-space is my specialty."

I tucked the taser in my pants pocket and walked toward the fracture. The heavy robe tangled around my legs.

"How come we're in such a rush?" I asked Smokey. "Is this guy in trouble?"

"He possesses knowledge of Between. The Council does not wish the inhabitants of his destination to gain this knowledge."

"Why's that?"

Smokey scratched his bovine cheek. "They do not make suitable neighbors."

"But—"

"Be sure you leave nothing behind," the big demon admonished.

"How's this going to work?" The fracture pulled stronger as I approached.

"Splendidly, Traveler."

"Are you coming with me?"

He raised his eyebrows and snorted contempt. "And associate with the soulless?"

2
〜〜〜〜

I didn't get to ask what he meant by *soulless*. D-space sucked me through a shimmering curtain and into an impossible place. I drowned in a pounding surf, or perhaps I was caught at the bottom of a waterfall, pummeled against the rocks and unable to come up for air.

I was slammed and tumbled and bounced off banks of nightmare clouds and crystalline spires and glowing brimstone-and-hellfire mountains like the ball in a demented pinball game. The bones in my arms and legs snapped in a hundred places. My ribs were crushed. My skull was battered until my brain popped out to swirl away in the flood of energy that carried me relentlessly on.

Then I burst through another curtain of glitter and smacked down on my chest. Dusty cheatgrass tickled my nose, and I sneezed, followed a moment later by retching as my stomach arrived, late as always. My head throbbed. I wiped a trickle of blood from my nose and squinted at my surroundings.

I lay in a weed-choked vacant lot strewn with snagged plastic grocery bags, empty drink cups, and the occasional dented pop can. Behind me, the fracture glinted. To each side of the lot, two-story brick buildings rose. An alley ran along the back with brick buildings beyond, and a sidewalk and paved street fronted the final side.

Across the street, more two- and three-story buildings stood, the bottom floors housing businesses, and the upper floors either offices or residences. The lower windows displayed signs for a hardware store, a hairdresser's shop, and an insurance company.

The sun slanted down on the street and reflected off the dusty windshields of two older-model cars parked at the curb. In my fifteen years traveling as a homeless person, I'd passed through a hundred rural towns just like this one.

I heaved to my feet and wondered what had become of my lost scientist. Humans who traveled through D-space unshielded ended up gibbering, drooling mad and unable to care for themselves—except for me. I'd thought that meant he wouldn't be mobile. The loco super-talents we'd rescued were incapable of even sitting up without assistance. But I didn't see my quarry.

Had someone taken him away? No pedestrians strolled the street. No kids on bikes pedaled past. In fact, the whole place had a deserted air. On closer inspection, I noticed a broken window at the hardware store, the street sign at the corner canted across the sidewalk, and a battered old station wagon farther along had two flat tires. The hair on the back of my neck rose.

I looked back at the fracture and around at my feet. After I'd run away from the orphanage at ten, I'd learned urban survival skills, like which days grocery stores put out their spoiling produce and how to avoid attracting the attention of cops.

I hadn't learned how to track a lost madman through weeds. I scanned the area looking for flattened vegetation and broken stalks, because that's what Indian guides did in novels, but I saw those everywhere.

There! Those looked like drag marks, and if I half-closed my eyes, a trail headed toward the corner of the building across the lot. Or maybe I saw a pattern that didn't exist. I could make a pattern out of *anything*. But nothing else looked as promising.

I tiptoed across the lot, my head swiveling in case anyone tried to sneak up behind me, my hands holding up the robe. I imagined I looked like Snidely Whiplash skulking off to enact a nefarious plan, except I didn't have a top hat or mustache.

A few feet from the corner, I spotted the first smear of red. Someone had spilled paint. Or perhaps emptied the remains of an old paint can onto the weeds. Not an environmentally sound way to dispose of a toxic product.

Easing up to the building, I peeked around. Three shops down, someone hunkered in a doorway, back to me. Droplets of red on the sidewalk turned quickly to a river of red leading to the figure and beyond, then around the corner at the cross-street. Someone would be pissed about spilling that much paint. It cost a bundle.

I slipped down the sidewalk checking each doorway before sidling past. The huddled person ahead wore filthy blue jeans, ripped running shoes, and a tattered red and white checked shirt. Gross tangled brown hair stuck out from the back of his head. He made ripping and grunting noises.

A homeless person, with less than polite eating habits. *No surprise there.*

I expected the ripe tang of an unwashed body. Instead, my nostrils stung from the stench of dead animal left rotting in the sun. My stomach flip-flopped. I would have held my nose, but I needed both hands to keep the damn robe from tripping me. Besides, it would have been rude talking to the guy with my hand covering my face.

"Hey." I stopped a few feet away.

He was just far enough into the doorway that I couldn't see what he was doing, although I could tell he had something in his hands. I glanced both ways on the street, but nothing moved. Except for the flies. There were a lot of flies. Clouds of flies, buzzing around the doorway and on the puddles of paint. Sniffing paint because they couldn't find glue?

When he didn't respond, I took a step closer. "Excuse me, I'm looking for a friend of mine. Maybe you saw him? He's about..."

What *did* the scientist look like? Would I know him when I saw him? All I knew was that he'd be naked and gibbering, drooling mad. I hadn't even asked his name. *Dumb, River.*

"He wasn't wearing any clothes. And he's a scientist, so he looks smart. Well, he probably looked smart before he went crazy," I said. "Did he pass by here?"

The grunting and ripping continued. I stepped past him hoping to get into his field of vision. That's when I saw the bloody foot in his hands—his gray, decomposing hands. I choked.

Not real.

He was just a grubby homeless guy, chewing on... chicken rescued from the trash. Yeah, a really grubby homeless guy with some kind of nasty skin fungus... or something. *Eww.*

I glanced around, hoping to spy a stroller. I relied on the reactions of sane people to sort out the hallucinations from the real stuff. If someone came by and ran away screaming, so would I. But the street remained empty.

Dang! I should have brought backup. I walked a tight circle, avoiding the paint pool, and stopped on the opposite side of the lurker. Maybe I just needed a new perspective to see the poor man as he really was.

He grabbed another chunk of flesh in his teeth and pulled. It came loose, and he glanced sideways at me while he sucked it through his puffy, peeling lips. His cloudy eyes were lidless and bulging, and his cheeks were lined with splits and cracks that wept serum. A loose flap of his skin hung under his chin.

His ugly gray hand lashed out. Nasty nails snagged my robe and pulled. His grasp jerked me into him. I smacked his shoulder and knocked him head-first into the shop door. I leaped back and heard the sound of my robe tearing. He had the foot in one hand, and a chunk of robe fabric in the other.

Not chicken. A real foot.

My eyes flicked to the paint lake on the sidewalk, to the river of paint leading away.

Not paint. Blood. No one could lose that much blood and live, could they?

My heart tried to beat its way out of my chest. *Soulless*, Smokey said.

Zombie. Oh, hell! Real!

I turned and ran, but only two steps before tripping on my robe and falling in the still-wet puddle of blood on the pavement. I scrambled up, sure he'd pounce on me. He seemed absorbed with his foot again and remained squatted in the doorway.

I wanted to run back to the fracture. Instead, my feet glued themselves to the pavement and I rocked. I couldn't leave a fellow human here. I had to find him, get him back to E-Prime. Besides, Smokey said I wasn't to leave anything behind.

I swallowed my rising panic and hurried along the street, startling at every little noise, real or imagined. And there were suddenly a lot of noises: clicking and tapping and whispers coming out of thin air. I deeply regretted my choice to come without backup.

At the corner, I flattened myself to the wall before peeking around. Down by the alley, three more zombies dressed in decomposing flesh and the ragged remnants of casual clothing engaged in a tug of war with what was left of my scientist. He was missing his head as well as his foot.

A husky country boy zombie ripped loose an arm with a great cracking and shuffled away to the middle of the street, where he crouched and gnawed on the bicep. A redheaded female zombie tore free the lower right leg and foot with a rending pop and tottered into a shady doorway. A beanpole blond guy zombie dug long nails and rotting fingers into the stomach and pulled, shredding the flesh and spilling loops of intestines onto the sidewalk. I barfed.

Did the poor scientist have a family that would want to bury his remains? Would they notice if he was missing an appendage or two? What was I supposed to do? I juggled the taser in my sweaty hand.

The zombies didn't seem to move too fast. If I stunned them one at a time, could I make off with the body parts before they recovered? On the other hand, I didn't move too fast in the damn robe, either.

I retreated back past the foot thief to the vacant lot, stripped off my robe, and weighted it down with a rock, just to be on the safe side. Then I unwrapped the second robe and harness, spread the robe on the ground, and weighted it with rocks, too. My preparations made, I jogged back to the corner, giving the foot thief a wide berth. I'd deal with the missing foot later, once I had the rest of the body.

I pussyfooted up the sidewalk, keeping an eye on all three zombies.

The stench coming off them choked me. I wished I had nose plugs. I didn't know how they might react to an attack on one of their kindred. If I was lucky, maybe they'd go after their fallen comrade instead of me, and I could make a clean getaway.

Okay, no way it would be a *clean* getaway. The tall, skinny torso guy had guts spilled everywhere. I clenched the taser and looped around behind him, my thumb on the button. With a quick jump forward, I jammed the taser in the back of torso guy's neck and let him have it.

He jerked, screeched, and collapsed onto the scientist's body.

Crap. Why couldn't he have fallen sideways? I grabbed the zombie's dress-shirt collar and hauled back. The shirt ripped free in my hand, the material as decomposed as the wearer.

The zombie twitched and flailed and rolled in his victim's guts, weird gurgling sounds coming from his chest. I grabbed his leg and dragged him across the pavement. Under his pants, his flesh shifted, like stewed chicken meat falling from the bone. I closed my eyes and kept dragging until he'd cleared the carcass. Then I returned to the scientist to survey the damage.

No way could I drag him back to the fracture in his present state. I needed to get his guts back inside him. Geez, I wished I'd thought to raid the hardware store for a pair of gloves. If I stuffed his guts back in, would they stay while he traveled through the fracture? No time to worry about it.

Screwing up my courage and closing my eyes again, I grabbed internal organs and loops of intestines and shoveled them back into the abdominal cavity. They were hot and squishy and slippery with blood and goo.

My hand contacted something small and hard. I thought I'd picked up a rock from the street, but when I opened my eyes, it was a rectangle about a quarter inch thick and three-quarters of an inch long, wrapped in bright yellow duct tape.

Some kind of medical device? Why else would it be in his guts? *Leave nothing*, Smokey had said. I jammed it in my pocket.

Torso guy was already on his knees and crawling my direction. I grabbed the scientist's remaining arm and hauled ass, er, torso down the alley. The arm wasn't in good shape. One of the zombies must have tried to remove it earlier. Halfway down the alley, it came off.

I cussed and swore and left the arm on a garbage can while I dragged the torso by the leg with the missing foot. I tried to look on the bright side: I probably couldn't have moved him whole.

When I reached the vacant lot, I positioned the body on the second robe and strapped on the harness. I was covered in blood by the time I'd finished. Quick as a bunny, I dashed back down the alley to retrieve the arm. Back at the fracture, I let the harness out as far as it would go, and jammed the arm through, pinning it against the ribs. Then I jetted back through the alley.

Torso guy wrestled with arm guy over possession of the right arm. I had no idea how I'd stun both of them at the same time. I started with leg woman.

She wasn't so oblivious as torso guy or the foot thief and kept her back against the building wall. If I was going to stun her, it would be a side approach. I edged closer.

She growled.

I backed away. I'm no fighter, and the whole idea of zombies being real scared the hell out of me. But this was my first mission as an official member of DPS. I had to keep this job if I wanted a life with Sammie. Had to impress everyone so they'd want to be friends. Normal guys had friends, and I wanted the trappings of normal, even if I wasn't.

"Hi ya." I inched toward her. "Nice day for a... um... Nice day, isn't it?"

Her eyes rolled, lips peeled back from blackened teeth, and muscles tensed. Well, they tensed as much as rotting, bloated flesh can tense.

"You live around here? Seems like a nice place." I gained another six inches, my knees knocking and my hands shaking.

In a burst of motion, leg woman swung the appendage. The ankle bone connected with my shin bone. I howled and hopped back on one foot. She lurched forward, raking long filthy nails down my forearm to shred my sleeve and gouge the flesh below. I dropped the taser and leapt back farther.

Zombies must be attracted to screaming, flailing behavior because they suddenly all had an interest in me. I bolted toward the end of the block. They abandoned the arm and leg and followed, tottering faster than I imagined they could go and emitting a high-pitched keening sound.

It occurred to me that I didn't need to stun them. I just needed to ditch them far enough away that I could collect the missing pieces and get back to the fracture before they caught up. Yeah, that should work.

"Hey, over here! Can't catch me," I hollered as I pranced up the street ahead of them, running backward and waving my arms. I was the Pied Piper; they were the rats. This would be a lot easier than fighting them for the body parts.

I danced into the next intersection. That's when I noticed the other zombies. Five came along the street from my left, six from my right, and when I turned around, four more shuffled in behind me. All of them had their heads in the air, sniffing. I looked down at the fresh blood on my shirt, and my hair stood on end despite my watch cap. *Shit.*

I dodged around the three original zombies, burned rubber back to the arm, grabbed it and the leg, and staggered down the alley. A whole ravening pack of zombies flowed down the alley behind me, pushing, shoving, and knocking over garbage cans. Had the rats eaten the Pied Piper? I couldn't remember.

I no longer cared what Higgins thought of me. Or anyone at DPS. I didn't care whether the mission was a success. I just wanted to get out alive.

No time to thread more limbs in the harness or fetch the missing foot. I pulled the robe around the torso and tapped the navigation plate to life. Just like that, the body vanished into the fracture.

I snatched up my own robe, jerked it on, and grabbed the arm and leg. I was still trying to close the robe over them when the first zombie reached for me. I side-stepped, tripped over the robe hem, and went down hard. The pack closed in. I stabbed at my control plate and screamed.

3

No ping-ponging around D-space this time. Just straight torture as my body dissolved in a shower of acid, soaking through my skin, then the underlying muscle, and finally eating away at my bones.

"Not real, not real," I chanted, my mental shield against the aberrant experiences of D-space.

Every transit of D-space seemed to take an eternity, but this transit seemed shorter than most. Before I'd dissolved to the molecular level, I plowed through the curtain of silver glitter to smack down in the E-Prime fracture chamber. The arm and leg wedged between my chest and the floor didn't soften my landing a bit. My head contacted the floor, and I saw stars.

The clop of hooves registered in my demented brain, and I rolled to face the fracture. The motion spilled the bloody, chewed limbs out of my robe onto the floor.

Three copies of Smokey strode to me and frowned down at the scattered body parts. I blinked a couple times, and the three demons merged into one. A long column of smoke flowed from his nostrils and drifted toward the ceiling.

Smokey flicked a taloned hand at the mess. "Where is the part containing knowledge?"

I struggled to my feet, wobbling like a drunk, and stared first at Smokey, and then at the dismembered scientist.

"You have failed, Traveler," the demon said, scowling. "The Council will not be pleased."

"But... but..." I'd done the best I could. Maybe I'd lost a few body parts in the attempt, but he had no call to ding me for it. I'd been outnumbered. I'd been wounded. The scratches on my arm still burned.

The demon spun on his cloven hooves and stormed back to the fracture.

"*Soulless*, you said." I took a crooked step after him, shook my fist in the air, and shrieked, "You didn't tell me they were effing *zombies*."

Smokey disappeared through the fracture.

I'd failed. Would DPS command see it that way? If I told them about being outnumbered, surely they'd understand my strategic retreat. If I told them about the zombies, they'd know for sure I was crazy. I'd edit the impossible creatures out of my mission report. I'd be a regular guy just doing his job.

For a moment, I thought the conk on the head had knocked out my hearing. The fracture chamber was dead quiet. I turned around, staggering a little to maintain my balance.

Armed guards pointed their weapons at me. Was it just me, or had they traded in their usual rifles for much bigger guns, ones with fat magazines? And they didn't usually wear flak jackets and helmets down here, did they? Was arriving drenched in blood, clinging to body parts not my own, and screaming about zombies a shooting offense?

Beyond the guards, an audience of a dozen people—er, *beings*—stared at me, their expressions frozen in surprise—or possibly shock. Well, the humans and the Neans had expressions of surprise. I couldn't read Rap faces, but they watched, unblinking.

So much for editing zombies out of my report. Maybe they hadn't heard me clearly. Maybe I could say they'd misunderstood. Maybe something logical rhymed with zombies that I could say I'd shouted instead. Nothing came immediately to mind.

Colonel Juarez stood in the center of the group. He was around fifty and looked like his hair had migrated south. He was bald on top, but had bushy black eyebrows that nearly met in the middle over hooded mocha eyes, a thick nose, fleshy cheeks, and a full mouth. His eyes shifted from me to the carnage and back.

I'd been told talents weren't expected to salute since they weren't part of the military, but I thought I ought to do something, if only I knew what. As head of DPS, he was technically my boss. I settled on a tentative nod and a half-smile.

He didn't smile back. Since he also didn't order the guards to shoot me, I called it a win.

A Nean priest no taller than me but years older stood beside Juarez. Like the other priests I'd seen, he wore an outlandish hat like a Catholic cardinal and a long golden robe. Tension showed around his eyes. He tightened his grip on his wooden staff. The symbols carved into the length of it took on a tiny glow. Just as quickly as it had come, the glow winked out, and his face became composed.

The four Nean priests behind the old one were anything but composed. One screamed something in Nean and pointed at me. Two of them burst into a guttural chant and thumped their staffs on the floor in time with the jumble of syllables. The fourth, a redhead who would tower over me even without his silly hat, joined in, but he couldn't get the rhythm right. A shimmering pool of light leaped up around the group.

The pool didn't encircle the humans—or the Raps.

The four dinosaurs weren't like any scary velociraptors I'd seen in books—not that the rows of sharp teeth in their muzzles or the pointy claws at the ends of their digits weren't intimidating. They stood on their back legs but otherwise looked like large dogs covered in the soft down of an ostrich chick. Sammie said that was because they'd mutated—er, evolved—from what they'd been when they'd gone extinct in our dimension.

The Raps had taken several steps back. Two of the little gray-brown dinos pointed wands my way, their postures stiff with tension. The other two gestured at me with their upper limbs and chattered like angry magpies.

The yelling priest I dubbed Hothead pointed his staff at me. A slow-moving beam of wavering light undulated my direction. It stopped six feet away and hung there. Hothead bared his teeth and put more focus into it. His face turned a brilliant shade of scarlet from the effort. The beam grew brighter but came no closer.

I stood as tall as my five-foot eight allowed and glared back. Their magic didn't work near me. I wouldn't back down, at least not from their light beams. If Hothead swung that staff instead of pointing it, I'd be far away in a nanosecond.

A slender, chalky white Rap stepped from behind the group of its fellows. It gave the light beam a wide berth and stalked like a flamingo to stand beside the body. Its gaze flitted between the beam, the dead scientist, and me.

Instead of the usual short, fluffy coat typical of Raps, this one's coat looked more like that of an Irish Setter, with smooth flowing fringes hanging down the chest, backs of the legs, and along the tail. It wore a tan vest that had a million bulging pockets and a tool belt hung with lots of shiny things I couldn't identify. I hadn't met many Raps, but I'd never seen one wear a stitch of clothing.

The head tipped to one side and then the other. Blue-white eyes took in my robe. I realized I stood barefoot on the concrete, my shoes and the lower half of my uniform pants missing. The bottom of the robe hung in tatters. My pale naked calves were crisscrossed with bloody scratches. Embarrassment warmed my face.

"The equipment performs even in this condition?" the white Rap said in speech so filled with clacks and trills that it was hard to recognize the words. "Pardon my frontness. We exchange names first. I am—"

A shrill whistle from one of the other Raps cut into my eardrums.

The white Rap glanced over its shoulder, dipped its snout at me, and stalked back to vanish behind the others.

The elderly priest watched the proceedings with sharp interest. He touched Hothead's shoulder and spoke a few words. Hothead clamped his jaw and broke off his attack. The others stopped their chanting and thumping. The light vanished.

The steel double-doors of the fracture chamber burst open, and the scariest man on the planet walked in: Capt. Samuels, head of DPS security and my girlfriend Sammie's dad. I still had the boot print on my stomach from our first meeting. He'd thought I was one of the bad guys then, but I didn't think that excused his behavior.

"What's going on here?" He strode the length of the chamber to draw up beside the corpse.

The guards took a step back to give him room and keep him out of their line of fire should they need to plug me. He snapped a salute to Colonel Juarez.

"Flight Leader Falcon," Juarez said to the heavier of the chattering Raps before turning to the elderly Nean. "Your Highest Eminence Sacred Leader Schlauzauber Frommanisch. I regret this unfortunate interruption during our welcoming ceremony. Please accompany me to our conference center while Capt. Samuels handles this matter."

"Unacceptable," Flight Leader Falcon squeaked. "The talent wears our equipment without our permission or knowledge. It must be returned immediately."

Hothead rattled off something in Nean to the old priest, who nodded.

"The Holy Order requires an explanation of the transgression in your dimension by a demon." The old priest pointed at what remained of the scientist, and his brow furrowed. "And of how a human comes to be in this state."

Juarez flashed an unhappy look at me. He plastered on a stiff smile and addressed the group. "An explanation will be forthcoming as soon as we've adjourned to a setting more conducive to discussions—and had time to investigate. Please, this way."

Juarez led the two groups out of the fracture chamber.

I reached up to wipe my bloody nose, but it gushed instead of trickling like it usually did, adding to the mess already smearing my uniform. Doc stepped forward from where he'd been lurking by the doors and offered his handkerchief, which I gratefully accepted.

Capt. Samuels loomed over me. He stared down with his steely blue eyes. His craggy face seemed more lined than before, but for someone who'd lost his son four days ago, he was remarkably composed. His nostrils flared, whether in anger or because of my stench, I couldn't be sure. I tensed and edged back.

"Explain yourself." Samuels leaned closer.

"Um... it's not my fault," I stammered. "The dismemberment, I mean."

The captain arched an eyebrow. His eyes raked over my uniform, and his nose wrinkled. "You have fifteen minutes to clean up and be in my office, where I expect to hear a coherent report of your mission."

Samuels turned to Doc and pointed at the scientist. "Get this man out of here. I want a preliminary report on cause of death by nineteen hundred hours."

The captain spun on his heel and marched across the chamber. The guards at the door snapped to attention as he passed. I sucked in a deep breath and let it out.

"Are you okay?" Doc gestured at my shirt. "How much of that blood is yours?"

"Not that much." I offered Doc his blood-soaked handkerchief.

Doc grimaced. "Keep it."

He shook his head over the remains on the floor. "If I'm going to have a COD by nineteen hundred hours, I could use some help. Give me a hint. How'd Smith die?"

"He was dead when I found him," I replied.

"So you didn't see what happened?"

"Just the taking apart part. His head was already missing. I brought back as much as I could."

Doc placed a gentle hand on my shoulder. "You did well, River. Without your help, we would never have found him. At least now his family will have closure."

I tried to push the horrible image of the zombies out of my head while I stripped off my shredded robe and harness. One of the soldiers took them from me without so much as a shiver. They were tough; real men, not wimps like me.

We crossed to the door. A blonde talent stepped well back at our approach. I guess she didn't like comrades who comingled with demons. Or maybe it was the odor from my uniform.

Outside in the quad, the sun had set, and stars twinkled overhead. The moon shown down on us, and I couldn't help thinking about the night Sammie and I made love by moonlight. I hoped we'd do it again soon, but I didn't want to push. I was half afraid she'd change her mind about me when she realized how crazy I was. Or her dad would find out and kill me.

Which reminded me that I was due to face the homicidal man in less than fifteen minutes. I bid Doc goodbye and ran like a banshee for my quarters, all the while trying to think of a word that sounded like *zombie*.

4

My room was neat as a pin. I hadn't mastered making those military corners on the bed yet, but otherwise, I'd kept the place scrupulously clean in my three days with DPS. I'd never had a room of my own before. Heck, for the past fifteen years, I mostly hadn't had a roof over my head.

I took pride in my tidy, beat-up desk, single bed, and twelve-by-twelve square of brown carpet, not that I had any possessions to leave lying around. Everything I owned fit in the bottom half of a backpack. But keeping things orderly helped me manage the schizophrenia.

I stripped out of my uniform and drank from the showerhead in the attached bathroom while I washed off the blood and gore. Soap and hot water removed the smell but not the memory of guts slipping through my fingers. I scrubbed my hands extra hard.

I wasn't sure what to do with my ruined uniform. I didn't want to leave it on the floor. If it stained the carpet, would I have to pay damages? Before I headed out the door, I scooped up the filthy shirt and tattered pants and dumped them on the shower floor. Then I scrubbed my hands again.

I dashed across the quad to Administration, another of the three-story stone block buildings. Lights shone from most of the high, narrow windows, which was unusual, given the late hour.

Losing the scientist seemed a very big deal. I hoped DPS appreciated my efforts to save him more than Smokey had. I just had to keep this job and make a few friends, for the sake of appearances. Then I'd be worthy of a wonderful person like Sammie. She'd never have to make excuses for me or be embarrassed to be in my company.

Samuels' office was on the second floor. I took the stairs two at a time despite my fatigue and pounding headache. The last thing I needed was Capt. Samuels angry at me for being late.

Samuels gave me the willies, but I was determined to keep it together while I told him my story. It wouldn't take long. I took three deep breaths, rolled my shoulders, and whispered *ohm* twice before I opened the office door.

My punctuality didn't help Samuels' mood. He glowered at me from behind his desk where he stood with his hands clasped behind his back. I quivered in my sneakers, the only footwear I had after losing my official boots in the zombie dimension. The soft overhead light hummed *Swing Low, Sweet Chariot* off-key.

"You will have noted, Mr. Madden, that high-level VIPs from the Raptor and Neanderthal dimensions are visiting us. They've assembled here to discuss recent events, of which you were a part."

Samuels placed his fingertips on the edge of his desk. "Because of the actions of you and Talent Samuels, we have the Raps over a barrel. They owe us. We'll use their debt to negotiate increased access to their technology."

He'd lost his son, nearly lost his daughter, and all he cared about was how he could leverage the loss? My stomach did a slow roll. I wanted to escape this monster and find Sammie.

"We don't expect to have the Neans on our side. They're a superstitious, backward tribe with little interest in technology. And I won't allow this latest accident to derail our focus on forcing the Raps to share their tech. Nor will I tolerate other distractions. *Don't* become a distraction, Mr. Madden."

I stood up straight and sucked in a breath, ready to assure him he didn't have to worry about me. I'd tell him my story and race back to my room. I was woefully behind in my reading and couldn't afford another screw-up in my classes.

He spoke again before I could say a word.

"I would have preferred a private debriefing of your retrieval efforts, but the Neanderthal and Raptor delegations insist that they be allowed to observe." Samuels leaned toward me, and his hard blue eyes narrowed. "Here's how it will go. You will answer their questions respectfully while telling them as little as possible. There will be none of your abnormal behavior or hysterical responses."

I would have swallowed, but my mouth was dry as the desert. Frightened as I was of Samuels, I would have preferred telling my story to him alone instead of reciting it in front of the Raps and Neans. But maybe they didn't know enough about humans to recognize lies.

And asking me to be normal under stress was like expecting an elephant to dance on the head of a pin. No amount of practicing normal behavior made it stick. I was doomed.

"Let's go." Samuels swept around his desk and out the office door.

I scrambled after him. We didn't go far—ten feet along the corridor and through another door marked *Conference Room.*

The room was fifteen by twenty-five feet. Venetian blinds covered the windows, and the overhead light bulbs left dark shadows in the upper corners. A conference table occupied most of the space. Swivel chairs and Rap crouching stools ringed the table.

The Raps, Neans, and humans all stood, their attention focused on the far end of the room where Hothead intoned a guttural chant. His staff and robe glowed soft yellow, and sheets of warm light flowed in waves over the table and seats. The light flickered and dimmed. My end of the table darkened.

A cry rose from the younger Neans. The waving light retracted to form a shield around the Nean delegation, and Hothead pointed his staff at me. I couldn't help it. I snickered.

Then I remembered Samuels' warning about being respectful. I could feel the captain's eyes boring into my temple. I resolved to act normal, make my report, and get the heck out of there. *What sounds like zombies?*

Colonel Juarez gestured to the chairs. "Now that the blessing is complete and Captain Samuels and Mr. Madden have joined us, please be seated so we can begin."

"His Highest Eminence Sacred Leader Schlauzauber Frommanisch cannot remain in a dimension where demons are welcomed," shouted Hothead, who still pointed his staff at me.

The High Muckymuck priest raised a hand, spoke a word in Nean, and then switched to English. "Let us hear the Colonel out. If the human is possessed against his will, it will be our duty to assist him. Humans may not be aware of the risk demons pose. It is our sacred duty to educate them."

Possessed against my will? *Me?* The demon would have gotten the short end of that stick.

Hothead fell silent, and the light snuffed out. The old guy rolled back a chair, gave it a curious look, and sat. The three shorter, darker priests eschewed seats and clustered around their leader's back, staring daggers at me. The tall redhead lingered behind them and seemed more interested in how the swivel chairs worked than in who occupied the room.

The chief Rap, Flight Leader Falcon, and his second-in-command settled on two of the backless Rap stools along one side of the table. The other two gray Raps, stunner wands still in paw, stepped back against the wall, eyes scanning the room. Their posture was unmistakable: *bodyguards.* The white Rap stood blinking at us all like an enthusiastic tourist at the zoo.

Colonel Juarez sat opposite the Raps. Professor Higgins positioned himself next to the Neans. He looked my way and sniffed in disdain.

A thin, dark-haired woman dressed in a tight black turtle-neck sweater and black slacks that accentuated her hourglass figure and extreme height sat to the left of Juarez. Her dark eyeshadow, high cheekbones, and pointy chin reminded me of a Halloween witch, although she didn't have the requisite hooked nose or warts. But she had the aura.

Samuels pointed to a chair next to the woman. I took the hint and sat. Witchy Woman gave me an appraising look but didn't speak. Samuels flanked me. I felt like an insignificant mole hill squeezed between two towering mountains.

The white Rap flitted past its own kind and nabbed a human-style chair directly across from me. It threaded its tail out the side and perched on the front edge. It couldn't be comfortable. The other Raps studiously ignored the white.

I scooted my chair forward until the edge of the table pressed hard against my ribs, and then I gripped the chair seat with both hands, determined not to rock. I'd play it cool. I wouldn't say anything to embarrass the brass in front of the others. I'd be in control. *Ohm.*

Behind me, the first whispers of an invisible chorus started. *Failed, interrogation,* and *torture* surfaced in the incomprehensible hiss of their conversations. I resisted the urge to glance over my shoulder. *Not real.*

"Today's meeting was called in response to the recent attack on the Raptor's home dimension, R-Prime," Colonel Juarez said. "In the interest of improved relations between all our dimensions, I would like to begin by letting Flight Leader Falcon elaborate about how Raptor-backed humans came to be in possession of E-Prime talents used as unwilling test subjects in fracturing experimentation."

The flight leader chirped, possibly to clear its throat. "We have already provided sufficient explanation. Of more importance is that humans possess our technology without authorization. After the attack on our dimension, your super-talent," he waved a paw at me, "raided the combatants' camp and stole our technology. You will return it at once."

"Did not!" I said. Samuels' head jerked my direction. Oops.

"You argue over possession of devices when demons breach the barriers of the human dimension?" Hothead said.

Juarez ignored Hothead and spoke to Falcon with calm determination. "We'd like to focus on how those criminals came to be in possession of *your* technology and *our* humans, and what measures we can institute to assure it doesn't happen in the future."

"We do not interfere in the cultural affairs of others." Chirps and whistles interrupted the smooth flow of Flight Leader Falcon's words. "If you wish to assure your safety from your own kind, take responsibility for it: change your brutal human ways."

"Not interfere?" I gasped. "You were supplying them!"

All eyes turned my direction. There was a pause. Higgins' words about starting a multidimensional incident blared in my head. I wedged my tongue between my molars and bit down. *Be cool, River.* It was an impossible goal.

"Perhaps, sir," said Samuels, "we should debrief Mr. Madden about the latest incident and continue this discussion after he's dismissed."

Yeah, debrief and get out, maybe look for Sammie. If her dad was back already, she must be here, too. Sammie would tell me what *on report* meant and how to fix things with Higgins. I didn't want to be fired after just three days. Keep the job. Make friends. Make Sammie proud.

"Yes." Falcon's flat black eyes looked into mine, and I shivered. "Begin with how you acquired the equipment you used to retrieve the unfortunate human lost from the platform."

"Sure." My hands tightened on my chair as I thought about what the Raps allowed to happen to the super-talents Sammie and I rescued. "One of your Rap buddies thought I was one of your *human* buddies and gave it to me when I visited R-Prime."

Falcon and his second exchanged chirps and squawks. For the first time since we'd sat down, the white Rap turned its attention from me to its companions. The head tipped left, then right, like a bird checking for an approaching cat.

"The theft of your precious technology is nothing." Hothead leaned over the table and swept his staff over the group. "The appearance of demons takes precedence over all."

The old Nean raised a hand that stopped his junior priest. Hothead bared his teeth at me. It's possible I bared mine back in an unfriendly smile. Behind Hothead, the redheaded priest narrowed his eyes, first at Hothead, and then at me. I looked away first.

"Mr. Madden, describe your mission to locate the missing scientist, John Smith," Samuels commanded in a louder voice than necessary.

This was it, time to tell my little white lies. But I'd meant to prepare better. *Zombie... what the hell rhymes with zombie?* Maybe I should stick to the truth. No, bad idea.

I cleared my throat and stammered, "Well, Smokey said I needed to rescue someone, but when I got there, he was in pieces. The scientist, I mean. So I gathered him up as best I could and came back."

I blew out a little sigh and waited to be dismissed. All I wanted to do was find Sammie. And take some aspirin. I'd forgotten to do that in my rush to make the debriefing, and my head throbbed in time to my pulse.

Samuels ground his teeth. "Smokey?"

"He's a demon," I said. Just to poke the Raps, I added, "I couldn't have saved R-Prime without him."

That wasn't strictly true. Smokey'd been less a help than a nag, pointing out that Sammie would die if I didn't save the multiverse. So I did. Save the multiverse. I'd do anything for Sammie.

The Nean delegation came unglued. I'd seen them get all het up about demons before. Maybe I shouldn't have mentioned Smokey. But it was them acting crazy now, not me. That should please Samuels.

I'd done my bit and given my report. I scooted my chair back, ready to leave. I couldn't believe I'd gotten off so lightly with only a few small omissions and no actual lies. Maybe I was getting better at acting normal.

"He admits it! He colludes with the unholy from the darkness!" Hothead leaned threateningly over the table. The two shorter priests began to thump the floor with their staffs and chant.

Capt. Samuels stared at me like a chained pit bull, all fierce eyes and taut muscles. I leaned away. Behind me, the invisible chorus ramped up its insidious whispering, and *life sentence, dungeon,* and *firing squad* floated above the murmurs. I glanced back, and then kicked myself for paying attention.

"Please." Colonel Juarez made calming motions with his hands. "We're trying to determine how a man was lost off a platform into D-space. We can take up your concerns with prior events when we've completed the debriefing of Mr. Madden."

His High Muckymuck lifted his chin, which silenced the rest of his delegation. "That is agreeable to the Holy Order, provided all parties recognize the seriousness of the accusations against Mr. Madden."

The priests stopped their racket and bowed their heads—all except the redhead at the back, who shifted in place and adjusted his hat.

Hothead wasn't mollified by the words of his leader. He glowered at all of us.

"Ignore the threat to your dimensions at your peril. The unholy from the darkness have already begun their attacks. It was one of them who threw your man Smith from the platform—the same one who approached—" he jabbed his staff at me "—this demon-clothed-in-flesh in the fracture chamber."

5

All eyes swiveled my way. I felt like a bug under a microscope, one the observers planned to squish soon. I squeezed the seat of my chair to keep from bolting for the door.

Samuels recovered first, not surprising for a guy with ice water in his veins. "Why wasn't this reported hours ago when the platform first returned?"

Hothead jerked back a fraction and went still. Confusion vied with worry in his expression. Perhaps he'd finally recognized the good captain as the real predator in the room.

Was that the start of a smirk on the redheaded priest's face?

"If you'd read my reports, you'd know it's against the rules of the Holy Order to speak of the dark or the things that reside there." Higgins glared down the table at Samuels and me. "Of course it wouldn't be reported. I'm surprised we're hearing about it now. My apologies, Sacred Leader, for the ignorance of my fellow humans. We don't mean to give offense."

"How is it possible for a demon to breach the shields to get to Smith?" Samuels asked without missing a beat. "I thought the whole point of the shields was to keep anything in D-space out, to protect everyone on the platform."

Falcon and his companion erupted in a burst of chatter, chirping, peeping, and cawing at one another. They waved their paws about, light glinting off their nasty, sharp claws. It didn't take a Rap expert to see they were terrified. The bodyguards at the wall tensed.

As one, the group of Raps swung to face the white. Falcon rattled off a series of staccato chirps and fell silent.

The white lifted its snout to the ceiling. One claw scratched its throat. Beside me, Witchy Woman leaned forward and hummed under her breath, looking interested in the proceedings for the first time. We all waited on whatever pronouncement the white would make.

The white did a wonderful imitation of a human shrug and held out a paw, pads up. The grays screeched loud enough I thought the windows might shatter. The white's lips quivered. It averted its eyes and straightened its vest. Was it laughing?

"Your Highest Eminence Sacred Leader Schlauzauber Frommanisch," Falcon said, "we had your assurances that your shields were fully capable of resisting the negative energy of D-space. Now you report that they can be breached? This creates unacceptable risk. All travel must be suspended until new shielding can be developed and tested."

"Impossible!" Hothead snapped. "His Eminence Sacred Leader Schlauzauber Frommanisch must return to N-Prime to prepare for the coming Celebration of Light. The continuance of our world depends on it. You cannot deny him transportation."

The debate raged around me while I thought about the Nean's fishy story. The demons might be pissed about the mess I'd made of their territory while I was saving the multiverse and retaliated by attacking a platform, but it didn't feel right. If Smokey attacked the platform, why did he have me rescue Smith?

Smokey wasn't here to defend himself, and that didn't sit well. Much as I wanted to leave, I had to stay and be his voice. After all, he was raising my nightmare. I didn't want the little cloud eaten.

I'd seen Smokey deal with a Nean attack. His mere presence didn't knock out their light shields like mine did, or everyone on the platform would be drooling, gibbering mad now. Smokey deflected the Nean light into an enormous spinning color wheel. It wasn't the kind of thing anyone on the platform could have missed—unless Smokey's defensive system was like nightmares, which were only visible to me.

Come to think of it, except for sticking his talon in human heads, Smokey never interacted physically with anything in our dimensions. He acted indirectly, by persuading a dimension's occupants to act on their primal desires.

But maybe it was different when he was home in D-space. Maybe he *could* get physical there. While they hadn't dismembered me, the Demon Council had directed me through D-space to Smith's location. Didn't *that* involve physical interaction? Or did it?

The more I debated with myself, the more confused I became. I resolved to keep my mouth shut and let the smart scientist people figure it out.

Colonel Juarez looked like he'd developed a headache worse than mine. He leaned back in his chair and furrowed his brow, glancing around at the other humans—except for me.

The door opened, and Doc stepped in. A flash of hope streaked across Juarez's face. He flagged Doc toward a seat at the end of the table.

"This is Dr. Polaski," Juarez said to the gathering. "Doctor, have you determined how Smith died?"

Doc sat and paused to survey the group. When he got to me, for just a moment, a reassuring smile touched his lips. It felt good to have a friend in the room.

"I've done only a cursory examination, and as you saw, Smith's remains are incomplete and in poor condition."

"Yes, yes." Samuels made a circular hurry-up motion.

Doc ignored Samuels. What a brave man!

"Preliminary cause of death is blood loss associated with dismemberment."

"Demons!" Hothead said with a snarl. "They ripped him apart and stole his soul."

For a guy who didn't want to speak of things from the dark, he sure seemed willing to throw *demons* into the conversation at every turn. Was it an ancient cultural prejudice or something more, something personal?

Juarez spoke up before Hothead could continue his rant. "The Neanderthals just told us that their priest saw a demon drag Smith from the platform during its transit through D-space. They contend that it's the same demon who conversed with Mr. Madden in the fracture chamber when he returned from his mission."

Doc nodded, calm as ever. "I can't see demons. Can someone describe it?"

The three young priests' eyes went wide. They made signs with their hands and muttered under their breath. The redhead showed a flash of uncertainty before mimicking the behavior of the other three.

The old priest shook his head. "To talk of the darkness is to invite it in."

I rolled my eyes. Samuels had that much right: Neans were backwards and superstitious.

"He's about eight feet tall, big bull head with teeth like a—" I looked across the table "—like a Rap. Only much bigger."

The Raps exchanged a glance.

"And curling horns like a mountain goat. Human torso, lots of bulging muscles, six-inch talons on massive fingers, hairy goat legs, cloven hooves. He blows smoke out his nostrils."

Doc rubbed a hand across his chin. "Can anyone verify River's description?"

Even the High Muckymuck priest averted his eyes.

"Talent Samuels gave a similar description of the demon she and Mr. Madden encountered at E-4," Samuels said. "I think we can assume it's accurate."

"Then I doubt it's our killer," Doc said.

The veins at Hothead's temple and throat bulged. His eyes bugged out.

"None of the injuries on the body are consistent with an attacker of that description, except possibly for the dismemberment, but I understand River witnessed that, and he didn't mention demons participating."

"Nope," I said. "Absolutely no demons participated."

"What *did* you see, Mr. Madden?" Juarez asked.

I sucked air through my teeth and wiped sweat from my brow. This was it, my moment to sound sane and reasonable, even though I wasn't. What was my story again?

"Um...wild animals. Big ones."

Doc looked perplexed.

Zombies, zebras. Nope, didn't rhyme. "Like lions and bears," I added. "Tearing him apart."

"You're sure?" Doc said. "You couldn't have seen something else and... misinterpreted? The bite marks on the corpse indicated something smaller."

Unmasked already. My stomach tied itself in knots. What would I say now? How would I explain human bite marks on Smith's corpse? *Zombies, hombres.* Close, but wasn't that racist?

"Headhunters."

Around the table, mouths gaped and eyes blinked. What was I thinking? *Zombies* and *headhunters* didn't even start to rhyme.

"Headhunters?" Higgins asked, his voice loaded with incredulity. "I thought you said wild animals?"

Uh-oh. I'd gotten my story mixed up already. My admiration for good liars soared.

"The headhunters drove them off. And then they started eating Smith."

"They didn't cook him first?" Higgins glanced around the table. The non-humans looked shocked. The humans looked fascinated.

It had to be a trick question. Higgins was an anthropology professor. He probably knew all about headhunters. Higgins didn't like me, but siding with the Neans against the human at the table was over the top, even if one—or two—of us were madmen.

But Doc would know that Smith hadn't been barbequed. Or boiled.

"No cooking. That I saw."

Higgins eyes narrowed. "And how many of these headhunters were there?"

I didn't want them to know I was a wimp, that I'd run away without finishing my mission. And I'd been chased by a dozen zombies. Twelve to one was pretty long odds, wasn't it?

"A lot." The humans didn't look convinced. I needed more details to make the story believable. The devil was always in the details.

"They carried spears. And they wore necklaces of teeth and shrunken heads. And war paint on their faces. Lots of headhunters armed with spears. And blowguns."

Wait. Did research show that liars talked too much?

The more I talked, the more Higgins smiled. It was an evil smile. "I see. How many armed headhunters exactly?"

Yep. I'd said too much. My chest thumped against the table edge. I'd started to rock and hadn't noticed. *Buck up, River. Ohm.*

"I didn't have time to count. I was busy gathering up the body parts. They were kind of scattered."

Higgins' eyes narrowed. "And what were the headhunters doing while you were retrieving the body parts?"

Crap. Even I wouldn't believe a story this crazy. I swore I'd never tell another lie the rest of my life. If DPS ever sent me on another mission, I'd be sure to take backup.

"I got them to chase me. I may be small, but I can run really fast." Finally, a bit of truth. "Then I ditched them and ran back for the pieces."

I thought about the gouges down my arm and my shredded pants. "Only they caught up to me at the fracture. I had to fight them off. With the taser Doc gave me."

Higgins sniffed. "I don't believe a word of your story. You could have killed and dismembered Smith yourself before you returned. After all, you were alone on your *rescue* mission."

"Just because I'm crazy doesn't mean I go around cutting up people," I replied with some heat.

Aw, hell. I wanted to bite my tongue. *Cool, River. Ohm.*

"When we have a full autopsy," Doc said, "we'll know much more about how Smith died."

Witchy Woman addressed Doc in a thick Russian accent. "Let us stick to ze evidence we have. You saw tool marks where ze limbs were severed?"

"The limbs were quite literally ripped off by someone with great strength," Doc responded. "The only marks were bites from human mouths and tears of the appropriate size to be made by human fingernails."

"More human savagery," Falcon squawked.

The redheaded Nean spoke, a touch of a smile on his face. "This human is no hunter. He's too weak to kill another in such a way. Or to win a fight with a human the size of Smith."

I couldn't miss the Nean's taunt, and I couldn't let it pass. If the

Nean wanted to cast aspersions on my story, I could play the same game. So what if he was right?

"Did anyone besides the priest see this demon?" I asked. "I mean, when he threw Smith off the platform."

The redhead thought a moment. Maybe he was slow processing English. Then he huffed up like a charging rhino. "You dare question the word of a priest of the Holy Order? May the darkness take you and your cursed race."

The two young priests tossed nervous glances at the redhead and made signs in the air. Hothead cocked his head toward the redhead before he pointed his staff at me again. The runes along its length blazed. The old guy pursed his lips and glared at me.

I'd done it, just as Higgins predicted. I'd started a multidimensional political incident. The light bulbs hummed the *Funeral March*. My head throbbed in time with it.

"I think," Juarez said, his voice cool, "Mr. Madden is suggesting that we have no conclusive proof of the cause of death at this time."

"That's right," Doc added. "We've had a number of super-talents fall through D-space without protection from your shields. While they all suffered from mental issues, none of them has received any bodily harm. I'm inclined to agree with River's report: Smith was not dismembered by demons but by the occupants of the dimension in which he landed."

"What does the Raptor delegation believe?" the old Nean asked.

"That dimensional travel involves unacceptable risks and must be discontinued." Falcon glanced at his companion. "And that all ties with humans must be severed."

6

~~~~~~~~~~

I rolled over on my bunk and stared at the ceiling. In the dorm rooms nearby, the sounds of my fellow DPS recruits filtered through the walls as they carried out their morning routines and donned their uniforms, still thinking they had futures at DPS. I'd ended those futures—along with my own—when I'd opened my mouth during the summit with the Neans and Raps.

There'd be no DPS. Humans couldn't navigate D-space without Rap technology. Worse yet, without the Rap-made cuffs we wore strapped to our wrists, I and the other super-talents could cause a fracture and fall through dimensional barriers unexpectedly. The cuffs, I'd been told, eventually wore out and had to be replaced. How would we get new ones?

While I wouldn't go gibbering drooling mad like the other super-talents did when they fell through a fracture, I couldn't risk accidentally opening a fracture with Sammie nearby. As with all humans who had a talent for fracturing dimensional barriers, if she got too close to a fracture, she could be dragged through by its tidal forces.

I couldn't let that happen. The only way to prevent it was to never go near her again. I couldn't face a future without Sammie.

There had to be a way to prove that Smokey hadn't pulled Smith off the platform in D-space. I had no idea how to contact the demon. No one else could understand him, even if he swore on a stack of bibles that he didn't do it. In the back of my head, I wasn't positive he hadn't.

The Demon Council thought that the human ability to fracture posed a threat to the multiverse. Get enough talents together in an older, weaker dimension, let them fracture at the same time, and voila! Instant cascading multiverse collapse. Because of this fear, the council had threatened to destroy the E-Prime dimension, thereby ridding the multiverse of talents.

Of course, they didn't need to destroy E-Prime to prevent multiverse collapse. All they had to do was prevent humans from traveling to other dimensions. I'd bargained enough with Smokey to know that demons were wily.

Had they arranged Smith's demise to shut down DPS and quarantine all humans in E-Prime? Had they miscalculated and accidently sent Smith to the zombie dimension? Why was that a problem for them?

And how would I get Raps to work with humans again? I had to discredit the Neans' claim that Smokey attacked the platform and make the Raps believe they could travel safely between dimensions.

If I couldn't get an explanation from Smokey—and who'd believe me if I did—my only other option was to make the Nean priest recant his testimony. Or find evidence to prove he'd lied. I'd need Sammie's help. The Neans definitely wouldn't talk to me.

The thought of seeing Sammie was all it took to get me moving. I jumped out of bed, dressed, and glanced down my schedule for today.

The first item was breakfast at 0700 hours. The second was fracture practice at 0800. I didn't have a watch, but from the sounds of preparations around me, breakfast would start soon. My stomach growled.

I jogged through the hall, down the stairs, and out into the quad, where I stopped with a lurch. I hadn't expected to find Sammie so easily, and I hadn't expected the quad to be filled with Neans.

Clementine Samuels—Sammie to her friends—stood twenty feet down the walk, lovely as ever. She was just a little slip of a thing, but good—no, amazing—in a fight. She reminded me of an elfin princess with her delicate, exotic features, dark hair, and short stature. She glanced my way, saw me, and smiled. That smile outshone the sun, which had just crested the horizon.

I walked over to her while the two dozen Neans on the dry grass of the quad performed the loopiest dance I'd ever seen. It looked like a cross between Tai Chi and western line dancing. In unison, the group grunted unpronounceable syllables, banged the ends of their staffs on the ground, and hopped about like the Easter Bunny.

"What's this?" I said to Sammie with a laugh. "Morning calisthenics?"

Sammie turned those pretty brown eyes on me and said, "This is a prayer ceremony to honor the sun. It's an important part of their religion."

"Oh." I wiped the smile from my face. I needed Sammie's help, but I didn't know how to ask. I watched the Neans while I tried to think of something intelligent to say, something that would impress her.

The tall, redheaded Nean priest looked like he had two left feet. He was never in step with the others, and I thought he might be lip-syncing. As the others swept from one goofy position to another, he fumbled his staff.

"What a doofus!" I quipped. The moment the words fell out of my mouth, I knew I'd screwed up. A little frown formed on Sammie's face. As an outlier on the bell curve of humanity myself, I knew better than to make fun of others. But I couldn't seem to stop saying stupid things around Sammie.

"Um... want to get breakfast with me?"

She turned her attention back to the field. "I'm on duty."

"But all the platforms are grounded."

"As they should be." She crossed her arms over her chest. "A man died because a platform was attacked in D-space. Until we know how to protect ourselves, it's not safe for anyone to travel. The Raps have sent message drones to all dimensions letting them know about the dangers."

"How do we know that's what happened? Maybe he fainted. Maybe..."

I knew darn little about platforms and how they worked. The crew always consisted of a Rap navigator who steered the platform through D-space, a Nean priest who generated light shields around the platform so no one went mad, and a human talent or two who could open a new fracture in case the original fracture closed before the platform got out of a dimension again. Add on a scientist passenger or two, and a platform became a pretty crowded place.

"Maybe someone bumped him, and he fell. And they don't want to fess up." And maybe I should just shut up before I said anything else really dumb.

On the field, the chanting and leaping accelerated.

"Can we go somewhere?" I said. "I need to ask you something."

"I told you, I'm on duty. I'm to mentor First Luminary Acolyte Schlauzauber Heshlibob." She nodded at the big redhead.

His name was a mouthful, more than I'd ever remember. But that didn't stop me from paying attention to its acronym: FLASH. With his flaming hair and gaudy gold robe, it fit.

"That lunk? What makes him so special?" *Uh-oh.* I'd done it again. I wanted to smack myself.

Sammie's jaw tightened. "He's Highest Eminence Sacred Leader Schlauzauber Frommanisch's son and a member of the DPS coalition. He'll train to work on a platform crew, the same as you. You'll be expected to treat him with the courtesy you would show toward any of your other teammates."

I'd never been part of a team. Heck, mostly I didn't feel like part of the human race. But I wanted to live up to Sammie's expectations.

"This was your dad's idea, wasn't it?" I said. The day suddenly seemed gloomy. If the Raps pulled out of DPS, the minutes I had left to spend with Sammie were already flying past, and now her father had found a way to occupy her time so she couldn't spend it with me.

"Col. Juarez assigned me this mission." She'd reached a full-blown frown. "We know so little about Nean culture or politics. They've resisted Professor Higgins' attempts at cultural exchanges. They took offense at whatever was said in the summit last night and might break off all contact."

Guilt flickered through me. I'd insulted them deliberately, and now everyone would pay the price.

"We have to see the multiverse through their eyes. We have to extend the hand of true friendship, not just partnership. We can help them, and they can help us." Sammie's face positively glowed with excitement. "Besides, if I'm going to resign as a talent and become an anthropologist, this is a unique opportunity. Imagine writing a master's thesis on a society previously unknown to humans."

She'd spent her whole life trying to meet her father's expectations, and now she wanted to break free to follow her heart. What if her heart carried her away from me? Thinking about that possibility was scarier than facing zombies. I wanted every moment of her time for the rest of our lives, and I'd do anything to make it happen.

All the priests dropped to the ground and bowed, first toward the sun, and then toward their elderly leader. Flash gave Sammie a wave and a smile. She returned a quick grin. The priest's eyes tracked to me, and his face hardened. Then he tuned me out to focus on Sammie as she walked over to him.

I stood on the sidewalk and rocked. I wanted to go after Sammie, drag her away from that jerk who'd called me a wimp, and tell him to leave her alone or else. I wasn't sure what I'd do if he called my bluff on the 'or else' part. I was a pacifist.

"Good morning, Mr. Madden," a heavily accented female voice said behind me.

I jerked around. Witchy Woman stood at my elbow.

"Uh... good morning, Miss... uh..."

"Dr. Natasha Filenkov. You may address me as Natasha. You are interested in ze Neanderthal religious practices?"

I was terrible at small talk. If Natasha had been at the summit, she must be someone pretty important. I didn't want to make a bad impression.

"No," I replied. "Are you helping Doc with the mad super-talents?"

She lifted her pointy chin. "I am a scientist, not a medical doctor. I deal in facts, not flesh. I study Rap technology. It is difficult. Ze Raps do not like to share."

"But we have a bunch of their technology, don't we? I mean the platforms, the stunner wands the talents carry, the harnesses and robes that Sammie and I brought back. Sammie said even the talent uniforms are Rap nanotech."

"Zey do not share knowledge of positive and negative energy, or understanding of how to travel between dimensions. Ze platforms defy gravity. How is it done? I am not allowed to take a platform apart to discover ze answers. I must observe and measure covertly."

"You're spying on the Raps?"

"What choice do we have? We have planted measuring devices in ze fracture chamber, but we have learned little. Talents have carried measuring equipment while in transit. Because of ze Nean shields, it is useless. Probes we attempt to launch from our dimension do not recognize ze fracture or enter it. We could learn much if only we could get data from D-space."

Natasha was one frustrated scientist. I'd given up trying to understand the mysteries of the universe early on. Heck, I wasn't sure which ones were real mysteries and which ones were hallucinations. But Natasha showed grit, and I admired that.

"Col. Juarez has asked me to look into ze loss of Smith. I have some questions. Tell me about zis demon you call Smokey."

Knowing that Col. Juarez hadn't blithely accepted the Neans' claim went some distance toward easing my anxiety. Maybe Sammie making friends with them was all a cover, and she didn't like the haughty Nean priest at all.

"I don't know a lot about him. He seems like an okay, er... demon, as demons go. Not that I know a lot of demons. Only three, and two of those in passing. Unless you count the soot-ball. It's only a nightmare, but someday, it will grow up to be a demon. If it doesn't get eaten."

Natasha blinked at me.

Oops. Too much information. How did normal people know what to say and when to shut up?

"You have known it long?"

I'd seen Smokey over the years when I'd fallen through fractures, but back then, I'd thought the Dark Place—what DPS called D-space—was all part of the hallucinations I experienced during psychotic breaks. Only recently had Smokey come looking for me in real dimensions.

"Four or five days?"

"How did you meet it?"

I didn't think it would help Smokey's cause to tell her the Demon Council was investigating DPS with an eye to destroying the E-Prime dimension, and Smokey was their agent. I'm also a terrible liar. With that in mind, I tried for something truthful but non-specific.

"He asked me to save the multiverse," I replied, downplaying all the parts I'd skipped.

One of Natasha's eyebrows rose. Of course she didn't believe me. I was an unlikely hero.

"Let us go to ze fracture chamber." She led me across the quad. "I wish to hear more from you about demons and inspect ze platform from which Smith was lost to find why he died."

Wow, she was serious about figuring out what happened to the dead scientist. Maybe I didn't need Sammie's help. Maybe Natasha would prove that the Nean priest lied and tell everyone what really happened—whatever that was. I hurried after her, my spirits rising.

7

Natasha took the elevator down. I took the stairs. I told her I needed the exercise. Her credentials were enough to get me through the guarded door at the bottom. The six armed guards inside kept a watchful eye on us. The blonde female talent I'd seen there before nodded to the doctor. When the talent looked at me, her hand drifted toward her wand pocket.

On the right wall of the chamber, the white Rap sat at the controls of a platform. The big stone slab hovered six inches off the concrete. With no priest onboard, the runes ringing the edge remained invisible.

Natasha pulled up. "Hmm. Let us watch for a moment."

The Rap slid off the crouching stool and pulled bits and bobs from pockets in its vest and tool belt. It scattered them around both the surface of the stone platform and the mushroom-shaped control panel column thingy in the center, and then climbed onto the stool again.

"Do you know about ze Raps?" Natasha asked.

"They're descended from dinosaurs," I replied. "And are accomplished liars who show no remorse."

She chuffed a soft laugh. "In zis we agree. Rap culture is a matriarchal society structured according to intelligence wiz ze smartest on top. High intelligence is associated wiz ability to detect positive and negative energy flows, ze trait necessary to navigate D-space, but also needed by energy researchers.

"Zey are also risk-averse. You know what zis means?"

"They have others do their dirty work for them," I replied in a flash of anger.

Natasha gave me an appraising look. "Zey consider dimensional exploration vital, but will not risk zeir most energy sensitive—and intelligent—individuals on platforms. In Raps, intelligence is paired wiz sex and plumage color. Darker color means a less sensitive and less valued individual, ze darkest being also male."

Natasha paused, watching me.

"So that white one is one of their *smartest*?" I found that hard to believe.

"And female. White females are extremely rare and have great value. Zey are never allowed to leave R-Prime."

The Raps I'd seen so far ran the gamut from black through dark gray to medium brown. I gasped as my conclusions settled in.

"They send their dumbest, least sensitive people, er—dinos—to be DPS navigators? They've got a lot of nerve telling us demons make travel unsafe!"

The white Rap splayed its—her—paw over the controls. The platform moved smoothly up and down a few inches. She touched another place, and the platform shifted toward the wall but didn't bump despite how quickly it accelerated. The little Rap didn't even sway with the motion. She blinked at the controls, hopped off, and bent to collect her gadgets.

"Ah," Natasha sighed, "so zat is why she is here."

"Enlighten me," I said.

"Her long feathers cover her deformity. See her tail? How it is truncated? Ze organs of energy detection are located in her tail. She must have experienced a tragic accident and lost a portion. To Raps, her high intelligence but low energy detection ability is useless. She is outcast. Zat is why Flight Leader Falcon acted as if she was not present. He struggles to adapt to her new, much reduced status."

"Okay," I said, still confused. "But why is she *here*?"

"A very good question, Mr. Madden." A cunning smile curled Natasha's lips. "Shall we find out?"

Natasha strolled across the fracture chamber with me close behind. The little white Rap stepped off the platform, saw us, and came to an abrupt stop. Her muzzle dipped in what might have been a nod of recognition.

"Dodo," the Rap said with a click and a wheeze.

Confusion flickered across Natasha's face and shouted from mine. Had the Rap just called the good doctor an idiot?

When neither of us replied, the Rap spoke again. "The customary exchange of names. Have I done it incorrectly?"

"You're... Dodo?" I asked.

The Rap dipped her muzzle again. "An elegant name. It has symmetry and repetition, a roundness without beginning or end."

It took everything I had not to laugh out loud. But something in my schizophrenic brain responded to her assertions about the shape of the word. Whispers of "Bo-bo-banana-fanna..." filtered down from the lights. I clamped my teeth, determined not to be dragged down a rhyming rabbit hole.

"Mr. Smith was lost from zis platform, yes?" Natasha stepped around the Rap and swept a hand over the vehicle.

"Possible," the little Rap replied. "Very, very possible. I was not present. I am a navigator recruit."

Dodo clacked her jaws. Her sharp teeth glistened white. I leaned back.

"When we came in, you were flying it," Natasha said. "Did you find it to be in good working order?"

Dodo cocked her head. "I am a navigator recruit."

"Yes, you said. Did it perform within normal parameters?"

The Rap tapped the pads of her digits against her muzzle for a moment before answering. "You can clarify?"

Natasha crossed her arms over her chest.

"Maybe the platform is broken, and that's why Smith fell off," I said.

Dodo looked over the platform. "No pieces are missing."

The Rap was thick as a brick. We'd learned nothing, and I didn't think we ever would. By now I must be late for fracture practice, and I'd missed breakfast.

"A visual inspection does not mean it flies correctly," Natasha said. I gave her credit for persistence.

"Ah! You want to fly." Dodo leaped onto the platform. "Come."

Natasha and I hesitated. She wanted us to join her on the platform? That *couldn't* be a good idea.

Dodo stalked to the controls and turned. "You displace the talent, I, the Raptor navigator, and Mr. Madden, the scientist. We require another to displace the Neanderthal priest."

Natasha's brow furrowed. Then her expression cleared. "You wish to emulate ze load conditions under which our scientist was lost."

Natasha waved at two of the soldiers. They crossed the chamber to her. One was tall, white, and on the willowy side. The other was dark and built like a tank.

"You will join us," Natasha told the heavier man. She stepped onto the six-inch thick slab of tan stone.

The two men exchanged a look. The tall one said, "We can't leave our duty stations, ma'am."

"Col. Juarez has tasked me to discover how our man was lost. Do you wish for me to call him?"

The heavy one grimaced.

"Go ahead," his buddy said. "She has clearance, and there's still five of us on the ground."

The soldier clambered onto the flying hunk of rock and looked daggers at his fellow guard.

"Mr. Madden?" Natasha said.

My hands clenched, my knees shook. The lights belted out *Eve of Destruction*. I didn't trust Raps—any Raps—and especially one a few feathers short of a duck. But I had a duty to help discover why Smith fell.

"We'll stay low, right?" I stepped onto the platform. My gaze jumped to the fracture, jagged and glittering, like the mouth of a hungry monster. "You'll keep us away from the fracture?"

"The *whistle-chirp-chirp* contains the flight path from the tragic journey," Dodo said. The platform lifted a few inches. "We will duplicate it, with modifications to remain inside the room."

The hair rose on the back of my neck. The only indication of motion had been us moving in relation to the walls and floor, which made it feel like they'd moved, not us. I'd had hallucinations where the walls moved. It wasn't an experience I wanted to repeat.

A sheen of sweat glowed on the brow of the soldier. He sent a pleading look at his fellow guard and tightened his grip on his rifle strap.

Natasha's brows lifted with the platform, and her eyes gleamed. She pointed to her feet and spoke to the soldier. "You must stand here, at ze edge. Mr. Madden, place yourself to his left."

The soldier swapped places with Natasha, putting him behind and to the right of Dodo at the control column, and Natasha in front of it, assuming we knew which way 'front' was. With a round platform, who could tell? I took my place to his left

"How will ze stress here compare to D-space?"

"Compare?" Dodo chirped.

"Would ze platform experience more stress in D-space?"

The Rap chattered her teeth and splayed her paw on her chest. "You wish to test stress limits?"

I didn't like the sound of that, but Natasha smiled and nodded. "Exactly."

"Possible. Prepare for flight."

Prepare? How? There was nothing to hold onto, no railing to prevent falling off. No wonder we'd lost Smith. For a safety-conscious species, the Raps seemed remarkably blasé about—

We angled up at break-neck speed. Our flight was soundless and motionless, as though the room revolved around the platform. No wind ruffled the few strands of hair trailing out from under my watch cap. The soldier ducked to avoid clonking his helmet against the ceiling.

I ducked because the soldier did. My whole body went rigid. My mouth hung open. My brain screamed that I should jump while I had the chance.

We leveled off and shot across the chamber. Our speed was too great. Even if we turned at the last moment, all the humans would be carried forward by their momentum and splatter against the wall. A yelp burst from my throat.

Three inches from the wall, we made a hard left for six feet, then dropped straight to the floor like a rock in free-fall. The platform made another sharp direction change inches off the floor and raced toward the fracture. A guard jumped sideways to avoid being hit.

I squatted low and dug my nails into the rock surface. The soldier kept his dignity and his feet, although he'd dropped into a permanent half-crouch. His face was frozen in horror, and his eyes showed a lot of white. I'd seen that look on the faces of the demented at the mental hospital where I'd been incarcerated for six months. It immediately preceded an explosion of insane behavior.

I caught Natasha's rapturous smile and sparkling eyes as she turned to watch the storage lockers whiz past. The soldier and I weren't the only lunatics on the craft.

When the platform swirled into a ceiling-bound spiral while whirling around in circles, my stomach rebelled. I closed my eyes and swallowed hard. My muscles, my balance told me we were standing still. *Impossible.*

I slit one eye open. The room gyrated around me, moving faster and faster until it was all a blur of light and color. *Pretend it's a hallucination, River. Ohm.*

The alarm system blared. Its wail came and went like a train whistle in the night as we zoomed by a wall-mounted speaker. The platform spun so quickly I thought we'd be thrown off. If this was how travel went in D-space, I wanted no part of it.

"It's gonna kill us!" the soldier beside me shouted, his eyes on Dodo.

The sheer panic in his voice sent a shiver up my spine. Nothing good ever comes from putting a gun in the hands of the insane. The soldier had crossed that line three turns back.

The soldier slid his rifle off his shoulder and pointed at the Rap. My heart jumped into my throat. My future with Sammie went up in smoke. If a human killed a Rap, the dinos would do more than take their tech and leave in a huff. They'd probably nuke our dimension.

Natasha's face was white, and her hands were raised in a stopping motion. She was too far away to do anything. I was closer, but what did I know about guns? Only that I never wanted to have one in my hands.

Dodo turned her muzzle toward the soldier and blinked. Her paw shifted on the control mushroom. If she carried a stunner in her vest or on her tool belt, she'd never have time to draw.

The soldier had already placed his finger on the trigger. When the bullets started to fly, they could go anywhere, hit anyone in the room, especially since we were still twirling like a top. I leaped.

It was like jumping into a vat of wet cement—mushy on top but unyielding beneath the surface. He must have weighed twice what I did, and it was all muscle. I'd have seconds to permanently disable him so he couldn't carry out his assault on the Rap. Yeah, right. I practiced meditation, not kung-fu.

I deflected the barrel toward the ceiling with one hand while I jammed my thumb inside the trigger guard. A gazillion bullets sprayed from the barrel. The sound waves pounded my head. A ceiling light shattered. Rock chips hailed down on us. His clip emptied. I prayed he didn't have some fast reload gizmo.

The soldier heaved, and I flew backwards. The platform was mere inches off the ground and at a dead stop. I slammed onto my back, all the air knocked from my lungs. Pain raced down my spine into my pelvis. The back of my head cracked the concrete. It hadn't gotten any softer since yesterday. My vision dimmed.

Lightning crackled through the air. On the platform, the soldier slumped to his knees, and then keeled over. Next to the platform, the blonde talent still pointed her wand at him, ready to launch a second bolt if necessary. Natasha took it all in, open-mouthed.

The other guards ran to the platform. They turned their guns first on the Rap, then on the talent, and finally on me. *Yeah, blame it on the crazy guy.*

Natasha made a snappy recovery. "Ze platform, it has inertial dampeners so no motion is felt by ze passengers, yes?"

Dodo settled the platform and hopped off her stool. She padded to the fallen soldier and looked down on him. Then she turned to me.

One claw-tipped digit pointed my direction. "The scientist has fallen."

8

Captain Samuels burst through the door of the fracture chamber like a tank smashing through enemy lines. A dozen soldiers followed in his wake. They scattered, fell to kneeling positions, and trained their rifles on me. I sighed.

"Someone shut off that damned alarm!" Samuels shouted. "What the hell's going on here?"

One of the new arrivals scurried away, and the alarm cut out. The five chamber guards all looked at one another, each hoping someone else would explain.

Natasha stepped over the unconscious soldier and right up to Samuels. You wouldn't see me get that close to him. *Ever.*

"We have conducted a flight test of ze platform from which Smith fell and concluded it is in perfect working order."

I rose to my feet, keeping a wary eye on the guards, and edged away from Samuels.

Samuels' face clouded over, and he pointed to the prostrate soldier. "What happened to that man?"

The talent snapped to attention. Her eyes looked straight ahead. "I stunned him, sir. He displayed unsafe weapon handling near the Raptor who operated the platform during the test."

Dang! She was good. I would have burbled on about the guy going crazy and how it wasn't my fault. I wondered if I'd ever master that kind of forthright evasion.

"Mr. Madden. Of course you'd be involved." Samuels' eyes narrowed. "What's your role in this?"

"Uh..." I wiped my palms on my pants. "I was the scientist. And I fell."

I'd played the scientist, and I'd fallen, just as the Rap said. Something about that nagged at me, but Samuels took a giant step closer and drove it right out of my head.

"Aren't you supposed to be somewhere?" he asked.

"Fracture practice. I think. Sir."

One minute I was walking away. The next I was racing through the chamber doors and leaping up the stairs three at a time.

I ran out the front door of the fracture facility into the quad, reversed course, and pelted out of the rectangular group of buildings onto the fenced sports field.

Wan morning sun warmed my shoulders, and fresh, crisp air filled my lungs. The ground raced by under my feet. The wind whispered on my cheeks. My surroundings vanished.

Nothing cleared my mind like running. I could see right away that Smith hadn't fallen because of a platform malfunction. I could also see that Natasha was looney, and that I'd run smack out of new theories to explain Smith's demise.

Wheels in my brain clacked and turned in time with my feet, something that happened when I thought hard. Either Smokey—or a demon that looked like him—had killed Smith, or the Nean priest lied to cover for something or someone else. To get the truth from the Neans, I'd need Sammie's help.

"Madden!"

I pulled up short and looked around, lost. I'd already reached the far end of the vast grassy area with its paved oval running track and infield striped for football games. I didn't remember how I got there.

A squat man a few inches shorter than me and wearing the standard black talent uniform jogged towards me, puffing hard. His half-moon eyes squinted at me. His high cheekbones and full cheeks shone rosy red. Strands of coarse black hair stuck to his glistening forehead.

"No one mentioned you were another Olympic runner." He offered a pudgy hand. "Talent Second Class Nick Pingayak. Call me Nick. I'll be your mentor for fracture practice."

I gave his warm, damp hand a quick shake. "River Madden."

At last, here was the person who could teach me how to control myself so I wouldn't fracture unexpectedly. Maybe if I studied hard, I could learn to live without the Rap cuffs. We walked back the way I'd come to join a group of recruits already on the field.

My mentor whistled quietly under his breath, the same short phrase over and over. It wasn't a song I recognized. The more I listened, the more I heard words in the sounds. *Not real.* I chided myself to stop creating hidden meanings where there weren't any.

Nick glanced my way. I must have been staring because he looked embarrassed.

"Sorry. I'm trying to memorize a phrase."

Wow, so he was crazy, too. There couldn't possibly be an entire government organization completely filled with nut cases, could there? Or maybe that wasn't such a stretch.

"It's Rap." He lowered his voice, even though no one was near us. "I'm a Yupik Eskimo. My people subsist on what we get from the sea. We developed a whistled version of our language that can be heard over long distances and a lot of environmental noise. Capt. Samuels thinks that background will help me learn the Rap language so we can eavesdrop on them."

And I thought I was the only one who didn't trust the Raps.

"How's that working for you?"

He grimaced. "Not great. The navigators hardly say anything, and when they do, they use English, even when they're off duty. Samuels says it's deliberate, to prevent us from learning their language. But those new Rap VIPs have been blabbing in their native tongue since they arrived."

I surveyed the landscape, checking for Raps who might be pointing wands—or sonic banana guns—at me. "You've seen them? The Rap VIPs, I mean."

Nick's grimace deepened. "I had a debriefing with them this morning. They wanted to know what happened on the platform yesterday, even though I already filed a five-page report saying I didn't see anything."

My eyebrows shot up. "You were on Smith's platform?"

"Yes, to my everlasting regret."

"And you didn't see anything?"

He looked at me like I was an idiot. "I stood on the front of the platform. Lark, our navigator, was directly behind me. The priest was at the back right edge, like always, and Smith was to his left, balancing the load—not that load distribution makes any difference on a platform. It's more like an elevator; everyone wants their personal space."

If load distribution didn't matter, then why had Dodo insisted we needed another person on the platform? Her statement about the scientist falling ran round and round in my head. I almost missed what Nick said next.

"It was an ordinary transit. The priest got the shields up, we entered the fracture, and ten minutes later, we exited at E-Prime. I'd cleared the security search before I realized Smith wasn't with us."

The fracture chamber was a big place. If the priest had seen Smokey pull Smith off the platform, he should have raised the alarm on arrival, long before Nick walked the length of the chamber and was frisked by the guards. I didn't buy the priest's reticence to speak about demons as an excuse to say nothing.

"Why didn't the priest warn everyone the platform was under attack when it happened?"

"Couldn't, not and keep his focus on the shields. If he'd broken his chant... Let's just say we'd all be nuts now, assuming we weren't dead like Smith." Nick thrust his hands in his pockets. "All the talents are rattled. We've seen what happens to super-talents who fall through fractures unprotected. None of us want to end up like that. Or in pieces like Smith."

If the demons wanted to halt inter-dimensional travel, they were well on their way. Raps weren't the only ones who could be risk-averse. If Smokey took the fall for Smith's death, there'd be no more DPS.

"You didn't see a rainbow-colored round disk thingy?" My question earned me an incredulous look. Maybe he thought I'd ask about unicorns next.

Ahead, the other DC recruits stood in a rough line, spaced out in pairs along the football field. The recruits focused on metal rings set atop poles at the opposite edge of the field. A middle-aged female talent marched around offering words of encouragement and instruction.

A knot of Nean priests stood behind the recruits. All of their eyes looked my direction. One pair of eyes belonged to Hothead. A glimmer of runes crept up his staff.

Nick pointed out Hothead. "If you want to know more, ask him."

He was the shield priest on the platform? Any hope of getting useful information from the Neans melted into the cool morning air. Maybe Natasha could pry information from them. Or Sammie, if she lost that starry-eyed look I'd seen when she'd told me about her important new assignment. *Friends, my ass.*

Nick stopped fifty feet from the recruits. "Slip off your cuffs while we practice creating fractures."

"*Creating?*" I said, aghast. "I thought you'd teach me how to stop."

My mentor rubbed his head and gazed down the line of recruits. "Talents are assigned to outposts in alternate dimensions to ensure that the research teams never get trapped. If an access fracture closes, the talents reopen it. To be at talent at DPS, you have to be able to fracture on demand."

"But..." I *had* to keep this job, but how could I keep it if I didn't fracture?

"Look," Nick said, "you watch and listen while I work with the others, and then we'll see what you can do."

Nick strode away. I removed my cuffs, despite my better judgment.

At the far end of the line, a nearly invisible sooty cloud of negative energy formed over the head of a tall, good-looking male recruit about my age. He'd created the beginnings of a nightmare, although no one but me could see it. Seeing nightmares was another of my unique, freakish talents. The little cloud drifted and thinned until it disappeared, too weak to have any effect on the dimensional barriers.

Mr. Lee, an older Asian guy, drew a deep, calming breath, folded his hands as if in prayer, and closed his eyes. Nothing happened.

I could have told him that. Smokey said nightmares were the result of negative thoughts: anger, fear, despair, pain. Lee's calm meditative approach wouldn't create the kind of powerful roiling nightmare capable of causing fractures.

Next to me, Hannah, a girl I pegged as in her late teens, tightened her fists and stared hard at the target. Lank chestnut hair framed a long, thin face dominated by haunted hazel eyes. Her slumped shoulders lifted with her effort.

One of the other recruits said she was the daughter of one of the super-talents Sammie and I rescued. If that was true, she had plenty of fodder to create a nightmare.

Sure enough, a black splotch of haze formed in front of her. Unlike the other nightmare, this one grew darker, drew itself together, and floated to mid-field. It hung eight feet off the ground, spinning slowly, as though it was getting oriented.

The hair rose on the back of my neck. Nightmares signified all that was wrong in the world. To create them deliberately sickened me.

With a jerk, the nightmare smacked against an invisible barrier. A tiny crack lanced across the sky. Glitter formed at its edges. The nightmare sieved through the crack and disappeared into D-space.

The recruits cheered. Nick jogged over to shake Hannah's hand. The other instructor joined them and patted Hannah's shoulder. The crack wasn't large enough for a platform, but if the girl teamed with another talent, together they'd be able to make a full-blown fracture.

The Nean priests scuttled forward and began to chant. Rolling sheets of slow-moving light washed over the newly formed crack. The glitter paled. It wasn't a very big crack, but the Neans made slow progress healing it. Maybe they were the second string.

I wondered what the Neans would think if they could see nightmares; if they knew that nightmares—the ones that weren't eaten by demons—grew up to become demons. They'd piss their robes.

A swirling black cloud squeezed through the crack into our dimension. It corkscrewed up and out of the Neans' light, paused, and then it dove for me.

It whirled around my head blocking my vision with its basketball-sized mass. I swatted at it to no avail. It stopped, moved two feet away, and hung in the air, quivering. Something about it seemed familiar.

"Soot-ball?"

My little cloud nightmare vibrated up and down. Like an over-excited puppy, it zoomed around me three more times. I'd created it when I'd accidentally fractured my way into E-4, where I'd met Sammie. My little nipper'd stuck like tree sap ever since.

But Smokey said the soot-ball had to migrate to D-space or starve. It likely wouldn't last long there on its own. I couldn't just abandon my offspring, so I'd made my bargain with Smokey to raise it.

I grinned, and then I looked around the field.

"Is Smokey here?" If I could get answers out of Smokey, maybe I could make sense of Smith's fall.

The soot-ball thinned, sank, and pulled back while drifting side to side. No Smokey. But something else was up.

"Does Smokey know where you are?" I asked, hands on hips. I had no personal experience with parents that I could remember, and no parenting training, but this was the stance the cook at the orphanage used when she wanted to know who'd lifted the cookies cooling on the counter.

The soot-ball sank more and drifted left, right, our agreed sign for 'no.'

Down the line from me, a new nightmare formed over Hannah's partner, Pete. Pete was tall and lean and black as the night. He'd been a marine and lost his lower left leg in Afghanistan. He'd also been an Olympic marathon contender. Now he walked with a limp on an artificial foot.

Pete's nightmare dropped over him like a shroud before it wandered aimlessly along the line of recruits. Smokey said nightmares tried to get their creators' attention. When they couldn't, they lost interest in humans and either wasted away or, if they were strong enough, fractured to get to D-space.

Watching his nightmare gave me an idea. Why create a new nightmare when I already had one? If the soot-ball helped me, I could remain at DPS without creating more monsters. After all, how many would Smokey be willing to raise?

"Hey, soot-ball, can you make a fracture again? Like you did when you were born?"

Nick stood behind Hannah and Pete, but he watched me—watched me talk to something he couldn't see. Heat crept into my face, and I half-turned away.

My little buddy skittered in a circle that eventually became a horizontal motion. What was that supposed to mean? If we were going to work together, we needed better smoke signals.

"This is important. Really important. I can't stay here without your help. And I want to stay."

Pete shook out his arms and frowned. His nightmare, smaller and less dense than Hannah's, expanded, contracted, and expanded again until it was so thin I thought it might disappear. It didn't have the mass to manage a pinhole, never mind a fracture.

The soot-ball drew into a compact sphere and darted behind my left shoulder. It jiggled like a pond in an earthquake. I couldn't figure out what had caused its reaction.

Hannah had her fists bunched and her head bent while she tried for another nightmare. A darker, more malevolent cloud coalesced above her. It traced a small circle around her, growing as she concentrated.

"I need a fracture," I pleaded. "It doesn't have to be big."

The soot-ball disappeared behind me and reappeared off my right hip. Dark waves rippled through its smoky interior. It inched forward, and then snapped back.

Near the center of the field, Pete's faint nightmare continued to thin. Hannah's nightmare wafted straight up, swaying softly as it rose. Its interior burped and bubbled and tumbled. It reminded me of the grotesque nightmare that had nearly eaten Smokey. I shivered.

The soot-ball bounced in place and shot forward. It streaked down the row of recruits, flew up from below Hannah's nightmare, and buzzed once around it. It headed towards Pete's fading nightmare at center field.

Hannah's nightmare thickened and gave chase. There was a hunger in its pursuit of the soot-ball that made my blood chill. It gained ground quickly, but not before the soot-ball reached Pete's creation.

The soot-ball circled Pete's nightmare, tapping itself against the soft edges of the other nightmare's spreading mass. Pete's nightmare retracted into something more solid—just in time for Hannah's nightmare to plow into it.

It looked like the Saturday night fights on TV. Pete's nightmare flew back, then reversed course, came at Hannah's nightmare, and ripped a handful of smoky substance away. Hannah's nightmare retaliated, pressing forward and ripping away chunks from its opponent. The soot-ball refereed from an orbit ten feet away.

It was a lopsided battle. Hannah's nightmare gave up the ripping strategy and engulfed Pete's diminished nightmare. The interior of the new, larger nightmare roiled violently while it hung in the sky for ten seconds. Then it began a slow revolution, a formless predator seeking its next prey.

"Soot-ball!" I waved my arms. "Get out of there!"

All the humans and Neans turned toward me. The soot-ball zigged and zagged before the victorious nightmare, a new contender taunting the seasoned champion. *Kids. They never listened.*

The Frankenstein nightmare lunged. The soot-ball dodged, but not fast enough. The monster pulled a gauzy blob of soot out of my nightmare. I sucked in a breath and held it.

The soot-ball fled, full-tilt. I'd never seen a nightmare move at its speed. It made a bee-line for the crack. As it rocketed faster and faster, it changed shape until it was a long, thin needle.

The monster nightmare poured on steam. It became smaller and denser, kind of like a cannonball. A cannonball headed toward a crack in the dimensional barrier.

"Fracture!" I screamed down the line of recruits. "Get back!"

I ran for the quad, digging my cuffs from my pocket. Nick watched me, open mouthed. Then his mouth snapped shut, and he shoved Hannah.

"Move!" he shouted. "Go, go, go!"

I looked over my shoulder. The soot-ball speared through the tiny crack. The behemoth splatted against the invisible barrier. The barrier shattered.

Jagged fissures ripped across the curtain that separated our dimension from D-space. Glitter silvered the surface of a center rupture twice as large as the aperture in the fracture chamber. Tidal forces dragged at my body.

The Neans' staffs came up. Their voices rose in unison. Alarms drowned the sound of their words, but they created a shield between the recruits and the gaping fracture, cutting the sucking sensation. I ran wide of them, frightened that I might disrupt their magic and doom the fleeing talents.

Humans, Neans, and Raps spilled from buildings and onto the playing field. Anyone with talent stopped dead well back from the edge of the field. The Neans ran pell-mell to assist their comrades.

The Raps backed away. Except for the white one, Dodo. She padded forward to within twenty feet of the Neans. Her truncated tail rose straight up like a flag pole, the long feathers flapping in the breeze. Then she turned her pale blue eyes on me.

9

I stood at the far end of the field and shivered as though it was forty below even though the temperature must have been near fifty. My fellow recruits could have been sucked into the fracture, never to be sane again. The soot-ball hadn't returned. Did it become the monster nightmare's lunch?

I checked the fasteners on my cuffs for a third time and vowed never to fracture again. Better to live homeless and loveless than to put others in so much danger. The decision tasted like ash in my mouth.

Col. Juarez rounded the corner of the building. The Rap, Falcon, and the old priest, His High Muckymuck, flanked him. The two Rap bodyguards trailed behind, eyes darting around and paws holding wands. Capt. Samuels caught up to them at the edge of the grass.

I glanced about for an escape route.

Then Sammie appeared, and my heart sped up. The redheaded priest, Flash, walked too close beside her and hung on her every word. It's a good thing I was a pacifist, or I might have stormed over and had words with him.

His High Muckymuck said something to Flash and pointed to the fracture. Flash got a surly look. He nodded to Sammie and trudged across the field to help the other priests.

Sammie saw me and jogged over.

"Did you do that?" she asked, awe in her tone while she gazed at the fracture.

I hung my head. "Umm..."

"It's amazing. I wonder if their shields are like miniature dimensional barriers. Or bandages that cover the wound while the fracture heals on its own."

My head snapped up. I glared at the Neans and crossed my arms. "Looks like Flash will be busy for a while. Maybe we could take a walk?"

"Who?" Sammie finally turned her attention on me. She had that little crease between her eyes that she always got when she wasn't especially pleased.

I waved a hand toward the field. "First-Light-whatever. His initials spell 'FLASH.'"

Sammie huffed up. "You could at least make an effort to learn his name. It's First *Luminary* Acolyte Schlauzauber Heshlibob."

"He started it!" I protested. Oops. I was coming across like the 16-year-old whiner I'd masqueraded as when I'd first met Sammie. It wasn't hard. I could do it without thinking. "Sorry."

Sammie's shoulders drooped, and she let out a breath. "He's just a kid, River, and his life's a mess. His mother is warrior caste, which means he's resented by the other acolytes, who are pure priest caste. And unlike the other acolytes who start creating light as soon as they can walk, he didn't show any signs of magic until recently. Once he did, he was forced to join the priesthood even though he had other plans. He's a sweet boy underneath, but he has a lot of anger issues. He could use some sympathetic friends."

"It's just that a lot has happened," I said, "and I don't know what to do. I feel like—"

"A fish out of water?" Sammie interrupted.

I'd intended to say 'like a psycho without his meds,' but if Sammie could overlook my mental status, I'd try harder to do the same. I smiled and nodded.

Sammie's expression softened more. "I know what a difficult transition it must be for you coming to DPS. I wish I could be more help, but right now, Col Juarez needs me to patch things up with the Neans. He's desperate. The recruits get a leave in town tonight. The bus heads out after mess. I'll ride along, and we can talk then. I've missed you."

Sammie flashed me a radiant smile, patted my arm, and hurried back to Col. Juarez.

The day brightened, and a weight lifted from my shoulders. She and I were going on our first date. The feeling lasted only a moment. I couldn't afford a date. I couldn't even go dutch. I didn't have any money.

I shoved my hands in my pockets and trudged back toward the quad.

Pete fell into place at my left shoulder. He grinned and slapped me on the back. "Nice job, Madden. If it hadn't been for you, we'd be out there doing nothing useful for another hour."

The tall, good-looking recruit pulled up on my right. He had an electronic tablet thingamajig with lots of numbers and squiggly lines showing on the screen. I had one of those in my desk. I hadn't figured out how to turn it on.

"JR," he said.

I barely had time to grasp his hand before he had it back on the tablet screen, tap-tapping on stuff.

A curvy, dark-haired woman joined JR.

"Veronica," she said. "Why don't you come back to my room, honey?"

I missed a step. Was she propositioning me?

"Later," JR replied. "Some interesting trades goin' down right now. Ought to get gnarly when the Asian markets open."

Veronica's lips pulled into a pout. "Trade, trade, trade. That's all you do."

Pete snorted and spoke to me. "I saw you come on the field. You look like you move pretty fast. Ever race?"

"I've run for my life a few times," I said.

Pete missed a step, and then he laughed. "Want to make a wager on which one of us is faster?"

I couldn't help it; I glanced down at his artificial leg. "Umm..."

"Don't think a cripple could beat you?" he asked. "Probably right. How about you give me two-to-one odds and a fifty yard head start? We'll make it a two-mile run. Look, you already got your kicks on."

I hung my head and mumbled, "Just started the job. No money."

JR's attention snapped from his tablet screen to me, his eyes glinting. "How much you intend to bet?"

"Well..."

"Fifty," Pete said. "Won't do it for less."

"Done," JR replied.

"But—" I shook my head.

"No worries," JR assured me. "I saw that caricature of Higgins you did. You do me a drawing of that demon friend of yours, and I'll give you fifty for it."

"*Dollars?*" No one had ever given me more than five bucks for one of my sketches.

Veronica rolled her eyes and peeled off from our group.

"I get the copyright," JR added.

"And you'll still owe me another fifty if I win," Pete said. "You can give it to me out of your next paycheck."

I rubbed my watch cap and thought about the kind of date I could take Sammie on for fifty dollars. No, a *hundred* dollars. Wow! She'd be so impressed that she'd stop worrying about relations with the Neans and realize I was the man for her. And I could ask her to interrogate the Nean to find out what happened on the platform. I grinned.

"Okay if I use pink stationery for the sketch?"

An hour later, I was back at the athletic field, sketch in hand. JR had provided a huge sheet of paper and *two* long, sharp pencils. I'd never had such luxurious art supplies. I'd drawn Smokey striding through the apocalyptic ruins I'd seen in my dreams when I first met Sammie.

I'd been surprised at how grateful the other recruits seemed because they thought I'd gotten them out of fracture practice. They must know how easily I could beat Pete in a race, but they'd gone ahead with the plan anyway. Wasn't that how friends acted? Having friends might be easier than I thought.

The Neans had finished healing the fracture and departed. They'd been replaced by a cadre of soldiers at the edges of the running track. No one carried weapons, which was a relief. There were a lot of looks my way followed by groans from half the troops and laughs from the other half. Had I missed something?

Pete returned to the track, JR walking at his side. Pete wore a white t-shirt over running shorts. What should have been his left calf was a plastic connector thingy and silver shaft, and the foot was a curved blade of flexible metal. He no longer limped.

JR took the sketch from me and unrolled it. His eyes shone with delight, and he nodded his approval. He passed a wad of cash to Pete, who grinned and stuffed it in his t-shirt pocket.

"You gonna run in your uniform?" Pete asked as we walked onto the track. He stopped and bent, stretching his muscled legs. "Four laps is a long way."

Stretching was a luxury for people who knew ahead of time when they'd need to run. While I'd been homeless, I'd remained prepared to go full out at a moment's notice, no stretching required. I stood on the asphalt track and waited, silent.

Pete finished his stretching and jogged casually up the track, gradually gaining speed. I opened and closed my fingers a few times to let out some tension.

"Go!" JR shouted from the sidelines.

I looked over at him. Then I looked back to Pete, and my heart jumped.

Pete ate up the track, his legs a blur. *Shit! Olympic marathon contender.*

They'd hornswoggled me, the new guy who didn't know any better. Not only would I be out the fifty I'd earned for the sketch, I'd owe Pete another fifty come payday, whenever that was.

I dashed away. Pete steamed down the backstretch by the time I reached the first turn. Was I gaining on him? It didn't look like it.

I narrowed my eyes, shut out all the cheering and jeering soldiers lining the track. Their ranks doubled, then tripled. Everyone who wasn't on duty must be watching.

Ohm. Ohm. My shoulders relaxed. My strides grew longer. My feet moved quicker. A little screechy buzz grew in my brain. I'd catch Pete if it was the last thing I did.

When we started the last lap, I'd closed the gap to ten feet. He must have heard me coming. Or maybe the noise of the crowd tipped him off. I could just hear them over the buzz in my brain. He glanced back, and surprise widened his eyes.

Pete tucked his chin down. His arms pumped harder. His stride lengthened. The gap between us grew.

I gritted my teeth and stepped up my game. The volume of the buzz in my brain jumped. We'd started the final turn when I pulled up at his shoulder.

Pete looked down at me. "You run like a girl."

In two quick strides, he pulled ahead again.

I poured on more effort, closed up, and gasped, "You run like a..." I didn't have it in me to call him a cripple.

"Crip?" he said, reading my mind.

"Turtle!" I choked.

"Fag!" he sneered and leaped ahead.

We both leaned into the turn, neck and neck. If he had a kick left in him, I was dead.

"Cheater!" I said.

"Fool!" he snapped, but he lost a few steps on me.

"Loser!" I shouted.

"What's burning?" He coughed.

The buzzing had gotten so loud that I almost didn't hear him. I was in the zone. I could run like this forever. Liquid lightning raced through my veins. Liquid lightning burned my wrists.

We crossed the finish line, me in front by a hair. Smoke curled from the Rap cuffs I wore. My feet faltered.

"Shit, Madden," Pete squeaked as he pulled even, his eyes locked on the blackening cuffs. "Infirmary, now!"

Pete grabbed my sleeve and pushed me off the track. He shouted at JR. "Call Doc! Madden needs new cuffs! And sound the fracture alert!"

We ran between the big stone hulks and across the quad to the infirmary building, alarms clanging. People streamed out and looked around, confused. My wrists got hotter, and pressure built in my head.

Suddenly Dodo was beside us. She loped along on her hind legs, easily matching our speed. Her paw slapped something onto my chest. She consulted a gadget in her hand. Her jaws clacked.

"You are disarmed."

Doc stepped out of the building that housed the infirmary, new cuffs in his hands and worry in his eyes. Pete and I didn't slow until we'd reached him. Doc pointed a Rap energy-measuring device at me. It gave off the slowest of ticks.

Dodo strolled up and addressed Doc. "Please replace his *caw-squawk* and I will remove the *chirp-tweet-tweet*."

Doc looked at her, and then at me. Unlike Nick, he didn't speak Rap.

"He burned up his cuffs." Pete pointed to the blackened strips on my wrists.

"Ah! *Cuffs*. Please replace his cuffs, and I will remove the *chirp-tweet-tweet*."

Doc shook his head. "How in the hell..."

When he touched the blackened cuffs, they disintegrated. Dodo scooped a sample into a glass tube. Out of nowhere, Natasha dove on the last of the burnt bits, a challenge in her eyes. Dodo only nodded.

Doc examined my wrists and then strapped on new cuffs. "Nothing serious. Use some ointment if the cuffs chafe the irritated skin."

Dodo snatched a silver spider-shaped doodad off my chest.

"What is zat?" Natasha asked.

Dodo blinked her big, blue eyes. "A *chirp-tweet-tweet*."

The Rap padded away across the grass just as Samuels arrived.

"You *again*, Madden?" He didn't wait for me to reply, just turned to Doc. "What happened?"

"Cuff replacement." Doc rubbed a hand over tired eyes. "I have patients to attend to."

Doc disappeared back through the building door. Natasha scurried away, her fragile sample of cinders cupped in her hands. Samuels gave me the evil eye and marched off.

"Dang, Madden, don't you know to stay away from Samuels?" Pete said in a hushed voice. "And where the hell did you learn to run?"

I appreciated that Pete had risked his sanity bringing me to Doc—if I'd fractured, he would have fallen through—but that didn't make me forget he'd tried to fleece me. *Not a friend.*

"You think someone *taught* me to run like a girl?"

Pete threw back his head and laughed. "Psychological warfare. You were outrunning me."

"I'm not a fag, either," I grumbled, my anger blunted by his admission that I was faster.

He laughed louder and handed me the wad of bills. "Yeah, well, I am. You want to make something of it?"

I wondered what Pete would think if he knew I was schizophrenic. I wasn't in the mood to share.

"Naw," I said. "I'm a pacifist."

Pete wrapped an arm around my neck and rubbed his knuckles hard against my watch cap before he let me go with a friendly shove. He sure acted like a friend. Was he?

"Come on, let's get lunch. Then I have to pay a bunch of soldiers a bundle of money."

I hadn't thought about what Pete had on the line and felt bad for beating a cripple. Should I have let him win, even if he was a cheater? What would a normal guy do? But without winning the bet, I wouldn't be able to take Sammie on a fabulous date.

"How much did you lose?"

He grinned. "Not as much as JR. Not by a longshot."

10

It was the longest afternoon of my life. Higgins cancelled class. He said he was busy working on détente with the Neans. He piled on yet more reading to keep us out of trouble. It seemed like an appropriate punishment after I'd screwed things up with the Raps and Neans.

I tried to be a good student and read in my room, but all I could think about was my date with Sammie. I'd heard about dates but never been on one. Couples ate at fancy restaurants or went to movies or made out in spooky woods where they were attacked by scary serial killers. While I wouldn't mind making love to Sammie again, I didn't fancy meeting a madman in the dark. Would Doc loan me another taser?

After dinner, Hannah wished everyone well and headed for the hospital ward to sit with her mother. Pete, JR, Veronica, Mr. Lee, and I walked to the front gates to board a bus.

Sammie wasn't there. I got on last and made sure I sat in an empty row so there'd be room for her beside me.

The driver started the bus.

We waited.

Where the heck was Sammie? What if the bus left without her?

We waited some more.

In the waning light, a group of people came toward us from the quad. The redheaded Nean, Flash, wore fatigues instead of his glowing robe and silly hat. He walked between Capt. Samuels and Sammie, just like he was one of our soldiers. Four real soldiers with pistols on their hips and MP armbands around their biceps marched behind them.

No! She couldn't bring *him* on our date. And her *dad*? Seeing Samuels made me shiver.

The entire group clomped onto the bus, filling the stubby vehicle. An older female MP flashed a quick smile and nabbed the seat I'd saved for Sammie. All my fantasies about an evening with my sweetheart melted into stewing disappointment.

Pete moved so Sammie and Flash could sit together in the first row, right in front of her father. She chatted amiably to the Nean on the way to town, pointing out landmarks through the windows. I stared hard, willing her to turn and face me, but she didn't.

We drove through an area of middle-class tract homes and into what passed for Lake Point's downtown. A few modern glass and concrete office buildings stood shoulder to shoulder with older brick and wood shops and stores. Some places were vacant, but mostly the town seemed to be holding its own against the flight of businesses and residents to larger cities.

Most of the downtown stores were buttoned up for the night, except for a McDonald's in the next block. I'd hoped for something nice, something with candles on the tables, but I didn't see any restaurant signs. The neon beer advertisements from a corner bar lit the pavement and drew everyone.

I'd never been in a bar. Because I looked like a teenager, no one would let me in without ID, something I'd never had. Besides, spending money on alcohol meant going without food. I voted for food every time.

But now I had a wad of cash in my pocket and government ID if anyone asked. I could impress Sammie with my good fortune and buy a round for everyone. That's how normal people treated their friends, and I wanted Sammie to see I'd made a lot of friends, even if they weren't really my friends.

One of the MPs entered while another held the door, eyes sweeping the street. Samuels led Sammie and Flash in. The rest of us trudged behind, except for JR and Veronica, who walked briskly down the block. The other two MPs brought up the rear.

The inside was dim and smelled of booze. A jukebox by the door winked and blinked in a gaudy display of neon. A bar ran along the left wall, a mirror behind it. Booths with hard wooden seats ringed the walls. Tables dotted the floor space at the front. Two pool tables took up the rear.

A thin, middle-aged bartender with dark hair and tired eyes squinted at us. He nodded to my fellow recruits, but his attention seemed more focused on the MPs, who spread out around the room where they could watch both the front and back doors.

A couple of college-age guys finished up a game of pool with a rowdy shout and moved to the bar for beer refills. A red-faced lush nursed a drink in a booth. Otherwise we had the place to ourselves.

Pete strode to the pool tables, inviting Mr. Lee to join him. I wondered whether Pete hustled pool as well as hustling races. I wouldn't be accepting any billiards challenges. Crazy, not stupid.

Capt. Samuels took a stool at the end of the bar. He looked more like a sentry than a patron. The bartender glanced his way every few seconds.

"How about here?" Sammie said.

She'd picked a table with half a dozen chairs gathered around it. Flash stopped craning his neck around and grunted approval.

I shoved past him and pulled out a chair for Sammie. She gave me a radiant but tired smile and sat. I hoped Col. Juarez wasn't overworking her. Losing her brother had really taken it out of her. She deserved time off, not being saddled with responsibility for the human relationship with the Neans.

Flash stood watching me. Watching and waiting for something. I grabbed the chair next to Sammie and plopped down, even though I wasn't entirely comfortable what with the big redhead looming over me.

"You will show your obeisance to the First Acolyte." He pointed to a chair.

"Like hell," I said. "Real men help *ladies* to their seats, not oversized orang—"

"River," Sammie said in a voice sharp enough to slice tomatoes. She had a death grip on my arm. "First Luminary Acolyte Schlauzauber Heshlibob isn't familiar with our customs."

Flash went all sappy. "It is my wish that you address me as Hesh." He turned hard eyes on me. "You will refer to me as First Luminary Acolyte Schlauzauber Heshlibob as is appropriate to your standing, demon spawn."

Demon spawn? How dare he! Sammie's nails dug into the zombie gouges in my arm.

"Yeah, whatever you say, Flash," I muttered.

I gave him the cold shoulder and leaned toward Sammie. Flash was around the table and sitting on her other side in two shakes of a lamb's tail. The jukebox in the corner played an Elvis tune, *Burning Love.* The recording was old and scratchy and not at quite the right speed.

"You want something to drink?" I fished the wad of cash from my pocket with a flourish. "I'm buying."

Sammie's eyes went wide. "Is that part of the money you stole? I thought you gave it all back? You can't use it in this dimension."

"So he's a thief as well as demon spawn." Flash wrinkled his nose.

I went stiff. "Not a thief. Or a demon. I won the money fair and square."

"You won it gambling?" Sammie's forehead furrowed, and her lips thinned.

"What is this *gambling*?" Flash asked.

Sammie gave me a look that said I should have kept my mouth shut. I guessed she didn't want Neans to know about our vices.

She shifted to speak to the Nean. "It's when two or more people wager money on the possible outcomes of an event. The person who correctly selects the eventual outcome keeps all the money."

Flash's eyes narrowed, and he crossed his arms over his chest. "What event did you wager on?"

I puffed out my chest and waved to the back of the room. "That I could beat Pete in a two-mile race. And I did."

Flash laughed, showing a mouthful of big, square teeth in what I had to admit was a square, powerful jaw.

"You beat a cripple in a race and brag about it? Neanderthal warriors would be ashamed to admit such a thing."

Sammie, who'd been looking at me with admiration, froze.

I gritted my teeth and reminded myself that I was a pacifist. And that I needed Sammie to get information from this high-handed turkey.

"I'm really thirsty," Sammie said. "River, maybe you could get the drinks now? I'll have sparkling water with a twist of lime please. First Luminary Acolyte Schlauzauber Heshlibob, may I recommend a virgin frozen strawberry daiquiri?"

The Nean gave a curt nod. I pushed out of my chair and swaggered to the bar. The bartender stopped polishing glasses and gave me his full attention.

"Sparkling water with a lime twist, a virgin frozen strawberry daiquiri, and, um..."

I had no idea what to order. I wanted something manly, something that would boost my bruised ego and impress everyone with my knowledge of alcoholic beverages, of which I had exactly none. I glanced to where Capt. Samuels sat, back to the bar, eyes constantly scanning for threats, short glass of clear liquid in hand. Now there was a man's man.

"And whatever he's having." I jerked a thumb at Samuels.

The bartender got a bemused look and hustled away. Glasses clanked, hoses hissed. The front door jingled.

A new guy stepped in. Moisture clung to his short brown hair. His sharp gaze traveled round the room while he shrugged water droplets off his bomber jacket. The drops splattered on his gray slacks and on the floor around black, rubber-soled, lace-up shoes.

A centipede of apprehension marched up my spine. Undercover cop? He was dressed too fine. Federal agent? In a tiny berg like Lake Point?

The bartender set three glasses in front of me. "That'll be nine dollars."

I goggled at him. Good thing I hadn't offered to buy drinks for everyone. There had to be a cheaper way to attract friends.

"Why so much?" It must be Capt. Samuels' drink driving up the price. It was probably some special old whiskey, the type that burned all the way down. Yuck.

The bartender pointed to each glass, starting with a slushy red drink. "Six for the daiquiri, two for the sparkling water with lime, and one for the tap water."

Of course, Samuels was on duty. I peeled off bills and left them on the bar while vowing I'd never buy drinks in a place like this again. It was a worse rip-off than McDonald's.

I juggled the drinks back to the table. They only slopped a little when I set them down. I got a quick thanks from Sammie, who listened with rapt attention to Flash, and nothing at all from the ungrateful Nean.

Burning Love ended, and *Stuck on You*—also scratchy and playing at the wrong speed—took its place. Perhaps the bartender was an Elvis aficionado, and the jukebox held nothing but the old rocker's hits. Still, he ought to get the machine fixed.

"Tell me about your Celebration of Light." Sammie sipped her sparkling water.

Flash's mouth twitched, like it was the last thing he wanted to talk about.

"Four times a year, the Holy Order conducts a group service that gathers the life given by the sun to strengthen what you call our 'dimensional barriers' that protect us from the dark. Without this act, our protections would wane until..." He shifted in his chair. "We don't speak of those things."

"Superstitious mumbo-jumbo," I muttered. Under the table, Sammie's foot stepped on mine.

"As the strongest priest in the order, His Highest Eminence Sacred Leader Schlauzauber Frommanisch is the focal point. Only he can transfer the power collected by the priests to the barriers of our dimension. He must return in the next five days to conduct the ceremony, or our dimensional barriers could be weakened and breached." Flash took a big pull on his drink.

Sammie frowned. "And that's why it's critical that the Raptors lift their ban on inter-dimensional travel, so he can get back in time. Is His Highest Eminence Sacred Leader Schlauzauber Frommanisch having any luck changing their minds?"

"Not so far."

"No surprise there. Hey, maybe they'll let your dad travel by harness and robe. And you could go, too... in a flash." I chuckled at my joke.

Sammie gave me a black look.

Flash drew himself up, not that he needed to. He towered over Sammie and me like a wizard over a couple of hobbits. "Unlike humans, we do not steal what the Raptors are unwilling to share."

"Because you can't make it work, eh?" I countered.

Sammie planted a swift kick on my shin. I jerked.

The door jingled open, and JR and Veronica walked in. Veronica fought a grin and JR sported a dark, brooding expression. It looked great on his handsome features. I could see why he'd attract a looker like Veronica.

The couple went to the bar. Pete and Mr. Lee joined them.

"Hey, JR, didn't think we'd see you here before last call," Pete said.

JR half-turned to Pete. "Wi-fi's down at McDonald's."

Behind JR's back, Veronica flashed a resplendent smile and gave Pete a wink.

When they'd been served, the whole mob ambled over to our table and sat down, snagging more chairs and squeezing everyone in. Pete put a stack of paper napkins on the table. Flash gave the others the once-over as Sammie introduced them, and then he ignored everyone, his focus exclusively on Sammie.

I had to do something to get Sammie away so we could talk. She'd promised. Besides, she looked a little bedraggled, like she'd had enough of playing babysitter for one day.

The late-comer at the bar watched us in the mirror. Capt. Samuels watched the late-comer. *Suspicious Minds* blared from the jukebox. Conversation in our group died.

"Show them your swan, Mr. Lee." Pete shoved a paper napkin over to the old Asian guy.

With a wan smile, Mr. Lee deftly folded the napkin, his thin, gnarled fingers surprisingly limber. A moment later, an origami swan perched on the table in front of him.

"How cool is that?" Pete waved his beer at the little creation. "Do another."

I snatched a napkin off the top of the pile, fished my pencil stub from my pocket, and began to draw while Lee folded. He finished first. A little elephant joined the swan.

In my sketch, Mr. Lee sat cross-legged on a bamboo mat folding something. Over his head, in the mists of his thoughts, butterflies and hummingbirds took shape. I passed the napkin across the table.

Lee's mouth opened in surprise, and delight twinkled in his eyes. He made a half-bow and started another project.

"Wow, Madden," Pete said. "Where'd you learn to do that?"

"Show them your magic coin trick." Veronica dug JR in the ribs.

JR tore his eyes from the sketch and turned to me. "You're the big winner today. Can you spare a quarter?"

Sammie shifted in her chair and glanced at Flash, who frowned at the others.

I dug out a quarter and tossed it to JR. Then I grabbed another napkin, certain that I'd never see the coin again.

JR pushed up his sleeves. He warmed up by walking the quarter across his knuckles, making it disappear in one hand and reappear in the other. In a final flourish, it vanished for good, just as I'd predicted.

I slid another sketch across the table. On the napkin, Veronica wore that glorious smile she'd flashed at the bar, her eyes on JR. JR's tablet lay on the table, forgotten, while he gazed with longing at Veronica.

When she saw the drawing, Veronica's eyes glistened and one hand covered her mouth. JR went still, staring at the paper.

"You see much." Lee looked at me in a strange way.

"A child's scribble," Flash sneered. "Any of my people could do better."

Sammie's jaw tightened. She said nothing. How could she let his dig go unanswered?

I slapped a napkin and the pencil stub on the table in front of Flash. "Go ahead."

Some of the arrogance fell away. *Gotcha!* I crossed my arms and waited to see how he'd worm out of the mess.

Flash pushed up his sleeves. He rolled the napkin into a compact tube, smothered it in his huge right fist, and placed his fist on the table, fingers up. He waved his left hand a few inches above his fist.

Nothing happened. I stifled a giggle, and the others exchanged glances.

Flash's expression set in concentration. A deep hum came from his throat, and a sheen of sweat formed on his brow. His left hand circled slower. He wasn't a half-bad actor, pretending to strain mightily while doing nothing.

In a single, sudden motion, his left hand snapped back, his right fist tossed the roll into the air, and the napkin vanished in a brief eruption of orange flame. A few cinders drifted to the tabletop.

For a moment, everyone fell silent. Then Pete cheered, and the others joined in with clapping and exclamations. Sammie smiled and touched the Nean's arm. Flash smirked, a king acknowledging the peasants gathered at his feet.

I ground my teeth. *Show off.* It was no more impressive than JR's disappearing coin. The Nean must have palmed the napkin and replaced it with flash paper, a stage magician's trick. The way everyone responded, you'd think he'd done real magic.

The jukebox switched to *Heartbreak Hotel,* a slow, blues piece. I needed Sammie alone.

How did a guy get a girl's attention? No grabbing her breast, not with her dad and the other recruits looking on. I'd never danced with a girl, but I figured if the music was slow, I could get away with shuffling my feet.

"They're playing our song." I wiped my palms on my pants. "Wanna dance?"

Heads cocked. Ears listened. All eyes turned on me.

Sammie leaned closer. "I don't hear any music."

"The jukebox. It's playing—"

Uh-oh. Not real.

I wanted to crawl under the table. They'd all know I was crazy and reject me. Shame heated my face. How could I hang around Sammie if I was such an embarrassment?

I jumped up. "Pit stop."

I scurried to the back and through a door marked *Restrooms.* I bypassed the two restrooms and burst out a third door into an alley.

Mist drizzled down, chilling me. The shapes of dumpsters loomed in the dark. The light over the bar's door crooned *Cold Kentucky Rain,* off-key. I ran for the street.

Several blocks later, I stopped under a dress shop awning and rocked on my heels. I'd been a childish fool to run away. I'd recently learned that running never fixed anything. But old habits died hard.

I'd man up, go back to the bar, and ask Sammie for a private word. Yeah, that's what normal people did. Then she'd tell me what *on report* meant, and I'd ask her to interrogate the Nean priest from Smith's platform.

I'd figure out what really happened. The Raps would settle down. Everything would be great. All I had to do was go back to the bar.

I squinted left and then right along the dark street.

Always have a Plan B. If Sammie couldn't help because of her important new job, I'd ask Natasha if I could work with her. Maybe if she learned enough about positive and negative energy, she could make a human version of the Rap cuffs. Even if DPS fell apart, the super-talents and I would still be okay. After all, humans didn't *need* to travel to other dimensions.

Or maybe Natasha could even figure out how to create shields, and then we wouldn't need the Neans to travel across D-space. I'd have Sammie all to myself. No priority mission occupying her time.

Rain dripped in my eyes. I rocked a bit more.

Crap. Which way was the bar?

A black SUV turned the corner and angled to the curb. I sucked in a breath and hurried away, shoulders hunched, hands in pockets, muscles tensed and ready to run.

Footsteps scuffed on the concrete behind me. I walked faster. The SUV rolled past and pulled to the curb again.

Where the hell was the bar?

"Mr. Madden," a male voice called at my back. "Mr. River Madden. I'd like a word, please."

11

I turned and faced the lush from the bar. He held up a leather wallet. A badge glinted in the streetlight.

"Special Agent Joseph Black, FBI," the lush said. He gestured ahead. "Please get in the car."

I swung around. The SUV's front and rear passenger doors hung open, a tall, All-American running-back type in a trench coat sandwiched between them.

I almost made a break for it. They wouldn't catch me on foot, but they had the advantage of the car and no doubt guns. I didn't know the town, could run into a blind alley. And normal white males didn't run from the feds. *Be cool, be normal.*

Agent Black and I climbed in the back of the vehicle. It was a squeeze, what with the big, hard-looking agent already in there. I couldn't see the ends of the seatbelt, and I didn't have the courage to fish for them next to the two men's thighs. God forbid they think I was feeling them up.

"Um... what's this about?" I asked, all deferential and quiet.

"We need your help, Mr. Madden," Black said.

There he went, using my name again. When I'd joined DPS, I'd signed a mountain of paperwork, including something about keeping secrets *or else.* The clerk assured me that the existence of DPS was known only to those inside it and the President. No blabbing to *anyone* about where I worked, especially those from the alphabet agencies.

How did this guy know my name? Had he bugged our table at the bar? But if DPS was so secret, how did he know to listen to our conversation? Lake Point, Idaho, was a sleepy country town, not a hotbed of sedition that would attract random covert surveillance. A queasy feeling like a snake sliding over my skin started at my sacroiliac and ended at my scalp.

In the back of the SUV, the invisible chorus murmured. *Hot lights* and *rubber hose* jumped out of their whisperings. *Not real. Not listening. La, la, la.*

"I think you have me confused with someone else." I wished I'd thought to say it *before* I'd gotten in the car. "You can let me out at the next corner."

The SUV swooshed past the next corner. The wipers swish-swished as the rain susurrated against the street. The darkness swallowed the headlights whole. Where were they taking me? *Grandma's house* and *wolf* leaked from the chorus.

"I hope we aren't going far," I said. "I don't want to be late getting back to base."

Oops. Did they know about the base? It was a big base in the foothills overlooking the town. It would be hard to miss. Still...

"No worries," Black said. "We're almost there."

We'd driven into an area of homes on acreage—an area without streetlights. Tall pines hid most of the dwellings from view. *Vampires, werewolves,* and *Freddie Krueger* rippled through the chorus. Deeper shadows flitted through the shadows between the trees.

The feds were no friends of mine. Heck, law enforcement officers of all stripes were no friends of mine. I didn't know what they wanted, but whatever it was, I wouldn't tell them *anything.*

Sooner or later, DPS would look for me. All I had to do was slip off my Rap cuffs, and they could use their tracking device to detect the negative energy fields I gave off—if I didn't fracture and fall through before they found me.

The SUV turned up a winding drive to a sprawling ranch home. Light shone through half a dozen windows. From its hillside perch, it must have a lovely view of the valley. The feds in this dimension definitely had a bigger budget than the ones I'd met in E-4.

We disembarked, climbed wooden steps to a spacious veranda, and entered through a carved front door.

The front hall had a hanging chandelier made from a wagon wheel. Fake lanterns shed their light on a gleaming hardwood floor. To the left of the entrance, what should have been the front parlor overflowed with desks and agents.

Black led me through a door to the right and into a study lit by a driftwood desk lamp. He pointed to one of a pair of cowhide chairs in front of a gas fireplace filled with fake logs and invited me to sit. The goon from the back seat of the SUV followed us in, shut the door, and stood with his feet apart and his hands clasped in front of him.

In the soft light of the study, I got my first good look at Black. He was a square-jawed, hazel-eyed, brown-haired guy in his mid-thirties who wore the rumpled suit of a boozer but a sharp expression that said he was far from drunk. He had that Superman persona about him: suave haircut, manly good looks, muscular physique under the suit.

"This is Agent Lloyd." Black waved to the man blocking the only exit.

Agent Lloyd was a square-jawed, green-eyed, auburn-haired guy in his early-thirties who wore a black suit like his boss, only without the rumples. No mistaking *him* for a lush.

They looked like brothers and definitely shared genetics with the other agents I'd glimpsed at the desks in the room across the hall. I wondered if the government had some clandestine cloning program they used to create their employees. The desk lamp quietly hummed the X-Files theme.

The room felt uncomfortably warm despite my wet clothes. I wiped sweat from my brow and took a firm grip on the chair arms. Shackles lashed out from the wood and encircled my wrists and ankles.

My heart raced. I squeezed my eyes shut and jerked my arms up to free them. They flew into the air, unrestrained.

"Something the matter, Mr. Madden?" Black asked.

I opened my eyes. Wicked spiked shackles dangled from the chair arms. *Not real.* The desk lamp cackled. Oh, boy, it was going to be a long night.

"Whatever you want," I said, looking anywhere but at Black, "I don't have it. Or know it. Or... anything. I'm the new guy. In town."

"Precisely, which is why we need your help." Black leaned back in his chair. The cowhide gave a strangled moo.

I waited. I would have told a lie but couldn't think of one.

"We know you work for Dimensional Protective Service. You're one of their 'talents,' and have been there only a few days. That's what makes you so valuable."

Black leaned toward me and lowered his voice. "You see, Mr. Madden, there's a mole at DPS."

In an instant, a man-sized mole stood beside the fire: upright, furry, wearing a cowboy hat, and carrying a Winchester rifle in its tiny paws. I sucked in a breath. A *blind* rodent with a gun? The desk lamp drawled *Home, Home on the Range.*

"Based on the information that's leaked, the mole must be high up in the DPS command structure. He—or she—has been selling secrets to the Chinese for over a year," Black said. His eyes tracked to the side of the fireplace where I still stared.

Oh. *That* kind of mole. The rodent morphed into a shadowy human silhouette dressed in a trench coat and fedora. The desk lamp transitioned to the James Bond theme.

"Isn't me," I said. My shoulders relaxed a smidge. I'd be out of their clutches in no time.

Black's well-groomed eyebrows lowered a bit, and his voice took on an impatient edge. "We're aware of that, Mr. Madden."

"And I don't know who it is. Can I go now?"

The agent's jaw tightened. "We need your help to identify the mole. It's your duty as a loyal American. Don't you love your country, Mr. Madden?"

What I'd love was for him to stop using my name, especially with that tone of voice. As far as my country went, what had they ever done for me? Chopped the budgets for community mental health services, closed the mental hospitals, moved the mentally ill homeless along because out of sight was out of mind.

"You would, of course, be recompensed for your services."

I sat a little straighter. He was offering a job? Things weren't going too well for me at DPS. Heck, I wasn't sure DPS would survive the whole fracas with the Raps given the Rap's distrust of the Nean shields—or their fear of demons.

If a job with Natasha didn't work out and DPS fired me, maybe I could be a spy for the FBI. Wasn't that the strategy normal people used? Have their eyes on the next job before they left the current one—or got tossed out? *Any* job was better than no job, even if it meant working for the despicable FBI. I had to hold onto Sammie, and that meant passing for normal with all the trimmings.

"What would I have to do?"

Black smiled, and it was a little scary. He drew a piece of paper from his suit jacket.

"I have a list of tasks. We'll start with basic surveillance. Agent Lloyd will provide you with listening devices that you'll plant in the offices of our primary suspects... and a few other potentially useful places.

"We'll also give you a phone. You'll call us daily to report anything you see or hear."

Ha! Like a Chinese spy would blab to me. And did I want to spy on the people I worked with? Except for Higgins and Capt. Samuels, everyone had been pretty nice. Still, I needed a steady job to buy a house and make a life with Sammie. I couldn't ask her to sleep in garden sheds and eat out of dumpsters like I'd done. She deserved better than a derelict.

"Who are these suspects?"

"Three people have been at DPS over the same time period as the leaks occurred and also have the kind of high-level security clearance to access the information: Dr. Natasha Filenkov, Professor Dennis Higgins, and Dr. Charles Polaski."

Doc a Chinese mole? Didn't seem possible. On the other hand, I liked to think *I* was a nice guy, and I was hiring on to be a spy. Now that I knew who I'd be spying on, doubts leaped into my mind. I pushed them aside.

A funny look came over Black. In a too-casual voice, he said, "We had our eye on one other person, but his presence at DPS doesn't match the leak timeline. Do you know a scientist by the name of Smith?"

The little hairs on the back of my neck stiffened. Prof. Higgins had been quick to accuse me of killing and dismembering Smith, even without knowing about the schizophrenia. Would the FBI be any different?

"Uh... I haven't been at DPS long. I think he might be... well... dead."

A flash of surprise streaked across Black's eyes and was gone. Or had I imagined it?

"What happened?"

"Don't know," I said, possibly too fast.

Black smoothed his rumpled shirt with a well-manicured hand. "You must have heard something."

"I'm the new guy. No one tells me anything."

Black didn't look mollified. I couldn't think straight with him watching. Heck, I couldn't think straight most of the time, never mind under pressure. Maybe that was why I was such a bad liar.

"Except that he was dismembered."

You could have heard a feather fall on the hardwood floor. Black looked less shocked than like a guy who finally understands the punch line of an old joke. What was that about?

Black's voice dropped low and soft. "Where and how did he die, Mr. Madden?"

The trench coated silhouette produced a gun and swung it my direction. I'd walked smack into that zombie trap again. Sweat popped out on my forehead. No headhunters this time.

"No one knows." Okay, the demons did, but did they count as people? I don't think so!

"If no one knows about his manner of death, how do they know he's dead?" Black's question had a suspicious undercurrent.

"Because someone brought back his body—parts of his body."

Black rubbed a hand over his lips. My brain added the clanking of wheels going around. "Was he gutted?"

"Oh, yeah. Definitely gutted." Oops, *TMI.* I needed to change the subject before I revealed my whole life story. I needed to get out of there and think when I wasn't under so much pressure.

"Why do you need me? Why don't you just tell Capt. Samuels? About the mole, I mean."

If Samuels knew he had a spy in his midst, he'd stop at nothing to find the culprit. I felt bad for the spy.

Smooth as silk, Black answered. "We don't know who we can trust. Perhaps our mole has an accomplice. By bringing in anyone from DPS, we risk alerting the traitor. We're keeping our cards close on this one, given the importance to national security."

"I'm not sure I'm qualified—"

"You haven't been at DPS long enough to be approached by the Chinese, nor do you have connections to anyone already there. We checked."

If he'd checked on me, did he know about my schizophrenia? Would he hire me as a spy if he did? Should I tell him? No, I needed the job as a backup plan. And I wanted to help DPS.

Black stood. "Agent Lloyd, bring the surveillance equipment and show Mr. Madden how it works."

Lloyd whipped out the door.

Black shook my hand. "Welcome to the team, Mr. Madden. Your country appreciates your service."

Wow, he wasn't as smart as he seemed if he hadn't figured out that I was crazy. Or else I was getting darn good at faking it. I almost smiled.

Lloyd returned with two dozen round metal buttons in a clear plastic bag and a cell phone. He couldn't quite keep smug satisfaction from curling his lips.

"Plant the bugs where they won't be seen, usually on the underside of an object near the subject's desk," Black said. He handed me a piece of paper. "Here's the list of where to place them. Use gloves so you don't leave fingerprints.

"You'll see 'Ike' listed in the phone's contact list. Call us at 2200 each day. If you learn something important, call immediately. But be sure no one sees or hears you make the call."

Lloyd took my elbow and ushered me out of the study.

"Don't I have to sign some paperwork or something?" Working at DPS was my first job, and they'd had reams of forms to sign. I'd also expected a bit more training before I tackled going undercover.

"No problem," Black said. "You're already in the government system."

Lloyd whisked me out the door and into the SUV. We rode back to Lake Point in silence. Well, he rode in silence. Creepy Halloween music played in *my* head while more of the menacing shadows slipped between the trees.

The listening devices burned a hole in my pocket. The plastic cell phone dragged like an anchor. I hoped Black's list wasn't written in invisible ink. I'd landed in a fine mess. Did DPS have rules against moonlighting? Was it legal to collect two government paychecks?

If Natasha was the mole, how could I help her learn enough to replicate the Rap cuffs and also prevent the information from reaching the Chinese? The super-talents and I needed those cuffs.

How could Doc possibly be a spy? Hadn't he taken an oath to help people?

If Higgins got arrested, would my essay fail still count against me? Scratch that. Heroes didn't focus on self-centered concerns with the stakes so high. Learn the secrets of Rap technology and save the mad super-talents from falling through another fracture to their deaths. Find the Chinese spy. Those were the jobs.

Lloyd pulled over in the same block where they'd picked me up. I stepped into the rain, and he drove off.

I rocked, a million conflicting thoughts and feelings swirling around in my brain. One surfaced.

Where the hell was the bar?

12

It was a dark and stormy night. I shivered, soaked to the skin. Despite hours of looking, I couldn't find that damn bar. For once in my life, I would have welcomed a run-in with a cop. Even they had more sense than to come out in the deluge.

A smart guy would find a dry bolt hole and start again in the morning. In the morning, I could ask someone for directions, run like crazy back to base, and hope no one missed me. But this was not a time for dreaming.

A single headlight pierced the darkness. The buzz of an engine cut through the fog and rain. A black figure on a racy motorcycle approached. I thought about flagging the rider down, decided a run-in with a biker was worse than a chewing out for being late back from R&R.

The bike glided to the curb. The rider, dressed from toe to chin in black leather, flipped up the visor on a shiny black helmet.

"Mr. Madden."

I snapped my jaw closed and cleared my throat. "Hey, Natasha. Kind of late for a ride, isn't it? Um... which way is the base?"

"So, you are lost? Zat would explain your failure to return. I will notify everyone searching for you." She drew a cell phone from her pocket and tapped once on the screen.

"I have found Mr. Madden. We are returning to base." She dropped the phone back in a pocket and gestured to the seat behind her. "Come."

Ride on the back of her motorcycle in the rain at night without a helmet? *Was she loony?* But I already knew that. I'd seen it in her face while we'd zoomed around the fracture chamber.

I got on behind her and attributed my shaking to the cold. I didn't know what to do with my hands.

Natasha revved the motor. The bike leapt away, fishtailing on the wet pavement.

My arms, having a mind of their own, wrapped themselves around

Natasha's waist like an anaconda around a crocodile. Rain stung my face and eyes. Wind pierced my clothing and chilled my skin until I was numb. Not riding a motorcycle again. *Ever.*

We roared out of town and up the hill to the base, a journey of less than half a mile. Water droplets on the chain-link fence sparkled under the sodium-vapor perimeter lights. If not for the storm, I could have seen the base from where Natasha picked me up.

Natasha paused long enough for the gatehouse guards to check our ID. She rolled through the parking lot to a spot that wasn't technically for parking, right next to the building that contained her office.

I scrambled off before she changed her mind and roared away again.

Natasha dismounted, opened a saddlebag, and withdrew a briefcase. Did she use it to smuggle stolen documents off the grounds?

I'd accepted the job as an FBI spy to determine whether Natasha was the mole. If the Raps found out that details about their technology had leaked to humans outside DPS, they'd take their toys and go home. Finding the mole meant we'd keep the Raps in the game while we worked on replicating their tech, thereby saving DPS. And I'd collect two government paychecks. I'd be able to buy nice digs for Sammie and me in no time.

Could I help Natasha crack Rap technology so the other super-talents and I would be safe from accidental fractures at the same time that I busted her as a spy? Sure, why not? I smiled. I had real plans. Practicing being normal worked.

Then I frowned. What did 'helping Natasha' mean exactly? How would I prevent her from passing secrets to the Chinese? Was I deluding myself? I rocked.

Natasha walked away.

I scrambled after her. "Hey, maybe I could help with your research."

She kept a brisk pace. "You have a scientific background? A physics degree?"

"Well, no." Maybe she was mad about coming out in the rain to find me. "And thanks for the ride. I could give your instruments a ride. Through D-space, I mean. I don't need shields."

Natasha swung her dark eyes my way. "You did not report zis. In fact, you did not file any report of events leading to ze assault on R-Prime. We have only Talent Samuels' statements."

More writing to do? Did they think I was a novelist?

"Wasn't part of DPS then," I said. "But I'll get right on it." *As soon as I find paper.*

Natasha pulled open the building door and a blast of warm air rushed out. "Good. Bring it directly to me. When I have read it, we will talk."

My suspicion level notched up. "Just to you?"

We arrived at an office, her name emblazoned on a plaque. She tapped numbers on a keypad by the door.

What if everyone kept their offices locked? The bag of bugs bulged in my pocket. How would I plant them? I barged in behind Natasha as she entered. She rounded her desk and faced me.

"You want somezing else, Mr. Madden?"

I thrust my hands in my pants pockets, fished around to isolate a single disk, and looked at the desktop. Keyboard, computer monitor with a cord leading down to a metal box under the desk, and mouse. Nothing to hide a listening device under.

"I was wondering whether you learned anything about what happened to Smith," I said.

"He was not jolted from ze platform. But you know zis."

The best I could do with her watching would be to stick the disk on the bottom edge of the desk near the floor. She leaned down to turn on the computer.

I leaned down and stuck the bug to the wooden desk edge. Only it didn't stick. It *clinked* on the floor. I snatched it up, flipped it over, tried again. Another clink. I plastered it on the back of the computer, next to a perforated area.

The computer hummed to life. It was louder than I expected. I straightened, smiled.

Natasha stared at me, eyes narrowed. She couldn't see what I'd done from her side of the desk, but she couldn't have missed me bending over.

I pointed at my feet. "Shoe's untied."

"Good evening, Mr. Madden."

I hustled out the door and closed it gently before collapsing against the wall. Then I remembered Black's instructions to use gloves so I wouldn't leave fingerprints. *Aw, hell.*

The clock on the wall said it was quarter past three. I wanted to change into dry clothes and climb into bed. But the buildings were mostly dark and quiet, the ideal time to plant the remaining bugs. My success in Natasha's office bolstered my confidence.

I examined Black's list of bug locations. Col. Juarez's office was first, and Capt. Samuels' was second. They might be Black's priority, but they weren't mine. I'd start with the prime suspects. I headed for the infirmary.

While I jogged across the quad, I reviewed my abduction by Black. He knew a lot about who worked at DPS. What value did the staff roster have for the Chinese? How did the FBI get a copy? Why was Black interested in Smith if he didn't fit the suspect criteria?

I slipped down the hall to the infirmary, checking over my shoulder every few steps. No light shone under the door. This ought to be easy.

The infirmary was unlocked and deserted. I let out a sigh. Spying wasn't so hard.

I flicked on the light and looked over Doc's desk. Stacking wire paperwork baskets stood on one corner. A big paper calendar/blotter covered the center of the desk. A black metal gooseneck light arched out from the upper right corner.

I pulled a bug from the bag, used my shirttail to polish off my fingerprints, and jammed the bug inside the lamp shade. I let out another sigh, switched off the light, and stepped into the hallway—right into Doc.

"Did you need something, River?" He glanced at the door behind me.

Doc had me flat-footed. Why did Black think I'd make a spy?

"Uh... no," I stuttered.

Doc checked his watch. Puzzlement colored his eyes.

"I got lost. In town," I said, a lie taking shape. "And I was worried. What if I'm away from base and my cuffs fail? Maybe I should carry a spare pair."

"Okay," Doc said. "I have some in my office."

I turned to enter the infirmary, but Doc walked away toward the stairs. I scrambled after him.

"Your office isn't in there?" I pointed back the hall.

"That's just the infirmary workstation. My office is upstairs."

Doc unlocked the door of a comfortable room on the third floor. A soft glow from a desk lamp cast shadows over two inviting visitor chairs, a solid mahogany desk, and walls lined with bookshelves sagging under the weight of medical texts. A rag rug in muted blues and greens gave the space a safe, cozy feel.

A heavy, well-worn volume lay on the desk. The title read *Studies in Chinese Acupuncture*. Before my eyes, Doc sprouted a pointy nose with whiskers and soft, gray fur. I stared down at the book, shutting out the hallucination. *Not that kind of mole.*

In my peripheral vision, Doc opened a desk drawer and pulled out a pair of the Rap cuffs.

"Keep these safe." He handed the cuffs across the desk. "The Raps make us account for every pair."

"Sure, sure," I replied. "I thought acupuncture was mystic mumbo jumbo."

Doc glanced down at the volume. Frustration carried through his voice. "I've been working with the super-talents who've fallen through fractures for over two years now. None of the diagnostic tests have given me any clues about what's wrong with them, and none of the treatments I've tried have brought any of them out of their catatonic states. I've tried Western medicine, alternative medicine, acupuncture, Asian herbs. There's nothing I wouldn't do to help them recover."

Did 'nothing' include selling secrets to the Chinese in exchange for medical advice? Was Doc the good-hearted physician who'd sell his soul to Satan if it helped his patients?

Doc rounded the desk, put a hand on my elbow, and ushered me to the door. "I should get back to the ward. If you need anything more, you can find me there."

I hadn't gotten a bug planted, but I didn't see a way to do it now. He locked the door, and we walked down the stairs. He peeled off at the second floor, headed for the full-blown hospital ward where the mad super-talents stayed. I clattered down to the first floor feeling a lot less jubilant about my new career as a spy.

13

I slogged across the muddy quad to Administration. My confidence washed away in the downpour. I'd tried Prof. Higgins' office and found his door locked. Didn't anyone trust anyone at DPS?

I stopped just inside the building and listened. No footsteps sounded on the stairs or along the hallway, but I'd seen lights in windows on my way here. I ought to have a story ready in case I encountered anyone.

I'd say I was looking for someone. No, scratch that. There wasn't anyone with an office here that I'd want to talk to.

I'd promised Natasha to write a report. I'd say I was looking for paper. Was that stealing? Was I supposed to buy my own?

My wet sneakers squeaked on the linoleum as my feet carried me—unbidden—up the stairs. *Uh-oh.* I was headed for Samuels' office.

What was the point of bugging his office? The FBI didn't seriously believe Samuels was a spy—or colluding with spies, did they? You'd never catch me making that accusation. If I did, he'd probably plant a slug between my eyes.

I stopped at the top of the stairs to peer along the hallway. The invisible chorus leaned over my shoulder to peer with me. I couldn't hear while they whispered at my back. *Water-boarding* and *rack* featured in their hushed tones.

No one in sight. I sneaked around the corner into the hallway. I'd gone ten feet when I heard clicking. I stopped, breath held. *Not footsteps. Just the heating system.* Or was it coming from the stairs at the far end of the long hall?

I backpedaled to a cork bulletin board mounted on the right wall and pretended to peruse the yellowed notices plastered on its surface. From the corner of my eye, I watched for movement. And I saw it.

A three-foot tall dark gray gargoyle flitted from one doorway to another. I let out a breath. The clicking must have been the sound of its stone toes against the floor.

I shook off the shiver that always accompanied my little vacations from reality and hurried forward. Samuels' office loomed.

I reached for the knob. The white Rap, Dodo, entered the corridor at the other end of the hall. Her hind claws tick-ticked on the linoleum, just like the gargoyle's. My eyes went as wide as the moon. I froze.

Dodo scrutinized the name plaque on the first door she came to. She had a device the size of a cell phone in her paw, which she compared to the plaque. Then she crossed the hall to the opposite door and checked the plaque beside it.

The Rap pulled a short cylinder from a vest pocket, crouched low, and spritzed a puff of vapor under the door. She replaced the cylinder in her pocket and spent a full minute tapping on the device, all the while whistling what might have been *Heigh Ho* from Snow White. Or maybe my brain thought Raps worked like light bulbs.

Dodo clacked her teeth, dropped her paw to her side, and stalked toward me. She stopped, mid-stride, and stared. Her jaws snapped shut, and her walk resumed. She pocketed the device.

"Ah, River Madden, pardon my failure of greeting. My kind find it difficult to distinguish members of your kind."

It sounded like a big, fat lie. She'd looked more shocked than uncertain even if I didn't know Rap body language. And what was she doing here at three in the morning?

"I thought I might find you at Capt. Samuels' office," she said, "given the base-wide alert when you were discovered missing."

"Lost," I said. "Not missing. And why would they alert your lot?"

"To ask our help to track you should you have fallen through a fracture," she chirped. "Impossible for us, of course, with the ban on D-space travel."

My eyes narrowed. "How does checking for fractures add up to being at Capt. Samuels' office in the middle of the night?"

Dodo blinked up at me with those big, blue eyes. "Your whereabouts were unknown, but you are here now. Therefore, you were off base without permission. Capt. Samuels is responsible for law and punishment, is he not?"

Aw, hell. So Capt. Samuels was gunning for me. I looked over my shoulder, sure I'd see him sneaking up behind. Imagine him catching me with a bag of bugs in my pocket and a flimsy excuse about getting lost.

"But why are *you* here?" I pressed. The little Rap's twisted answer didn't quite make sense.

"To thank you for preventing the soldier from using his weapon to harm me. The pursuit of knowledge can be dangerous, as your own experience demonstrates."

Was she warning me, making a veiled threat not to investigate

Smith's death? Were the Raps involved? I couldn't see how, but knowing them, it was a serious possibility.

"My experience?"

"You faced death to retrieve Smith. You were then accused of his killing and dismemberment."

There I stood, the FBI's electronic ears listening to every word. I gritted my teeth. I'd been a dunce. I should have ditched the bugs in the first dumpster I came to and never left the base again.

But if I did, how would I save DPS? I'd made no progress unraveling Smith's misfortune. And now DPS faced the added threat of a Chinese spy.

"You will see Capt. Samuels now?" The little Rap shifted from paw to paw.

Not if I could help it. I grasped the knob in my shaking hand, twisted.

Locked.

My shoulders relaxed a smidge. "Guess I'll catch him tomorrow. Today. Later."

The Rap and I exchanged a nod and walked in opposite directions while I chewed through my options.

I had no skills useful for catching a spy or unraveling a mystery. I couldn't suss out the physics behind the Rap devices. I needed help. Like it or not, I had to work with the feds. Would I face a firing squad for lying about my part in Smith's rescue? Or just be thrown in jail the rest of my natural life?

I trudged up to the third floor, although it seemed a useless exercise. Col. Juarez had an office there, but it would be locked, too. If I had to come back later, how would I explain what I was doing? I wished I was a better liar. Then I could sneak in on the pretense of reporting something.

I entered the hallway and strode briskly but silently along its length, anxious to get my spy chores over. Three rooms down on the left, light filtered under a door, along with the strains of a radio tuned to a jazz station. Someone working late.

Juarez's office was closed, dark, and locked. As I released the knob, I caught movement in my peripheral vision. *Another gargoyle.* But it wasn't.

Dodo appeared at the end of the hall, treading more quietly than before. She had the little device in her right paw, and the cylinder in her left. She spritzed toward the corner of the ceiling and checked the device.

What was the Rap spraying? Air freshener? Anthrax? Bird flu? Who knew?

No teeth clacking this time. Just a cautious turn down the hallway and an abrupt halt when she saw me.

We stared. We nodded. We made synchronized turns and each went back the way we'd come.

I should report her suspicious activity. I could imagine how that conversation would go: Me accusing her of something-or-other while I explained why I was sneaking around in the wee hours of the morning. Spying was a lot more complicated than in the James Bond book I'd read.

I trotted past the second floor and swung around the landing headed for the first floor. Below, Capt. Samuels jogged up.

My foot missed the next step. I stumbled, grabbed the rail, recovered. My hand shook on the banister. I stuffed it behind my back.

Samuels' skin had a gray pallor. His eyes were red and irritated, and his shoulders drooped. Water droplets glinted on his hat and jacket shoulders. He glanced up. His jaw stiffened.

"Madden. In my office."

Samuels continued past me and disappeared into the second floor hallway. I wiped a sudden sheen of sweat from my forehead and dragged myself after him, looking for a place to ditch the damn bugs.

Samuels had the door unlocked and was waiting behind his desk by the time I arrived, still carrying a pocketful of illicit listening devices in a super-secret government facility.

"Close the door."

I closed it, not that it did much good with the FBI monitoring the conversation. What could I do to prevent them from hearing my chewing out?

Samuels spread his feet and clasped his hands behind his back. His shoulders had squared, but I had the impression it was costing him. He was Superman, I was kryptonite, but he wouldn't admit it, and it wasn't anything intentional on my part.

"Report."

The temperature in the small, stuffy office plummeted. How did he know about my meeting with the feds? Handcuffs, a cat-o'-nine-tails, and a bloody pair of pliers appeared on the desktop.

I couldn't help it. I rocked. What had I gotten myself into?

"Mr. Madden!"

"Sorry. Sir." My pulse thumped in my ears. I thrust my hands into my pockets and fingered the bugs. Rubbed the bugs, making sure they scraped and clanked against one another, but not so loud that Samuels would hear.

Samuels leaned forward, big, strong hands flat on his desk. "Where did you go when you left the bar?"

"I don't know," I said. Truth was always easier than lies, I'd heard. The captain glared, and I continued. "I've never been in Lake Point before. I meant to walk a few blocks and see the sights. But I got lost."

"For six hours?"

Had I stumbled around in the dark that long? I hung my head. "Yes, sir."

Samuels straightened and squinted. "When you left the bar, a man followed you out. Did you see him?"

My lungs refused to inflate. My mouth opened and closed, but no sound came out. He'd seen Black disguised as the lush, knew he'd targeted me.

"Man?" I squeaked.

"The one at the bar, in the black leather jacket and gray slacks."

"Who?" I blurted. Black had worn a rumpled tan trench coat over his rumpled black suit.

He slid open the top desk drawer, pulled out a photo, and tossed it on the desktop. It showed the late-comer to the bar in profile, the picture snapped surreptitiously by one of Samuels' MPs.

I swayed a little, dizzy with relief and dropping blood pressure. "Nope. Didn't see him. Except in the bar."

The late-comer had that look about him, though, the lean, polished look of a federal agent. A clone twin of Special Agent Black and his helper, Agent Lloyd. Was he working with Black, too? I wondered whether Samuels had Black's picture hidden in the desk drawer.

"Who is he?" I asked, rubbing the bugs together more vigorously.

"None of your concern, Mr. Madden. If you see him again, you're to report it immediately. And may I remind you that DPS is a top-secret operation. You are not to speak of it even if questioned by representatives of other governmental or law enforcement agencies. Consider yourself on report. Dismissed."

On report? *Again?* One of these days, I'd find out what that meant.

Right now, I'd race for the nearest dumpster and get rid of the bugs in my pocket. This was a game way out of my league.

14

I awoke feeling like road kill, all my glorious plans shattered. I hadn't solved the mystery of Smith's fall. I hadn't convinced Natasha to take me on as an assistant. I hadn't completed my mission for the FBI. I hadn't even managed a first date with the love of my life.

With so many failures piling up, how could I prove myself worthy of Sammie? I wanted a life with her. At my current rate, I was headed straight back to being a lonely, homeless drifter who hawked sketches to get by. That wasn't good enough for Sammie.

Helping the feds was out. Colluding with them meant squaring off against Capt. Samuels. Crazy, not stupid. I'd call them at the appointed hour and tell them I was through. They could find someone else to be their cannon fodder.

I couldn't think about Sammie without thinking of Flash monopolizing the little time we might have left together. He and his Nean buddies made my blood boil. Boiling blood led to frustration, which led to fractures. I glanced at the spare cuffs on my desk.

Natasha wanted a report. I still hadn't found paper. Once I gave her the report, then what? She could send me away, and I wouldn't be any closer to saving DPS.

My discontent all traced back to Smith. I'd spent many a homeless afternoon curled up with a book in a public library. A fair share of the books had been mysteries. The detectives always started by investigating the victim.

What did I know about Smith? He was a scientist, a big, fit guy in his mid-thirties. He'd done something that caught the FBI's attention. Did he have friends? Enemies? A penchant for finding trouble? An allergy to peanuts? Who could I ask?

I leaped out of bed, dragged on my uniform, and wolfed more aspirin for the headache thumping behind my eyes. I stepped out of my door as Pete stepped out of his.

"What was it, Madden, booze, dope, or women? JR put his money on dope, but dopers don't run like you."

Heat rushed up my face, and I made a study of the floor.

"Lost," I mumbled. "I went jogging to see the town and got lost."

Pete laughed. "Next time you take a late night run, let me know so I can wear the right appliance. Then you'll have a running partner to drag your sorry ass back on time."

We traversed the hall side-by-side. Pete hadn't mentioned my bizarre comment about the jukebox. The memory made me squirm. He also seemed willing to be seen in my company, but I didn't know why.

"Um... what does *on report* mean?" I asked.

"Means a demerit was added to your record. Earn too many demerits and you'll get kicked out. If you have demerits, you're confined to base until you've erased them. Capt. Samuels put you on report for your little stunt last night?"

I nodded, wondering how many more I'd earn when Samuels learned that I already *had* a demerit from Higgins when I left the base.

"No biggie. You can work it off."

We headed down the stairs. "How?"

"Depends on what the CO assigns. Sometimes it's kitchen duty or grounds cleaning. Sometimes it's twenty-five perimeter laps."

"Scrubbing toilets with a toothbrush?"

"Sometimes, if you've been extra bad."

I gulped. "My toothbrush?"

Pete laughed long and hard.

Outside, the sky was still drab gray, but the rain had stopped. We stuck to the sidewalks and avoided the soggy grass of the quad. At the far end, the Nean priests hopped and slipped, performing their ritual and splattering their robes with mud. Sammie watched from a safe distance. I gritted my teeth and looked away, too embarrassed to meet her eyes.

"Did you know Smith?" I asked.

"The dead guy? Only by sight. Big, blond Nordic type, probably a Viking in a previous life. Handsome dude. All the ladies drooled over him. Me, too, but he wasn't interested. He wasn't here much, spent most of his time at M-Prime. I hear it's a real weird place."

"What's M-Prime?" I hoped the M didn't stand for Monsters, the way the 'R' in R-Prime stood for 'Raptors' and the 'N' in N-Prime stood for Neanderthals. Humans, of course, made themselves the center of the multiverse by using 'E' for Earth, even though both the Raps and Neans lived on versions of Earth, too.

"It's a moonless alternate dimension. The brainiacs think intelligent life developed late because there aren't any tides. There's still debate about whether the hive-dwelling amphibians qualify as 'intelligent.' But mostly they're trying to measure what else is different about the M-Prime solar system and figure out what happened to make it that way. One theory is that the asteroid that took out the dinosaurs obliterated the moon instead."

All the high-end observatories I'd seen in pictures were big and complex and loaded with computers and telescopes. They weren't the kind of thing you could easily hide from the locals. "DPS built an observatory in an alternate dimension?"

"Clever, eh? Humans don't have the technology to set up an unobtrusive science post, but the Raps do. It gives us a chance to see more of their equipment. They can cloak a whole building, just like in Star Trek when they hide spaceships."

Had Smith learned something about Rap technology that the Raps didn't want humans to know? Could the Rap navigator on Smith's platform have engineered Smith's fall? Or had a cloaked Rap pushed the scientist off? And projected a holograph of Smokey to make demons look responsible?

What was the white Rap spraying in Administration this morning? Some kind of mind control drug so they could manipulate us into doing what they wanted?

Pete opened the door to the mess hall. I gave him a wave and jogged toward Natasha's office. I didn't find her there. A woman in a white coat suggested I try her lab farther down the hall.

I walked to the indicated place and knocked. After an age, Natasha cracked the door open. She had safety glasses perched on her head, a long, thick apron covering her torso, and heavy tongs in her gloved hands.

"You have ze report?" she asked.

"Not yet, but soon. I had a question about Smith, and I thought you might be able to answer it." I flashed a cooperative smile and considered sticking my foot in the door.

"What does he have to do wiz your report?"

"He asked about it." I rushed to expand my answer. "My report, I mean."

The door inched open. "I did not know you had met him."

"Oh... well... we didn't. I heard he asked about it." My palms felt damp, and it seemed hard to breathe. I was the world's worst liar.

"He was an astrophysicist. Why would he be interested in your experience of D-space?"

"Exactly what I asked myself." I moved closer to the door. "I thought you might have an answer. Can I come in?"

Natasha stepped back. "You can speak to no one of what you see in my lab."

I held up two fingers on my left hand and crossed my heart with my right index finger. "Scout's honor."

She snorted and walked deeper into her lair.

The room was four times the size of her office. Counters ringed the walls, a worktop ran down the center, and overhead fluorescent lights shared secrets in whispered mathematical formulas I couldn't comprehend.

Computers vied with fancy lab machines for space on the countertops. A single tall stool stood beside a workstation. Natasha marched to it and sat.

"You believe it is important zat Smith asked about your report?"

Natasha was good at asking questions, but I could play that game too. "Don't you?"

"Why do you wish to pursue Smith's death?"

"Why not?" Okay, maybe I wasn't as good at the game as Natasha. "I mean, I rely on Rap technology to stay in this dimension. If Smith's loss sends the Raps back to R-Prime, I'm screwed."

Her lips pursed, and her eyes slid sideways to a tiny dab of ash on a silver tray. "You believe Smith learned about Rap technology, and what he learned related to your experiences?"

It sounded as plausible as anything I could dream up, so I gave a vigorous nod. "Maybe Smith left clues behind at M-Prime. I could go there to check. And I could carry your instruments so you could measure... well... whatever."

I chewed my lip. I'd come to the stumbling block in my plan. "We'd need the coordinates of M-Prime to program the robe."

She waved a dismissive hand. "Our talents have collected coordinate symbols for ze M-Prime dimension. But ze Raps have barred use of ze robe technology."

Excitement lifted my spirits. "So don't tell them."

The guards in the fracture chamber looked none too happy to see us again, especially with the wad of gear that Natasha lugged along. She had the credentials and the balls to bully her way in. I trailed in her shadow, glad that no Raps or Neans hung about.

A guard pulled a robe and a harness from the locked cupboards. Natasha dumped her equipment and snatched them from him. Her face glowed, and her hands rubbed the chest plate like it was the softest fur.

"Perhaps when you return, I will study it in my lab," she said.

"The equipment can't leave the room, ma'am," the soldier said. When she glared at him, he ducked his head. "By order of Col. Juarez."

Natasha ground her teeth.

I tapped the plate to life and switched to the navigation screen. Natasha's eyes got round. She stared at me and ran her tongue over her lips.

"When you return, Mr. Madden, we should have a long chat."

I felt like the Thanksgiving turkey ready for carving and took a half step back. "Sure, sure. Whatever you say. Can you find the right symbols for M-Prime?"

She refocused on the chest plate, and I drew in a deep breath. I hoped she knew what she was doing. I didn't want to end up lost in D-space because she'd gotten a symbol wrong.

She entered the destination. I shrugged into the too-big harness, pulled on the robe, and brought up the shields.

Natasha added a second harness that must have weighed fifty pounds. Idiot lights twinkled in shades of red and green from black cubes and gadgets. I looked like a Christmas tree done up for a funeral.

Natasha checked that everything worked and gave me a thumbs-up. I staggered across the chamber to the fracture. I'd better not have to run from zombies in this getup. They'd have me for lunch before I'd taken three steps.

The fracture drew me in. A giant anvil pressed down on me, snapping my bones like twigs and squashing my mass into a foot square cube. My blood exploded outward in a spray of mist. The pressure continued, shrinking me smaller and smaller.

Not real. Well, sort of. Somehow, my old mantra didn't comfort me the way it did before I knew about D-space. If I survived, I'd give some thought to a new focus that would see me through the torture of dimension hopping.

The curtain of glitter parted, and I splatted on a metallic floor. My stomach arrived doing triple handsprings, and my head pounded like a rock in a cement mixer. Blood poured from my nose.

But at least there weren't any armed guards pointing rifles at me. In fact, there weren't any guards at all. Was that typical for outposts in alternate dimensions?

After a couple of minutes, I pushed up to my hands and knees. The room spun. The dull glow of ceiling lights dimmed.

When my vision cleared, I wobbled to my feet more easily than I expected. But then, I no longer wore Natasha's equipment harness. It had vanished in D-space. Boy, she was going to be mad.

I hiked up my robe and tied the ends around my waist. I'd learned my lesson in the zombie dimension: always be prepared for a quick exit.

The fracture room was small and cramped. One of the car-sized, rectangular Rap supply platforms was shoved against the side wall. There was barely room for a standard platform between the fracture and the exit. I staggered forward, not wanting to be a casualty should a platform shoot through unannounced.

The ceiling in the fracture chamber might be high, but the exit door was scaled for Raps. On the other side of the door, an open shaft rose several stories. *Uh-oh.* A Rap anti-gravity elevator contraption.

I closed the door and prowled the fracture chamber while keeping what distance I could from the glittering fracture. There had to be stairs somewhere. Or a ladder. Or *something* I could use to access the rest of the facility.

I found nothing.

Back at the shaft, I rocked. What terrible safety! Didn't the Raps know it was a bad idea to take an elevator in a fire? What if there was a power outage? Anyone in the tube would end up like Humpty Dumpty. For a risk-averse race, they took a lot of risks.

I gripped the wall and leaned into the shaft, hoping to catch a glimpse of someone above who might throw down a rope. Nothing moved, and no sounds filtered to me. I didn't get any lighter, either.

Had the facility been abandoned and no one told me? Then why leave the lights on? How would they have left if all platforms were grounded? Maybe they'd gone for a walk?

I edged into the shaft and scooted around the wall looking for handholds. More nothing.

I rubbed my head. "How the hell do the Raps get up this thing?"

The walls moved. No, scratch that. It was me moving, drifting casually up the tube. My arms wind-milled, my legs kicked against all-too-thin air. I stifled a yelp.

"Stop!"

I stopped. The floor steadied three feet below. More of the second floor showed over the edge of the shaft. *Voice activated?*

"Up," I commanded, my voice shaking and my fingernails digging into the flesh of my palms.

I floated higher. When my feet reached the level of the second floor, I grabbed a post beside the shaft and pulled myself out. Gravity returned.

I stood in the center of a sixty foot diameter room. The walls sloped inward to the ceiling. It must be a tower, like the ones at the Rap base on R-Prime, the sides rising to a point high in the sky. I shivered, remembering the scary float to the top.

Equipment ringed the walls. What I first thought were windows but soon realized were viewing screens looked out on a marshy meadow punctuated by tall mud mounds twice my height. They must be the hives Pete mentioned. Something fist-sized, green, and frog-like hopped through the vegetation nearby. A mountain range jig-jagged along the horizon.

I turned my attention back to the room. Nothing screamed 'Clue!' I appreciated the uncommon silence of the electrical equipment.

I screwed up my courage, ordered the anti-grav tube to take me up, and stepped off the edge, making sure I didn't look down. Sweat broke on my forehead. My stomach rolled. My robe floated around my chest.

I pitched out on the next floor and gulped a deep breath. Unlike the previous level, this one had a closed floor plan. I confronted three doors spread around the shaft, each marked with Rap symbols, a scrawl I assumed was Nean hieroglyphs, and English. I opened the door labeled *Human.*

A wedge-shaped space lay beyond. A couple of easy chairs and a TV sat in a long, narrow space to the right. Three doors along the left wall opened into tiny odd-shaped bedrooms. One was marked *Talents* and was fitted with bunk beds, one room had a label marked *Milburn*, and one bore Smith's nameplate.

I stepped into Smith's room. The sheets and blanket were wadded on the mattress, which was askew on a shelf jutting from the wall. The drawers of a bureau hung open, their contents draped over their edges and strewn on the floor beneath.

I waded in and stabbed a toe at a pair of tighty whities. *Eww.* I should have brought latex gloves like detectives wore. Or any gloves. No more traveling D-space without them.

The top and second drawers were empty. The third drawer contained a white t-shirt still folded, a tube of petroleum jelly, and a package of condoms. I had a girlfriend now; wearing a rubber was the responsible thing to do. It wasn't like Smith would come back for them. I stuffed the package in my pants pocket.

Did Smith have a girlfriend? Or a boyfriend? Here at M-Prime? I added that to my mental list of questions.

The fourth drawer contained half a pair of socks and a roll of bright yellow duct tape. I threw up my hands, frustrated that I hadn't found anything important, and kicked the drawer.

It jammed on something. I knelt and tried to close it again without success. I pulled the drawer out.

A plastic baggy taped to the back of the drawer snarled in the track. I grinned. I wasn't such a bad detective.

I pulled out the baggy and ripped it open. A driver's license and passport spilled into my hands.

The driver's license pictured a dark-haired, bearded man. His name was Boris Kirdan, and his address was Waco, Texas. The passport had the same name and picture and was issued by Nigeria.

Were passports required to travel D-space? I hoped I wouldn't earn more demerits for coming to M-Prime without one. Did coming here count as leaving base? Big black checkmarks swarmed across my vision.

I closed my eyes and focused on Smith. Had he switched rooms with this Boris character? Was I looking in the wrong place?

My eyes shot open at the sound of a thunk somewhere above me. Guilt warmed my face. I dropped the documents in the bottom drawer and scurried out of the bedroom.

The thunk came again, and then again, building to a slow, steady rhythm. A low, warbling voice ground out guttural syllables. I tiptoed to the suite door. The chant definitely came from up the shaft.

Should I announce myself? Or search the other rooms and be gone before anyone realized I'd arrived? Neans hated me on sight, and interrupting someone at prayer was rude. I opted to avoid a confrontation and backed away from the door—until I fell over an armchair and toppled to the floor with a thump of my own.

The facility went quiet. I tiptoed to the door and peeked up the shaft. A Nean looked down from two floors above. From his expression, I'd given him a good fright.

"Hi ya." I cast around furiously for an excuse to be there. "I just dropped by to see if you needed anything here, what with the travel ban."

"Who are you?" The priest pushed his hat back a bit as he leaned over to get a better look down the shaft.

"DPS sent me. By robe." I swept a hand down my body in case his English wasn't too good.

His surprise changed to keen interest that made me squirm. "You travel alone?"

The creepy quiet of the facility settled around me like a smothering blanket. Where the heck was everyone? I moved to the edge of the shaft.

"Sorry to interrupt your ceremony, er, prayers. If there's nothing you want, I better move on. Too many outposts, too little time."

"Wait!" The priest threw up a hand in a stop motion. "We need more... I don't know your word. If you come up, I can show you."

I wiped sweating palms on my pants, ordered myself not to look down, and entered the tube again, all aquiver.

The priest's eyes lit with excitement. He shifted to a two-handed grip on his staff and raised it to rest across his shoulder. His jaw muscles flexed.

I'd seen that stance on the streets. It meant violence was coming in a burst of murderous rage.

"Down!" I shouted at the tube, my head already rising above the level of the priest's floor.

The priest swung the staff like a pro golfer taking a tee-shot. The staff whistled over my head. The anti-gravity tube reversed course, the walls creeping by oh so slowly.

The priest growled a syllable. I stopped drifting down and started back up. He showed me his big, white teeth.

"No! Down!" My stomach flipped over. "Down, down, down!"

I drifted down. The Nean dropped into the shaft with me. I got a look up his robe that I could have done without. I kept my eyes on the bottom after that.

My sneakers touched down. I bolted through the door while I fumbled to activate the harness and set my destination. Sandals slapped on the floor behind me. No time to straighten my robe. I dove into the fracture.

15

My body turned inside out. It was just as painful as it sounds. My trip through D-space was filled with ghouls and ghosts and galloping ghasts. Just when I thought it couldn't get weirder, a nuke went off.

The mountains, valleys, shimmering crystalline structures of D-space shivered, split, sundered. They all dissolved into the sparkling glitter that shaded a fracture. I watched in horror and wonder. Is this how the end of the multiverse would look?

Then the glitter solidified into an enormous jagged tube that grew in seconds to encompass half my field of vision. I rocketed along its surface and bounced against the serrated spikes rising from it. Felt them rip through flesh and stab into my head, like a giant hand dissected me with a dull steak knife.

Around me, the discordant buzzing harmonics of D-space turned to screams of panic. Nightmarish creatures fled from certain destruction as the new structure expanded, but few moved fast enough to escape their crushing fate.

D-space had never been this torturous. I wanted out. The part of me that always held together on a transit flickered and faded. My thoughts scattered like debris in a high wind, torn away in the punishment of ricocheting along the wicked, white surface.

Pressure smacked into me, pressure not caused by the jutting lances that grew longer with each passing second. I skipped over a few of the smaller protrusions, crashed into a larger, sharper spike, screamed in agony.

More pressure. More distance. Another collision. Less and less of myself. Just a whimper now.

A ragged black comet whirled past, ducking between the menacing spires and racing up to explode against me, creating the same pressure I'd felt earlier. Once, twice. Each nudge moved me away from the deadly thing birthing in D-space. Each pass near the aberration shredded the comet until it resembled a collection of streamers instead of a single mass.

The soot-ball! It hadn't been eaten. A flicker of relief kindled into a flame of hope.

Suddenly free from the insidious appetite of the tube, I shot away in a new direction. Destruction gave way to normal demented D-space landscape. I tumbled through it, fading in and out of consciousness. A curtain of glitter did nothing to slow me.

I slapped down chest-first on concrete, the air knocked out of my lungs. I couldn't see, couldn't hear, couldn't feel. Was I dead?

Then my stomach arrived, twisted in a knot and doing the cha-cha. Cannons fired in my brain. Every inch of my body ached. Blood poured from my nose.

Black high-heeled boots clicked on the concrete beside my head.

"Mr. Madden, where is ze equipment harness?"

Pandemonium broke loose in the fracture chamber. Angry Raps whistled and chattered loud enough to drown a group of chanting, shining Nean priests, their staffs charged and aimed my way. Twice the usual complement of guards had their rifles pointed at me. It was good to be home.

I rolled over, and the room rolled with me. Except the floor still pressed against my chest. I'd developed telekinesis during my journey through D-space and could now make the walls rotate at my command. Or maybe I was just nuts.

I blinked a few times and tried for hands and knees. Hand and knees wasn't a bad position to collapse from provided I didn't hit my nose. Two nosebleeds per day was my limit.

No one rushed to help me up. Standing was overrated anyway. I settled for sitting on my heels, knees solidly in contact with the concrete. Bare knees on cold concrete. Naked knees sticking out of pant legs missing from just below my crotch. *Crap. I'd ruined another uniform.*

"Demon!" Hothead shrieked.

A beam of eye-searing light jumped from his staff and crawled across half the distance between us. The Raps stopped their ear-splitting racket to watch. Hooray for Hothead! All that screeching made my headache worse.

When the light halted and hung in the air, Hothead grimaced and bore down. "You have disturbed the balance between light and dark! You must pay the price!"

My wits gathered like cotton wool stuck in molasses. "What?"

"Ze Raps have recorded an unexpected dimension split at M-Prime."

"Split?" I mumbled.

"A cataclysmic event occurred zat has caused ze dimension to fork into two dimensions, each representing a different possible outcome. M-Prime and a new M-2 will be unreachable for hundreds of years."

"It's not my fault," I said.

Natasha arched an eyebrow. Col. Juarez joined Natasha, and Flight Leader Falcon joined Juarez. Capt. Samuels stood behind them. His stare turned me to stone.

"You have again used our technology without our permission," Falcon squawked. "We demand that you return it now and are prepared to take it by force if necessary."

The two guard Raps had their stunner wands in their paws and looked ready to spray the chamber. At the barest nod from Samuels, the soldiers turned their weapons from me to the Raps.

"We used your equipment to further investigate ze disturbing incident in D-space," said Natasha. "Are you not curious about ze result?"

"Travel in D-space is filled with unacceptable risk," Falcon tweeted. "We will no longer participate in such a venture. Return our equipment or face the consequences."

Before she could reply, my wrist tattoos flared into intense itching, and Smokey stepped through the fracture.

The big demon clip-clopped straight to me, his pointy teeth bared and his bulging muscles flexed. Long clouds of smoke shot from his nostrils and wreathed his head.

The Raps backpedaled until they were against the walls, except for the white female, who held her ground and stared intently at the gadget she'd used in the hallway the previous night.

The Neans powered up their staffs another notch, and the room brightened like a mini-supernova had gone off. Humans and Raps shaded their eyes. I struggled to stand and face the demon.

"Traveler, what have you done?" Smokey roared.

"It's not my fault!" I whined. "Not this time!"

All Nean and Rap eyes shifted from the demon to me. I wrestled with the knot in my robe, embarrassed by my semi-naked state. My fingers were too slick with blood from my nose to get it untied. Most of the humans looked confused since they couldn't see the demon. But the talents quickly alerted them by pulling their own stunner wands and shouting, "Demon in the chamber!"

"It is because of your kind traveling Between that we contend with the soulless," Smokey said. "Now your meddling has caused untold damage in the territory of a powerful overlord. The Council votes for the recycling of this dimension."

I'd done everything I could to protect E-Prime. And I wasn't guilty. Anger bubbled up, taking my blood pressure with it. My head felt like someone rapped it with a mallet.

"The *soulless* problem is your fault." I stabbed a finger toward his muscle-bound red chest but given our height difference and my wobbliness, I pointed more toward his rippling abs. "After all, you pulled Smith off the platform. I tried to clean up your mess because I thought we were friends."

Oops. Did I really just accuse an eight-foot tall demon of nefarious acts based on the word of a bigoted Nean? What was I thinking! What would he answer?

Smokey reared back, his brows pulled low. "I am not to blame for the lost soul. Had you not failed to retrieve the part with knowledge, Between would not be plagued by the soulless. It's your fault."

I crossed my arms and glared at the demon. How exactly would I tell if he lied? He'd reared back. That was one point for lying. He didn't shuffle his feet, er, hooves. One point against. His breathing didn't change—he'd huffed smoke at the same smog-alert rate since his arrival, so another point against. He definitely stared unblinking, but did he ever blink? If I split a point, I'd be lost. I wasn't good with fractions.

"Fine, give me the blame. Just... give me a clue how to make it right."

Smokey's glassy bull eyes narrowed. "You wish to make a bargain, Traveler?"

Aw, hell, not another bargain. But maybe I could leverage a little something extra. The Raps wouldn't continue to travel D-space unless they had reassurances they would be safe. I and the other super-talents relied on the Rap tech. I had to keep them in the game, much as I disliked them.

"We'll fix your soulless problem if you agree to give platforms safe passage through D-space, er, Between. No jostling the passengers."

Smokey scratched a jowl. "Done."

"Okay, then," I said, surprised he'd agreed so readily.

"You will stop the soulless before we recycle this dimension."

"What?!"

"It is a fair trade for the loss of resources caused by the growth of a new dimension."

"*We* didn't cause the split." What had Natasha said? "It was a cataclysmic event. Out of our hands. Nothing to do with us. How would we start a cataclysmic event?"

I knew the answer to that one. I'd prevented a human-driven cataclysmic event that could have destroyed the multiverse. I hoped Smokey wouldn't think of it.

"Are you sure one of your warlords or overlords or whatever-lords didn't do it?" I asked.

Smokey pointed to himself, talons flashing. "We don't *create* new dimensions! We *recycle* them."

I lifted my chin. "Well so do we. It wasn't us."

Uh-oh. I shouldn't have said that. My head hurt so bad I couldn't think straight. But I couldn't let the demons destroy E-Prime.

"How're we supposed to fix the soulless problem?" I asked, playing for time.

"You must go there and make fractures until the barrier to Between is destroyed."

I goggled at him. "You said recycling was *your* job."

"The soulless create no nightmares for us to marshal against the barriers."

"Can't you just round up a bunch of nightmares and herd them in through the fracture?"

"They are difficult to herd into a dimension, or chase far enough from an existing fracture to create a new one when they exit. It is an exercise in futile organization."

An idea formed despite my semi-conscious state. "Let's say we agree to help. Wouldn't that free up a bit of space Between?"

The big demon nodded his massive head.

"So you'd get back what you lost in the split, right?"

After a moment, Smokey nodded again.

"Sounds like if we take care of your soulless problem, we ought to be square. Tit for tat. An eye for an eye. You leave us alone, and we'll leave you alone. Will your demons, er, Council agree to such a bargain?"

More smoke flowed out of Smokey's nostrils, but in an annoyed puff instead of an angry stream. "Only if you act soon, before the infestation spreads."

I'd already destroyed one dimension, admittedly by accident. What would DPS command say when I proposed we destroy another? But I couldn't do it by myself, and I didn't see another way to save E-Prime.

"I'll take it up with my people and get back to you."

16

I wanted to crawl into bed, pull the covers over my head, and wake up to find that my day thus far had been a vivid dream. Instead, I sat at the conference table thinking its surface would make an excellent pillow and trying to pay attention while the lights crooned twisted, dire versions of familiar lullabies. A cool draft circulated around my bare legs, making goose-bumps rise.

The Neans had taken their station at the head of the table, Higgins at their side. Hothead kept his staff glowing. It was a silly display since I could knock his light out by simply moving closer. Flash stood behind him, that annoying smirk on his face.

The Raps sat opposite me. To soothe their ruffled feathers, Juarez had handed over the robe and harness I'd worn. Did the Raps know how many more robes we had stashed in the fracture chamber cupboards?

I was the filling sandwiched between Natasha and Samuels. She seemed oblivious to the mess she'd stirred up by sending me to M-Prime and tapped a long, red nail on the table.

Samuels sat too still, like an earthquake gathering its strength before jolting a continent. Maybe we didn't need to send a whole contingent of talents to the zombie dimension. Wouldn't Samuels be enough? If only he were a talent!

"Mr. Madden." Col. Juarez had dark smudges under his eyes, and new strain lines etched his face. "Report."

"Um... well..."

I glanced at Natasha, my face half-hidden behind a wad of paper towels that didn't seem to be slowing the dribble of blood running from my nose. She ignored me, no more a team player than I was. Fine, we'd both face the firing squad.

"I volunteered to travel to M-Prime to help Natasha—Dr. Filenkov— with her investigation. Into the loss of Smith, I mean."

"By using *our* technology even though you knew it was forbidden.

Another reason to break our alliance with humans," Falcon chirped. "We will arrange a tactical withdrawal."

Joy sparked in Hothead's eyes. "You will return His Highest Eminence Sacred Leader Schlauzauber Frommanisch to our dimension as your first priority."

Falcon turned his fleshy muzzle to the Nean. "All platforms will return to R-Prime, where we shall remain. If your people wish, they may use automated cargo vehicles to continue to N-Prime. Should you decide to avoid the risks of further D-space travel, you may remain at R-Prime."

The sparkle vanished from Hothead's eyes. "Unacceptable."

His High Muckymuck raised a hand and silenced his minion. "What was discovered at M-Prime?"

Hothead's jaw clamped shut. Flash leaned forward, no longer smirking.

Your murderous priest needs to practice his long drive. But I couldn't say that. I needed to patch up DPS, not rip it apart with allegations I couldn't prove and no one would believe. Raps and humans needed Neans to travel safely, much as I wished it weren't true.

"Smith was a slob."

Natasha and Samuels both turned their heat-ray vision on me. Oops. Neither important, nor appropriate. I'd never get the hang of the whole team business.

I studied the tabletop. "I didn't learn anything that might explain his fall."

Dodo examined her nails, and then buffed them against her vest like she had nothing more important to do, but her stubby ears cocked my direction. "Nothing to explain why the dimension might suddenly split?"

"Seemed fine to me." I thought about my excruciating trip through D-space. "At least it was when I left."

"The demeanor of my kind was as expected?" she pressed.

"Didn't see any of your kind. Or my kind, either." Now that I thought about it, that seemed odd. "Guess they were on an away mission."

Falcon turned to his second and twittered something. Over my head, Capt. Samuels and Col. Juarez exchanged a look I couldn't fathom.

"And ze demon," Natasha said. "What did it want?"

This was my chance to shine. I sat straight and gave the room a timorous smile. "Smokey wants to trade. The demons will ensure safe travel in D-space if we do a little favor for them. I said I'd have to ask, but it's a great deal. For us. And for everyone." *Except the zombies.*

"What would this *favor* be?" asked Prof. Higgins. "And why would we expect demons to honor any kind of agreement?"

"The, uh, headhunters are causing problems in D-space. Because they ate Smith. Or something. Smith was our guy and on one of our platforms, so the demons say it's our fault. Now that they know about D-space, the zom—the headhunters have to go."

Higgins leaned over the table. "What do you mean by that?"

"They want the talents to create enough fractures to collapse the dimension."

The room went still. Higgins' face got so red I thought he might be having a seizure. I'd hoped for a more agreeable response.

"The demons demand genocide of a human dimension in exchange for safe passage?" Higgins asked. "Preposterous!"

"They *are* aggressors," Samuels said. "They killed Smith and attacked Mr. Madden without provocation. If they are also aware of D-space and develop the capability to travel across it, they are a threat to all our dimensions."

I wondered how eager Samuels would be to nuke the zombies for the demons if he knew the demons wanted to recycle the E-Prime dimension. It seemed like a good time to keep mum.

"*Another* hostile human culture. Intolerable," squeaked Falcon. "They cannot be allowed to spread."

"A dimension collapse will destroy more than a single planet," Higgins said. "It will destroy an entire universe. What of other potentially intelligent species on other planets that will be caught in the destruction?"

Uh-oh. The whole multiverse thing was impossibly complex. Were we about to kill a lot more than a single planet of zombies? But Smokey said the zombies were bad for all the multiverse.

"Your technology can ascertain where fractures occur in their dimension," His High Muckymuck said to the Rap leader. "Can we not simply deny access to these areas by using your impenetrable metals to shield them?"

I hadn't thought of that. The demons wouldn't find that solution acceptable. They wanted real estate, not just an end to whatever mischief the zombies were up to.

"Um, that won't work. The headhunters are too advanced. You know, buildings and clothes and such." The humans turned disbelieving looks my way.

"Too advanced?" Higgins' face set into a smug smile. "You said they were armed with spears and blowguns."

I did? I'd told so many lies, I couldn't keep them straight. In for a penny, in for a million bucks.

I plowed on. "And maybe they can fracture."

"Did you *see* them fracture?" Higgins asked.

Had I stated the sky was blue, Higgins would have argued that it wasn't. "Smokey might have mentioned it. I wasn't there long."

Col. Juarez ran a hand over his bald pate. "We cannot commit mass murder. We'll locate their fractures and build barriers that will prevent them from accessing other dimensions, and we'll monitor those containments to ensure that the inhabitants don't escape. Is everyone agreed?"

The Raps and the Neans didn't argue with Juarez's solution. He stood and turned to me.

"Mr. Madden, when the demons contact you again, you're to negotiate for containment. If that doesn't appease them, we'll review other options."

I was darn sure it wouldn't, but I couldn't push harder without telling them the headhunters were flesh-eating zombies. They'd lock me up. Crazy, not stupid.

Everyone filed out around me except for Capt. Samuels. When I stood, he said, "My office, now."

Samuels strode down the corridor, punched in a code on the lock pad, and swung the door open, waiting just inside for me to enter before closing it. He rounded his desk and glared at me, feet apart and hands behind his back.

"Report on your excursion to M-Prime. And this time, don't leave anything out."

"Well... Natasha and I were discussing how she wasn't getting far with her D-space research. I suggested—"

Samuels waved a hand. "Skip your flimsy justification. Begin when you arrived at M-Prime."

It occurred to me that as head of security, Samuels might have all the DPS offices bugged, and he already knew about the conversation between Natasha and me. What if something I said now wasn't what I'd said before? Sweat dampened my face, and my stomach twisted in a knot.

"Um... it was quiet. There was a Rap elevator shaft thingy—"

Samuels' mouth pulled into a tight line. "I'm familiar with the layout of the M-Prime facility."

"I went up to the next floor. Above the fracture chamber. It looked like a control room with lots of equipment. No one was there."

He placed his palms on the desk and leaned forward. "No Raps?"

"Not unless they were invisible." I shifted my bare feet on the cold wood floor. "So I went up another floor. To the crew quarters. No one was there, either."

Samuels straightened and gazed at the office wall over my head. After a moment, he pulled out his swivel chair and sat, while motioning me to do the same. I perched on the edge of the metal-framed, armless chair.

"Then what did you do?"

Should I tell him about searching Smith's room? Assuming it was Smith's room. I was such a bad liar.

"I still didn't find anyone. I heard—"

"You said Smith was a slob. On what did you base that statement?"

"I went in the human area. The doors were all open. Smith's room was a mess."

"Describe it."

The package of condoms suddenly seemed like a boulder in my pocket. I shouldn't have stolen them, especially since I planned to use them while I had intimate relations with Samuels' daughter. Another boulder formed in my throat.

I coughed. "The sheets and blankets were wadded up. Clothes were tossed on the floor. Drawers were half-open."

Samuels face tightened, and he swung his chair slightly left and right while he stared at his desk.

Since he was lost in thought, I hurried on. "And then I heard something coming from above. A thumping noise. And chanting."

The captain brought his attention back to me. "A Neanderthal priest?"

"Yeah, praying or something. He wanted me to come up. He seemed..." The last thing I wanted to admit was that I was scared of a Nean. "They don't like me much."

"You didn't see or hear any Raps or humans?"

"Just the one priest. One unfriendly priest." I shifted in the chair, shivering. The room definitely wasn't at a comfortable temperature for shorts. "I went down and through the fracture instead."

Samuels nodded. "Anything else?"

"I lost my pants," I said. "The legs, I mean."

Samuels scowled at my alabaster shanks. "See the supply clerk for a new uniform. Dismissed."

I jumped from the chair and rushed to the door. I didn't stop to think until it closed behind me. Where was the supply clerk's office? I wasn't going back to ask Samuels.

Why had Samuels been so interested in the state of Smith's room? Should I have told him it might not have been Smith's room?

Why had he asked whether I'd seen anyone else at M-Prime? Why was the white Rap, Dodo, so interested in the behavior of the Raps stationed at the facility?

Why had the priest attacked me? Sure the Neans hated me, but they hadn't taken a swing before. On the other hand, I'd never been cornered by one alone before.

I was supposed to find answers, but the questions multiplied faster than fleas on a feral cat and were just as irritating. I'd heard there were mail-order private investigator courses. I wondered how fast I could get one.

A soldier on the stairs pointed me in the direction of the supply officer's hidey-hole. It was housed in the basement of the building that also housed the infirmary. I raced across the compound and pounded down the stairs, thinking of how wonderful pants and shoes would feel on my frozen feet and legs.

The supply clerk was a short, hard-faced man with a salt-and-pepper buzz cut and a gravel voice. He shook his head at the state of my clothes and waved me through his office to a storeroom lined with deep shelving.

Mountains of military uniforms bulged from racks. Rows of boots stood at attention in the next section. The overhead fluorescent lights sang, "Over hill, over dale, as we hit the dusty trail..."

We quick-marched all the way to the back of the sprawling space and stopped before a locked cupboard. The clerk pulled a bunch of keys from his pocket and opened the doors to reveal neat stacks of black talent shirts and pants. The clerk sized me up with a look and withdrew a pair of pants.

"Um... how much?" I asked.

"How much what?" the clerk snapped.

"Money," I replied. "I don't have any cash on me..."

"Don't they teach you kids anything?" At my befuddled look, he continued, "You don't pay for the uniforms, but you do have a limited yearly allotment. Exceed it and you'll need permission from your CO to requisition additional supplies."

"Right, right," I said. "I ruined two pair in the last two days. Can I get one more? And some shoes and socks?"

The clerk's mouth turned down. "Anything else, Your Highness?"

I winced. "Um, a coat? If you have any?"

The clerk turned away, grumbling. He led me through the maze of supplies, collecting new socks and a black rain jacket before pulling up at a rack of low boots.

At the end of the aisle, a soldier tottered on a step-ladder while he wrapped bright yellow duct tape around a sagging square metal heating conduit. The soldier glanced down and then looked again. A smile formed on his lips as he perused my naked legs.

"What the hell's that?" The clerk pointed to the conduit.

The soldier's smile vanished. "You told me to fix it with duct tape, and that's what I'm doing, Sarg. If you don't like the color, you should have ordered something else."

"I did." The clerk pointed at the boots. "Better try these on."

I stared at the yellow tape, reaching for but not quite finding an association. The clerk crossed his arms and turned his glare on me. I grabbed a pair of boots, shoved my bare feet in them, and whisked them off again. No wearing shoes without two pairs of socks, my delusion about foot rot rearing its ugly head.

The clerk marched back to the exit. He made me sign forms in triplicate and turned his back on me. I didn't see a changing room, so I unfolded a pair of pants and pulled them on over the remnants of my ruined pair. Two pairs of socks, boots, and the jacket made me feel whole again.

My plans were in shambles. DPS looked less likely to survive. The questions in my head tumbled over one another like cars in a demolition derby competing for my attention. I ought to do something about my bloody nose before I ruined my new jacket. I trudged upstairs to find Doc.

17

Exhaustion carved deep lines in Doc's face. He doled out a couple of packets of ibuprofen and packed my nostrils with bits of gauze, which he called sponges. When he'd finished, I hopped off the exam table and reached for my coat.

"Do you always get nose bleeds when you travel in D-space?" he asked.

I thought back over my homeless years when I'd fallen through fractures once every year or two.

"Maybe a trickle if it's a long, rough transit."

Doc rubbed a hand over his jaw. "If you don't mind talking about it, what's a transit like?"

I shuffled my feet and glanced around the empty aid station, mindful that the FBI bug was still jammed up the lamp shade. I should have retrieved it and let it join its brethren in the dumpster. I felt like I owed Doc an answer. Maybe if he understood what D-space was like, he could help the mad super-talents.

"I could use a coffee," I said, "if you have a few minutes."

In truth, I didn't drink coffee, but going for a hot chocolate didn't sound like the kind of activity a hard-boiled detective spy engaged in.

Doc's weary brow lifted and a glimmer of interest shone in his eye. "Sounds good."

We headed for the mess hall. I was glad for my new coat. Light mist drizzled over the quad.

"D-space is like..." I shrugged. I didn't have the words. "It's different from here."

Doc waited for five or six steps. Then he patted my shoulder. "If D-space causes people to go mad, it has to be a traumatic place. I understand why you might not want to talk about it."

I sighed. "It's not that. None of this," I waved a hand over the quad, "exists there. It never did, and it never will. Nothing that's real here is real there."

Doc frowned and mulled this over. "Like a state of psychosis?"

My face heated. "I can't speak for everyone, but when I'm psychotic, the reality of the world still exists. There's air and gravity and... normal stuff. The disturbing part of psychosis is when the normal stuff acts weird. In D-space, there isn't *any* normal stuff."

"And that departure from reality is so extreme that the mind goes into shock," Doc muttered. He looked at me. "How do you stay sane?"

I laughed, pleased that he thought of me that way but uncomfortable with the lie. "I only ever have one foot in reality. Every minute, I'm choosing to ignore things I've learned can't be real no matter how real they seem. I get fooled a lot."

"That's remarkable. It must be exhausting."

The thought of the demons recycling E-Prime and killing a good man like Doc ate at me. I had to stop them. I had to unravel what happened to Smith.

"Did you know Smith?" I asked.

"Not well. I did his physical when he joined DPS eight or nine months ago. He didn't have any medical issues in case you're wondering whether a sudden bout of vertigo might have caused his fall. There was an unusual virus on his body, but I think he picked that up in the dimension where you found him. I'm testing samples."

"He couldn't have seen another doctor about something, especially if he thought it might get him kicked out of the program?"

Doc shoved his hands in his pockets and hunched his shoulders against the chill. "It's possible, but unlikely. The scientists don't have high physical health requirements to do their jobs. And he lived on the base when he wasn't at M-Prime."

"He did?" I couldn't believe my luck. "Where?"

"Over there, third floor." Doc pointed to the same building where I lived. "Lake Point is short on housing, and with the secrecy level of DPS, most of the staff live in the compound when they aren't away on an assignment in another dimension."

"How'd he come to be at DPS?" I opened the door of the mess hall.

"Higgins recommended him. They taught at the same university sometime in the past."

That tidbit got my attention. Agent Black warned that the spy might be in cahoots with someone here. Were Smith and Higgins partners in crime?

"Or maybe it was Dr. Filenkov who brought him on board." Doc headed for the beverage station.

"Um... maybe we can do that coffee another time," I said, overcome by the desire to get to Smith's room.

Doc gave me a curious look. "Sure, River. Thanks for the information about D-space. It's sparked some new ideas."

He shuffled away on leaden feet. I jetted out the door and through the mist to the dormitory building.

No one walked the halls, which probably meant more demerits for missed classes or training activities. The third floor hallway echoed with my footsteps. I resisted the urge to tip-toe.

Some of the doors had formal nameplates. Some had pieces of adhesive tape with names scrawled in black felt pen. A few had no names. Smith's place was the last one on the left.

I tried the knob. To my surprise, the door opened. I glanced down the hall to be sure I wasn't observed and stepped inside. *Hell, I'd forgotten gloves again.*

Smith's room was twice the size of my cozy little nook. One wall sported wood bookcases filled with volumes of physics texts. The other had a twin bed covered in a floral print spread, a nightstand, and a desk with three small drawers along one side. A bureau stood beside a window that looked out on the playing field.

The bed was neatly made and the desk tidy. In fact, except for a computer monitor that wasn't plugged into anything, the desk was bare. Had DPS already cleaned out the place?

I opened the desk drawers. A yellow legal pad and a couple of pens were the only contents in the top drawer. In the second drawer, I found two small black plastic rectangles with metal ends. A worn phone book and a map of Lake Point lay in the bottom drawer.

I was too late. Whatever personal items Smith might have had in the room were gone. But good detectives never gave up. I moved to the bureau and opened the top drawer.

White undershirts, neatly folded. The second drawer had briefs, a jock strap, and two pairs of flannel pajamas, also tidily folded and stacked. My breath caught in my throat.

No wonder Samuels was so interested in the state of Smith's room at M-Prime. The scientist wasn't a slob. His room had been searched, and by someone who wasn't concerned about the search being discovered. *By someone who knew he wasn't coming back.*

I looked over my shoulder, that creepy feeling of being watched crawling up my spine. I shoved the drawer closed and race-walked to the door. The hall stood empty, but I didn't slow down until I was safe in my own snug room.

Progress at last! I wanted to dance a jig—until I realized I didn't know what the search meant. Who searched Smith's room? Why? I groaned. Not more questions.

I kicked off my new boots, hung my new coat in the closet, and stripped out of my new pants. I wiggled out of the remnants of my old pants and chucked them in the wastebasket. Then I remembered the stolen condoms and fished the pants out again.

I dug the condoms out and thought about where to put them. No leaving them on the desk for everyone to see. I slid open the top drawer, spied the last of the pink stationery with the happy dancing flowers, and closed the drawer. It didn't seem decent keeping those innocent blossoms in the same drawer with rubbers.

I opened the second drawer and stashed my illicit prize. Then I pitched the ruined trousers in the trash again.

Ruined pants. Ruined pants with something bright yellow in the pocket. Something that had been embedded in Smith's guts. Yellow like the tape in Smith's drawer. *Not a medical device.*

Where were the ruined pants I'd worn in the zombie dimension? I'd left them on the shower floor. But they weren't there when I got up this morning. They weren't there yesterday before dinner, either, were they?

Where was my uniform? Had the spy taken it? What was the yellow doodad I'd found in Smith's corpse? I shoved my feet in my boots and dashed from my room.

Veronica strolled along the corridor toward me.

I screeched to a halt. "Hey, Veronica, I had some messed-up clothes in my room, and they're gone now. Any idea where they went?"

Veronica sniffed. "The servants probably stole them."

Was she joking? We didn't really have servants, did we? At least I hadn't seen anyone in a butler's coat treading the halls, but then we recruits were out of the building much of the day.

"Where would I find these servants?"

"In the servants' quarters?" She marched to her room and disappeared through the door.

"Servants' quarters. Right. Thanks."

Had she learned about my schizophrenia? I cringed at the thought and scratched her off my list of potential phony friends. I intended to surround myself with normal people, not a bunch of lunatics. Who else might give me a more helpful answer? I turned my feet toward the mess hall. If you want to know what's up with the servants, ask another servant.

In ten minutes I had my answer. The dorm janitor was right where the cook's helper said he'd be: taking a smoke break on the athletic field.

The janitor was a bent and grizzled old guy with a raspy voice punctuated by a smoker's hack. I positioned myself upwind of his cancer stick and introduced myself.

"I'm wondering whether you saw a torn uniform on the floor of my shower."

"You mean those blood-drenched rags?" he wheezed. "They don't pay me enough to work with hazardous materials. No sir. Had to get a second pair of gloves and one of them surgical masks, just to be safe."

"Sorry," I said. "I didn't know what to do with them. And I hadn't emptied the pants pocket yet. Where are they now?"

He coughed up a gob of phlegm and spat it ten feet away onto the running track. *Eww.*

"In the dumpster, o' course. You think anyone would want those smelly things? Stunk up the whole building. Had to wash my collection can when I was done. If I weren't due to retire at the end o' the month, I'd be in Col. Juarez's office complainin' right now."

"Sorry to be such a bother." As a pacifist, I'd learned that even if it isn't your fault, apologize. Some might consider it wimpy. I liked to think of it as a diplomatic skill—my *only* diplomatic skill.

I hung my head and shuffled my feet, just to make my apology seem more authentic. "Which dumpster?"

The old janitor looked at me like I was crazy. He was a solid judge of character. "How should I remember which dumpster? Whichever one was open, over by the kitchen, where the garbage truck does its collection."

I thanked him, although not profusely, and jogged back to the mess hall. Three large green dumpsters were parked just outside the kitchen's back door, their ripe contents wafting in the humid air.

I hoisted the lid on each unit and took a good sniff. *Ah, the sweet essence of eau de garbage bin.* None of the receptacles smelled like my ruined uniform. I'd have to dig. I hoisted myself on the edge and dropped in.

Having lost all my belongings and my clothes each time I'd fallen through a fracture unexpectedly, I'd become a connoisseur of trash. Wrapping in garbage bags was superior to trotting about in my birthday suit when I arrived in a new dimension.

To my disgruntlement, DPS used a cut-rate bag, thin as tissue and easily torn. It wasn't a brand you'd find me modeling. I made a mental note to speak to the supply clerk, just in case I overran my yearly allotment of uniforms.

I found my zombie-shredded pants in the bottom of the second dumpster. The hard, yellow-wrapped medical-device-that-wasn't still hid in the front pocket. I grinned and crawled out from amongst the garbage.

Back in my room, I realized that I'd ruined yet another uniform on my treasure hunt. At least this one wasn't shredded. I put the curious yellow lump on my desk and stepped into the shower, sans boots but still wearing my grubby, stinking new uniform. I applied shampoo everywhere except on my watch cap, rinsed, and undressed. I hung my washed clothes on hangers to dry and donned a fresh uniform.

The yellow lump on the desk drew me like the dessert bar at an all-you-can-eat buffet. I washed the blood and gore away and picked at the yellow duct tape wrapping until it loosened.

The next layer proved to be a condom. Made sense. It would keep the contents waterproofed for someone whose man-purse was their... Yuck. It didn't bear thinking about.

A black plastic metal-tipped rectangle lurked in the condom, clean and dry. I turned it over in my fingers. I'd seen more of these in Smith's desk upstairs. What were they? Why did Smith need to smuggle this one in his bowels? Had it gotten him killed?

I didn't have answers, but I had an idea of who to ask.

18

I was absolutely certain that Sammie wasn't a spy. I also owed her an apology for running out on our date after acting like a weirdo. I'd drag her from Flash's clutches, apologize, and ask her about the plastic device jiggling in my pocket.

I found her in the quad, watching a group of Neans do... something. They'd stuffed a pair of camo fatigues with straw and propped it against a running hurdle. The dummy's creator had added gloves with long spikes sticking out the tips of the fingers. It looked like the decapitated progeny of a cross between a scarecrow and Edward Scissorhands.

Hothead had the Nean priests organized into a line twenty feet from the effigy. One by one, they'd charge their staffs and fire their slow-mo light beams at it. Those priests who hit the scarecrow backed up five paces and tried again.

Flash stood at one end of the line and ten feet closer to the target dummy than any of the others. He had a white-knuckle grip on his staff, and sweat dripped into his eyes from his prominent brow ridge. Light flickered through the carved runes on the staff, but that seemed to be all he could muster.

Sammie watched from the sidelines. She looked more frazzled than the previous night. I wanted to rush over and hug her. But I'd seen her fight, and I wasn't sure what welcome I'd get. I sidled over, head down.

"Hey."

I needed a better way to open conversations, especially with Sammie. I promised myself I'd make a sketch of her, tape it to my bathroom mirror, and practice until I had a witty, romantic opening down pat.

Sammie gave me a relieved smile and quick hug. "River, there you are! I heard you were in D-space when the split happened. The Raps say the turbulence is horrific. I was so worried about you. You're not invincible, you know."

Bolstered by her concern and the way she'd skipped over my

embarrassing disappearance the night before, I returned her smile.

Her gaze strayed to the field, and my smile vanished. Flash had given up his efforts and moved another five feet closer to the target. I restrained a smirk and focused on Sammie.

"What were you doing at M-Prime anyway?" Sammie asked. "Did Dr. Filenkov send you there? Things were bad enough between the humans and the Raps without her adding to the misery. She shouldn't have used the Rap equipment without their permission."

I'd intended to take credit for what I thought was a brilliant idea. Now I mentally backpedaled but failed to regain my footing. Sammie waited, the little worry line between her eyes starting to form.

"Well, um..." Sammie's dad loomed from my subconscious, probably because I was worried he'd seen her hug me. My brain took a sharp left turn. "Why does everyone keep asking me about who I saw at M-Prime? Except for one Nean, I didn't see anybody."

Yup, that worry line on Sammie's forehead grew deeper by the second. But it didn't seem to be me causing it—for once.

"M-Prime is a covert outpost. From the outside, it looks and feels like a natural rock formation, thanks to Rap tech. All observation is done from inside the facility and with minimum staffing. That's standard operating procedure on a world with intelligent life.

"The Raps never leave their equipment unattended. You should have encountered at least one of them while you were there."

With all the spying we were doing on the Raps, I could understand why they wouldn't leave us alone with their equipment. But where was everyone?

"How many people, er, beings stay at M-Prime?" I asked.

"Three Raps, two priests, two talents who never leave the facility regardless of the dimension—it's a safety thing to keep them available should the fracture close—and usually two scientists, Smith and Dr. Ross Milburn." Sammie's eyes took on a haunted expression. "The Raps say we won't be able to get into the dimension again in their lifetimes. We've had so many losses recently."

I could tell that Sammie included her brother in the count. My heart wept for her. I wished I could say something that would ease her pain. But what did I know about the care and feeding of friends and lovers?

Frustrated with my social skills, I looked out on the field, where Hothead harangued Flash over his lack of focus. "What are they doing?"

Sammie wiped a finger over the corner of one eye. "They're practicing for the coming war with the demons."

My mouth dropped open, and my eyebrows shot up. "What war?"

"The Neans and demons fought ages ago. Eventually the Neans pushed the demons out of their dimension and closed the barriers with their light magic, all except for one persistent fracture. They've lived peacefully for hundreds of years, but they've always kept the Holy Order alive in case the demons returned."

I couldn't help it. I laughed. "Yeah, well, good luck with that. Smokey creamed three of their priests at E-4."

Sammie turned hostile eyes on me. "It's no laughing matter. And why are you on the demons' side? They may have killed Smith."

Flash stomped across the squishy grass of the quad, splattering mud with each sandal plant. The color of his face matched the flaming color of his hair. He glared at me.

"It's all right, Hesh," Sammie soothed. "You're new at this. It'll get easier when you've had more practice."

Flash poked his staff my way. "The demon spawn should not be here. He'll report our weakness to his demon companions."

My hands clenched, my shoulders rose. My pacifism flew out of my head on great, green wings.

"What's the matter, Flash? Low battery on your staff?" I scoffed. "Too much of a baby to get it up?"

If Sammie hadn't ducked between us, I would have been ducking another Nean staff swing.

"You're not helping," she said before she grabbed Flash's arm and dragged him away.

First I fumed. Then I wondered what the hell I was thinking acting like that. Then I remembered that the Nean started it. Yeah, it was his fault.

I stormed back to the dorm and into my room. I paced. I rocked. I'd never asked Sammie about the plastic rectangle still hiding in my pocket. *Crap.*

I sighed. I was a dunce. I slumped on my bed. Then I moved to my desk chair. The bed made me think of Sammie. I missed her.

What had I learned? There should have been a bunch of... beings at M-Prime. Except for the one priest, I hadn't seen or heard anyone.

If the staff members weren't allowed out of the observatory, then they hadn't been on an away mission as I'd assumed. The humans at least weren't sleeping. The sound of my conversation with the Nean should have carried up the gravity shaft to anyone above. Wouldn't they investigate a new arrival?

What about Boris? Sammie called the second scientist Ross Milburn, and that was what I'd seen on a nameplate. Was Boris a talent, on station to keep the fracture open? Or a visiting scientist who'd left his ID behind? Why was it hidden?

Feet clomped by in the hallway. From the uneven tread, it had to be Pete back from whatever class I'd missed. More black checkmarks swirled before my eyes. I pushed them away. They pushed back. I missed the knob on the first try and opened the door.

"Hey, Pete, do you have a minute?" I called to his retreating back.

Pete turned and flashed me a grin. "You missed fracture practice. You hiding out so Nick won't find you? Or maybe you don't need more practice after that monster you created yesterday."

"That wasn't really—"

"I want to be you when I grow up. You really know how to blast those barriers. Hey, what was it you were muttering before you cut loose? Was that some kind of spell or something? Will you teach it to me?"

I ought to set the record straight. Pete had contributed more to the fracture than me. Instead, I stuffed down my guilt, flagged Pete into my room, and closed the door. Then I dug the plastic rectangle from my pocket.

"Do you know what this is?"

Pete looked at the rectangle, balanced on my palm. He looked at me and back at the rectangle. A smile split his face.

"Is this a joke? Everybody knows what one of those is."

I set the thing on the corner of my desk. "I don't."

Pete's smile faded. "Sorry, man. I thought you were pulling my leg. It's a USB drive."

I squinted at the rectangle. "For...?"

Pete's expression was nothing short of incredulous. "You stick it in a computer and transfer files to it. Then you stick it in another computer and move the files to the second computer. Or maybe you just keep it around in case the files on the first computer get damaged. Do you know what's on it?"

When I shook my head, Pete asked for my tablet. I reached in the desk drawer and pulled out the pretty pink stationery.

Pete stifled a smile. "No, the electronic one that DPS gave you when you signed on."

I expected the heat in my face to singe off my eyelashes. I dug the device out of another drawer and handed it over.

"Log on." Pete handed it back.

"Um..." I wanted to disappear into the floor. I shrugged. "I've never used a computer."

"*Never?* What school did you go to?"

"Amish," I said. Yeah, that would cover my deficiencies with computers without making me seem abnormal.

"So... do you have a religious objection to using this?" Pete asked.

Aw, hell. I hadn't thought of that.

"I've converted," I said. "Can you show me how?"

Pete pointed to a tiny button on the side. "That's the power. DPS should have given you a user name and password. Do you have that?"

I scrounged in the desk for the book-sized stack of paperwork copies and drew them out.

"That red slip. You didn't change your password after you got that?" Pete grimaced. "If Samuels finds out, he'll have your head. Never write down your password."

The screen on the device lit up. Pete showed me how to get to a keyboard and type the information from the red note. He turned his back while I entered a new password, per the instructions. When he left, I'd add it to the note, just so I wouldn't forget it.

"Let's see what's on your drive," Pete said.

He plugged the rectangle into a hole on the side of the tablet and tapped on the screen. The display changed. Pete frowned over it, tapped more, and then handed me the device.

"Whatever is on the drive is encrypted. Without the password, it can't be accessed. Where'd you get this?"

"Dumpster," I said.

Pete gave me a long look. "Okay, maybe it's not encrypted. Maybe the files are corrupted. That's probably why someone threw it away."

Corrupted, as in evil, law-breaking files? Because they were influenced by demons while they traveled through D-space and therefore went to the dark side?

At my blank look, Pete continued. "The drive's broken, and the data is scrambled so it can't be read. Doesn't look right for corruption, though. A computer expert might be able to retrieve something."

Pete turned to the door. "Higgins cancelled class again. If you want, I could teach you how to use your tablet this afternoon. But first we get some lunch."

"Do you know a talent named Boris Kirdan? Dark hair, dark beard?" I asked.

"Doesn't ring a bell." Pete pulled the door open.

"How about a scientist?"

Pete shook his head and shrugged. "Your description's kind of vague, and I don't know everyone at DPS."

I pulled the pink stationery across the desk, grabbed a pencil, and sketched the face from the ID in Smith's room. Pete watched over my shoulder.

"You sure the name's Kirdan?" he said. "Except for the beard and dark hair, that looks like Smith."

19

I counted down to my 2200 phone call with the feds. Pete had spent the afternoon teaching me about computers, the kind of thing that one friend does for another. Would he want to be my friend if he knew about my mental illness?

I couldn't focus. Too many puzzle pieces whirled around in my head. Questions stacked on questions only to crash down and shatter any theories I built.

Smith had to be the spy, despite the feds' reservations. Why else would he sneak computer files through DPS security in his bowel? Or was he hiding the drive from the Raps? Samuels might know, but if I asked, I'd have to tell him everything. I didn't want to die of old age in prison.

The feds were my only resource, much as I wanted nothing more to do with them. Agent Black had been right to worry about the possibility of a spy ring and not a single lone wolf. The spying at DPS began several months before Smith arrived. Someone else *had* to be involved. Maybe the FBI could unravel something on the drive that would point to the identity of Smith's cohort.

Spying for the Chinese didn't explain why Smith fell from the platform, though. If I didn't solve the mystery of his demise, the Raps would break off relations with us. And if the Raps found out Smith died because he'd been spying for the Chinese, they'd claim we broke our promises to them and go home mad.

Or maybe the Raps already knew, and *they* tossed Smith into D-space. Smith's fall gave the dinos the perfect excuse to leave DPS while keeping whatever secrets Smith carried out of our hands. If we blamed demons instead of the Raps, the dinos would be safe from retaliation, especially if they suspected we had more robes and harnesses that we could use to launch an attack on R-Prime.

Inter-dimensional war was too glum to contemplate. I'd be fifteen minutes early, but I couldn't wait any longer to call Agent Black. I checked to be sure the cell phone rested in my pocket, pulled on my raincoat, and crept into the hallway.

A door to my left opened, and Pete emerged. I ground my teeth.

"Hey, Madden, sneaking out to see your woman again?" Pete joshed.

"Can't sleep," I said. "Going for a jog."

Pete's head tilted right. "Got your cuffs on?"

I pulled back a sleeve to show him the Rap devices covering my tattoos.

"Good. You owe me a rematch. Wait right there."

Pete ducked into his room. I shuffled my feet and thought about breaking for the exit. No, he'd just follow me. I'd make it a short race, claim a cramp, lose quickly. I'd stay outside to walk the cramp off and call the feds.

Yeah, that ought to work without raising Pete's suspicions. It was a good lie, my best all day. I was getting the hang of the spy business. If I mastered spy lies, how hard could it be to lie about the schizophrenia? Lots of crazy people passed for normal. I could, too.

In a minute, the tall, limber marathoner returned, dressed in running shorts and a windbreaker. He slapped my back and led the way to the stairs.

Outside, wet fog blurred the security lights at the upper edges of the buildings and along the perimeter fence. A few guards in long trench coats and dew-speckled helmets patrolled the otherwise empty quad. Each nodded as we passed.

We trudged around the corner and out to the athletic field. Pete waved his arms, drew in and puffed out deep breaths, and jogged beside me, knees pumping. He could prance all he wanted. I refused to be intimidated by his psychological warfare.

With only the perimeter lights to guide us, we stumbled onto the asphalt track. Swirling gray mist cloaked the infield and hid the backstretch. Beyond the fence, towering evergreens forested the foothills and disappeared into a black sky.

"How far?" Pete asked when we reached the track.

"A mile," I said.

"A mile's for sissies. How about five miles?"

No point arguing over the distance when we wouldn't do more than a lap before I feigned my leg cramp. "Sure, why not?"

Pete squinted at me, the whites of his eyes, the reflective stripes on his shorts and shoe, and a gleam from his fake foot all that showed in the darkness. "You want to make a bet?"

I chuckled. "Not tonight. Not *ever*."

Pete swung his arms more, stretched his legs, and dropped his coat at the edge of the grass. Since I wasn't going far, I kept my coat on. I didn't want to forget it and explain to the supply clerk why I needed a new one.

We lined up, Pete taking advantage of the inside position. I didn't mind. After all, this wasn't a real race.

He went off like a Doberman chasing a cat. I sprinted after him. Our feet slapped the asphalt and echoed back from the distant building walls, the sound muffled in the high humidity.

The wind cooled my cheeks. Warmth flowed through my body. Running felt fabulous. I'd give it a few more laps before I quit, just to work out the frustrations of the day.

We rounded the second turn and ran shoulder to shoulder toward our starting point. The ground fog thickened to sooty blackness. The building lights dimmed to pin pricks, and the structures disappeared from view.

Pete grunted and lost half a step on me. I ran on, in the zone and loving it. Cold air wheezed in and out of my lungs. I could run all night, although it was darn hard to see the track.

When I came out of the curve onto the backstretch, I glanced over my shoulder. Pete ran a good four paces behind. His face was drawn into a grimace, and his chest heaved. It hadn't occurred to me that *he* might be the one quitting with a cramp. I felt bad outrunning a cripple and slowed my pace.

Pete made a gradual recovery as we completed another circuit and came into the home stretch again. He was a black shadow given away only by his labored breathing and the slap of his feet.

Either I was going blind, or we were in for one heck of a deluge soon. The quality of the darkness reminded me of—

"Nightmares," I whispered.

A nasty chill slid over my body despite my cozy new coat. I drew back my sleeves, but the cuffs looked the same as ever. No burning sensation ringed my wrists. It wasn't me creating the gloom around us.

Pete gasped and pitched over onto the grass. He rolled until he landed on his back, arms and legs akimbo.

I crouched beside the stricken marathoner. *Heart attack?* That didn't explain the darkness that thickened to stygian soup around us. What would cause the very air to blacken?

With each breath, Pete faded. His eyes pleaded with me before rolling back in his head.

"Help!" I shouted. "Someone help. I need an ambulance. He's dying!"

A dark ball streaked past, momentarily dispelling a gloaming ray of anti-light and revealing that, if not for the beam, the evening was no darker now than when we'd entered the field—except for the roiling masses of nightmares sliding past the perimeter lights and headed my way.

Pete sucked in a breath. His eyes fluttered open. "Madden, no strength. What's wrong with me?"

The huge crowd of nightmares posed a fracture threat. If they broke the dimensional barrier too close to us, we'd be sucked through. Pete wouldn't survive, at least not as the sane, funny con man I'd come to know. Panic swamped my thought processes.

The nightmares were the least of our worries. The beam of black held us in its grip, the source of the beam a point near the gate to the field. The glob spiraled around again, scattering the beam, but slowing on each pass.

I recognized the whirling dervish. "Soot-ball! What the hell's going on?"

The valiant little demon-wanna-be jiggled as it swept by, but it couldn't turn the tide of black death around us. Was it safe here, in the presence of so many of its own kind? Where were all the nightmares coming from?

I needed reinforcements. And to get Pete out of the death ray.

"Soot-ball, get Smokey."

Something human-sized shifted in the shadows by the source of the beam. Faint guttural sounds cut through the fog. The anti-light became so dense I could barely see my hand in front of my face.

I grabbed Pete's wrists and dragged him across the wet infield grass, shouting for help as I went. The beam lagged but followed. *Damn!* Why did it affect Pete and not me?

I caught another glimpse of the growing mob of nightmares collecting over the athletic field. I tore my cuffs from my arms and strapped them on Pete. They might hold him in this dimension if a fracture opened. I'd be sucked through in a heartbeat.

I didn't feel any different without the devices, but Pete's chest stuttered and rose. Because of the cuffs?

"Help me," I shouted again. I needed a plan. I'd make a run for it, draw the attack away from my fallen comrade. Then I'd flank the figure at the gate and do it grievous bodily harm. Would I be too late to save Pete?

A streak of fire blazed through the night, burning its image onto my retinas. A thunderous boom followed. A second later, a metal trash barrel clanged down on the asphalt track with a reverberating bang. When my vision returned, the barrel's dented and melted side burned like a furnace where it lay just a few feet away from me, tossed there by the explosion.

A lumpy shape lay on the ground near the gate. The strange dark beam had vanished.

Alarms split the night. Soldiers poured out of buildings, tugging on uniforms and strapping on weapons as they came. As soon as they saw the glow from the blaze, a group of them ran my direction. I screamed again for medical help.

Lights along the football field popped on. Pete's face had gone slack, his eyes half closed. His chest no longer rose and fell with his breathing. I stared in stunned silence.

The first soldier to reach me took one look at Pete and radioed for Doc. He set his weapon aside and began CPR. More men and women arrived, their rifles at the ready and pointing into the night.

Someone guided me back toward the buildings. At the gate, two soldiers helped a swaying Nean to his feet, his robes and staff scorched and blackened.

I tore loose from my escort and rammed the priest in the chest. He took a steadying step back, barely moved by my charge. His face twisted with hate, and he swung his charred staff to club me. The soldiers jumped between us before he connected.

Hothead ran to our happy little group and shook his glowing staff at me. He got a step too close, and the staff snuffed out. "Demon! By your attack on one of ours, you have declared war against the Holy Order."

"He killed Pete!" I shouted, struggling against the men holding me back.

A mix of Neans, Raps, and humans formed a circle around us. The Raps tilted their heads every which direction, like birds watching for danger but uncertain where it might come from. The Nean faces ranged from bewildered to outraged.

Capt. Samuels pushed through to stand beside Hothead. His High Muckymuck followed. Doc barely glanced our direction as he ran by onto the field, a nurse and two soldiers with a stretcher just behind him. I was torn between going back to Pete and slugging the Nean who'd attacked us.

His High Muckymuck's gaze went to the burning barrel and lingered there before he looked around the circle. At last he turned to me.

"Speak, human."

"Be concise," Samuels warned.

I pointed at the priest. "He murdered Pete."

Samuels glared. "Details, Madden."

"Pete and I were running. This guy," I waved a hand at the priest, "blasted us with a black death ray. Pete fell. And died."

The rattle of stretcher wheels silenced everyone. Doc rode astride Pete, applying CPR, while two soldiers hustled the litter through the gate. My heart stuttered in my chest. Troops peeled off our group to join those moving the stretcher. It accelerated to a fast run.

His High Muckymuck's face paled at the sight, and one gnarled hand went to his chest. His eyes caught those of his son, who now stood at the outskirts of the group. Flash's face reflected barely controlled rage, but he looked at the attacking priest, not at me.

His High Muckymuck turned on the priest. "What happened?"

The Nean lifted his chin. A garble of words came out of his mouth, sounding a bit like German. He went on at length, gesturing at me during the narrative. Any Neans who hadn't looked hostile before certainly did by the time he finished. A growing murmur of discontent rumbled around the circle.

His High Muckymuck wheeled to me, but his words held less accusation than I expected. "He says you are a demon and tried to steal the soul of your companion. He couldn't stop you in time to save the talent."

"Not entirely accurate." The little white Rap stepped into the circle, one paw smoothing her damp chest feathers. "I observed the humans running. The priest hid by the gate, generated a negative energy field with his staff, and directed it at the humans."

Samuels looked at the priest, and then at the wreckage of the trash barrel. "Is that what caused the explosion?"

Dodo lifted her muzzle to the sky as though she'd never noticed it before. She scratched her throat with a claw. "Metal attracts lightning. The priest survived. The container did not."

Her muzzle dropped. Her eyes rested briefly on Flash before they turned to blink at me. She seemed suddenly conscious of the square device in her paw and tucked it in a pocket.

His High Muckymuck plucked the staff from the priest's reddened and blistered hands. The other Neans gasped, whether over their boss's behavior or the priest's, I couldn't tell.

"You have used forbidden magic. You are outcast," His High Muckymuck said.

At that moment, a cry went up from the group. They all stared at something over my shoulder. My wrist tattoos flared into intense itching. I turned.

Smokey strode across the field, his cloven hooves leaving no impression in the soggy grass. His big bull brows pulled low. His chin tucked close to his chest. His bulging muscles looked carved from rock. An enormous column of smoke billowed behind him.

Overhead, the nightmare clouds jittered and dashed, roiling back from the enraged demon—except for one compact puff of nightmare that quaked just behind the demon's left shoulder. *Soot-ball, bringing reinforcements a little too late.*

Smokey stopped beside the smoldering debris of the trash barrel and eyed the group. "Traveler, why have you gathered the nightmares here?"

"Shields!" Hothead cried. "Prepare to attack!"

Flash pushed through to take a place at his father's side, feet braced, staff pointed at Smokey. He and the demon locked eyes, and both of them growled. The trace of a smile touched Flash's lips. The furrows above Smokey's eyes deepened and his fat cow lips pulled back from his pointy teeth.

His High Muckymuck placed a hand on Flash's arm. "Fall back. Let the human, Madden, deal with the demon."

Flash gave his father an incredulous look before turning his hostility on me. He eased his stance, but the aggressive glitter still danced in his eyes.

I'd never seen Smokey this mad and wished that someone, *anyone* but me, could understand the big guy. As Higgins had so rightfully pointed out, I sucked at diplomacy. How was I supposed to soothe a savage demon?

I moved out of the group so they would be less likely to hear what I said, just in case something incredibly dumb—or crazy—fell out of my mouth. My limbs shook like a sapling in a hurricane. I swallowed the lump in my throat.

"Hey, Smokey, thanks for coming. False alarm." *Always apologize even when you didn't do anything wrong.* But did that work with demons? "Sorry if I pulled you away from something important."

The big demon gazed up at the overcast of nightmares covering the field. "Do the Unholy Children gather the nightmares here to attack the soulless? It is a strategy fraught with danger. Better to birth them in the soulless dimension."

So Smokey blamed the gathering nightmares on the Neans. Interesting.

I studied the ground. "Yeah, about that attack. A dimension is a whole universe, filled with billions of stars and planets. It doesn't seem right to destroy all that to get rid of a single planet of soulless."

A flicker of orange flame flared in his nostrils. More smoke erupted.

"The dimension is too widely contaminated to be saved, Traveler. Few souls anywhere there remain untouched by its ravages."

One less source of guilt to worry about. But Juarez said I had to offer the demons an alternative.

"The brass want to build cages around the fractures to prevent the soulless from escaping into D-space, er, Between. They want to know if your Council is okay with that."

Smokey snorted. "Millions of fractures are scattered over the soulless dimension. You cannot cage them all."

"But..." Wow, the whole scope of the multiverse was hard to take in.

"The Council will not agree to a change in terms. They want an eye for an eye, tit for tat, this dimension for another, as you promised."

"But..."

Smokey stretched out his wicked talons to the sky, lifted his muzzle, and roared. The gathered nightmares flinched back. No mistaking the panic in their reaction. As one, they fractured.

A gazillion glittering cracks ripped across the sky. The nightmares sieved through, crowding and jostling as they went. A gazillion tiny invisible hands plucked at my being, dragging me forward a step.

The talents in the group at the edge of the field cried out and ran from the insidious tidal pull. I wanted to run with them. The Neans and Raps stood, dumbstruck, watching the catastrophe unfold.

"It begins," the demon said, menace in his growling voice. He turned from me and paced toward the worst of the cracked area.

I should have told DPS command about the zombies. I should have warned them about the threat the demons posed. If E-Prime dissolved, it would be my fault. And for what? So I could look normal for Sammie? How could I be worthy of her love if I let the demons destroy E-Prime?

"Wait!" I ran after the demon. "I'll do it. I'll do it alone. Just stop this."

Smokey paused. He swiveled his big bull head to look over his shoulder. "You'll go now?"

I could jump into a fracture this very minute and be guided to the zombie dimension by the Council, where I'd have to create enough nightmares to collapse the barriers. But I'd prefer to arrive clothed and wearing a good pair of sneakers in case I had to dodge zombies before I got the job done. I needed to finagle a robe. And I'd like to say goodbye to Sammie before I disappeared forever.

"Tomorrow. First thing. I promise."

The demon nodded and strode on toward the greatest area of barrier weakness. "I'll be back."

20

With Smokey gone, His High Muckymuck's voice carried over the group. He intoned a series of syllables that brought bright, warm light to his staff. In seconds, all the other priests joined him, and a huge bubble of healing shield light spread—until it contacted me.

Dodo paced to where I stood on the field. "You must remove yourself to allow reconstitution of the barrier by the priests."

She didn't carry any large objects clipped to her belt—objects large enough to cause gouts of flame. But I knew she'd lied about the lightning, and she hadn't mentioned seeing anyone else on the field.

Fire, not electricity, had streaked horizontally across my vision. Maybe the Raps had miniature flaming banana cannons? Or molten meteor throwers? Was she keeping mum about using it so she didn't have to reveal its existence? Why was she on the field anyway?

I trudged off, the Rap unwelcome at my side. We gave the Neans a wide berth. Before we reached the group, their old leader turned away. With two younger priests in tow, he hurried ahead of us back to the facility while the other priests continued their work.

"What did the demon say?" Dodo asked.

I wanted the Rap to leave me alone. Pete gave his life because he'd extended his hand in friendship. I'd done too little to save him. His sacrifice tore at my soul.

To honor his name, I'd do the right thing. I'd call the feds. I'd pump Agent Black for all the info I could get, and then I'd leave a note for Samuels telling him everything—which wasn't much. He'd have to find the spy without me.

I'd get a robe and go to the zombie dimension, where I'd create enough nightmares to collapse the dimension or die trying. I wasn't sure I could withstand the ride through another collapse so I'd die trying regardless. If I failed, there'd be no E-Prime to come back to. No Sammie to come back to.

"Look, no offense, but I'd like to be alone," I said. "My friend just died."

The Rap fluttered her baby blues at me. "His Highest Eminence Sacred Leader Schlauzauber Frommanisch believes he lives. He goes to perform the ceremony of *grunt-slurg-schwitz* if your doctor will allow it."

I frowned at the Rap. She spoke Nean as well as English? "Doc won't let a priest within a mile of Pete."

"Unfortunate if true. I shall test your theory." The Rap padded away toward the infirmary.

I turned off behind the mess hall. There weren't any suitably dark corners to lurk in while I made my call, not with every light in the facility blazing. The smelly nook by the dumpsters would have to do.

After a few tries, I found the cell phone's directory and selected Ike. The phone rang just once before Agent Black picked up.

"You're late. What's going on there?"

Did the feds have the place under observation? Given their hideout's location, a good-quality telescope might well give them a view into the DPS facility.

"Target practice," I said. "Why were you interested in Smith?"

I hadn't meant to blurt my question out like that. I'd intended to be clever and circumspect. Clever and circumspect, like cunning and careful, clambered into a car cruising away to Constantinople. I drew in a deep breath. *Ohm.*

Silence dragged on for a full thirty seconds, allowing me time to meditate and Black to squirm.

"He had access to some of the leaked information," Black said at last, an edge in his voice. "About the explosion—"

"Nothing to do with moles or mice or men," I snapped.

Black's voice hardened. "You lied to us, Mr. Madden. You said you didn't know Smith. What really happened to him?"

My shaking hand squeezed the phone, frustration at my illness building. *Shit.* I'd given my cuffs to Pete. I had to get a grip or risk an unplanned exit from E-Prime.

"He fell off a platform in D-space, and zombies ate him for dinner. Or maybe lunch. I'm not clear on the time zone difference between here and there." That ought to convince them they'd hired a madman—in case they had any remaining doubts.

"We don't seem to be getting anything from the bugs you planted," Black said.

"What a shame."

What a shame! the invisible chorus muttered behind me. *What a shame!* the building lights echoed. *Shame, shame, shame on you!* they chanted in round.

I rubbed my forehead, a monster headache throbbing behind my eyes. *Not real.*

The feds had a treasure trove of details about everyone at the base. They'd picked me, the crazy guy, to stitch up into a turncoat. Why? They thought I was gullible enough to fall for their offer? They were right about that.

Who'd willingly hire a schizophrenic to save the US from a Chinese threat? Even *I* wasn't that crazy.

They needed someone inside DPS because they'd lost contact with their spy—and any warm body would do.

"Smith was your inside man. When he didn't report back, you cast around for a replacement. I was the first person to walk out of the bar alone. Your background check turned up no connections to anyone at DPS because I don't have a background to check, and Smith hadn't handed over my file yet."

"You can't reveal your conversations with us to your superiors without also revealing your willingness to spy on your own people," Black threatened. "You have no choice but to do as we say."

A brief, maniacal laugh burst from me. Okay, maybe it was more than brief. I broke the connection and tossed the phone in the dumpster.

No more lying. No more hiding my condition to keep a job or make friends. I had just one goal: save E-Prime by destroying the zombie dimension.

But first, I had to know whether Pete made it, as the little Rap claimed. I hustled across the quad to the infirmary building and took the steps up two at a time. A short walk along the hall brought me to the door of the hospital ward. Low chanting came from inside.

Had Doc let the traitorous Neans minister to Pete after they'd tried to kill him? Indignation bubbled up in my gut, and I pushed through the doors.

A soft yellow glow emanated from the back left corner of the large space, providing illumination. Ten hospital beds lined each side of a center aisle, each bed separated from the next by curtains. Mad super-talents slumbered under blankets. Colored lights twinkled on medical monitors above each bed.

Wisps of nightmares periodically oozed from the super-talents, like lazy smoke from a cigarette. The sooty clouds coalesced near the ceiling or squeezed out cracks around the windows. They avoided the lighted area in the far corner.

The nightmares sent a shiver up my neck. There was something twisted about them, something wrong I couldn't put my finger on. Something mad. I glanced over my head to see whether I created the same sooty trail, but the air around me was clear.

Hannah sat beside one of the beds, holding the hand of the female super-talent Sammie and I rescued. The woman in the bed was little more than a bag of loose flesh, her bones pressing against tissue-thin skin. I fought back the urge to gag. Tears streaked Hannah's cheeks. She didn't look at me.

In the back corner, His High Muckymuck stood chanting at the foot of Pete's bed. The two younger priests had their hands on the old priest's shoulders. The old leader's staff was extended over Pete's still form and created a pool of sunlight that stirred feelings of cloudless summer skies, wildflower meadows, love, and laughter.

Doc and Dodo stood back a few feet. Doc had a relaxed rapturous expression on his face. The Rap had her device in her paw, but she wasn't looking at it. She seemed as caught up in the proceedings as Doc.

My hands curled into fists, and I marched toward them. Dodo turned her muzzle my direction. In a split second, she'd launched down the aisle and intercepted me.

"No closer, River Madden." She planted herself in front of me and placed a front paw on my chest. "You must not interfere if you want your friend to live."

I raised an arm to shove her aside. The doors opened behind me.

Flash strode in. His gaze moved from me to the Rap to his father, and his face morphed from worry to rage. He stalked to me.

"Get out, demon spawn, before I take you apart," he whispered.

The door opened again, and Sammie squeezed in. Her lovely features scrunched into a frown. Seeing her fanned the flames of anger in my heart.

"Screw you." I leaned toward the towering Nean. "Take your murdering Holy Order and go to Hell."

"River, stop it!" Sammie rushed down the aisle to us.

Flash took a deep breath and a half step back, his eyes never leaving mine. "My father gifts his life to a *human* while good Neanderthals die for lack of care. Bow and kiss the ground we walk upon, for it is sacred."

Footsteps tapped on the floor behind me. I turned.

His High Muckymuck approached, leaning heavily on the two young priests. Pale and gray, his ancient face looked decades older. The shine was gone from his eyes. His feet dragged on the linoleum.

The young escorts chanted softly and maintained a small glow around their leader. The closer they got to me, the more strained their faces became, until the light in their robes and staffs flickered.

"He fades," Flash whispered, a touch of fear coloring his voice. He pointed his staff at the door. "Go, demon. You disrupt the energy."

"Maybe if you ask real nice." I stiffened my posture and lifted my chin.

A growl erupted from the tall redhead. In one quick motion, Flash had both hands on his staff and rammed it into my gut. I flew backward and slapped down between two hospital beds.

The air whooshed from my lungs. My head cracked the floor. The dim ward went dark and quiet and made a lazy turn.

I sucked in air and passed a hand over my eyes. My vision cleared and the room righted. I wished it hadn't.

Sammie peered up at Flash, her hand over her mouth, sympathy in her eyes. *Sympathy for Flash.* No worry about me sprawled on the floor. My heart froze.

Doc hurried to my side and stared into my eyes.

"You'll live," he pronounced.

Doc rose and turned to His High Muckymuck, who had advanced to reach his son.

"I'm so sorry. After all you've done— If you wish, I can speak on your son's behalf," Doc said. "I'm sure Talent Samuels would, too."

"As would I," said Dodo.

"How can I punish one and not another?" His High Muckymuck whispered with effort.

His shaking hand reached toward his son and grasped the boy's staff. "You are outcast."

Flash dropped his eyes and released the staff. He spun and darted to the doors. Before stepping through, he tossed his goofy priest hat to the floor.

I climbed to my feet and swayed.

Sammie stared at me, brows pulled down, nose wrinkled in revulsion. "River, how could you?"

She fled after the Nean.

My frozen heart shattered.

His High Muckymuck tottered along the aisle leaning more heavily on his helpers. Their robes and staffs resumed their glow when they reached the door.

Doc watched me, lips in a hard line.

"What?" I said. "He started it. Besides, one of them tried to kill Pete and me."

Doc's fists went to his hips. "*One* of them, River, not *all* of them. The Sacred Leader has already sentenced the guilty man *and* made restitution. He saved Pete's life."

I crossed my arms and glared at Doc. Pete wouldn't have been near death if not for the Neans. Whatever they did for restitution, it wasn't enough.

"The Neans don't have modern medicine. The members of the Holy Order are the Neans' only healers. There aren't enough of them to go around. Life-saving treatment is rationed to those who've proven worthy. There's unrest because their sacred leader assigns priests to shield platforms so we and the Raps can travel between dimensions instead of using those resources for his own people. Now he's tapped his own strength at a critical time in order to heal a human."

"Not my problem," I said. I'd be leaving soon to save E-Prime. What did I care about Nean politics?

Doc lifted his arms in exasperation "Your little tiff here has as good as killed his son."

I opened my mouth, closed it. "How?"

"Their staffs are more than a tool to focus their magic. They're a symbol of all the priests believe in and swear to. It's the worst sacrilege to use one as a weapon except in a battle against demons," Doc said softly. "The penalty for misuse is horrific—the same as it is for the priest who used dark magic against you and Pete.

"To prevent the boy from using magic to harm others, they'll cut out his tongue. To ensure that he's removed from the gene pool, he'll be castrated. No one will be allowed to acknowledge his presence. He'll spend the rest of his life sweeping the temple. He's an angry teenage kid who tried to protect is father, River. Does he deserve that?"

21

I awoke to knuckles rapping on my door.

"Mr. Madden, briefing in Administration in ten minutes," a female voice called.

Boots clomped away down the hall. I squinted at the lack of light coming through my window and judged that it was oh-dark-ugly or thereabouts. I sat up. A bomb exploded in my head. I staggered to the bathroom, wolfed some aspirins, and dressed.

I'd tossed in my bed for hours, reviewing my actions over the past couple of days. They were despicable. I'd let my jealousy and anger do irreparable harm to another—a kid, even if he did tower over me. I couldn't look myself in the mirror, never mind facing the other recruits or Sammie.

My mind shied away from my guilt and shame. Smokey could turn up at any minute and I had no plan, no robe, and no sneakers. I sighed. I'd run for my life in bare feet before. On the bright side, I'd never have to do it again. My death while saving E-Prime would be no more than I deserved.

When I arrived in Administration, the conference room was packed. Falcon and his second chirped quietly between themselves. Nick should have been there. He would have gotten an earful.

Dodo perched on a Rap stool. One claw traced patterns on the table. She glanced up at me. Something in her acknowledgement dripped disappointment. I'd thought of Raps as less than human until that moment. Now I saw it was me who didn't meet the 'human' bar.

His High Muckymuck had only Hothead at his back. I wondered where Flash was. Had they already invoked his punishment? A big, barbed spear of guilt drove through my stomach.

The old Nean's shoulders drooped. Gnarled hands lay still on the table. The usually keen interest was absent from his eyes. I wanted to apologize to him, but I couldn't find the words.

Higgins sat to his left, speaking in a low voice. The professor seemed oblivious to the priest's weakened condition. Whatever lecture he delivered, it fell on deaf ears.

Natasha watched everyone with bored indifference. She didn't greet me as I slid into my chair. Samuels stood behind Juarez and murmured to the DPS commander. When he spotted me, he took his usual seat to my left.

"Thank you all for coming," Juarez said. "I've been in contact with the President regarding the events of yesterday."

Juarez focused on His High Muckymuck. "She sends her thanks to the Holy Order for going above and beyond the call of duty to aid Talent Peter Wilson. We understand what a grave sacrifice this was at such a critical time for your world. Dr. Polaski assures me that Mr. Wilson will make a full recovery. She suggests we put the matter behind us."

The old priest sank lower in his chair and made no acknowledgement of Juarez's words. Hothead fought some inner battle with the muscles of his face and prevented a sly victory smile from doing more than tugging at the corners of his mouth. What had he won?

"Turning to the demon, the President thinks it's time for a coordinated plan that will protect each of our dimensions from its incursions." Juarez directed his gaze across the table to Falcon. "Do the Raptors have anything to offer that might safeguard our installations or prevent a repeat of last night's damage?"

"No," Falcon squawked. His claws made visible indentations on the tabletop.

Everyone waited for him to elaborate. When he didn't, Dodo shrugged.

"We cannot create barrier energy as the Neanderthals do, nor destroy it as human talents do," she said. "We detect and manipulate it."

Juarez looked at His High Muckmuck. "Do the Neanderthals have the capability to protect our dimensions from the demon?"

Hothead couldn't keep the sneer out of his voice. "We warned you of the danger, but you allowed the demon—" he gestured down the table to me "—to walk among you. You can never be safe until he is expelled, until your people walk the paths of the Holy Order."

Juarez turned to me and raised an eyebrow. If I were him, I'd be weighing the safety of a whole dimension against just one whacko, and the whacko would not get favorable treatment. If it helped saved this dimension, they should agree to sacrifice me. I planned to leave as soon as I had a robe anyway. Or even if I couldn't procure a robe. Let my leaving serve some higher purpose.

Hothead's spine stiffened. "Our numbers are small, and our people's needs are great. We have no priests to spare to protect your dimension.

You must suffer the consequences of inviting the darkness in."

"We have never interacted with the demons," chirped Falcon. "We have been strong allies of the Neanderthals. We require your assistance to defend against this threat."

Dodo spoke to the tabletop. "Be cautious of where you build your nest, Flight Leader. The Neanderthals were unable to prevent a demon from breaching the shields on a platform."

Falcon's head came around so fast I thought he might snap his neck. He leaned away from the white Rap and shivered. The same alarm came over the other dinos.

"Other suggestions?" Juarez asked. He looked at Natasha, but she only shrugged. No one offered answers. The lights hummed *The Battle Hymn of the Republic* in hushed tones. I squirmed in my chair.

"What did the demon want, River Madden?" Dodo asked in a voice little above a whisper.

I hung my head. "He wanted us to stick to the original agreement."

Samuels leaned closer. "Refresh our memories, Mr. Madden. What were the specific terms of your agreement with the demon?"

I swallowed hard and reminded myself that it no longer mattered what these people thought of me. I'd promised myself to be honest, no matter the personal cost.

"If we destroy the zombie dimension, the Demon Council won't recycle E-Prime. Otherwise, E-Prime is toast. Last night was the beginning."

Stunned silence dropped over the room. Samuels was the first to break it.

"They threatened our dimension, and *you neglected to mention it?*"

"*Zombie* dimension?" Higgins cried. "What zombie dimension?"

"The demon stopped its attack. What did you agree to, River Madden?" Dodo asked in the same low voice.

I glanced around. They waited.

"Um... if the demons would leave E-Prime unharmed, I'd collapse the zombie dimension. By myself. Since DPS didn't want to."

"Destroyer of worlds!" Hothead shouted.

"I have to agree with the Holy Order," Higgins said. "Madden cannot be allowed to collapse a dimension filled with countless billions of innocent beings just because he didn't have the diplomatic skills to communicate with them."

Natasha had morphed from bored to fascinated in less than a second. "You can do zis?"

Falcon screeched something so filled with trills and clicks that I couldn't understand any of it. Dodo cocked her head at me. I should have kept my mouth shut and jumped in a fracture last night when I had the chance.

"Is that why the demon stopped the destruction?" Samuels said.

"How do you create ze negative energy to collapse dimensional barriers?"

"He's a super-talent," Samuels said with a frown. "It's what they do. Haven't you read any of the reports?"

Natasha gave the officer a slit-eyed look.

"Please, everyone," Juarez said while tapping his knuckles on the table to restore order. "One question at a time."

When the room quieted, Juarez continued. "In your report, you stated that the dimension was inhabited by headhunters. Now you say they're zombies?"

Under the bright lights of the conference room, it sounded like lunacy to me, too. I clenched my jaw.

"That's preposterous," Higgins said. "The man's delusional. Zombies aren't real."

My cheeks warmed. I clamped my hands on my chair seat and avoided eye contact with everyone.

The door opened, and Doc joined us.

"Sorry to interrupt, Col. Juarez, but I have some information that the group should hear."

"Excellent," said Higgins. "Let's see what Dr. Polaski has to say about Mr. Madden's mental state. After all, the good doctor's a trained psychiatrist, and Madden is clearly in need of treatment."

Higgins folded his hands on the table. Doc glanced at me before returning his attention to Juarez.

Juarez shifted in his chair. "Mr. Madden claims that the dimension where he found Smith is populated by zombies. In light of Mr. Madden's mental condition, I'd like you to address the veracity of his claims."

Doc ran a hand over his chin. "I can't discuss my patient's medical condition without his permission. Do I have your permission, River?"

I couldn't believe my ears. Doc was the greatest. But I had to fess up. No more hiding. The cost was too great. I nodded.

"River suffers from psychotic schizophrenia. For those of you unfamiliar with the condition, it means he receives sensory information from his subconscious which he experiences the same as if it had come from the surrounding environment. From his point of view, he struggles to differentiate real from imagined."

"He sees things," Higgins said in a triumphant voice. "I knew it. Zombies! What a crock!"

"Tell me about the zombies," Doc said.

I wanted to run from the room. Failing that, crawling under the table would do. Why hadn't I jumped in a fracture last night, before I'd sentenced Flash to a living hell?

"They're like us... only dead," I said. "I mean, they live in a town and wear clothes. But their flesh was rotten and hanging off and the town looked... abandoned. No one took care of things anymore. And they ate people. At least, they ate Smith."

Looks of disbelief went around the table. Doc gave them a minute to digest my statement.

"You're sure they were real?"

Were they? I rubbed my arm, still scabbed over from the claw marks. Doc's gaze followed my motion. Hallucinations never caused physical damage.

"Yeah, they're real."

"No one will believe this hogwash," Higgins said. "He should be locked up where he can't hurt anyone. Where he can't destroy an entire dimension."

"I believe him," Doc said. "It explains what I found in Smith's autopsy."

Everyone sat a little straighter.

"I discovered an unusual virus around the bite wounds on Smith's body. I've done some early testing with rats. Whatever the pathogen is, it attacks the host's nervous system, digesting the neurons and replacing them with its own nerve-like structure, but less efficiently."

"So they're sick," Higgins said. "They're still human and deserve compassion, not annihilation."

"That's debatable. Once all the human nerve tissue has been replaced—including the brain—what makes an individual a self-aware person is gone. While the creatures he saw may remind River of Hollywood zombies in appearance, they're really parasitically controlled human remains. The virus is highly contagious. If it spreads to E-Prime, it could wipe out the entire animal population in a matter of weeks." Doc sat back in his chair. "In fact, its potential for catastrophe is so great that I've already incinerated Smith's remains and all my samples. I advise against sending anyone there."

My heart stopped beating. I'd already gone to the zombie dimension. Was I infected? Would I join the ranks of the walking dead?

Doc flashed me a reassuring smile. "If you were infected, we would have seen symptoms within hours of your return. It moves that quickly."

I slumped in my chair and sucked in air. Any death would be better than becoming a zombie.

Juarez wiped a hand over his tired face. "We may not have the option to stay away. For reasons that remain unclear, if we don't destroy the zombie dimension, the demons will attack E-Prime."

Worry clouded Doc's eyes. "Anyone who goes there must wear a biohazard suit. And we'll need a quarantine protocol for the returnees. We can't assume we'll be as lucky as we were with River."

Juarez looked down the table to me. "Mr. Madden, we saw the fracture you created at E-4 and again here on the practice field. How confident are you that you can collapse the dimension by yourself?"

Collapsing dimensions wasn't something I practiced. In fact, I'd only done it once and then with a lot of help. Now that I understood more about fractures, I wasn't sure I could destroy a dimension alone, especially a dimension with strong barriers.

"Not confident, sir. The fracture on the practice field wasn't mine." I squirmed in my seat. "Hannah and Pete did it. But I promised the demons I'd try. I have to go."

"This mission is too important to rely on a single green recruit," Samuels said. "We need a comprehensive solution."

Juarez shifted from diplomat to strategist marshalling his troops. "We'll send a recon patrol first, one platform with heavily armed units in biohazard suits. When they report back, we'll use their intel to plan the assault."

Higgins addressed Juarez. "You've decided? Based on the word of a madman and test results that can't be independently verified because they've been destroyed? And what about the potentially billions of innocent creatures spread over the other planets of their universe?"

"Smokey says the virus is everywhere. There aren't any intelligent species left." I looked around the table. "If there were, the demons wouldn't need us."

"My people will not participate," Hothead said. "The threat does not affect us. We must be returned to our own dimension so His Highest Eminence Sacred Leader Schlauzauber Frommanisch can conduct the Ceremony of Light. With the resurgence of demons, the ceremony is vital."

His High Muckymuck roused from his stupor. "We will assist if we are satisfied that the plan provides adequate safeguards."

A sour expression twisted Hothead's features. His grip tightened on his staff, but he held his tongue. Why hadn't I noticed the power struggle between them before? I should have paid more attention in Higgins' class.

"We don't even know where this dimension is," Higgins protested.

Dodo trilled, "I have recovered the coordinates from the equipment used to retrieve Smith."

Falcon gave a single strangled squawk and turned his muzzle toward his white comrade.

"Do the Raptors agree to participate?" Juarez asked.

Dodo regarded Falcon. "Damned if you do, and damned if you don't,

Flight Leader."

Falcon's feathers stood on end. After a moment, he ran a paw over the top of his head and down his neck, smoothing his ruffled coat. "We must conduct a risk assessment before we can agree. If the results are favorable, we will ask for a volunteer navigator."

Dodo clacked her jaws, eyes twinkling. Falcon looked shocked by her behavior and turned his muzzle away.

22

I waited in the fracture chamber, pretending I didn't hear the *William Tell Overture* coming from the lights. Except for double the usual contingent of guards and four armed talents, I had the place to myself. Or I did until the little white Rap stork-walked through the door.

Dodo's vest pockets bulged to overflowing, and tons of extra gadgets clinked on her belt as she padded to join me.

"You await the demon?" she asked.

My gaze went from the Rap to the chamber doors. Where in the heck was everyone? How long did it take to mount a recon mission?

"Your leaders will be here shortly," Dodo said with a whistle and a lisp.

"Not your leaders?"

"They continue to discuss the risk assessment." She placed a paw on her chest and made a shallow, apologetic bow. "They lack numerical understanding and struggle with the conclusion."

"So... they're too scared to go and won't admit it?"

Dodo lifted her muzzle and clacked her teeth. For the first time, I realized that was how she laughed.

"Possible. Very, very possible," she said. "Their participation is not required for the initial mission."

"How's that?"

"Only one platform will be dispatched. I will provide the navigation."

"Shouldn't they send a real navigator, not just a recruit?"

"None volunteered."

I thought about the crazy flight around the fracture chamber I'd taken with her at the controls, and sweat broke on my forehead.

"Uh... you'll be careful, right? No scaring the soldiers this time?"

She clacked her teeth again. "It will be a mission fraught with danger."

Oh, boy, she was mad as a hatter. I knew how to pick 'em. I couldn't think of a way to prevent her from driving the bus.

Smokey stepped through the fracture and the four talents brought their stunner wands to bear. He ignored their ineffective weapons and clip-clopped to me. Tiny puffs of smoke spilled from his nostrils. His glassy black eyes stared down.

"Traveler, you are prepared?"

"Hey, Smokey, um, there's been a change of plans."

The big demon's chest swelled, and his brows thickened. "You will not keep your bargain?"

"No. Yes! I mean, the others," I gestured around and rushed on, "want to help, too. Everyone's very excited to be part of such an important mission to help the Council. But we need to know more about what we're facing."

Smokey's eyes narrowed and the slit of his mouth showed the tips of wicked teeth. "You face the soulless. Already they have released their spores into Between."

"Wait. What's that mean?"

The demon growled. "Those who devoured your lost soul now have awareness of fractures. They spread the knowledge. As more gain awareness, more seek to pass through the fracture to find new food supplies."

I rocked back. "They ate Smith and became talents? Can they fracture?"

"They are not souls and create neither nightmares nor fractures. They take advantage of existing fractures. If they spread to new dimensions, they will replace all the souls in each with their own kind. Without souls to generate nightmares, the dimensions become impervious to recycling, and all Between starves. Destruction and renewal cease. The multiverse dies."

"Wow," I breathed.

"They are difficult to contain. You must act quickly, before any pass beyond those who guard."

"We will. We're sending a platform to look the situation over, and then we'll throw everything we have at the soulless," I said.

"This bodes well, Traveler. The barriers are strong and will require large amounts of damage to ensure a full collapse, which must occur quickly so that the soulless are destroyed as the barriers fall. Do not delay."

Smokey turned on his hooves and trudged back to the fracture. When he'd disappeared through it, the talents holstered their wands.

"What did the demon say?" Dodo asked.

I wiped my brow. "No time to lose. The zombies have learned how to spread to new dimensions. It's curtains for the multiverse if they succeed."

The chamber doors swung open, and Capt. Samuels and Doc entered. Behind them, two soldiers in full combat gear pushed a bin heaped with white fabric.

"Everyone listen up," Samuels said in a voice that carried to every corner of the gigantic room. "We're about to launch a mission to an infected dimension. To ensure the safety of this dimension, no one enters the chamber or goes through the fracture without full biohazard gear, regardless of race. No one exits this chamber without going through full decontamination in the hallway. Anyone who fails to comply with decontamination is to be shot on sight. Questions? Good. Gear up. Doc will instruct you about how to wear these things."

I gulped. I could have brought the virus back with me when I'd retrieved Smith's body. If I had, I'd be responsible for billions of deaths.

While the guards and talents pulled on suits, more men and women erected a portable clear plastic wall on the other side of the doors. I caught glimpses of more construction farther along the hallway.

When the soldiers were kitted out, the Rap and I walked to the bin. Doc pulled out a garment for me. He smiled at Dodo and handed her a suit.

She held the suit up. "It does not conform to my biology."

While I flailed about donning my suit, Dodo shed her vest and belt. Doc stuffed the Rap's hind paws in too-big rubber galoshes and adjusted the fit of a human-sized suit by applying generous strips of the hideous yellow duct tape around the sleeves and legs. The supply clerk must have gotten one heck of a deal on that stuff.

Doc chopped a sleeve off another suit to cover Dodo's tail and secured it with more tape. He placed a hat like a beekeeper's with a clear plastic veil over her head. Her breath fogged the glass. She looked like a snowman decked out in crime-scene tape. The two combat soldiers exchanged a wary glance.

The little Rap donned her vest and belt. "Where are the robes and harnesses?"

While Doc retrieved the items from one of the locked cupboards, Dodo pulled her atomizer from a pocket and spritzed the inside of the veil. My curiosity soared. What was that stuff?

Doc handed robes to the soldiers and to Dodo.

"What's this about?" I asked, surprised to see them putting the robes on.

"The Neanderthals are few in number and divided about how to respond. They will save their strength for the main assault," the Rap said. "We will use this equipment to provide shielding on our journey."

"Whose idiotic idea was that?" I didn't believe what I'd heard.

Dodo cocked her head. "Mine."

Undaunted by my criticism, the little Rap showed the soldiers how to activate the robes and set them to return to E-Prime at a touch of the chest plate. Under her expert manipulation, the robes took on a shimmering glow. If the Raps never used them, I wondered how she knew so much about their operation. She gave a happy chirp, buckled on a harness, and slipped into her own billowing robe.

The soldiers followed Dodo onto the platform. She didn't trip or anything, despite the too-long robe and clunky galoshes. A twinge of envy sprang up in me, but I stomped it out.

She lifted the platform from the concrete floor and glided it toward the fracture. The soldiers clenched their rifles where they were shielded under their robes and adjusted their feet. I swore I heard the Rap whistling *Heigh Ho* again just before the platform broke through the curtain of glitter.

Doc clapped a gloved hand on my back. He'd pulled on his own hazmat suit while I'd watched the Rap depart.

"Let's pull back to the doors."

I followed Doc down the room, casting worried glances over my shoulder.

Falcon and his entourage looked into the fracture chamber through the newly installed plastic curtain. Just behind them, Higgins and Natasha conversed in low voices. They appeared to be in disagreement about something.

His High Muckymuck watched the proceedings, too. Hothead was notable by his absence, but two priests waited to do His High Muckymuck's bidding. Or maybe they were there to catch the old guy if he fell. He didn't look good.

"They should have a priest with them," I said. "The robes could fail. They *do* fail. That's why the Raps won't use them."

"The Raps won't use them because they couldn't achieve ten nines of reliability." Doc laughed at my bewildered look. "That means they have to work 99.99999999% of the time before the Raps consider them safe. And even then they're cautious."

"She didn't seem very cautious to me," I grumbled. "Besides, there must be two dozen priests here. They could have spared one."

"Most of them are untrained acolytes," Doc replied. "And there's a lack of consensus from the Neans about what they owe us. Their Sacred Leader has enough on his plate without facing an open rebellion."

We stood by the doors and waited. Time dragged by. I fidgeted.

"Is there anything I can do? About Flash?" I asked in a hushed voice, not wanting to be overheard by His High Muckymuck.

"Who?" Doc said.

"First Light... whatever. The old guy's son. He's just a kid. I egged him on. It's my fault. He didn't hurt me. He doesn't deserve to suffer such harsh punishment."

With the masks covering our faces, I saw the lifted shoulders of Doc's sigh more than heard it. "We have to respect their culture and their laws, just like we want them to respect ours. That's a tenet of our working agreement with both races. We follow the rules of the culture we're visiting while we're there. When in Rome..."

"We're in Idaho," I muttered.

It occurred to me that Flash wasn't the first priest to swing his staff at me. The Nean at M-Prime had done his best to bash my skull in. Knowing the penalty, why had he done that? I hadn't done anything to warrant that kind of reception or prod him to take that kind of risk.

The fracture pulsed with light, drawing me back to the fracture chamber. Wands snapped up, and after a short delay, rifles followed. I stiffened and held my breath.

A second later, the platform shot through the aperture. It sped down the floor at an unbelievable rate, too fast to stop before ramming the wall. The alarm system howled.

Only it wasn't the alarm system. The noise came from the platform. How did that work?

One soldier lay prostrate on the stone near the control console. The other knelt at the back edge of the vehicle and wrestled his rifle from under his robe. The little Rap was half twisted on her stool, one paw on the controls, the other holding a heavyweight version of a talent stun wand, also pointing at the fracture. Her robe hood was thrown back, and her hat was missing.

"Incoming! Open fire!" Dodo screamed in a voice that sounded exactly like Capt. Samuels. Or maybe I imagined that in the heat of the moment.

The soldier kneeling on the platform sprayed a salvo of bullets into the fracture. They passed through unimpeded and ricocheted off the back wall of the chamber, chipping the stone and ping-ponging between the walls, floor, and ceiling. The Rap's wand shot basketball-sized knots of crackling white lightning at split-second intervals. Had they gone mad in D-space?

The Great Dane from hell burst through the fracture.

I froze. So did the guards and talents in the chamber. The soldier and the Rap fired unabated.

The dog landed on unsteady paws and plunged forward in hot pursuit of the platform. It jerked from bullet and lightning collisions but still covered ground in galloping strides. Grotesque patches of skin and underlying tissue hung from its back and flanks. Half the neck had been pulped. The head jiggled like a bobble-head doll.

The chamber guards opened fire. Streaks of lightning leaped from talent wands. The source of the screaming alarm shifted to the wall speakers. The noise thrummed through my chest and made me cover my ears.

The zombie hellhound's body exploded under the hail of lead and lightning. Chunks of bone and goo flew in the air and drizzled down again, splattering the floor all the way to the fracture. I gagged on the putrid smell of decay.

Despite being pulverized to pieces no larger than my fist, the dog's flesh continued to squirm and thrash. My stomach rolled over. Was I hallucinating the churning remains, or did they still retain life after dismemberment? From the horrified eyes I could see through Doc's mask, they were real.

Once the dog was no more than writhing mush, Doc rushed forward. Dodo parked the platform ten feet from the chamber door, well away from the contaminated combat zone.

The siren cut out. A striding figure in a biohazard suit that could only be Capt. Samuels pushed through the plastic door, pistol drawn. He ordered the chamber guards to take prone positions in a line halfway down the chamber, their weapons trained on the fracture, which none of them could see. The talents stood behind them, wands at the ready.

More soldiers in suits rushed in and set a machine gun on a tripod behind the guards. Even more soldiers ran in with sandbags and built a short wall to shield their comrades.

I marveled at the amount of military equipment appearing in the chamber. What next? An F-35 fighter jet? A missile-destroying laser system? Captain America?

Satisfied with the progress of the fortifications, Samuels joined Doc. "Doc, what's his condition?"

The fallen soldier had his eyes open, but they were unfocused. His protective goggles were knocked askew, and a big bruise purpled his cheek. A ragged tear hung open at the shoulder of his suit.

"Mild concussion," Doc said. "His suit has been compromised, but I don't see any indication of bite marks. We'll keep him in quarantine just to be safe."

While men loaded the soldier on a gurney, Doc turned to the Rap. "We'll need to quarantine you, too."

"Not necessary," Dodo replied. "The head device was lost during the D-space return."

The Rap faced Samuels. "We must hurry. We have underestimated our enemy."

"We'll debrief in the conference room," Samuels said to Dodo and me.

As we exited, a soldier came in. He wore what looked like scuba tanks over his hazmat suit. The hose from the tanks led to a long metal tube in his hands.

"What's that?" I asked.

"Flamethrower," Doc answered. "To sterilize the fracture chamber."

I wished I hadn't asked.

23

We watched the images projected onto the conference room wall from the electronic device in Dodo's paw. We all wondered how she'd managed to capture the scene when we hadn't seen any obvious video equipment in her gear. The Rap claimed her footage would be more detailed than anything the soldiers' recorded.

The video started with a stark white screen. Then it flicked to the vacant lot in the zombie dimension. Dodo paused and zoomed the image in on shimmering silver strings strung helter-skelter through the weeds at mid-calf height. Samuels noted that they didn't seem to be tripwires for explosive devices or booby traps.

"Zey are a falling hazard only, much like ze wire employed in trench warfare during World War I. Zey expected more individual humans on foot, not a flying vehicle."

Samuels sent a thoughtful look along the table to the scientist.

"They learn," Dodo said. "Resistance will escalate. We must return quickly."

In the video, the first rock whizzed past. A paw crossed the screen to brush back the robe hood, and the field of view doubled. Did the Rap have bionic eyes? We were definitely seeing from her perspective.

At least two dozen zombies lined the open sides of the vacant lot. Their peeling flesh and rotting clothes brought a gasp from everyone in the room. A few of the zombies shook sticks. Most dipped into piles of rocks at their feet and hurled them at the camera.

The country farm boy zombie hefted a bowling ball and launched it. The ball cracked the soldier on the side of the neck. The soldier lurched and staggered. The camera closed on the soldier and Dodo's gloved paw snaked out. Her action saved the man from a head-first plunge off the platform. The platform reversed, and a hail of bullets and lightning balls covered its retreat.

The hellhound rounded the corner of the lot. My fingers dug into the armrests of my chair, and my breath caught in my throat. It rivaled any creature I'd seen in D-space for sheer ugliness.

Saliva trailed from the monstrosity's jaws. A single bound carried it over half the weeds and wires. It launched a second bound before the video washed white.

Dodo pocketed her device. No one spoke for a full minute.

Then it hit me. *Had I gone alone, I would have died before unleashing a single nightmare.*

My death would have been pointless. The only way to defeat the zombies was to work as a team—humans, Neans, and Raps. We'd have to trust and help one another to survive, the way friends helped and trusted one another.

"How the hell do we fight those?" Juarez asked under his breath. His gaze went to Samuels.

"I suggest the nuclear option," the captain said.

"You've got to be joking!" Higgins spluttered. "They're clearly sentient. We haven't even attempted communication."

"More important," Doc said, "we don't know that the virus is susceptible to radiation. We might make the fracture zone too hot for talents to enter while the zombies come and go as they please."

"The excursion was made without a shield priest," Hothead said. "My people are not required and will not participate."

Falcon had that downy new chick look again, all his feathers standing on end. "The navigators will not volunteer."

"They will, when they fully understand the danger," Dodo chirped. Falcon let out a squawk, but the little Rap ignored him and continued. "As for the priests, they will be vital to success. Robes are insufficient for the amount of weapons and shielding we must take."

"Now zat ze zombies have seen a platform, zey will improve fortifications. Talents are not trained to fracture in combat situations. Zey need undisturbed time to focus."

Samuels gave Natasha another assessing look and nodded. "She's right. But there's little point in holding the existing fracture if we're there to create more. As soon as the platforms exit the fracture, they should gain altitude and move to a safe location where the talents can work undisturbed."

"River Madden cannot be transported by platform because of his effect on shields, and he is not flight capable," Dodo chirped.

All eyes fell on me. I shrugged. Not being born with wings was hardly my greatest failing.

"Leave him behind," Natasha suggested.

"I'm the only one who can see nightmares or talk to the demons," I said. Given the expressions around the table, you'd think I'd said I could see dead people. "Smokey said the dimensional barriers are strong and would take a lot of energy to damage. He also said we need to be quick so nothing escapes once we create more fractures. But the platforms need to leave before the dimension collapse gets too far along, or they'll get caught in it. You need me to warn you when the collapse is near."

"River Madden is correct," Dodo said with a nod.

Samuels nodded. "Understood. We'll send through heavy ordinance first to clear the field in front of the fracture. The manned platforms will launch in a second wave, and Mr. Madden will bring up the rear. Three of the platforms will provide covering fire while the fourth platform picks up Mr. Madden. Once all the platforms reach a safe location, the talents can create a new escape fracture."

His High MuckyMuck lifted a hand in warning. "Mr. Madden cannot be on or near the platforms as they leave, or he will impair the shields. He must leave as he arrives—alone and last."

"Agreed," Samuels said.

Dodo hopped off her stool. "No time to waste."

Welding gear and steel plates appeared in the fracture chamber as if by magic. I couldn't imagine why the base had either. Maybe the supply clerk built full-scale DIY tanks in his spare time.

Capt. Samuels and Dodo directed the construction of armored turrets atop four of the six platforms parked along the sides of the fracture chamber. One platform would remain behind to take word to R-Prime about the events of the past days, no matter the outcome. One would carry the biggest, baddest bomb that Samuels had the explosives to build.

The turret walls of the four armored platforms sat back a foot and a half from the edge of the stone so they'd remain inside the Nean light shields, which the priests would generate from outside the turrets during transit. The priests faced a dangerous few minutes on arrival while they moved inside the armored area.

Solid walls rose to waist height, punctuated by gun slits at kneeling height. Expanded metal mesh covered the turret's upper half and the top. The mesh would stop rocks—and bowling balls—without impeding the navigator's line of sight. My confidence in the success of the mission grew with the construction.

The expeditionary force arrived in the chamber in a state of uproar. The Raps looked like a bunch of overweight, kid-sized ghosts ready to head out for Halloween trick-or-treating. They wore ill-fitting body armor under their biohazard suits and exchanged squawks while waving their beekeeper hats in the air.

The Neans' faces were dark and stormy. A soldier trailed behind them dragging a bin of suits and another steered a bin of body armor. The priests, still clad in their usual robes and sandals, stopped in front of Samuels.

"The Holy Order will not participate," Hothead said. "The required garments are unacceptable. A priest cannot generate shield light without robes. They are integral to the natural order."

Samuels frowned at Hothead. He wasn't much better at the diplomacy stuff than me. If I were a betting man—which I wasn't since my race with Pete—I'd bet on him slugging the infuriating Nean.

Dodo swept a low bow. "Sekunde Selig Deputy Bischoffs Oswin, your confirmation of my concerns is appreciated."

I pushed my jaw shut with a hand. So Hothead had one of those convoluted names, too. But what was the Rap on about?

Dodo waved a paw at the bins of biohazard and combat clothing as she led Hothead over to them.

"Of course you must wear your robes. Without them, your priests would lack their required conduit to the Light of all living things," Dodo said. "It is their strength, their reason for being."

Hothead lifted his chin. "It is good to speak with one who understands why we cannot simply discard our robes like an old cloak."

Dodo leaned closer to the priest. "Your robes are sacred, required for the creation of shields, and must be protected at all costs. How else are you to travel the multiverse in search of the Source?"

"Yes." Hothead agreed with an emphatic nod. "At all costs, so that we may find the one true Source."

"If the undead of the zombie dimension were to assimilate your robes as they assimilated your bodies, they might well learn the Way of the Light. And knowing the Way, they might well learn how to defeat you when they reach your dimension, which by my calculations will occur no sooner than two turns of the moon and no later than five."

Hothead blanched. The disgruntled Neans froze in their sandals and stared at the little Rap.

"How can you know this?" Hothead whispered.

"Numerical computation, based on D-space currents and the *whistle-chirp-tweet*. Rap computations are never wrong. We warned you about the unusual storm season you would experience, did we not? And about the earthquake that shook your temple, which survived because you took our advice to reinforce it? Your robes must be protected from the touch of the zombies. Cover them with the white garments, and cover those with the armored garments. Together we will stop the scourge that threatens the Holy Order and the Light."

All the Neans dug into the bins—except for Hothead, who marched from the chamber. Samuels looked both perplexed and relieved by the little Rap's solution. He walked Dodo a few feet away.

"Is that true? The zombies will reach N-Prime in the next two to five months?" Samuels asked.

Dodo blinked up at him. "Yes."

Goose bumps rose on my arms. "You're sure?"

"It is a short hop from E-Prime to N-Prime. Given that they will arrive here in one month, a spread to N-Prime is inevitable—as is their invasion of R-Prime within the week."

"The week? *This* week??" My head felt light, and I couldn't draw in enough air to make the dizziness subside.

The color drained from Samuels' face. Then his jaw tightened. "Not on my watch they won't."

Before they could return to supervising the construction, the group of Rap navigators approached. For once, the Raps didn't bother speaking English. They carried on like a flock of crows arguing over the last corn cob. Dodo listened, tipping her head left and right between nods and the occasional chirp.

When the last navigator ran out of steam, Dodo pulled her atomizer from her vest, unsealed the tape fastening the improvised biohazard sleeve around each Rap's tail, and gave the inside of each sleeve a squirt. Then she resealed the tape, stepped back, and sang like a nightengale.

The Raps closed their eyes and hummed like contented cats. After a few seconds, their eyes popped open, and they all moved to the side of the chamber, silent.

"Problems?" Samuels asked.

"Raps believe that covering their organs of energy detection will interfere with their ability to detect positive and negative energy, making navigation hazardous. Of course, that is not the case. Nonetheless, they believe. I have applied an amplifying solution to compensate for their lack of understanding."

Her explanation sounded like gobbledygook. I was pretty sure she'd used the same spray bottle she'd use in Administration and on the inside of her hat. When this mission was over, I'd have to tell Samuels about her nocturnal wanderings and nefarious activities—and admit my own. Life as a truth-teller was harder than I'd ever imagined.

24

They were an army of ghost warriors sailing over an unknown horizon. Four platforms were jammed with human soldiers and talents, Nean priests and acolytes, and Rap navigators, all draped in biohazard suits that my demented brain interpreted as funeral shrouds. I, dressed as the Grim Reaper, would follow.

Dodo, recognizable only because she was the shortest ghost present, tapped the controls of the demolition platform and hopped off. The platform, carrying its robe-wrapped package of explosives, glided through the fracture.

The little Rap scurried to her own platform, pushed through the crowd of humans and Neans stuffed into the turret, and climbed onto the navigation stool. The priest clinging to the outside of the turret rapped his staff and intoned a chant. A curtain of light sprang up around the platform. The other priests followed his lead.

I stood with my back to the chamber wall, staying as far as possible from the vehicles. My helmet tapped against the stone as I rocked in time to the chants. One of the guards nearby mumbled a blessing and crossed himself.

Someone had found me a pair of sneakers. Between the robe, the body armor, and the biohazard suit, I had the mobility of a redwood—I'd sway in a stiff breeze but was otherwise rooted to the ground. No one offered me a gun.

Despite her protests, Capt. Samuels held Sammie back to crew the reserve platform should the main assault fail to return. Someone would need to reach R-Prime with a warning. She watched the departure from behind the plastic curtain, along with the other VIPs.

I hadn't gotten the minute alone with her that I'd hoped for. Or found the courage to apologize to His High Muckymuck for what I'd done to his son. I'd go, I'd return, and then I'd make it right with everyone... somehow.

Rap tweets sounded in my earpiece, and one by one, the platforms vanished through the fracture. I tapped my chest plate to life, hiked up my robe, and lumbered down the chamber.

I'd left my cuffs with Doc, determined to help create the nightmares needed to destroy the zombie dimension. By the halfway point, the fracture dragged at me. I set my jaw and picked up my pace.

Well before I expected it, the fracture sucked me in. I spun and rolled, stretched and compressed, thumped into unforgiving cliffs of brimstone and crystal spires and gauzy nightmares. I split into a thousand copies of myself, each sprinting off in a different direction and taking a chunk of my reasoning with it.

Not real. Not real.

A cat raced past, in pursuit of a house-sized spider that dripped venom from its gigantic jaws. A cat with lidless eyes and trailing strips of rotting flesh. A zombie cat.

Real.

The creature from the Black Lagoon strode after them both, his gill slits rippling, his clawed hands opening and closing. His head twisted to glance at me before he refocused on the cat.

Real? Not real? My grip on sanity leaked away. Fear washed over me. My head ached.

I swept through a glitter curtain and slammed down on my chest. The world around me was black and silent. Black and silent and peaceful. We'd come in the middle of the night, and all the good little… were in bed fast asleep.

Good. I needed a nap before I got up to… Why was I here?

Thunder rolled over. A storm coming in. Hail striking a metal roof. Dawn breaking, a red dawn. Not the middle of the night then?

I should find shelter. I choked. Something thick and liquid and coppery blocked my breathing. Pain flashed from a spike driven into my brain.

"Madden, get up! We gotta go!"

I floated off the ground. The liquid drained away. A sunny afternoon washed in red appeared before my eyes. My back slammed against something unforgiving. A metal ringing reverberated inside my hat. Funny, my watch cap never made that metallic sound before. Had my delusional ants acquired cymbals?

My traitorous body said we weren't moving, but it lied. The ground dropped rapidly away. I floated in the clouds with the angels.

I looked down on a garbage dump surrounded by decrepit brick buildings. It must be a garbage dump, why else the mess? Chunks of steel cable draped over the edges of the surrounding ruins, as though they'd once linked the buildings, but a giant pair of scissors had snipped them in two. In the center area, broken timbers, broken cinderblocks, broken bricks, broken furniture, broken bodies. Who put bodies in the dump?

The scent of lavender and sweet tea wafted over me. Was one of those bodies the orphanage cook? Or was she one of the bystanders on the rooftops, waving and pointing at me? In the afternoon, the cook always smelled of sweet tea. I smiled at the memory and waved.

A stick sparked in the cook's hands. Metal pinged next to my head. A distant firecracker popped. Not a stick—a rifle.

"Shit!" the ghost sitting next to me roared. "More altitude!"

"Sure, sure," I replied. "No problem."

I leaned toward the edge of the stone we sat on and lifted my arms, ready to take flight into the clear blue yonder. My arms didn't cooperate, though. Hands held me back.

"Madden's acting weird. We need to set down and get him inside the turret. I can't hang onto him out here."

"Not weird," I said. "Mad. Mad as a hatter. Mad as a mad dog. Mad as a mad scientist's mother. Mad as..."

The view of the sky changed, the ground swirled up. A second later, the ghost had me over its shoulder. A solid ghost? Hinges creaked. I was sitting on stone again. They'd taken away my view of the sky. All I saw now was a crush of ghosts. A crush, a crowd, a clump. What were a group of ghosts called?

One of them squatted before me. "Madden, can you hear me? How many fingers am I holding up?"

Count the fingers. I could do that. One, two... I lost count, couldn't figure out why it mattered, started again. One...

"Is that blood on his goggles?" a female voice asked. "Maybe he can't see your fingers."

"Incoming!" the disembodied voice in my ear shouted.

"Where?" a different voice asked.

"What are those?" yet another voice said.

"Turn on your heads-up displays. Use the magnification option."

I lifted my head up. My headache magnified. I'd had some strange, psychotic dreams, but this one took the cake. It was the bee's knees, the be all and end all, the cat's pajamas. Cat's pajamas... Cat.

Zombie cat, escaping the zombie dimension.

I had to stop the cat. No, the creature from the Black Lagoon had it under control. I had to... do something.

"Birds," the voice in my ear said. "Hundreds of them, maybe thousands."

"What's that in their claws?"

"Rocks?"

"Rocks don't squirm."

Squirming rocks. Someone was madder than me. Hard to believe. Lots of somethings rained down from above. Someone shrieked.

"Mice! Don't let them bite you!"

Feet stomped, voices swore, ghosts jostled and swatted at rodents on other ghosts' backs. The bang-bang of a gun sounded, followed by the pinging of bullets ricocheting. A voice cried out in shock and pain.

"Don't shoot! Don't shoot!"

A fat rat landed in my lap. It bared long, sharp teeth and leaped for my face. I flinched back, smacking my hat against iron. A new wave of pain rolled through my head.

The rat's teeth glanced off my goggles. A gloved hand snatched the varmint and crushed it before shoving the body out a gun slit.

"High speed maneuvers, *tweet-caw-chirp* off," Dodo's voice whistled. "Passengers, secure yourselves."

The previously motionless plate of stone jerked. My back pressed into the metal turret. Wind whistled across me, and the sky spun like I rode the tilt-n-whirl at the county fair. Feathered bodies smashed against the turret and were flung off like cake batter from an egg beater. I puked, and then I choked.

I clawed away the goggles and mask covering my face. The red film coating my vision vanished. Blood poured from my nose and spilled like a waterfall down the front of my robe.

A body slumped down next to me. Gloved hands gripped an ankle. Blood oozed through the fingers. Pained eyes looked into mine.

"Nick," I said. "You're Nick."

"Get your mask on, Madden," he said through gritted teeth. His half-moon eyes narrowed to a squint. "How do you feel?"

"Great." And I did. Now that I could breathe, new energy coursed through me. I had a job to do. I had to save... What's it called? That's right, the multiverse.

"There's something wrong with your head," Nick said.

"Yeah, I have schizophrenia." I wondered if his x-ray vision could see the confusion in my brain. What did it look like? A mass of crossed wires and burnt out circuits?

The face plates of the other ghosts snapped around to gaze at us.

"Your head's tilted, and one of your pupils is larger than the other."

"Oh." The world *did* look a little crooked. Didn't matter. Those things we made... fractures, yeah fractures didn't have to be straight. We ought to get started.

A tendril of smoke tickled my nose. The platform lurched and dropped a couple of feet. Its twirling motion shifted to a wobbly downward spiral. Panicked tweets, caws, and whistles filled my ears.

"Prepare for hard landing," Dodo chirped over the racket.

Seconds later, the heavy stone hit the ground. A painful jolt ran up my spine and rattled my brain. The ghosts around me staggered and toppled. Dirt flew in the air and rained down again. The central control column sent up a thin puff of green smoke.

"Abandon ship!"

Ghosts grabbed Nick under his armpits and dragged him toward the turret door. No, they were talents, not ghosts. They had wands holstered on one hip and pistols on the other. Two more of them lifted me to my feet.

"I'm good." I shrugged off their help. I took a step and crashed to the deck. Damn robe. Or maybe my foot was asleep. The right one didn't quite sync with the left. More hands hoisted me. We squeezed out of the... metal thingy on the platform.

The four platforms sat in a row on a dirt track separating a desiccated corn field from a dehydrated soybean field. Black and brown and white feathers mixed with blood and fur and stuck to every surface of the... thingys that flew. The humans and Neans who'd ridden with me milled about, eyes on the sky, weapons raised.

"Let's get to it," I said, although I couldn't quite put my finger on what it was we were supposed to get to.

Dodo clomped to me and pointed a claw my face. "Are you wounded?"

I raised a hand and swiped it across my nose. It came away covered in blood. "Nose... nosebleed. It happens. What's wrong with the..."

Dodo swiveled to look at the smoking rock we'd abandoned. "A design oversight. The control column was not shielded and took fire. As predicted, the zombies escalated their capabilities."

"More incoming," a soldier said and sighted down his rifle.

In the distance, an amorphous black mass fluttered crookedly toward us. Panic slammed into me. I panted and grew dizzy. My feet wouldn't move.

"They are persistent and organized. Onto the other platforms," Dodo squawked. "Get the injured inside. Everyone else hold onto the mesh. Make sure River Madden is secure."

We scattered like wind-driven leaves. I was dragged to the nearest platform, lifted onto the stone, and pressed face-first against the metal by arms linked behind my back.

Paralyzing fear swelled in my gut. They were coming, and I couldn't see them from under my hood. They'd kill us all. No, they *wouldn't* kill us. We'd turn into viral specters. And then we'd fall through holes and poison the... that other place.

There was an initial sense of motion and rush of air. Dodo cawed and it stopped. A glance over my shoulder showed the dead cornstalks whipping past in a blur. How fast were we going? How fast could the birds fly? Weren't we supposed to be *doing* something?

A light bulb came on, illuminating the vast empty cavern inside my brain. I blinked at the glare. So much space, so little knowledge. A familiar screeching buzz echoed off the walls. *Not real.*

An ancient tome appeared, floating in the air. The title sparkled the way a... whatever those things were. The title read, *Don't Run*. The cover drifted open, the way books did in Disney movies. Pages turned. Each page had two words: Don't and Run.

"Stop!" I screamed. "Stop now!"

In a heartbeat, the platforms stopped their forward rush and dropped to the ground. I stepped backward off the stone. Someone snagged my arm and kept me upright. That darn right leg. Dodo was there, peering at me.

"There." I waved left, then right. "There."

They all stared at me.

"Here." My voice shook with my frustration and my finger stabbed at the ground. "Make..."

"I think he's had a stroke. If he has, he needs medical attention soon to avoid permanent brain damage," Nick said, limping closer. "You want the talents to fracture here?"

Fracture. That was the word. I nodded and waved a hand toward the distance. "There." Waved again, harder. "There."

"A series of fractures to weaken a substantial area," Dodo said. "Followed by a final large fracture at the center to begin the cascade. Yes, the numerical possibility is high for such a plan, provided the talents can produce the necessary energy."

"Alpha teams, step forward," Nick commanded.

A stroke? Brain damage? Bad things, very bad things. I leaned on a talent I didn't recognize, possibly the blonde woman who'd guarded the... She steered me to a platform and pushed me inside the cage thingy.

The malevolent black cloud in the sky drew nearer. Black wisps leaked from the six talents in teams of two spread fifty feet apart along a line, as though they were at practice on the playing field. Nick stood in front of them. Dodo had her square gadget in her paw, watching.

"Focus, talents," Nick said. "This is just another day on the job. Reach for your strength and blast it out there."

The flock of death came closer, the faster species of swifts and raptors outpacing their avian relatives. The soldiers formed a line between the talents and the birds. The talents spun up sickly nightmares that drifted away, thinning as they went.

"More!" I cried.

Dodo shook her muzzle. "The negative energy is too low, and the barrier energy too high."

Nick checked the distance to the approaching swarm. "Mount up! We'll try again in another location."

The soldiers filled the sky with lead and ran for the platforms. No more than a handful of birds fell. I clung to our cage and watched the birds dwindle as we raced away.

My eyelids drooped. So tired. Needed a nap. Then I'd... whatever. Everyone would be safe.

I was in the cavern again. The screech like fingernails on a chalkboard resonated around the walls. My wrists itched. A jagged... hole opened. A shadowy figure beckoned.

Wake up, River. Tell Dodo what to do. But my eyelids refused to obey. The infernal invisible chorus murmured mixed messages. *Death, demons,* and *dog food* floated in a sea of gibberish. Someone shook my arm.

"It isn't working," Nick said. "We can't break the barrier. Why?"

"Try again," I slurred.

"We have, three times." Behind his mask, pain and exhaustion lined Nick's round face. "You have to help us. You have to fracture with us."

How was I supposed to do that? I was just a crazy guy—with brain damage—one who couldn't seem to stand up straight. With a mad itching on my right wrist. Itching tattoos. Just one side? Because of the stroke?

I twisted as far as I could. Blam! The itching switched sides.

"That way. I pointed across the cage. "Help is that way."

Nick pulled back. "What help?"

"Demons," I said.

25

"My sensors do not detect the presence of demons," Dodo said.

Nick shifted his weight and rubbed a hand on his thigh. "Nothing else has worked."

Dodo looked from me slumped on the rock, to the direction I'd pointed, and then to the device in her paw. She cawed, and the rocks lifted off.

"How will the demons help?" Nick asked.

"They'll, uh..." I managed a shrug and a lopsided smile. "No idea."

"The talents are fatigued," he said to Dodo. "They aren't strong enough to go much farther. We need Madden to help."

Not good. A half-wit like me wouldn't save the day. We needed an army of strong talents, and instead we'd wasted what we had on futile efforts.

"We approach the city," Dodo said.

The itching increased in one wrist.

"Go left," I said. We veered. "Uh... the other left."

A puff of soot blew through the cage.

"Slow down!" I shouted.

"The flock from Hell isn't far behind," Nick warned.

"The soot-ball can't keep up. Pull over."

Nick and Dodo exchanged a look, but we stopped anyway. Farm land stretched on all sides. A mile away, the edge of the town rose from the dirt. Already a mob of zombies rambled toward us.

The soot-ball blasted back to hang before my face, jiggling all over.

"Where's... Smokey?"

My little buddy zipped a few feet and floated back.

"Is he at the..." I cursed my brain. Where the hell were the words? "The other place where we came in?"

Left, right.

"But he's here? In this dimension?"

Up, down.

"Do you see anything?" Nick asked Dodo.

Her muzzle pointed to her device. "My *chirp-caw* detects nothing. My tail says otherwise."

"Take us to Smokey," I said. "But we can't go near the soulless. And hurry."

The soot-ball zoomed away, headed off at an angle to the town.

"That way," I said. "Warp speed."

Dodo cocked her head.

"Never mind," I muttered. I used the wall to brace while I got to my feet. The soot-ball led us at a good clip to a hill overlooking the town. Dead brown lawn crawled up a slope dotted with headstones and the occasional stunted tree.

Smokey stood at the top of the cemetery, billowing smoke pouring from his nostrils. His friend the ogre stood on one side, and his other friend the troll stood on the other side. They dwarfed the demon, who wasn't exactly a shrimp. They were still as ugly and scary as the last time I'd seen them.

A gasp went up from the talents inside our prison or clinging to its edges. The guards peered around looking for an invisible enemy. Runes glowed along the length of Nean staffs. Light curtains flashed on at the edges of the platforms.

Dodo ordered our fleet down in the middle of the long hillside. The occupants poured forth in a flood. On the plain below, the zombies had changed direction and charged for the cemetery. In the far distance, the evil flock arrowed our way.

Smokey strode down to meet us.

"Traveler, you must——before——" The big demon swung an arm toward the town.

His mouth kept moving, but I couldn't understand the words. Scratchy noises came out instead. There was no mistaking his unhappy expression.

Dodo stepped up, her gadget pointed at the sky. "The barrier is weakened here, especially near the top."

"Is this it? Is this where we need to fracture?" I asked the demon.

"Madden, you're talking gibberish," Nick said. "Nod if we're in the right location. The zombies are coming."

I nodded.

"Alpha team, open an escape fracture at the top of the hill."

Smokey pointed toward the town, toward the place where all my misery started. I could see the sparkle from our hilltop location.

I grabbed Nick's arm, pointed up the hill, and then down. I spread my arms to indicate a line between the two points.

"Got it," Nick said. "Bravo team, mid-hill. Charlie, try to get a fracture as near the bottom as you can. Be sure you're behind cover. They'll be in rifle range soon."

One of the soldiers gave a few terse commands, and they deployed across the hillside, using grave markers as cover and acquiring targets amidst the leaders of the zombie horde, the members of which carried everything from hunting rifles to pitchforks. One wore a long black robe and carried a scythe.

I sank to the grass, exhaustion so deep that I thought I might fall asleep again. The soot-ball spun past and then ping-ponged back and forth in front of me like a kid hopping from foot to foot.

"Am I talking gibberish to you, too?" I asked.

The soot-ball hung motionless for a few seconds, and then it slid emphatically from side to side. A crazy guy created it. Of course it spoke fluent gibberish.

"I need to help. The barrier is too strong and the talents can't... Their nightmares fade. I have to..."

We were in for a lovely sunset. I could take a quick nap if I hurried. The sudden bang of gunfire snapped my head up. More followed. The first five zombies jerked, but only one of them went down, its head gone from its shoulders.

Behind me, cheers rang out. Something tugged at me. I twisted to look up hill.

Smokey and his posse were gone. A line glittered across the sky. Two talents danced a jig. Then they settled, balled their fists, and stared at their creation. The thinnest of lazy clouds drifted out of them.

"Not enough. Soot-ball, give 'em a kick. Make that... thing bigger, or we can't get the... thingys through."

My nightmare rushed away. It flew in a circle around one of the clouds, forcing the directionless mass to contract. As the nightmare became denser, it strengthened and became purposeful. The soot-ball widened its circle, bringing in the second, weaker nightmare.

The first nightmare pounced. It enveloped its newly created companion. Its center darkened and roiled. I grinned. Now that was a nightmare.

It pounced again, going for soot-ball. I sucked in a breath, but the little tyke dodged easily. After what looked like an ass-wagging jiggle, the soot-ball struck out for the far end of the glittering crack. The nightmare followed.

The soot-ball threaded the eye of the needle at the end of the split. Its pursuer rammed the barrier at speed. The main line burst open, and a big circle of splintered area spread. The pull on me increased.

"I'm hit!" a female voice screamed.

"Talent down!" yelled another.

The talent team at the bottom of the hill cowered behind a tall stone angel. One of them held a hand to a neck. The zombies pressed forward despite heavy fire from the soldiers. In another minute, the talents would be overwhelmed.

The talents from the top of the hill charged by me, their wands up and firing. They got only as far as the platforms before the Nean priests intercepted them."

"Talents, keep fracturing!" a Nean voice ordered.

Four of our eight priests abandoned their staffs to their companions and leaped on the back edge of a platform. It lifted off and skimmed zigzag down the hill, the suicidal white Rap at the controls. I held my breath, expecting it to stop by the downed talent.

The platform shot over the cemetery wall and on over the heads of the zombies. Little silver balls the size of marbles rained down from the priests' hands. They exploded on contact with the zombies, taking out the frontrunners. A geyser of flesh and body parts burst into the air.

The platform reversed course. It paused long enough for the priests to retrieve the talents, and then it shot up the hill again. Bullets pinged off the metal as it became the zombies' favored target.

The priests laid the wounded talent on the grass. The other talent stripped away the biohazard hood and combat helmet. Blood burbled from a slash on the neck of the blonde woman I'd seen in the... Damn.

On hands and knees, I crawled to them.

"Can you help?" I asked the priests. "Can you heal her?"

All I got were confused looks. I was gibbering again. I pointed to a staff, pointed to the talent.

"We do not have the power," one of them said. "Even His Highest Eminence Sacred Leader Schlauzauber Frommanisch could not heal such a grave wound in time to save her life."

Dodo appeared at my shoulder, her biohazard suit torn open, a paw fishing inside for something.

"She'll die if she doesn't get help now," I said.

"A necessary sacrifice. We must continue to fracture. The flock will arrive soon."

"Send her back." I waved at one of the stone thingys.

"We are over capacity for the remaining platforms. We cannot afford to lose another."

I clawed at my robe, finally getting it undone. Cursing my fumbling fingers, I stripped my gloves and worked on the harness buckles.

"River Madden, you cannot return to E-Prime without your equipment."

"I can," I said. "I will. Help."

The priests exchanged a look and a nod. One of them bound the talent's wound while another helped me undress. They secured the robe and harness on the talent, and Dodo set the coordinates. While they lugged our wounded companion up the hill, a glow formed around them. I hoped it would be enough to sustain her for the journey back. Near the fracture, the talent vanished, and the priests rushed back.

Smokey strode to join our group. The Neans backed away, growling, but none of them raised a staff to the demon.

"Traveler, more." He pointed to the growing web of fractures.

"How much more?" I asked.

I couldn't understand a word of his reply. He walked up the hill and slipped away, just as the talent had.

The soldiers were pulling back under covering fire from the talents' wands. Nick limped over and looked up at the cracks stretching above our heads. Our eyes met. His looked strange.

"Smokey says soon." Or at least that's what I hoped he'd said.

"It better be. Everyone's given all they have. Any chance you could help?"

"My head. I can't... find the place..." I hammered a fist into my leg. We were so close.

"Pull the platforms back," one of the soldiers ordered. He and his brethren were still firing down the hill. They'd thinned the ranks, but a dozen zombies worked their way forward, learning from us and using the headstones for cover.

Dodo turned to Nick. "Evacuate all talents who are too exhausted to continue."

"No one is willing to run from this fight," Nick said.

"We will be pressed against the fracture soon. The talents are at risk. Better to make an organized retreat than lose resources unnecessarily."

Nick didn't like it, but he didn't argue. A crew organized, and the first platform, crowded with talents, ran up the hill and through the fracture.

A bullet scored the dirt beside me, and I jumped.

The soldier who knelt beside me returned fire. "We have to move you higher."

"Can't," I said. "Too close to the..."

He glanced up the hill to the thing he couldn't see and dragged me behind a nice, big marker for Fred Bowker, brother, husband, and beloved grandfather. The remaining talents scattered around the hilltop, miniscule wisps of nightmare rising from them. Not enough.

"Evacuate everyone," I said.

Dodo replied over the com. "Do you have confirmation of collapse?"

"No. You'll have to bring them back to finish the job later."

"That is unacceptable, Traveler," Smokey said from behind me. "Already we struggle to prevent the soulless from escaping through the other fracture. We cannot prevent escape there and here."

When I'd recovered from the fright his sudden appearance had given me, I thanked my lucky stars that he no longer cut out like a bad radio transmission. The confusion in my head cleared a little.

"We can't, Smokey, not right now. Dodo, get moving, before the talents get pushed too close to the... fracture and get sucked through."

The remaining talents loaded up, and another platform glided away, stuffed worse than a tin of sardines. One platform remained. It would take Dodo, two priests, and the soldiers, who insisted it was their duty to be last out.

Last out was coming any minute.

26

The soldiers, with help from Dodo's exploding marbles, dispatched the zombies to the point where those that still squiggled would be a long time getting up the hill. They waited beside the platform near the fracture.

The birds came on like a lopsided, drunken tornado. The soldiers' limited supply of bullets wouldn't make a dent in their numbers. They should go, before the birds swarmed down, infecting us with every peck and rip. I hunkered on the grave I'd soon share with Fred Bowker.

"A conveyance comes."

I jumped. The damn demon had snuck up on me again. Why would a platform be headed this way? Who'd be insane enough to crew it?

I judged the distance to the fracture. Judged the distance to the wall of birds. *Crap.* At my crawling speed, I had no chance to make the fracture unless everyone cleared out immediately.

The reserve, unarmored platform zipped through the fracture, causing a sonic boom as it exited. Five unarmed humans made a tight ring around the Rap navigator, who hunched over his center console. A Nean priest held a blinding shield from a position at the back, much warmer and brighter than any I'd ever seen. It reminded me of the light the old priest created while he healed Pete and gave me a moment of peace.

At the front edge of the platform, a big fellow wore the flamethrower equipment over his biohazard suit. The flying rock shot down the hill to me and halted. The light shield snuffed out. One short human rushed to the edge of the platform and leaped off.

"Talents dismount!" Sammie's voice said in my com.

I was hallucinating. I wanted to tell her I loved her, tell her goodbye. *Not real.*

Dodo sped the remaining platform down to join us. She vaulted across the gap between the two vehicles and shoved the Rap navigator aside. Her voice sang out, and the Rap sprinted up the hill to the fracture where the soldiers and the two priests still waited.

The other humans gathered around me. The short one crouched and brought her face close to mine.

It was Sammie, my beautiful perfect Sammie.

"River, are you hurt?"

Tears welled in my eyes. The group dropped so I could see them better. JR, Veronica, Mr. Lee, and Hannah hovered over me. My fellow recruits. My fellow, untrained recruits were here to die with me. How sweet. How stupid.

"What the hell are you doing?" I asked.

Sammie went from overjoyed to mad in an instant. "Dodo sent a message saying you needed fresh talents. We're here to finish the job."

"Tell us what to do," Hannah said. "You told Samuels that we made that big fracture on the practice field. How? Nick says we just have to visualize the fracture and it happens. That's never worked for any of us."

"Incoming!" Dodo whistled.

Everyone turned to look. Dodo had one paw on the platform controls, and one on her gadget. The empty armored platform spun like a top and charged out to meet the oncoming flock. It mowed a path of destruction through them, but there were too many.

And they were getting smarter. The flock split and flowed around the destructive platform like a stream around a boulder. The platform plowed through them again on a return trip to the top of the hill.

The soldiers' guns barked and rattled. They held their ground until their ammo ran out, and then they mounted the vehicle. The priests clung to the edges, raising shields. The newly arrived Rap navigator scrambled into position at the controls, and they all disappeared through the fracture.

"Forget making... one of those." I raised a hand to wave at the top of the hill. "Think bad thoughts."

All eyes turned to me. Terror showed on faces, bodies stiffened. These were my friends, and I was about to ask them to do something horrific, something I should have done but couldn't.

"Remember the bullies who beat you. The buddies who betrayed you. The loved ones who didn't live. Feel the pain. Gather it. Grow it. Make it *angry*. Then throw it away," I said. "And run like hell."

The flamethrower belched. A stream of fire reached out and disintegrated the leading edge of the flock. As with the spinning platform, only a small fraction of our enemies died. But it slowed the onslaught and further dispersed the birds. They climbed and formed a donut formation over the cemetery.

Hannah straightened first. Her fists balled at her sides. Her shoulders rose. Her breath whistled through clenched teeth. Her eyes focused on the sky, where the birds circled out of the flamethrower's reach. Did our foes know he had limited fuel?

Sammie and the others looked dubious. She was their leader. They'd do whatever she said.

I whispered, "Think of what we found in Black Robe's dimension. You know how it works. Think of your brother, Griff, and what they did to him."

Tears welled in Sammie's eyes. She spoke to the others. "You heard him. Do it."

They all stood, each facing the outside of their loose circle, me collapsed and useless in its center. Their bodies flexed. JR's hands lifted to shoulder height, his hands fisted as though he strained at the top of a chin-up. Mr. Lee took a kung-fu stance, his dukes up, hands open. Veronica screamed a raw sound filled with pain and rage.

Sammie... My beautiful Sammie wept. Her sobs broke my heart.

Nightmares rose above our group. Roiling, angry storm clouds filled with hatred and aggression.

Hannah's grew fastest, feeding on a continuous stream of power from its creator. DPS hadn't recognized it yet, but like her mother, the teenager was on her way to becoming a super-talent. If she didn't release her nightmare soon, it would fracture too close to our group and drag us all through.

The birds plunged down in a funnel-shaped assault on Dodo's platform. A jet of flame reached out, the platform twirled, and the air filled with the stench of burning flesh. I gagged and struggled to my knees while burning bird carcasses rained down. Where they fell, the dry cemetery grass ignited. The birds peeled off and regrouped above the reach of the flamethrower.

Hannah's nightmare tried to envelop JR's birthing monstrosity. The two entities swirled together, drifting a little away from our group.

Mr. Lee's nightmare rose in a long thin column that resembled a black sword. Veronica's nightmare mirrored her scream: raw and jagged and filled with frustration and rage. It cut into Mr. Lee's elongating blade. The sword sliced back. They dissolved into a single churning cloud.

Sammie's nightmare had none of her softness and all of her steel. It birthed like an opaque warrior bent on finding its foe. It spun a slow circle, ignoring the other nightmares and drifted uphill.

Uh-oh. We couldn't afford to lose that much negative energy through the existing fracture. Everything had to hit the weakened area overhead, and at the same time.

"Soot-ball!" I shouted. Hazy smoke and chemical fumes made it hard to see and impossible to breathe. I finally spotted my nightmare hovering at the edge of the cemetery, clearly fearful of the huge abominations the recruits had created.

"Keep it away from the fracture!" I pointed down the hill to an area crisscrossed with thousands of cracks. "Take it there. Take 'em all there."

The soot-ball gave a shaky bounce and set out for Sammie's nightmare. It blasted past Sammie's creation but was ignored, just as it had ignored the others. The soot-ball looped back and clipped the nightmare's outer edge. A cat fight erupted with soot-ball ducking and dodging wicked-fast moves by its opponent.

Smokey stepped through the fracture at the top of the hill and stopped. "Splendid, Traveler. Nightmares of strength and substance. Your souls have done well."

The big demon called into the fracture. A human zombie rocketed through with such force that it continued to bounce and roll all the way to the bottom of the cemetery, limbs ripping loose as it went. The troll and the ogre appeared beside Smokey and earned his approving nod.

Overhead, the birds spread into a new formation. Two hundred feet up, they created a hollow spinning cylinder thirty feet high and wide enough that the sides were out of flamethrower reach. They intended to sink down around the platform and come from all directions at once. The flamethrower couldn't repel an all-encompassing attack.

Dodo rattled off rapid Nean words. The priest moved close to the shrouded soldier with the flamethrower. They conferred while they watched the flock.

Overhead, the Hannah/JR nightmare attacked the Veronica/Mr. Lee nightmare. The soot-ball continued to evade Sammie's nightmare, but only just. My little demon-in-training led the dance downfield to where the two larger nightmares battled. I lifted a hand to warn the soot-ball, bit back my cry. A moment's inattention would cost the soot-ball everything.

Smokey stopped fifty feet away. The troll and ogre spread out to his left and right and walked farther down the slope, creating a rough triangle with the nightmare free-for-all and the platform in the center.

"Dodo, evacuate now," I said.

"Impossible, River Madden. We much dispatch the flock first or risk an attack of opportunity."

The zombie trap dropped out of the sky, a deadly cage meant to finish us all. The soldier raised the flamethrower wand. Flames licked out and set the ground alight on three sides of the platform. The birds would have to pass through those to come in low, but the puny wall of heat and smoke wasn't enough to stop the birds that would spear in from greater height.

The soldier released what remained of his fuel to create burning side channels leading uphill toward the fracture. I cursed under my breath. What a useless tactic. He had half the cemetery burning, but none of it hot enough to impede the coming attack. He should have waited until they were close enough to hit.

"Talents, mount up!" Dodo said in the com.

The recruits ran for the platform. Sammie squeezed my shoulder, tears welling behind her goggles. "Good luck, River. Come home to us."

She darted after them.

The soldier with the flamethrower dropped his spent equipment. The priest thrust his staff into the soldier's hands. *No, he couldn't mean for the soldier to defend them by clubbing the zombie creatures to bits!*

The plague carriers spun down and in.

Dodo screamed for everyone to flatten and cover. The priest dropped with the talents. The Rap hugged the control console.

The soldier raised the staff, and it burst into flames. The sickly fire ring and corridor roared into the air fifty feet high. The heat singed my face and all the oxygen in the air vanished. My biohazard suit hissed and popped. I grabbed the ground, stunned.

Intense heat cooked the birds before they reached the inferno engulfing the cemetery. Their carcasses touched the flames and vanished.

Smokey, the ogre, and the troll screamed and pulled back from the conflagration. The tussling nightmares fled, hitting the dimensional boundary hard. A million glimmering cracks splintered across the sky. A large fissure streaked toward the fracture in the town.

The platform skimmed over my head, racing between the flaming channel walls to the fracture. The soldier collapsed to the stone. The priest retrieved his staff and hoisted himself to his knees. The staff cracked the stone, runes glowed, and a radiant light shield flared.

A figure at the back pushed up on its elbows. A hand extended toward me. A cry lodged in my parched throat. *Sammie.*

The platform vanished through the fracture.

With no air left to breathe, I slumped to the dirt. Of all the ways I'd thought I might die on this mission, suffocating hadn't been one of them. The fractures shone their glittering light on me, their web spreading inexorably. Then everything faded to black.

27

I drifted underwater. No, floated on top of water. No, floated in a boat that rocked gently beneath me.

"If you can hear me, try to open your eyes," a calm tenor voice said.

Eyes. Tries, lies, spies. Why? Wasn't I dead?

"What's wrong?" a female voice asked.

"His EEG shows increased activity, but it's too soon. His brain needs more recovery time," the male replied.

"River—" the woman called.

"Don't use his name, or call me by name, either. We'll want to evaluate what he remembers on his own."

Float, boat, moat. No, a river the voice said. *River, shiver, swim, drown.* Drown, because I didn't know how to swim. Ack!

"Are his vitals supposed to go that high?" the female asked.

"You're safe," the male responded. "You're safe. Open your eyes."

Window shades raised. A shadowed ceiling distilled overhead. My chest rose and fell in heaves. A little ballpeen hammer ran around on stumpy legs inside my head, hitting the walls, testing their strength. A crack appeared. The hammer scampered on, giggling.

Not real. Can't see inside my own head.

A face moved into my field of vision. "Do you know who I am?"

Soft brown eyes. Thinning hair. Fatigue fighting with laugh lines. Beyond him, beds filled with smokers. I'd died and gone to Hell? Surely Heaven didn't allow smoking.

Another face. Lank chestnut hair, tear-stained cheeks, red-rimmed eyes. A wall, a window, a bright moon in a dark, cloudless sky.

"What's your name, son?" the man asked.

I opened my mouth, tasted blood, felt burning in my throat, croaked, "Float, boat, moat."

I'd stumped him. The kindly face couldn't follow my lightning-fast response. Or maybe *I* couldn't follow my lightning-fast response. What was the question?

A drinking straw touched my lips. Sweet, cool water slid between my teeth and over my burning throat. Water. Running water. Oh, yeah, my name.

"River?" The fog lifted a little.

"What's your last name?" Doc asked.

"Madden," I said, more sure of my answers. *Madder, madness, mad as... me.*

"When's your birthday?"

I opened my mouth. Closed my mouth. Opened it again. "Don't know."

The girl frowned and whispered to Doc, "Is that bad?"

Doc gave her a reassuring smile. "It's what he put on his paperwork."

"Hannah." I looked down the row of beds in the dim ward. Trails of nightmares drifted up from the slumbering super-talents. "How's your mom?"

Hannah's eyes widened, and a hand covered her mouth. She had a funny band around her wrist, just like the ones I had around mine.

"She's holding on," Doc said. "It's late. Hannah, you should get back to barracks and get some rest."

Doc waited while she scampered out. Then he turned to me.

"Can you lift your right hand?"

I lifted a hand, put it down, lifted the other hand, and mumbled, "Sorry."

Doc smiled and uncovered my feet. "Wiggle your toes?"

I wiggled.

Doc replaced the sheet. "That'll do for now. Tomorrow we'll do some further tests."

"What happened?" I asked.

"We're not sure. What's the last thing you remember?"

Evil swarms of birds roasting on a rotisserie. *That couldn't be right.* Evil swarms of birds flambéed in the fires of Hell. Were all those souls in the cemetery burning in Hell? Had the soldier in the suit been Satan? Had an angel of God created the light?

"It's a bit jumbled," I said.

"Since you'd given your robe to Elana, we didn't know how you'd get back. Do you know how you did it?"

I thought about the Demon Council routing me to the zombie dimension, about the soot-ball saving me from the M-Prime split. They must have helped. Much as I hated to be in their debt, it beat being dead. I shook my head.

"When you arrived, you were unconscious from a brain bleed. We went in through your nasal passages to repair it. You probably have a sore throat and a headache, but those will pass. You've been in a coma the last two days. You need more recovery time, but you've made exceptional progress already."

"What about the others? The blonde talent with the wound... Elana?"

"She'll be fine, thanks to your quick thinking and the Neans. The mission succeeded. The dimension collapsed. The demon hasn't come back."

Happiness blossomed in my chest. I'd finally done something right.

A shadow passed over Doc's face, and he turned to go. "You should rest now. We can talk more in the morning."

My joy guttered out, and my heart hammered. "And everyone else? Did they all come back?"

Doc turned to face me again. "Nick Pingayak didn't make it. He'd been hit by a bullet in the ankle. The platforms were heavily contaminated by all the— His wound gave the virus a way in."

Nick? He was one of the good guys, one of the last to leave, one of the best of us. Tears burned in my eyes.

"I'm sorry, River," Doc murmured, squeezing my forearm.

"Are the Neans still here? What about Flash? Have they... ?"

"There's been too much turbulence for anything to travel in D-space. The Neans leave tomorrow. They have to get back for their ceremony. They'll take the boy with them."

We'd saved the multiverse, but my job was far from over. Here I was, stuck in bed, when I needed to figure out how to rescue Flash. And I needed to tell Samuels about the FBI and my spying. And catch the Chinese spy.

No rest for the wicked. Probably I should start with Flash. I wouldn't be alive to help him after Samuels heard about my gigantic screw-up with the feds.

The ward doors burst open. The overhead lights came on. Agent Lloyd marched down the center aisle, shoes slapping on the linoleum, secret-agent trench coat swirling behind for his grand entrance. Two of his clone twins followed.

Doc stiffened, and then he tucked his chin down, squared his shoulders, and strode toward the interlopers.

"Get the hell out and get those lights turned off," he said in a whisper that cut like a knife.

"Federal Agent Lloyd." The jerk waved his badge in the air and spoke in a voice that boomed off the walls. "Dr. Charles Polaski, you're under arrest for treason against your country."

Doc came to an abrupt stop. "What kind of BS are you shoveling? You don't have jurisdiction in this facility, and you sure as hell can't be in this ward."

"We have jurisdiction now," Lloyd said with a smirk, "thanks to our little buddy over there."

Doc spun to look at me. Betrayal flared in his eyes when he saw confirmation of Lloyd's accusation on my face. What had I done?

They escorted Doc out, hands cuffed behind his back. Around me, the super-talents cried and gibbered with a mournful note that set my teeth on edge. Their nightmares thickened. Lights flashed on monitors. A nurse rushed in.

I had to do something, had to stop Lloyd. I wiggled my legs free of the covers, levered up until my feet hung over the edge of the bed, and slid out. I did a slow melt to the floor, my head spinning.

My scalp went crazy with the dancing feet of ants. They tap-danced in complex formations from my forehead to the nape of my neck. My fingernails dug into my hair, which was no longer covered by a watch cap. At least my delusion had ditched the cymbals they'd acquired in the zombie dimension. I must be on the mend.

I crawled the few feet to the window and dragged myself up. Below, Lloyd and his companions escorted a protesting Doc toward the parking area. Across the quad, Agent Black watched, hands stuffed in trench coat pockets. Then he entered Administration.

Had to stop them. Had to stop them *now*. I turned around.

The nurse hadn't noticed me. She'd turned on soothing music and cut the lights. She talked on her cell phone, calling for reinforcements from the snatches of conversation I heard.

I wobbled three steps back to the bed and paused to gather my strength. I didn't have any. Oh, well. A cold draft shot up my back. Hell, I wore a hospital gown, open and exposing my skinny ass. No time to search for clothes. Had to get to Administration.

I yanked on the cotton blanket covering my bed. It weighed a ton. A bit of tugging convinced me that the sheet weighed half a ton. In a last-ditch attempt, I grappled with the pillow, wresting the cover free. Yeah, the pillowcase couldn't be more than five or ten pounds. I tied it around my waist to make a skirt.

I pushed off my bed, ordered my feet to move, waited. Not much happened. *Crap.*

I leaned and hoped I'd reach the next bed before I hit the floor. It worked... sort of. Shuffle, fall, shuffle fall. I'd progressed three whole beds when I spotted the chair Hannah used for visits with her mother. It had wheels.

In nothing flat, I rolled down the center aisle. The nurse cried out, but she was too slow and otherwise occupied. The ward door gave me a moment's pause.

The stairs gave me more than a moment's pause. The elevator, while more chair friendly, was absolutely out. I could scoot down the stairs on my behind, but then I wouldn't have the chair when I reached the bottom. I'd never make it across the quad on foot.

I eased down to sit on the first stair, reached behind me, and pushed the chair over the edge. It made an unholy racket tumbling down. Quick as I could, I bumped down after it. Then we did it again.

The pillowcase and gown didn't do much to keep me warm as I fought to push the lopsided chair along the sidewalk. I felt bad about its bent base and missing castor. I didn't get far before I bumped into a security patrol, literally rolling into their legs when they rounded the building corner.

The soldiers both gaped at me. Or maybe at the sad state of my wheeled companion.

"I thought the crazy ones weren't mobile," the taller one said.

"Look, fellas, I need to get to Col. Juarez's office and could use some help."

They exchanged skeptical looks.

"It's a matter of life and death." *My death, when Samuels hears I spied on DPS for the feds.*

One of the soldiers activated his helmet mike. "Capt. Samuels, this is Ramirez. There's a guy here who says he has to see the colonel on a matter of life and death. What should we do with him?"

I couldn't hear the response over the com.

"I don't suppose you have ID," the second soldier said.

I gave him a weak smile. "Left it in my other pillowcase. Tell him it's River Madden."

The first soldier relayed my identity. After a pause, he said, "He's not in the hospital, sir. He's in the quad, on his way to Administration."

The soldier signed off and looked down at me. "Can you walk?"

Would I be cruising the quad in a crippled chair if I could? "Um..."

They didn't wait for a better answer. They hoisted me, bent chair and all, and packed me over the frosty grass of the quad to Administration. One held the door while the other one rolled me inside.

It felt great to be out of the chilly air, but now we faced the issue of how to get up the three flights of stairs to Juarez's office. Their solution involved the elevator located in the center of the building.

"Wait, wait! Thanks for the lift. I can make it from here," I lied.

The soldiers stopped propelling me along the hallway. "Honestly, sir, you don't look like you can stand up by yourself, and we have orders to deliver you to Col. Juarez."

"Um... I hate to ask, but can we take the stairs? See, I have climacophobia. I could have a heart attack if you make me ride in an elevator."

Fear of elevators didn't have a fancy phobia name, but I didn't think the soldiers would be too impressed if I used the plain English term, so I'd substituted the fancy phobia name for fear of stairs. Both were about getting up, after all. A twinge of guilt poked my brain. I'd promised I'd stop lying.

After a short hesitation, the soldiers rolled the chair back to the stairs. They sweated and grunted their way up all three floors. I hoped they weren't some of soldiers who bet against me in my race with Pete. At least I was a runt and not a two-hundred pound goon.

They deposited me in front of Col. Juarez's door. One of them rapped knuckles on the wood. I swallowed hard and prepared to meet my Maker.

28

Juarez stood behind his desk, fingertips just touching its surface, uniform a bit rumpled. His mocha eyes steamed, and tension stiffened his facial muscles.

Samuels stood beside the desk doing his controlled earthquake simulation again. What a scary guy. If I were the fed, I'd be running like hell for the car by now.

Black had his back to me and turned when I rolled in. His self-assured sneer shone almost as bright as the 'I win' neon sign floating over his head. The light belted Rocky's theme off-key.

Then my appearance sunk in, and Juarez and Black switched to quizzical expressions. Samuels' face went volcanic: red with a black overlay.

"Mr. Madden," Black said, recovering his aplomb, "glad you could join us. I was just about to tell Col. Juarez how helpful you've been to our investigation of Dr. Polaski. You'll be a pivotal witness at the traitor's court martial."

I squirmed in my chair and tugged at my too-short gown and pillowcase that left my knobby knees and scrawny calves exposed. Naked before my enemies wasn't my idea of a fair fight.

"What jury would believe the ranting of a crazy guy?" I swept an arm down my state of undress.

A flash of uncertainty passed over Black. "It'll be a court martial. No jury to be swayed by emotions. A group of officers will listen to the facts and make a decision. He'll be convicted."

"Sure, sure. They'll convict on the word of someone who's bona fide, certified insane." I crossed my arms and gave him my best smug grin. "What, didn't Smith tell you? Oh, that's right. He died before he could pass you my file."

More of Black's confidence crumbled. Samuels' ears positively pricked up, and Juarez's expression shifted from defensive to hopeful.

"DPS wouldn't hire someone who's insane." Black, I noted, skipped quickly past my reference to Smith.

"Our people have a rare skillset." A predatory gleam shone in Samuels' eye. "We'll accept anyone who possesses it, regardless of mental health status. Mr. Madden is a psychotic schizophrenic uncertain of what's real and what isn't. He hears things, Agent Black, imaginary things. You'd better have hard evidence against Dr. Polaski that doesn't rely on Madden. I'm guessing you don't."

Black's angry gaze shifted from Samuels to me. "We'll charge Madden, too. He leaked secrets about your operation. I assume he signed the usual Secrets Act paperwork. Or is he too mentally deficient to write?"

Samuels jaw tightened. His stare scorched the skin on my face. I shrank back into my chair.

"Madden provided nothing of value to you." Samuels took a threatening step closer to the agent. I had the feeling there was something personal going on between them. "He may be crazy, but he isn't stupid. He strung you along, reported your contact, and then I played you for a sucker.

"I know about your listening devices. One's planted next to a computer fan. You're getting nothing intelligible from it. The other is stuffed in a lamp in a disused room. The rest are in the dumpster. I left them in place so you wouldn't know we were on to you."

He knew about the bugs? But I didn't report anything to him. It was a bluff, a bald-faced lie. Could he get away with it? And did he really think I wasn't stupid? I almost grinned.

Samuels smiled. It wasn't friendly. "I thought it would be harder to drag your sorry spying ass into the light, Black. I guess I was wrong."

"Release Dr. Polaski," Juarez said. "And get your people out of my facility."

Black huffed up. "I have evidence that proves Polaski's been in contact with the Chinese, evidence developed outside of DPS. I won't release him."

Black stormed out and slammed the door.

Juarez and Samuels spent a long, uncomfortable minute staring at one another. If Samuels had known I was a spy, he would have reported it to Juarez, wouldn't he? But Juarez looked as surprised as Black to hear the news about my affiliation with Samuels.

"Did the President notify you?" Samuels asked Juarez.

"Five minutes before that bastard showed up." Juarez waved at the door. "She's promised to make them hand over any evidence they've collected. That'll give us an idea of how much they know. We've got to get the situation under control before the Raptors realize what's happened.

We may have worked together to stop the zombies, but it hasn't cemented good will between our races."

They both turned to me. I shivered.

Juarez slumped behind his desk and pointed his security chief to a visitor chair. Samuels glared at me like he'd prefer to loom and intimidate, but he did as Juarez indicated.

"Let's hear it," Juarez said. Samuels tried to answer, but the colonel put up a hand in a stop motion.

I blubbered it all out, about my kidnapping by Black, my fears of failing at DPS, my desire to have a job and friends and a shot at a normal life. I skipped the part about being worthy of a life with Sammie, what with Samuels glaring at me.

I told them Smith was Black's inside man at DPS. Juarez brought my ramblings to a halt and asked for my reasoning.

I explained why I thought Black recruited me. I hadn't been at DPS long enough for Smith to steal my full dossier yet, which was why my mental illness came as a surprise to Black.

"And there was Smith's phony ID," I concluded. "Why would he have it unless he was undercover?"

Samuels blinked. Oops. Maybe I'd forgotten that when I'd told him about searching Smith's quarters.

"At M-Prime. Taped to the back of his drawer. In the name of Boris Kirdan. Only his hair was black, and he had a beard."

Samuels leaned forward. "You never met Smith. How do you know they were his? Did you bring them back?"

"Um... that would be stealing." I tried hard not to think about the stolen condoms. "I sketched the picture from the ID. Pete said it was Smith."

Samuels' brow pulled down. "You told Talent Wilson about the ID but you didn't report it to me?"

Crap. Had I gotten Pete in trouble? Friends didn't get friends in trouble.

"We'll overlook that lapse for now," Juarez said in a calm voice. "Is there anything else you haven't mentioned?"

"Uh... there was a U-something or other thingy... car... drive. It was in Smith's guts when I found him in the zombie dimension." I shifted at the memory of Smith's hot squishy guts in my hands.

The way they both looked at me, I thought maybe I'd morphed into a demon and vanished from their sight since neither of them were talents. If only.

Samuels found his tongue first. "*A USB drive? In Smith's guts?*"

"Um... his colon, I think. His intestines were kind of... I haven't studied anatomy much. Or computers. At all. I didn't know what it was."

A drop of sweat traced a path along my temple. The ants went into overdrive, waltzing in concentric circles. I rubbed at my scalp. Strands of thin blond hair drifted down. That didn't stop me from rubbing again.

I wanted to make things right, be helpful. "Pete said the files were dead... in a coffin... er, a crypt." Eyebrows rose on both men; I wasn't sure why. "Or they might have gone to the dark side, um, been... scrambled."

"Wilson thinks they're either encrypted or corrupted?" Juarez translated after a thoughtful pause. He was almost as good as soot-ball at sorting out my gibberish.

"Where's the drive now?" Samuels asked.

"In my desk drawer."

Samuels left in a hot minute. I hoped he didn't notice the condoms.

"What will happen to Doc?"

Juarez rocked back in his chair. "They'll interrogate him, try to pry loose as much information as they can about DPS. He's not a young man. It'll be rough."

A worm of anger curled in my belly. "How can they convict Doc if he's not a spy? They won't find any proof. It doesn't exist."

Juarez frowned at his desk. "I doubt it will ever come to that. Under the Homeland Security laws, they can keep up the interrogation for as long as they want without formally charging him. That's their real goal, to weaponize Raptor technology. Arresting Doc is justification for delving into our files to determine the extent of the leak. That will give them access to information we've so far managed to block."

The thought of Doc being waterboarded sickened me. The only way to spare him was to find the real spy, something I'd failed at. A wave of shaking rolled across me.

Juarez stepped to a couch that stood against the wall of his spacious office and grabbed an olive green blanket off the back. He draped it over my lap with surprising gentleness. It was wool and scratchy, but I pulled it tight.

Fatigue rushed over me in an avalanche. My eyelids drooped. My spine turned to jelly.

Strong hands tightened on my upper arms and lowered me to a hard, drafty surface with a lovely view of the dust bunnies under the desk. DPS ought to fix the heating in their buildings. I'd camped in garden sheds that were warmer. I'd find a new bolt hole later, after I had a nap.

Far, far away, Juarez's urgent voice said, "Medical emergency. Madden's collapsed in my office. Send a stretcher."

29

Gray morning light filtered through the window next to my bed. I'd awoken back in the ward, my head filled with bubble bath: lots of foaming and churning, but mostly empty space.

The nurses, all three of them, scurried from one mad super-talent to another trying to calm them. Their patients moaned and groaned and screamed. Some of them thrashed. A non-stop stream of sick nightmarish cloud oozed from each one. Somehow, they knew they'd lost Doc, and they slipped farther and farther into madness. I had no idea how to prevent it, except to get Doc back.

The ward doors opened. Sammie stopped just inside, her gaze scanning the horror before her. Even without the nightmares, it was a nightmarish sight.

My heart stuttered in my chest. Crazy *and* stupid, no matter what Samuels thought. I'd let my jealousy and anger ruin the best thing I'd ever had.

Sammie bit her lower lip and hurried through the room. She stopped at the foot of my bed. Pain marred her perfect features. I'd done that to her, and I couldn't forgive myself.

"Hi, ya," I said into the awkward silence.

"I'm leaving," she said. "I wanted to tell you myself."

My hands trembled on top of the blanket. Words wedged in my throat. Air couldn't get past.

"His Highest Eminence Sacred Leader Schlauzauber Frommanisch wants to improve relations between our races. I'm going to N-Prime as the human ambassador. I'll study their customs and teach them about ours. It's important work, probably the most important I'll ever do." She looked down at my feet. "And I'll keep Hesh company, if they'll let me. We can both learn sign language. He'll need someone to talk to."

"Good," I choked. "That's good. Tell him... tell him I'm sorry."

I couldn't look at her anymore, tears welling in those beautiful eyes.

I gazed out the window at the drizzle starting to fall over the quad.

"How soon do you leave?" I asked.

"In an hour." She sniffed. "I have to go."

With that, she race walked out of my life.

An hour. My life ended in sixty minutes unless I found a way to rescue Flash. I could kidnap him at gun-point, steal a jeep, and whisk him away to the woods. No, scratch that. I didn't know how to drive.

I could offer to trade myself for him. I'd gladly sweep the Nean's temple for eternity if it meant they wouldn't harm the kid. They wouldn't want me, of course, me being demon spawn.

Ah, maybe I could get Smokey to put in an appearance to distract everyone while I kidnapped Flash. Then we'd don costumes and run for it. If only I could run. I'd progressed to walking upright this morning, but not far.

The ward door opened again, and Capt. Samuels strode in. He seemed oblivious to the super-talents suffering in their beds, but took a moment to confer with each of the nurses.

How could such a hard man have created such a soft and lovely daughter? Moisture gathered in my eyes. I wiped it away.

The older, colder Samuels replaced the younger, lovelier Samuels at the foot of my bed. He had a file folder tucked under his left arm, which he opened on my lap. A blond version of Boris Kirdan stared up from the folder.

"Is this the same man whose photo you saw in the ID at M-prime?" he asked.

Hadn't I told him this last night? I had important thinking to do. I had to save Flash, and then I'd work on saving Doc. One crisis at a time, for Pete's sake.

"Our computer analysts are looking at the drive."

Goody for the analysts.

"Anything else you've failed to mention?" he pressed.

I wished he'd go away. "No. Yes. The passport was Nigerian."

Samuels gave a sage nod and glanced around the room. "Dr. Polaski is a valued member of the DPS team. He came out of retirement to help care for the super-talents we've recovered. If he hadn't... well, his long and distinguished military career would still be intact. He wouldn't be facing a *court martial.*"

Samuels liked to pulverize a guy when he was down, and he didn't need his jack-boots to do it. I was shrinking by the second, taking a beating I richly deserved, worse than anything I'd experienced in D-space.

"I'm sorry," I mumbled. "I never meant to hurt Doc."

"As a talent, you aren't military. If Black carries through with his threat to arrest you, you'll be tried in a *civilian* court."

A nurse walked over and dropped a striped bathrobe on the foot of the bed next to mine. Were they taking the occupant somewhere?

Samuels' laser vision penetrated to my very soul. What the heck? Did he hate me that much?

"That's how it works," he said, leaning over the foot of my bed. "Military court for the military personnel, and civilian court for everyone else. If one talent assaults another, it's a *civilian* matter requiring *civilian* arrest, trial, and penalties. It wouldn't involve the MPs—or their chain of command—who can be ordered to ignore certain laws for the sake of diplomacy and treaties."

Somehow, this conversation had veered wildly off the rails, or else my brain was more damaged than I thought. Doc wasn't a talent. I couldn't imagine him assaulting anyone. Well maybe Agent Lloyd after the way the man stirred up Doc's patients.

Samuels face got stormy. "After all, Mr. Madden, this isn't Rome. *It's Idaho,* where *citizens* can demand the arrest of criminals."

He snatched the folder from my lap and walked out.

Idaho. It rang like a big cathedral bell in my head. Grew centipede legs and raced around inside my brain—until it collided with *Rome.*

How much time did I have? I had to get to the fracture chamber.

I eased out of bed, stole my neighbor's bathrobe, and shuffled along the ward. A nurse raised a hand, checked herself, and turned away. I stared in surprise. I'd expected more resistance.

I pushed through the ward door, teeth gritted, stairs coming soon. How would I get down and across the quad to the fracture chamber? Would they let me in?

A big pendulum clock tick-tocked in my head with each stair that bumped on my bum. Down, down I went, less and less in control until I reached the bottom and ended in a heap.

The security guards I'd encountered the previous night stood at parade rest on each side of a real wheelchair. Was there a wheelchair shortage in the facility? Did they usually store it here with armed guards? It hadn't been here last night.

The guards glued their eyes to the far wall. I wondered where they'd been looking while I'd come down the stairs like a two-year old. I prepared to tell them a whopper about why I needed to borrow that chair.

When I tried to rise, I wobbled like an off-kilter top. They scooped me up, planted my butt in the chair, and hustled me out the door without a word. Never look a gift horse in the mouth—they have big, wicked teeth, and they know how to use them.

Rain pelted down. One of them draped his raincoat over my lap. My teeth chattered in the cold breeze. They pushed the chair over the sidewalk at a brisk jog. Probably the guy without a coat instituted our haste.

We reached the building that housed the fracture chamber in record time. The guards on duty nodded to my escorts. I, apparently, was invisible. No one asked for ID or authorization. I began to understand what life was like for cripples who lived in wheelchairs.

My escorts stopped in front of the fracture chamber doors, set me on my feet, and discreetly melted away. Were they real? Where had they come from? Why did they help? No time to figure it out.

I pushed through the doors.

Raps waited at the control columns of three platforms. Two talents stood on the stone of each platform. A smattering of armed guards watched. By the wall, Dodo looked on alone. Her ears pricked in my direction.

Closer to the door, Col. Juarez shook hands with His High Muckymuck, on whom sadness hung like a wet blanket. From his position behind the leaders, Samuels studiously ignored me.

Nearby, Sammie waited, silent and serious. Pain twinged in my heart. Next to her, Hothead fingered his staff, his face set and grim. Funny, he didn't look overjoyed to be going home.

Behind Hothead, the rest of the priests gathered. Behind *them*, the slightly crisped death-ray priest stared daggers at me. Next to him, Flash stood, head bowed. I'd never seen anyone more miserable—until his eyes met mine. Then he filled with rage.

I lurched across the floor. The overhead lights hummed *Jailhouse Rock* off-key. All eyes turned to me. *Oh, please, let me stay upright while I get through this.*

"Mr. Madden," Juarez scowled at me. "What are you doing here?"

I lifted my chin and nearly tipped over. "Making a citizen's arrest. Sir. It's my right, as a resident of Idaho."

Was it? I knew a lot about loitering and vagrancy laws in every locale along the West Coast. It was a survival skill. But I knew nothing about making a citizen's arrest. Mostly I avoided the legal system like the plague.

I rushed ahead before they could drag the raving lunatic in the bathrobe away. "I understand we have an agreement with the Raps and Neans that we'll abide by their laws when we're in their dimensions."

"We'll take it up later, Mr. Madden," Juarez said, "after I've seen His Highest Eminence Sacred Leader Schlauzauber Frommanisch off."

"No, sir. I believe he's attempting to help the culprit flee before charges are filed."

His High Muckymuck's craggy old face wrinkled in puzzlement. "Perhaps I do not understand your ways. The one whose name we no longer speak, who attacked you and Talent Wilson, faces harsh punishment when we return home. Restitution has been made."

Dang! I'd forgotten we had *two* priest culprits. Death-ray guy deserved whatever awaited him.

"Um, I can only identify the criminal for one crime—positively. It was too dark to see faces on the athletic field. Dodo" I waved at the Rap "had a better vantage point. And I wasn't the injured party in that event."

My rambling, illogical gibberish confused everyone, as I'd hoped. No one did gibberish better than me. Except maybe Dodo.

A glimmer of hope ignited in the old priest's eyes. "To what criminal do you refer then?"

"Him." I pointed to Flash. "First... whatever. I'm filing assault charges for his attack on me in the hospital."

Sammie's mouth dropped open. Shock, anger, and finally, understanding rippled across her expression. Her eyes smiled, even though she kept it off her lips.

"It's a civilian matter, Sacred Leader. Col. Juarez and I have no jurisdiction in civilian matters. Mr. Madden is within his legal rights to detain the boy. Your son must remain here," Samuels said in a quiet voice. "There will be a trial, and if he's found guilty, he'll be required to serve a sentence as the court orders."

His High Muckymuck gave a slow nod, his face a neutral mask. "I have no son. If these are your laws, the other whose name we do not speak must stay."

To my surprise, Hothead came forward, a satisfied smile playing across his expression. "Yes, let the other remain here, Sacred Leader, and face the human trial as the human law requires."

The guards, who'd been tensed like chained hounds ever since I entered the chamber, leaped forward to escort Flash away. The kid kept his eyes on the floor. He growled as he passed me.

The old priest bowed to Juarez and led his group to the platforms. Sammie joined him. Before she disappeared into the fracture, she gave me the tiniest nod and mouthed, "Thank you."

I collapsed in a heap.

30

I awoke to soft moonlight brightening my corner of the ward. No, it was the light from Dodo's gadget, which she used while she sat by my bed.

The rest of the ward was dark but not quiet. The super-talents continued their plaintive cries and muted moans. Despite the low light conditions, the nightmares were easily visible and getting thicker.

"River Madden, you are awake," Dodo chirped just above a whisper.

I blinked at her. "What are you doing here?"

"Monitoring the shifting negative energy. It is an unknown phenomenon and worrying."

Not good. She was headed down the bunny trail toward harvesting negative energy from super-talents, something we humans preferred the Raps not explore—again. Sammie and I had seen how that turned out.

"The supply of cuffs runs low. I have requested more be shipped immediately via unmanned platform since all Neans are currently at N-Prime for their ceremony." She raised her muzzle from her device. "Where is Dr. Polaski?"

"You're asking me, the guy who's been unconscious most of the day?" I hoped it hadn't been more than a day. I had to get Doc away from the feds.

"Asleep, not unconscious, according to the monitoring equipment." She returned her attention to her device. "The nursing humans also evade this question. Who is Lloyd, and what is the 'FBI' he claims?"

I'd sworn blind I'd stop lying. But was I supposed to tell a Rap about our family squabbles? On the other hand, it was darned hard to help Doc from flat on my back.

I'd also seen what humans, Raps, and Neans could do working together. And Doc's words of caution about how I judged people based on group stereotypes instead of individual behavior still rang in my ears.

I'd worked with Dodo under pressure. She was every bit as crazy as me. Maybe we had something in common. Still...

"What were you spraying in the hallway?"

Dodo lowered her device. "Pardon my lack of understanding. Are we bonding by the exchange of guarded information?"

"Uh... sure. In human cultures, ladies go first. That's you."

The little Rap clacked her teeth in a laugh. "Progress. You accept me as one of your kind."

I was pretty sure I didn't, but I wouldn't argue if she told me what she was up to. I scooted a little higher to see her better.

"The same as you," she said. "My *chirp-caw* detected the transmitting devices in your pocket. I distributed my own. They are an advanced design and not so crude as yours or those distributed by your Capt. Samuels."

Busted. Wait a minute. Samuels had listening devices planted around the place? Since when? *Did he know about Sammie and me?* If I weren't already white as a ghost, I would have turned whiter still.

"The FBI are a bunch of black hats who planted a spy at DPS and want to convict Doc of selling secrets to the Chinese," I said. "They took Doc away, and it's kind of my fault. I need to get him back."

The Rap's forehead wrinkled. She consulted her device. "I find only 'a color of headwear' in my database. What are black hats?"

"Uh... they're people who work for a different branch of the US government from DPS. And they don't play by the rules. Smith, the scientist who fell, was their inside man."

The Rap went silent for a very long time before she said, "That does not fit my numerical assessment. Are you sure?"

"Yeah. And Capt. Samuels agrees."

"How does your theory account for Smith's fall in D-space?"

I tugged at my blankets and mumbled, "I haven't figured that part out yet. I've been busy saving the multiverse. And then saving Flash."

"Why did the Nean priest attack you?"

"He was mad because I got too near his dad when—"

All the clicks and whistles and tweets dropped away. Exasperated perfect English replaced them. "The *other* priest. Did you not question why it happened?"

"They think I'm demon spawn and don't like me much."

The Rap lashed her chair with her tail. "My numerical model predicted the attack once you traveled to the M-Prime dimension and it split."

I resented her attitude. Raps had had thousands more years than us to develop their advanced technology, and I had four years of grade school to figure out math. "Well bully for your model."

"I hoped to prevent it, but I was too late. Think, River Madden. What did you do earlier on the day of the attack?"

My head ached. I wanted to go back to sleep, not think about nasty priests and their nasty death rays.

"You went to M-Prime," Dodo prompted. "What did you see?"

"Uh, not much." I ticked items off on my fingers. "An empty facility. Hidden documents."

"Documents?" The Rap leaned closer. "You did not report this in the meeting. Tell me about them."

"It's what convinced Samuels that Smith was a spy. Smith had a set of identity papers with his picture but a different name. If Samuels spies on everyone here, that's probably why Smith kept them there."

I scratched at my head. The delusional dancing ants would drive me around the bend if I didn't get a watch cap soon.

"And there was the computer thingy," I added. "That helped, too."

Dodo twitched like a cat ready to pounce. "Of what do you speak?"

"Smith had it in his guts. So he could get it through security. We thought he'd gathered information about..."

"Rap technology," the little Rap stated. "What was on the device?"

"Don't know. Samuels is working on it. Or has people working on it. There's something wrong with it so they can't figure out what it says."

Her tail lashed again. "Where is it kept?"

"Uh..." That look in her eyes scared me. She'd had the same wild look when she'd taken on the zombies. "I don't know."

"We must find it."

I gulped. "Couldn't we just ask Samuels for it?"

"Col. Juarez and Capt. Samuels have traveled to a place called Spokane to retrieve Dr. Polaski. We cannot wait for their return, and they would not approve such a request without lengthy discussion." The little Rap hopped off the chair. "Others will know the location of the device?"

"Well, sure, but no one who'd tell me. And I'm not very mobile at the moment."

"Easily fixed. Who can answer our question?"

"Maybe Pete. He's good with computers and knows a lot about how the military works."

Dodo consulted her device. "Talent Wilson? He resides in his room, next to yours."

On the second floor. I wondered whether the security guards were busy and where they'd stashed the wheelchair. I didn't fancy another drafty ride around the quad, but the Rap was in a state, and she seemed farther ahead in the detective game than me.

I worked on getting out of bed while keeping a few shreds of dignity intact. Dodo pulled a short metal stick off her belt and gave it a snap. It opened like a fan into a round, thin metal plate. When she let it go, it hovered at chair height.

"Did you design this?" I cast a jaundiced eye at the floating bit of tinfoil.

The little Rap flattened her ears and dipped her muzzle in what I took to be modesty. "A toy to amuse me."

"Um... before or after your accident with your tail?"

"After." Her eyes widened. She held a digit to her lips. "Shh! If they find out I am not disabled, they will send me back to R-Prime. I wish to see the multiverse, River Madden. My 'accident' was the price."

She'd chopped off her own tail and given up her high-society place to leave R-Prime? Couldn't she just pack a bag and run away from home?

I didn't see the bathrobe nearby and suspected the nurses would be a lot less cooperative about a third escape. I snatched my blanket—amazing how much lighter it had become—and wrapped it around myself toga style. Then I lowered myself to the hovering tinfoil frisbee. It was like sinking onto a firm cushion.

"To move it, lean in the direction opposite to which you want to go," the Rap directed.

Uh-oh. I'd flown a Rap supply transport with a similar control system. It had been a disaster.

"Does it have an autopilot?" I asked.

The Rap scrunched up her face and tapped a digit on her muzzle. "An interesting addition. Perhaps for now, I should guide you. Try to remain centered."

Dodo placed a paw on my shoulder and nonchalantly pushed me down the center aisle. The nurse, her back to us while she worked with one of the super-talents, never noticed. Once we cleared the ward doors, Dodo rushed down the stairs.

"What happens if we meet a security patrol?" I asked.

"Act normal," the Rap advised.

I laughed. She didn't get it.

Sure enough, the moment we got out the door, we bumped into a patrol. It wasn't my wheelchair buddies from the previous trips. One brought his rifle to bear until his companion placed a hand on his arm.

"Dog needs a run." I gave them an apologetic nod.

Dodo clacked her teeth in a hard laugh, which all the humans found disturbing. She pushed me across the quad while frolicking on all fours and barking. She did a heck of a dog imitation.

As we zoomed along the second floor hall of my building, I pointed a blanket-wrapped arm at my door. "Stop there first."

The anti-gravity frisbee glided to a gentle halt. I opened the door, dismounted, and stepped in. When the Rap followed me, I was glad I kept the place so tidy. No piles of laundry on the floor, no bloody uniform in the shower. It looked just like it should for company.

Dodo didn't seem to understand that it wasn't polite to watch a person dress. I managed to get briefs on beneath the hospital gown without exposing my private parts. My watch cap was my second item. I heaved a sigh and wiggled into shirt, pants, and coat.

It occurred to me I'd lost yet another uniform on the way back from the zombie dimension, and someone's loaned sneakers. I'd also arrived in the fracture chamber naked. Sometimes being unconscious was a good thing.

Dressing took more out of me than I expected. I rode the frisbee to Pete's door and knocked.

"It's open," Pete called.

Dodo floated me in and closed the door behind her.

Pete, who'd been sprawled on his bunk reading his tablet, scrambled to his feet, er, foot. His fake foot lay on the floor beside him. He seemed to realize what he'd done, grinned, and sat long enough to get his leg on.

"Hey, Madden, I thought you were supposed to be hospitalized a couple more days."

He seemed incredibly happy to see me. After my pronouncement about my mental illness in the zombie dimension, I expected to be as popular as taxes. But Pete didn't seem fazed.

"And what's that thing you're riding?" Then Pete's eyes shifted to the Rap.

"Pardon our intrusion." Dodo made a sweeping bow. "I have a question about human computers that River Madden is unable to answer."

Pete's curiosity shot through the roof. "Hit me."

Dodo blinked her baby blues. "You would be damaged."

Pete howled. "Sorry. It means ask your question."

"Where on the base would humans keep a secret computer device they attempt to decipher?" Dodo asked.

The grin fell from Pete's face. His eyes slid to me before returning to the Rap, his expression dead serious. "If I told you, they'd shoot me."

"Look, Pete, it's important," I said, painfully aware that I could be getting him in terrible trouble. "Samuels took that U-drive thingy I showed you. It was Smith's. Dodo thinks it has something to do with why he fell."

"Why can't you ask Samuels for it?" Pete said. Suspicion replaced curiosity.

Samuels would deny it existed. He didn't believe in sharing secrets. But Juarez said we needed to cement good will with the Raps if we wanted to retain their cooperation. The lying, the spying, the secrets had to stop. Sammie had it right. We had to be friends, and friends trust friends with their secrets.

"Trust her." I looked him in the eye. "It's the right thing to do. Besides, Samuels and Juarez left the base to rescue Doc."

Pete folded his arms and frowned at me. Eventually he shrugged, went to his closet, and pulled out his jacket.

"The computer lab will be locked," Pete said. "You won't get in."

The little Rap's nose quivered. "What of kind of lock?"

We encountered another patrol on our way across the quad to Administration. Clothes *do* make the man. Now that I dressed like a normal person, the soldiers simply nodded acknowledgement despite my mode of transportation.

Pete held the door, and Dodo steered me through. We stopped at the stairs leading down to the basement.

"You don't have to come with us," I said to Pete. I was pretty sure that breaking into the super-secret lab would rate more punishment than a few demerits.

"And miss all the fun?" He headed down the stairs.

At the bottom, we all paused. It didn't take Dodo's fancy gadget to detect the security camera mounted in the corner and pointed down the hallway. Had it been there before, when I'd come to the supply clerk looking for new pants? Did they have footage of me half naked stored in some archive?

We all exchanged looks. Pete took a deep breath and strolled on. I wished he wouldn't. I didn't want to get him in more trouble.

Without hesitation, Dodo joined him. "I am curious to see the organization of your stores. As you know, the organization of objects can be modeled by *chirp-caw-tweet-tweet* and applied by *click-click-clack-caw* to predict *warble-trill-tweet*. I wish to know if this theorem also applies to human populations."

Pete glanced over the little Rap's head at me. I shrugged.

Pete nodded and smiled at Dodo's pronouncement. "Would you be interested in placing a bet on that?"

The Rap blinked. So did I. "Trust me, you don't want to bet with Pete."

"Aw, Madden, where's your sense of adventure?" Pete asked with a grin.

"You would enjoy R-Prime, Pete Wilson," Dodo chirped. "My kind also think numerical modeling is adventuresome. Large groups of them do little else."

Pete slid his eyes to a door marked *No Admittance* across from the supply clerk's office. He jerked a tiny point with his chin, and then he turned to the supply clerk's door.

"See." He tapped a finger on a sheet of paper taped to the door. "I told you they wouldn't be open this late. 9 a.m. to 5 p.m. only. You'll have to come back in the morning if you want extra blankets."

I studied the sign, taking care to read each and every letter.

Beside me, the Rap studied the computer lab door, the floor, the ceiling, and the hallway running both directions. She pulled her square gizmo from a pocket, and her atomizer dropped to the floor. She bent to pick it up, and as she did, she puffed colorless spray toward the bottom of the computer lab door.

We regrouped and moved back the way we'd come. Dodo kept her paw on my back and her eyes on her gadget until we reached the end of the hallway. Pete kept his eyes on the Rap. I kept my eyes on where we were going. *Someone* had to.

We turned the corner and bumped into another security patrol coming down the stairs. Their rifles were neither hung comfortably on their shoulders nor pointing at us, but in a kind of semi-raised state of alert.

"This is a restricted area," the female soldier said, hard eyes watching us. "What are you doing here?"

"Us?" I squeaked. All my practice as a spy hadn't stuck any better than my practice at being normal. "Uh..."

"We seek additional blankets," Dodo said with a whistle and a trill. "River Madden recovers from *caw-caw-tweet—*"

"That's Rap for being a sissy," Pete said with a smirk and a wink at the soldiers. "Good thing the talents don't have to pass basic training. They're a bunch of wusses."

"—but the supply area is not accessible," Dodo finished.

"The infirmary should have spare blankets you can use for tonight," the woman said, unaffected by Pete's endearing manner or Dodo's race.

The two soldiers parted like the Red Sea, and we squeezed between them. They fell in behind us and made sure we exited the building.

"Told ya," Pete said when the soldiers had resumed their patrol. "You'll never get in."

"But we have," Dodo said.

31

Dodo projected images of documents and data on my dorm room wall. Pete watched, full of curiosity and possibly to gather information about how easily Raps could crack human computers. I worked hard to stay awake, pencil stub and pink stationery ready to jot notes.

"How's this work?" Pete asked. "You didn't go into the room. Everything in there is isolated from any outside connections or access. But you've got a copy of everything on every computer in the lab."

"I use a mobile and self-organizing version of the technology in your uniform," Dodo replied, never taking her eyes from the images flickering past in rapid succession.

Pete rubbed his chin and thought for a minute. "You get nanites in through the crack under the door. Once they're inside, they invade the computers and steal the data? How do they get the information out?"

"The nanites reform into a transmitter, which broadcasts to my *chirp-caw*." The image steadied. "This is the start of the information Smith carried."

It looked like a lot of mumbo-jumbo to me, but my demented brain shifted gears and scanned for patterns anyway. Before I could make sense—or nonsense—of any of it, the display moved on.

"Standard observational recordings of M-Prime phenomena," Dodo said. "Nothing of note."

The display flicked past a grainy photograph. The Rap stopped, reversed, and clacked her teeth in a laugh. Pete peered closer. Because he did, I did, too. It still wasn't anything I could name.

"Is that a circuit board?" he asked. "In a Rap electronic device?"

"It is the wiring that controls the… the closest in your language would be microwave oven." Dodo tapped her device. Another image of the same thing from a new angle showed on my wall. "It has a failed *squawk-click*. See the discoloration there. The technician has gone for a spare part, giving Smith the opportunity to take these pictures. The technician's flight leader would consider leaving the device open and unattended a serious breach of security."

The picture shifted to yet another view of the same trashed oven, and then another, this one farther away and capturing part of the counter to the left and behind the device. It gave a sense of scale.

The angle made for an interesting composition, the kind that drew my artist's eye. Soft light gleamed on the metal corner of the device. Shadows formed at the back edge of the counter, cast by overhead cupboards that were beyond the field of the camera lens. I glanced down at my dancing-flower tablet and doodled while Dodo moved on.

Four more images whizzed past. I yawned and doodled between glances at the display. More numbers, graphs, and dense reports slipped over the wall. None of them seemed worth killing for.

"Ah," Dodo said, "a record of John Smith's observations."

I abandoned my doodling to read Smith's diary. Talk about dry! Good thing he'd gone into science—and spying. He'd starve as a novelist. Way too much passive voice.

Smith shared Capt. Samuels' low opinion of Nean capabilities, noting that the two priests in residence seemed to go stir crazy during the past week, eschewing food, drinking a smelly brew from bowls, and chanting around the clock. On his final day, they'd been shooting him frigid looks.

"That's it?" Pete asked when the final image faded. "I don't see anything that would explain why Smith fell unless your technician saw him snapping those pics and tossed him from the platform for it."

"The technician in question is incapable of the higher order thinking required to concoct such a plan, and the navigator too risk-averse to leave the control console during a traverse to carry it out," Dodo tweeted.

I glanced down at my drawing. I'd doodled the kitchen scene. The glint shone from the edge of the oven. The cupboard shadows communicated a surrealistic foreboding. Drawn in heavy lines, a piece of paper lay next to the bowl, complete with indecipherable scribbles. Barely visible in the steam cloud above the bowl, Hothead's face scowled at me.

I was the scientist, and I'd fallen.

"Hothead did it," I said. "He knocked Smith off the platform."

"Who?" Pete asked.

"The shield priest." I sat straighter and stared at my drawing.

Dodo scratched her muzzle. "My numerical processing indicated he was positioned correctly, assuming he used a sweep of his staff, something priests are conditioned never to do. But we have discovered nothing to verify this theory."

"How could he keep the shields up and hit Smith at the same time?" Pete asked. "I thought shielding took too much focus? And wouldn't he get in trouble if he got caught using his staff as a weapon? Look what they intended to do to the Sacred Leader's own son."

"He wouldn't have a problem with the shields," I said. "The Raps send their dumbest individuals to be navigators while they keep the smart ones safe at home."

Dodo nodded her agreement, unruffled by the implied insult.

"Neans have taken a page from the Rap play book. They send their weakest priests to DPS while they keep the strong ones home to heal their own people. But Hothead isn't weak. He's Second something-or-other and powerful."

"You are correct," Dodo said. "He creates far more positive energy than the average priest. His assignment as a shield priest is unusual. He was also precisely positioned to attack Smith without being seen by either the navigator or Talent Pingayak."

The Rap stalked to the desk and looked at my drawing. The feathers over her eye ridges flinched up. She whirled around, tapped her device, and found the series of oven snapshots. She stopped on the wide field view, and then she zoomed in, not on the oven, but on the bowl steaming in the background and the note beside it.

"Neanderthal hieroglyphs," she said. "The picture is of poor quality and the note partially covered by the bowl in the foreground. From the visible fragments, the paper is a religious text, but I do not understand the significance."

Pete frowned at the image. "Smith photographed a religious text, and the Neans killed him for it? Harsh."

"Possible," the Rap mused, "but unlikely. In their efforts to convert us to their belief systems, they have widely shared their teachings. We must consult an expert."

"Um... you have a Nean expert here at E-Prime?" I asked.

Dodo blinked at me. "No, but *you* do."

"Not here." Sadness shot through me. "Sammie went to N-Prime with His High Muckymuck."

Pete punched my shoulder. "No, fool, we have the real deal. The acolyte you arrested."

My mouth dropped open. "You're dreaming!"

"He's right upstairs." Pete pointed to the ceiling. "Wouldn't hurt to ask him."

Of course it would hurt. The angry Nean teen had decked me in a heartbeat. I still had the bruise on my spine to prove it. Now that I'd messed up his whole life, he'd want to do more than shove me around. I swallowed hard, imaging how his meaty hands would feel wrapped around my scrawny neck.

I didn't get a chance to argue. Pete pushed me out the door, and

Dodo followed.

"Any bets on what he'll say?" Pete asked. "Or how long Madden will last?"

"At another time, I would be interested to know more about how you make your numerical predictions," Dodo replied.

"And give away my system? Never!"

We went up a floor, to the hallway that housed Smith's room. A guard stood at ease at a door halfway along. He glanced our direction and stifled a yawn. Then he noticed how I floated, and his posture came to alert.

"We have come to see First Luminary Acolyte Schlauzauber Heshlibob," Dodo trilled as she stopped before the man. "Is this permitted?"

Uncertainty washed over the guard's face. "Capt. Samuels didn't say. He just ordered that we keep the kid in his room."

"Great!" Pete flashed his endearing grin, rapped knuckles on the door, and reached for the knob. "We won't be a minute."

I'd intended to dismount my frisbee and walk in like a man—one with enough mobility to duck. But Dodo derailed my plan with a big shove in the middle of my back. We were through the door before I could react. Pete closed it behind us.

Flash wore fatigues and stretched on the bunk. Half a dozen candles flickered on the desk, dresser, and nightstand, providing the only light in the room. An untouched dinner tray sat on the corner of the desk.

Flash's expression registered surprise, and then he was on his feet. His jaw clamped, his hands came up in front of his chest like he held an invisible ball between them, and his feet spread. The candle flames leaped six inches high, pushing back the shadows. The air warmed. My hair stood on end.

"Hey," I said, my throat desert dry.

A flash of flame glowed in the empty space between his straining hands. His face hardened, his eyes pinned me, and the glow became a blob of flame, twisting and spinning in the air, hungry and alive. He drew back a little, like a ballplayer setting up to throw long.

"Go ahead." I slipped off the frisbee and stood swaying. Less than six feet separated us. "Give it your best shot. I deserve it."

A low growl rumbled in Flash's throat. Sweat beaded on his forehead. A drop trickled down his temple. Raw hatred lit his eyes.

"I screwed up, no excuses. I cost you your family, and nothing is more important than family. I'm sorry." I hung my head in shame and waited to die.

"First Luminary Acolyte Schlauzauber Heshlibob, your mission is not complete," Dodo tweeted. "You must help us."

The growl cut short. The flaming blob snuffed out. The candles danced a jig but shrank to normal size. I took a deep breath of overheated air and coughed.

Flash turned his back and moved to stare out the window. "Do not call me that. I have no name."

Dodo strolled past me and took a position at one side of the room. "You were tasked to observe Sekunde Selig Deputy Bischoffs Oswin, were you not? To convince him that your loyalty lay with the old ways of the Holy Order and not with your father and his progressive policies?"

Flash wheeled around, anger lining his face. His hand pointed at my chest while he answered the Rap. "And that... demon spawn ruined everything."

"Wait... you were spying on Hothead?" Was I in the wrong story?

"Who?" the Nean asked.

"Um... Second whatever..." His stare made me squirm. "We were never formally introduced."

"We believe he is responsible for Smith's fall. We lack motive." Dodo pointed her gadget at an empty wall, and the oven scene appeared. "Does the document on the counter provide the necessary reason?"

Flash tore his eyes from me, glanced at the image, and froze. After a long minute, he stepped closer. His huge hand reached out and touched the bowl. He squinted at the paper.

"Pardon the lack of quality," Dodo said. "Human technology is not sufficient to—"

"Where is this?" Flash whirled on the Rap, his eyes wild.

Pete took a giant stride forward so he stood next to the diminutive Rap. His readiness to tangle with the Nean came through loud and clear. He'd protect the Rap from any assault the hostile teen might launch, crippled or not. I suddenly saw Pete's fit body as more lethal than lean.

"M-Prime," the talent recruit said.

The Nean shook his head, his voice expressing his confusion. "It is the Prayer for the Dying. When is this?"

"The day Smith fell," I said. "Smith said the priests were, um... praying a lot and drinking stuff from bowls for about a week."

"It is an ancient ceremony, passed down from the demon wars. It cleanses the warrior before battle, in case he dies in the fight. Old priests who know that their end is near use it as a way to purify themselves before they join the Light." Flash looked more confused than before. "But the priests at M-Prime were young and strong. Why would they..."

"The question is not *why*," Dodo chirped. "*How* did they know they were to die soon?"

"New guy." I waved a hand. "Who died?"

Dodo turned to me. "Possibly no one. Possibly everyone."

The Rap turned off her gadget and pocketed it. I sensed a lecture coming, a lecture I mostly wouldn't understand.

"Dimensions split when cataclysmic events occur. Each offshoot dimension represents a potential outcome of the event. An individual object may exist in all, some, or none of the new dimensions, depending on their significance to the outcomes.

"To protect multiverse integrity and prevent a paradox, the new dimensions have exceptionally dense dimensional barriers to prevent an object crossing the barriers and colliding with a clone of itself in the near-duplicate dimension. As the objects degrade—age—and are lost into the environment, the dense barriers become unnecessary, and they weaken. We won't know the cause of the split or the outcome at M-Prime and its sister dimension for hundreds of years, until the barriers develop fractures and we can enter."

"Kind of like time travel," Pete said. "If you go back in time, can you give yourself knowledge that you need in the future in order to make the trip back in time? It creates a chicken-or-egg paradox."

My head was spinning. I dropped onto the frisbee, too tired and wobbly to stand. For the life of me, I couldn't see the connection between chickens and splitting dimensions—unless it had something to do with breaking eggs. But I lived in a world where very little made sense. I accepted the laws of the universe, er, multiverse, on faith.

"And there is the issue of the missing Raptor and human staff members. They would not leave their stations willingly. If only one priest remained on-station, we must assume that the others were either drugged into unconsciousness or dead."

"The priests expected to die because they knew the dimension would split," I said. "But the Raps didn't, despite all your technology."

"Much about the Neanderthals is unknown to us," Dodo said. "First Luminary Acolyte Schlauzauber Heshlibob, do the priests—"

"Don't call me that," Flash said, his face darkening.

"Even 'hey, you' is a name." I crossed my arms over my chest, anxious to hear what Dodo had to say and growing tired of the kid's martyr complex. "If you don't like the old name, pick something new."

Dodo continued as though the interruption never occurred. "Can priests use the Way of the Light such that they could detect a coming cataclysm?"

"And if they could, why the heck didn't they tell someone and evacuate?" I asked.

"No. We have no way to tell the future."

Dodo puffed out her cheeks and stroked the fringes on her chest. "Most perplexing. Data is required, but data is unavailable. A recursion is created."

"What?" I blurted. I should have spent more time in the science section of the library and less time reading fiction.

"We need more information to know why the split happened, but we can't get more information because we're on the outside of the split," Pete translated.

"Oh." I rubbed my watch cap. "Can't we just go there and take a look around?"

Pete sighed. "What part of 'thick barriers, no fractures' didn't you understand?"

"Oh." Boy, I really didn't understand anything Dodo said. "Um... no fractures, or no fractures big enough for a platform?"

Dodo stopped preening her feathers. "What do you propose?"

"The soot-ball doesn't need much more than a pinhole to squeeze through. It could take a look and report back. Assuming I can contact it. And understand it when it returns."

Dodo's eyes narrowed, and one digit tapped the side of her muzzle. "Is this the same 'soot-ball' to which you spoke in the zombie dimension?"

Pete looked worried. "Do we need to get him back in bed? He's not having another stroke, is he?"

"Crazy, not stroking," I lifted my chin and swayed on my frisbee, almost losing my balance.

The Nean brat stifled a laugh. Dodo hopped to and pushed me toward the door. Pete followed.

"How do we contact the soot-ball?" Dodo said, once we were well clear of the guard.

My nightmare seemed to turn up whenever I was in close proximity to a fracture. Or possibly just at random, since it had appeared the night Pete and I were attacked, well before Smokey did his thing scaring all the gathered nightmares into creating mini-fractures.

"I need a fracture to call it. Think the recruits could make one on the practice field for me?"

We stopped at the second floor.

"The four recruits and Talent Samuels created more negative energy in their single attempt than all the trained talents together on the mission. Gathering them to fracture at a time when E-Prime has no priests, is short of cuffs, and has a high negative energy level in the hospital ward is not advisable," Dodo chirped. "We will use the existing fracture."

"What the hell happened on that zombie mission?" Pete said. "And why didn't anyone invite me? No one wants to talk about it."

"Wait here, Pete Wilson. I cannot get both you and River Madden into the fracture chamber undetected."

32

With that, the Rap swept me down the stairs, out the door, and across the quad at such speed that it took my breath away. We stopped before I ricocheted off the fracture building doors, but only just.

Dodo dug in a vest pocket, pulled out nothing, and gave it a shake. It seemed like a strange time to take up performance art, and this late, who'd be around to drop coins for a mime routine anyway? Besides, she didn't have a tip jar.

The Rap lifted both paws high in the air. Something soft came down on my head. It draped over my shoulders, across my lap, and brushed my feet. The quad looked a little dimmer than a moment earlier, and a little fuzzy. I lifted a hand and touched fabric.

"Um... what's this?" I asked.

"A cloak of invisibility," she said. "What were you expecting? Avoid touching it. The *trill-clack-caw* needs further refinement."

Not real, my brain said. *Real,* my hands argued. *Not real. Real. Not real.*

Dodo didn't wait for a winner. She whisked me inside, dismissed the upper and lower level guards with a wave, and slipped into the fracture chamber.

A talent I didn't know sat on a chair just inside the door. I assumed he'd been posted to watch the fracture for a demon invasion since the regular guards couldn't see them. He had a paperback book on his lap and couldn't look more bored. Must be nice collecting a steady paycheck to read pulp fiction.

Four guards were spread around the chamber, which seemed quite a lot bigger with only one platform parked against the wall. Not a speck of blood or gore remained on the interior. The lights broken in the great zombie hellhound shoot-out had all been replaced. The new bulbs sang even farther off-key than the old. They serenaded me with a version of *You're Still the One*.

Dodo stork-walked down the floor. The drag from the fracture took hold and urged me forward. I leaned back just a little, and the flying frisbee shot ahead. I yelped.

Dodo whistled, at a pitch so high and so loud that I expected the new light bulbs to shatter. The frisbee returned to the Rap's side like a disobedient puppy skulking back to its owner. Or at least that's how *I* felt.

"Go ahead, River Madden."

How did she talk without moving her lips? I glanced around at the guards. They all watched her. What else were they going to do? Practice hula dancing?

"Pssst, soot-ball," I whispered.

I waited.

Dodo puttered around the lone platform like she did meaningful work—in the middle of the night. Nothing suspicious there.

I waited some more.

I was a good fifty yards from the fracture. Maybe I needed to be closer. Or speak louder. Come to think of it, how did the soot-ball hear without any ears? No, now wasn't the time to question my reasoning.

"Soon, River Madden?"

I cleared my throat and called louder. The guard closest to us turned full on and paid closer attention. Dodo burst into song. It sounded like opera, complete with male and female voices. Not that I've ever been to an opera. Or would be caught dead at an opera.

A moment later, a furious ball of black energy zoomed through the fracture and spiraled around me. It wiggled and jiggled like a junkie high on meth or an over-caffeinated Starbucks patron. I guess nightmares can see through invisibility cloaks. But how do they see without eyes?

I dragged my wandering, exhausted brain back on point. "Hey, soot-ball, you got out okay?"

The soot-ball made frenetic up-down movements.

"And Smokey?"

Some of my baby demon's enthusiasm leaked away, but I got an affirmative answer.

"Listen," I said, despite my concerns about its lack of ears echoing in my head. "I need your help. Can you go to those new dimensions, see what happened, and then come tell me?"

My nightmare thinned, flattened, and dropped a foot.

"I know it's hard, but if you can find a tiny hole and squeeze in for a quick look, I'd appreciate it."

My words weren't having the desired effect. "Is this something Smokey says is against the rules?"

A slow drift up and down. *Ah, ha!*

"It's important that you do what Smokey tells you because he knows best. But you have my permission this one time to do what I ask instead, okay? If Smokey doesn't like it, he can take it up with me. Now if you could get going, we're kind of in a hurry."

The soot-ball reformed into a rounder, compact shape and zoomed into the fracture. Dodo switched to a three-part harmony a cappella version of *Sweet Adeline*. Where had she learned this stuff? The light bulbs joined in, creating six-part disharmony. My headache pulsed in time to the chaotic beat.

"You drift, River Madden," Dodo whispered. "Please remain centered."

I dragged my eyes open to discover I'd bumped into the wall a good ten feet from where I'd been. It was a startling realization. What if I fell asleep and floated through the fracture?

I was saved from more worry by the reappearance of the soot-ball. It plunged through the fracture going a million miles an hour, made a sloppy zigzag while it located me, and then rushed over, its energy spent.

"Hey, soot-ball, are you okay? You look a little droopy."

A slow drift up, nothing down.

"What happened? What did you see?" *What was I thinking?* Our conversations didn't include lengthy explanations from my nightmare. I needed to teach it Morse code—if only I knew Morse code. And could the little tyke spell?

"How long?" Dodo asked.

I sighed. "It's going to be a while."

"We create interest here that becomes intense."

The Rap was right. The guards were keeping a closer eye on us. They wouldn't let Dodo mess about forever without becoming suspicious.

"Soot-ball, can you come back to my room with us?" It jiggled in what I hoped was the affirmative. "Okay, let's go."

We made another fast pass through the quad, me shivering in the cold under the thin sheet of invisibility. If it were really a cloak, it would be warmer. My nightmare lagged when the Rap bounded up the stairs to my room.

Dodo perched on my bunk and studied her gadget. The soot-ball and I both floated beside the desk. I pondered how to word questions so the nightmare could answer without taking all night.

"Did you get into both of the new dimensions?"

A quick pop up and down.

"Were there souls in both dimensions?"

Circles. Lost already. *Crap.*

"Were there souls like her?" I pointed to Dodo.

A definite no.

"Nean souls? The guys with the pointy hats and sticks that make light? The ones Smokey calls the Unholy Children?"

Another no.

"Souls like me?"

More circles. Maybe I was different from other humans because I'd created the soot-ball?

"Human souls? Like Sammie, my affiliate?"

No.

"No survivors? No souls?"

More circles.

"Survivors but not humans, Neans, or Raps?"

Yes.

"In both dimensions?"

No.

Had to be those frog people living in the mud mounds, unless there'd been some other undetected form of intelligent life. They survived in one dimension. In the other, the event, whatever it was, signaled their extinction.

"Can it say where the survivors were in relation to the original fracture facility?" Dodo asked. "Or what kind of cataclysm occurred?"

"I don't think the soot-ball can hang around in E-Prime long enough to answer an open-ended question like that. It's already looking a little peaked."

"Can it detect images and indicate whether they resemble conditions in the new dimensions?"

I hadn't thought of that. Dodo flashed a picture of the M-Prime meadow as seen from the observatory on the wall. I pointed to the picture and asked, "Does it look like that now?"

The soot-ball drifted around aimlessly, first to the wall, and then to the window. I thought it might be looking for an escape route.

"I don't think it sees the picture." I grabbed my pencil stump and did a lightning fast sketch of the meadow. Then I did a second sketch of the same scene while rain poured down and the meadow disappeared under water.

The soot-ball wafted over to my shoulder. I pointed to the first drawing. "Like this before, right?"

Yes.

I pointed at the second drawing. "Like this now?"

No.

I did another sketch of the meadow, this time engulfed in a wild fire. "How about this?"

No luck with that one, either.

"Meteor strike?" I muttered, ready to put pencil to paper again.

"Unlikely," Dodo chirped. "An approaching meteor would have been detected by the observatory."

I threw up my hands. "Then what?"

The soot-ball floated a few feet away. It spread into an oval. Dark and light areas formed. Shapes grew. I sucked in a breath and copied what I saw to the pink stationery.

Dodo padded across the carpet to look over my shoulder as the drawing developed. A low whistle filtered through her lips.

The soot-ball shivered, and the image it created collapsed. It sank slowly toward the floor.

"Hey!" I slid off the frisbee and staggered to the window. "Come on, out you go, back to Between, right now. Go find Smokey. And eat something. No junk food, either."

The exhausted nightmare pulled itself together and slid out the window where it disappeared into the night.

Dodo still stared at my drawing. I joined her, slumping in the desk chair.

"What the hell happened?" I asked in a whisper, my gaze on the horror before me.

A giant had played jackstraws with several square miles of forest. Uprooted and snapped off tree trunks lay in jumbles, some on the surface, others half-buried in mud. The flattened landscape stretched back to end at a mountain where a wide column of dense smoke belched into the sky. In the foreground, a tiny, bent spire protruded from the mud; it marked all that remained of the Rap observatory.

"A hurricane did this?" I asked.

"Based on the surrounding topography, a volcano." The Rap consulted her gadget. "The observatory location recorded minimal seismic activity. The volcano's existence was known and monitoring equipment placed. It has been doormat."

"Uh, you mean dormant? This looks like a bomb went off."

"According to numerical analysis, the volcanic eruption created two thousand times worse destruction than the atomic bomb dropped during your World War II," the Rap said. "How did the Neanderthals know such an event was imminent?"

"The same way birds and wild animals do?" Oops. Was it politically correct to compare the traits of animals with an intelligent non-human species?

Dodo blinked at me. "Do they? A discussion for another time. We must ask First Luminary Acolyte Schlauzauber Heshlibob."

I groaned. Once more into the den of the fire-breathing teen with the anger management issues. The skin on my face still felt crisped from our last soiree. I considered Flash while the Rap pushed me upstairs.

Capt. Samuels may have spirited the boy away from his family and fate, but what came next? Was I supposed to escort him to the police station? How would we get there? I didn't drive. Well, except for one time when the bus driver died unexpectedly. Maybe Dodo had a second tinfoil frisbee I could borrow, one with an autopilot.

We were barging past the guard at Flash's door before I knew it. Inside, the Nean youth sat on the edge of his bed, concern on his face. He stood immediately.

Dodo made a bow. "Pardon our interruption, First Luminary Aco—"

"So Flash," I said before the Rap could utter the kid's name, "do your people know how to blow up a volcano? Because it kind of looks like they did."

Flash couldn't have shown more surprise. He dropped down to sit on the bed again.

Dodo tipped her muzzle toward me and then pointed it at Flash. "My kind are unaware of any innate Neanderthal abilities or Neanderthal technologies capable of triggering such a calamity."

The irritating smirk blossomed on his face, and he rose to face us, arms crossed over his chest. "No, *we* have no such technology."

"If you imply that my kind—" The little Rap broke off with a squawk that made the Nean's smirk grow broad and smug.

"You little prick!" I said. "Your thieving Holy Order has been spying on the Raps and stolen their technology!"

"The humans and the Raptors see the Holy Order and think it is the whole of the Neanderthal civilization. Because priests live simply, all Neanderthals must live simply. So you pay no attention to where we go and what we see. We watch and learn."

"And blast other civilizations out of existence!" I said.

His smug attitude dropped away. "If a Neanderthal did such a thing, it is wrong and would never be condoned by—"

His brow lowered, and his mouth turned down. "Why would they do it?"

Dodo had her gadget in her paw, tapping on the screen. "Only one technology has the ability to wreak havoc sufficient to trigger a volcanic eruption."

"An A-bomb?" I said.

"A Raptor power supply. They are one hundred times more powerful than your A-bomb. A check of inventory shows that a spare power supply was shipped to M-Prime three weeks ago and failed to arrive. A replacement was shipped in the next cycle."

"You didn't think that was odd?" I asked.

"There are insufficient talents and priests to send all cargo via manned platforms. Therefore, automated platforms are used. They cannot compensate for changing D-space currents as a live navigator can. Because of this, some shipments fail to arrive."

I envisioned something the size of a nuclear power plant. How the heck did they get it on a shipping platform, which wasn't even as big as a manned platform? Wouldn't the Raps at the observatory notice something that large lying around?

"How big is one of these things?" I said.

"The size of a breadbox," Dodo replied.

If I hadn't already been sitting down, I would have nabbed a spot on Flash's bed. Imagine the terrorist potential to something that powerful but that small. I hoped we never learned another thing about Rap technology. We weren't ready.

"So the Neans intercepted the shipment, offloaded the power supply, and then sent the supply platform away before the Raps realized it arrived?" I asked

"Most troubling," Dodo said, still examining her device, "N-Prime also requested a backup power supply that never arrived."

All the color drained from Flash's face.

"Why would Hothead want to blow up N-Prime?" I said in a whisper. All I could think about was Sammie, there with His High Muckymuck.

"He is what you call the 'old soldier.' He wishes to maintain the Holy Order as it has always been," Flash said. "He ignores that with each generation, less acolytes qualify as priests. As the Holy Order shrinks, it is less respected by the common people. More and more people believe that the priests' stories of demons waiting in the dark are children's tales meant to scare them into obedience. What they see come from the dark are humans and Raptors who bring better ways of doing things."

"How does blowing N-Prime to smithereens get him what he wants?" I said.

Dodo pocketed her gadget. "He seeks to seal N-Prime from outside intrusion. No doubt he believes that he and his followers, because of their devotion to—and manipulation of—the Light, will save themselves while the non-believers perish."

"But *everyone* at M-Prime died, including the priests!" I was losing it. I had to get there, had to rescue Sammie.

"Is this true?" Flash said.

Dodo nodded. "My numerical calculations predict that he will place the power supply at the foot of the volcano near your temple and set it to overload. Your volcano is already unstable. The devastation will eclipse the event at M-Prime. The N-Prime climate will change to a degree that will make your world uninhabitable."

"He's bonkers. He has to be stopped. Let's go," I said. I slid off the frisbee and stumbled to the door.

"If you travel there by robe, you will die," the Rap said.

"The priests are all gone. What choice do we have? Just pin a note to the harness so if I'm dead when I get there, they'll know what to do."

"Numerical assessment indicates low odds for your successful arrival. Because of the recent turbulence, all programmed coordinates require adjustment."

I stared at the Rap, tears stinging my eyes. "I have to go."

"And you will. We'll take the remaining platform." She turned to the Nean. "You will be our shield priest. I'll drive."

33

I swallowed the lump in my throat and squeaked, "Him?!"

To his credit, Flash didn't squeak. He just stared, speechless.

"No time to lose." Dodo padded toward the door.

"I've seen him try to conjure light. He's crap! I'd rather take my chance in a robe. I can ask the demons to help."

Scarlet crept up Flash's cheeks. "The demon spawn is correct. I cannot create light."

"As the humans say, there is more than one way to uncover a cat," Dodo replied, new urgency in her voice. "First, we must get past the guard in the hallway."

Dodo ordered me back onto the frisbee and flagged the Nean to the door. Then she draped her invisibility cloak over him. It reached mid-calf level, leaving his fatigue pants and army boots sticking out the bottom.

"Unsatisfactory," the Rap chirped. "River Madden, you must give up your place on the *trill-tweet* until we reach the stairs."

The cloak came off, the Nean and I exchanged places, and the cloak went on again. Dodo threw back the door, and I bumped the kid out, catching one of his overgrown body parts on the jamb in my hurry. He grunted under the cloak. Dodo cawed and squawked and flailed her paws, keeping the guard's attention on her while I bobbed and wove down the hall.

Once we rounded the corner and reached the top of the stairs, Dodo removed the cloak and motioned Flash to stand. She waved me onto the frisbee. The kid gave me an evil look and offered to push me to the fracture chamber. Dodo set a brisk pace to the bottom, keeping herself between me and the angry Nean.

"What's the plan when we get to the fracture chamber?" I asked. "We won't all fit under the cloak."

"Order the guards to let us through," Flash said. "Shoot them if they fail to comply."

Sammie was at risk. I had to save her. But I drew the line at shooting guards. And I didn't have a weapon.

"Not required," Dodo said. "I will create a diversion once we reach the fracture chamber."

By then, we were in the quad. A pair of soldiers made their rounds on the opposite side.

"Slow down," I warned. Nothing screamed 'Fugitive!' like running. The Nean's long legs ate up the ground anyway, and the Rap loped to keep up.

We ducked around a corner of the building. Flash and I swapped places again. Dodo dropped the cloak over the Nean, and we all returned to the quad for the final leg to the fracture chamber. No hustling this time. I barely made it through the doors.

The guards inside stopped us with their suspicious looks and rifles at the ready. It seemed unfair that Raps got a free pass to roam the base and plant surveillance devices at will, but when they were accompanied by an innocent madman like me, they had to explain what they were about. I would have shoved past and bolted down the stairs if I hadn't known more guards waited at the bottom—and that I'd collapse before I reached the first landing.

"State your business," one of the men said.

Dodo responded with speech full of clacks, trills, warbles, and the occasional English word. She blinked up at the guard's puzzled face. When he didn't step aside, she repeated it, adding waving paws for emphasis.

The guards exchanged a look. They weren't buying it. Oh, no, she intended to leave the lying to me. She had no idea.

"She thinks she left the..." Boy, I was so bad at this. "What's it called?"

Dodo answered with a shrill, "*Caw-squawk!*"

"Yeah, the, uh... what she said... turned on. When she was here earlier. Working on the platform. In the fracture chamber."

The air stirred beside me. Flash getting ready to lunge? Or laughing? *Smug bastard.*

The guards exchanged another look.

"Wouldn't want to leave it running," I said. Cool dampness sheened my face. "Not environmentally sound. Wastes energy. Don't want to mess up the environment do we?"

They didn't budge. Not environmentalists. Soldiers. How could I motivate soldiers?

"Capt. Samuels probably wouldn't like if we wasted energy. Reduced efficiency and... whatever." I hoped they were as scared of the man's wrath as I was.

Apparently they weren't. They hadn't budged an inch. Soldiers, soldiers... Donuts? No, that was cops.

"No problem," I said. "We can come back in the morning, after it explodes. You might warn the guys downstairs to stand well back."

Their suspicion turned to anxiety. *Ah, ha!*

"You wait here while she fixes it," the second guard said.

"Sure, sure. I would, but she needs me to hold the, uh... wrench." Oops. Maybe a super-advanced race using wrenches didn't sound completely believable. "Hold the... not a wrench. It's a..."

"*SCREECH!*" Dodo's paws waved around in urgency that couldn't be misread.

I covered my ears. The soldiers grimaced but kept their hands on their rifles.

"Yeah, that's it. What she said." I gave them a weak smile

In unison, they stepped back, whether it was because they believed my outrageous lies or because they didn't want to experience another of Dodo's ear-splitting utterances.

"Can you let them know downstairs?" I asked over my shoulder as I stumbled down the first few steps, a death grip on the handrail.

While they swiveled to look at me, Dodo backed up a few steps, grabbed the invisible Nean, and shoved him forward past them. One of the guards radioed to their twins three flights down, warning them of our approach and the need for immediate clearance.

The moment the lower guards responded, Dodo pointed her lightning-ball wand at the soldiers and fired. It created no more intense a beam than a typical talent stunner wand. The guards crumpled to the floor. My mouth hung open.

"Time grows short," Dodo said. "Sit on the Nean."

I gaped at her. Invisible arms encircled my chest and mashed me back against something I didn't want to think about. My feet dangled a couple inches off the floor. My head got light from the vice grip around my torso. We all shot down two flights of stairs, where Dodo brought us to a halt.

"Wait here," the Rap ordered in a quiet voice. "River Madden will require the *trill-tweet* now. Make the exchange while I disable the next pair of guards."

It all seemed like something out of a military commando thriller, one starring Rambo, not a wimpy crazy guy like me. Would Capt. Samuels hand out demerits for our escapade, or cut straight to the firing squad? There'd be no lying my way out of this mess.

Light flashed, things thumped. A moment later, Dodo was on the landing waving us down. Flash grabbed my sleeve and hauled me after her, returning the bumps and bruises I'd given him when I'd driven.

Two more soldiers lay unconscious on the floor at the foot of the stairs. Dodo waited by the fracture chamber doors. She indicated we should cover our ears and look away. Two silver balls glittered in her paw. I hoped they weren't the lethal version she'd used in the zombie dimension.

Almost before we could respond, the Rap cracked open the steel door, lobbed her balls inside, and slammed the door shut. Two loud bangs followed, easily heard through the steel, and a flash of light shone through the cracks at the edges of the doors. The alarm system wailed.

"Hurry," Dodo said. "The guards will arrive soon."

They darted inside, towing me with them. Guards groaned on the floor and rubbed at their eyes, unaware of us.

Dodo had her gadget out and pointed at the platform. On its own, it rose and sailed across the floor to intercept us, like it had a ghostly mind of its own. She and Flash leaped aboard, pulling me with them.

"You must dismount, River Madden," Dodo said. "Stand beside the control console. First Lum—Flash, raise the shields. Fracture entry in thirty seconds."

The platform began a slow float toward the fracture. I slid off the frisbee onto unsteady feet. Dodo snatched the device and stowed it on her belt. The kid stood at the edge of the platform, unmoving. My throat closed.

"I have no staff!" Flash shouted. "I can't raise shields without a staff. I can't raise shields at all."

"Not light." Dodo tapped the console. She glanced over her shoulder at the fracture chamber doors, and then turned to the Nean. "Fire. Raise a curtain of holy fire. Your fire is a more potent form of positive energy and will shield us from the dangers of D-space even more efficiently than light."

The kid and I both looked at her like she'd lost her birdbrain. Then it hit me. It wasn't a soldier spouting fire in the zombie dimension. It was Flash. Smokey and his friends had screamed and retreated from those flames.

Holy shit! The kid was a Class A holy fire pyromaniac. And the priest who'd handed off the staff was his dad. The old guy risked everything to save us.

A second realization dawned. All those times Flash had been out of sync with his fellow priests or unable to create light hadn't been attempts at light at all. He'd been struggling to keep his fire in check. It was his curse, just as creating fractures was mine. Shame at how I'd made fun of him blossomed in my chest.

"I can't work without a staff!" Panic shone in the Nean's eyes. "I have no source of flame! I need a starter flame! And the demon spawn is too close."

He hadn't needed his staff to burn the napkin in the bar, or a source of ignition. And he'd done it with me sitting just a couple feet away. He was just that powerful. But he didn't believe it. He needed his psychological crutches.

"Give him your wand," I told the Rap.

Dodo blinked. "An electronic device is not sufficient."

"What the hell *does* he need?"

"Something from the natural world that will connect him to the Source. That is why the platform is made of stone and their staffs from the wood of living trees grown at their temple."

Something old, something new, something borrowed, something—this wasn't the time for rhymes. I looked around the chamber and saw fallen soldiers with their weapons made of metal alloys. I looked down at my Rap nanotech uniform. Nope, nothing natural.

I reached in my pocket, wobbled the two steps to the frozen, frightened teen, and thrust my pencil stub at him while the tidal pull of the fracture strengthened.

"It's wood," I said. "Take it."

His brow scrunched down. If he took it, I'd probably find it shoved down my throat—or in some alternate unpleasant location. He'd made fire before without any stupid stick. How'd he done it?

"Still can't get it up?" I taunted him. "Fine, I'll get a robe and save Sammie without your help. You were never gonna be her hero anyway."

Flash loomed over me, bared his teeth, and snatched the pencil.

"Back away, River Madden." Dodo's voice rang with warning.

"What?! From this..."

Jeez, what a time to run out of insults. *Think, River.*

"...this worthless excuse for a..."

The kid squeezed the pencil in his fist. His fist beat the air in time to a chant that started in the back of his throat. His chant rolled off his tongue like a curse and roared in my ears. Maybe it *was* a curse. I backed up until I bumped into the control console.

"Well done," Dodo said as a ring of fire ignited at the edge of the platform. A second later, the flames leaped ten feet in the air.

Had the kid thought she meant 'well-done' as in 'barbequed'?

Soldiers with weapons drawn burst through the fracture chamber doors. A split second later, we slid through the fracture.

34

We were going to die. Sweat ran from every inch of my body. The air blistered my lungs. The soles of my boots smoked. The little Rap was either clinging to the control console with her last breath or slumped unconscious, I wasn't sure which.

And the idiot Nean just kept the heat coming. Never again would I doubt the power of insults—or get on a platform with the teen. Or even stay in the same room with him. Or the same continent. *Never ever.*

Blazing like a meteor, we burst through the glitter at N-Prime. What an entrance!

But there was no one to see it.

The platform stopped ten yards from the fracture, on an area paved with natural stone laid in a basin twice the size of the E-Prime fracture chamber. Flash killed the wall of flame. I tossed the Rap over my shoulder and staggered away from the sweltering rock to a bench set under a flowering tree twenty feet away.

Dodo's breath came in shallow ragged gulps, and her flowing feather fringes were curled and scorched. She looked up at me with dazed eyes and struggled to a sitting position. I let out a breath I'd been holding and took in the surroundings.

The sun lit the horizon, turning it a pink-tinged blue as night shifted to day. Tropical trees swayed at the perimeter of the cobbled area, and lush ferns and shrubs huddled beneath them. Twin stone pillars inscribed with Nean hieroglyphs bracketed the fracture, and three platforms were parked beyond them.

Near the platforms, nine bodies—six human and three Rap—sprawled on the ground. My throat closed, my chest tightened. The world stopped.

"Sammie?" I croaked, although all the human forms were too large to be her. If we could just grab Sammie and get back through the fracture...

Flash rushed to the fallen. "She's not here."

He bent over each body, and the worry on his face eased. "They sleep."

Flash trotted to a burbling fountain made to resemble a waterfall that stood at the edge of the clearing. He filled an earthenware bowl at its edge and drained it twice. When he'd finished, he brought water to Dodo.

"Drink." Flash thrust the container toward the Rap.

I stumbled to the fountain and cupped water in my hands, slurping the cool, clear liquid until I thought I would burst. Water had never tasted so good.

Dodo coughed. She pointed to the horizon. "The sun rises."

Flash's head jerked up. "Sekunde Selig Deputy Bischoffs Oswin will time his bomb to go off at the ceremony's end, when the Light is greatest."

I looked around, crazy with worry for Sammie. "Where's this effing temple?"

"It's the volcano we must find. That's where the device will be." Dodo padded back to our platform and stopped beside it. She placed one hind paw on the stone and snatched it back. "We'll take a cooler model."

I dragged along behind the Nean and the Rap, who both sprinted to a fresh vehicle. Dodo whipped out her gadget and turned a slow circle, watching its screen.

"The power supply already reaches critical levels. We are too late to disarm it."

"We have to warn everyone, clear the area," Flash said.

"Evacuation is not a viable option." The Rap took the control stool, and our new platform shot out of the basin, skimming the treetops as it headed west.

"Then what's the plan?" I asked. My stomach churned, and my head throbbed. I couldn't get enough air. *Sammie dead.*

"Move the power supply as far as possible in the time remaining," the Rap replied. "Sufficient distance and altitude may prevent its explosion from triggering a volcanic eruption."

The platform's speed increased until our surroundings were a blur flashing by beneath us. The sky lightened. A mountain rising in the distance grew larger. To the right of the mountain, a cleared area dotted with thousands of buildings nestled.

"What's that?" I asked.

"Temple City," Flash replied, his face grim, "our largest trade center and home to many, many Neanderthals."

The scope of potential destruction hit me like a fist in the gut. Hothead would kill uncounted numbers of his own people to keep the status quo? To keep his precious Holy Order in power?

Flash pointed ahead to a cluster of stone buildings located in the center of a landscaped area half a mile square at the base of the mountain. "The temple is there. My father has invited Sammie to watch the ceremony, a privilege never before extended to those outside the priesthood."

"How long until the power supply blows?" My voice shook.

Dodo consulted her gadget. "Five minutes. It resides on the hillside above the temple."

The idiot Hothead had made the temple ground zero? What fool would believe he could survive the explosion, never mind the subsequent eruption? My hands balled into fists. Fanatics and their magical thinking; they were all alike.

Or were they? Something about the situation struck me as a little *too* crazy. No time to dwell on it now.

We hurtled over the temple complex. At its center, a hundred priests gathered in rings. Each priest rubbed shoulders with the priest to his right and left, and each had one hand on the shoulder of the priests forming the next ring closer to the center while the other hand tapped a staff on the cobblestone surface beneath the assembled throng.

Their robes shone, creating light as bright as the noonday sun. The light traveled inward through the rings so that the robes of the outer priests gradually returned to normal as the inner rings brightened to a blinding glare.

At the center of the circles, His High Muckymuck waited for the arrival of the light, eyes closed and staff held aloft. His mouth moved, but I couldn't catch the sounds.

Hothead stood an arm's length away, his face turned up, watching our approach. He looked across the priest circle to someone and motioned at us. A priest in the outermost layer responded by running toward a parking area next to an orchard. Three Rap supply transports waited there.

Sammie's black uniform caught my eye. She stood near an ornate two-story stone structure at one side of the field. A hand shaded her eyes, which were focused on us, not the unfolding Nean ceremony.

I wanted to warn her, tell her to run. I pointed to the supply platforms and hoped she'd understand. My heart pounded. *Go now, Sammie.* Her head turned in the direction I indicated, and then the temple scene fell behind and out of view.

We cleared a grove of trees and slowed.

Flash pointed to the trees and a ravine. "The Holy Wood, from which all staffs come, and beside it, the Grotto of Renewal."

Dodo spun the platform and pointed to the ravine. "There, near the bottom, in the grotto."

Flash's face pulled into a grimace. "To place the destruction of our race in such a location is sacrilege."

Dodo set us down. "I will retrieve the power supply. Wait here."

The Rap shook out her tinfoil frisbee, tucked it under her butt, and streaked away over the edge of the ravine.

A pop echoed behind us, and something chipped the stone of the platform near my feet. I spun around.

A Rap supply platform cruised our direction, just above the tops of the trees. A young priest hunched over the controls in the cab at the front of the flying, wheel-less pickup truck. A second young priest and Hothead stood in the open flatbed and leaned on the roof of the cab, like drunken red-necked hunters out for a bit of nighttime deer spotlighting. The priest beside Hothead had a pistol pointed at us.

The gun barked again, and a bullet pierced the control console of our platform.

"Into the trees!" I gave Flash a shove that barely moved him.

Another shot rang out. Flash flinched and reached for a slash in the fabric of his pants. Blood blossomed under his hand. He tossed me an angry look and shoved me back.

"Get away, demon spawn. I'll deal with them."

I took a run at him. It was more like a stagger and fall and moved him a foot closer to the trees still twenty feet away.

"Take cover first, you idiot. Then you can fry the bastards with my blessings," I said.

A bullet whizzed past my shoulder. I abandoned the stupid boy and reeled toward the trees. In a second, Flash was at my side. He grasped my arm and flung me under the branches. I tumbled over damp soil and stopped when my ribs smacked a sturdy trunk.

The supply platform maneuvered closer to get a clean shot at us. Flash grabbed a low branch in his massive fist, gritted his teeth, and muttered under his breath. Heat filled the air around us.

"You're going to burn down the whole effing forest!" I said.

Flash glanced around and broke off his chant. Before he could take further action, lightning crackled in the air from our left. We both craned our necks to see the source.

Sammie ran up the hill from where she'd parked a second supply platform. Her stunner fired. The priest next to Hothead took a hit and disappeared from behind the cab. A second later, his limp body dropped thirty feet to the ground.

The driver of Hothead's platform executed a swift turn, sparing Hothead from his own appointment with a stunning blast. Hothead barked something in Nean, and the vehicle dropped to settle on the grass.

Sammie's wand zinged. The lightning bolt bounced off the vehicle.

Hothead popped out the side of the vehicle and fired his own salvo. The black beam of anti-light shot out, dark and fast like a mamba, to engulf Sammie.

Beside me, Flash gasped. I clawed at the tree, trying to rise. I'd seen how quickly the death ray had drained Pete's life. I had to stop Hothead.

Hothead's driver jumped out of the cab, gaped in horror at the black beam, and broke for the trees. Nightmares flooded the sky, coming from all directions and dimming the light from the rising sun.

In the distance, another supply platform approached, one crowded with silly hats and golden robes. They wouldn't arrive in time. Already Sammie lay still on the ground, her wand in the dirt beside her.

Flame sputtered as Flash strained to conjure a fireball between his hands. Too slow! I staggered forward, pushing out of the trees. Had to reach Hothead. Had to save Sammie. Where the hell was Dodo and her lightning ball shooter? How long until the power supply exploded?

"Stand aside, Traveler." Smokey strode past, making me flinch. "This one is mine."

The big demon covered the ground to Hothead in the blink of an eye. He sank his talons into the priest, who turned too late to face his new enemy. The priest screamed and writhed and began to glow, switching his power from his death ray to his light shield. It did him no good.

Crackling drew my eyes to Flash. He had a full-blown fireball ready to toss, and his eyes were locked on Smokey.

"No!" I gave his arm a thump. "He's on our side!"

The fireball fell to the ground and ignited fallen leaves and grass. The Nean turned on me, his hands enormous fists.

"The tree!" I pointed to where the fire already crawled up the bark. Flash released me, dropped to his knees, and tossed dirt on the flames. I lurched away while I had the chance. The third transport closed in, a shining ball of light.

Smokey dug deep in Hothead's chest and pulled, a snarl curling his fat cow lips. Black... something... swirled under the priest's robe, pushing out through the fabric here and there.

"The console is damaged. The platform is not air worthy," Dodo squawked.

I tore my eyes from Smokey to look at Dodo. She'd placed the bread-box sized power supply on the platform and gazed with desperation at the control console. I walked crookedly closer to the platform. Screams made me turn back to the battle.

The black thing in Hothead's chest separated from his body, which fell like a discarded coat. *A demon hiding inside the flesh? How?*

The new demon stood upright on two legs, but any similarity to a human ended there. The head was elongated with a piranha's mouth.

The bones were all on the outside instead of hidden by skin. The arms ended in four fingers tipped with wicked claws. Spurs grew from the heels of webbed feet, and a long, bony tail swung behind the creature's back.

It leaped at Smokey with blinding speed and sank its teeth into his shoulder. Smokey barked a challenge and swiped his razor-sharp talons across the monster's back, tearing loose streamers of... I didn't want to know. The creature lashed around with its tail, but Smokey blocked with another sweep of his claws, amputating the appendage at the center.

The horrible, impossible thing released its grip on Smokey, screamed, and struggled to flee. Smokey followed, relentless and *angry*, more angry than anything I'd ever seen in my life. His talons flashed left and right without mercy, turning the abomination into chop suey.

The nightmares swirled closer, engulfing scraps tossed aside by Smokey's powerful strokes before racing away again. In seconds, the battle ended. The big demon raised his muzzle, and howled his victory. The nightmares scattered as quickly as they'd appeared.

The arriving priests spread in a line well back from the fight, revulsion in their expressions and staffs raised. Unlike the youths who'd served DPS as shield priests, they were old and tough and positively incandescent. Their chant was one finely tuned drone of building power. It sent ripples of goose bumps across my skin.

His High Muckymuck knelt by Sammie, one hand on her shoulder, light washing over her. Could he save her?

No use at all if the power supply exploded before we got it away.

I whirled to face Dodo and pointed to Hothead's vehicle. "Use a supply platform."

"Not fast enough. Prepare to die, River Madden." The little Rap hung her head.

I took a couple steps closer. "Can you make the platform... fall through a fracture? Does that much still work?"

Dodo's head snapped up. She tapped on the console and nodded. "It is in transport mode now."

"Get clear," I said. "Get everyone clear."

"You must stand back, too, River Madden, or be sucked in with the platform."

I ignored her. I had no idea if I could make a fracture where I wanted it, but I'd made enough of them accidentally during my life to know that I could make one where I stood.

I clenched my fists, closed my eyes and thought about Sammie. Saw her fall in the grip of the death ray. Saw her blown to smithereens by the exploding power supply. Saw her fragmented remains buried under a million tons of rock and ash and lava. *Gone forever.*

It *hurt*, more than any trip through D-space. More than any of the beatings I'd taken from the other boys at the orphanage. More than knowing I'd been abandoned as a child.

I gathered the pain into a ball, twisting it in on itself tighter and tighter. It came to life, ripping at my soul. I thrust it away. It wouldn't go. I opened my eyes.

The second most malevolent cloud of nightmare I'd ever seen hung before me, churning in a way that was wrong on every level. It stood as tall as Smokey and reached for me with sooty tendrils. Fear shot up my spine.

A paw on my belt dragged me back. "Come away, River Madden. The negative energy is sufficient. A fracture looms."

The obscene cloud followed me back, extending more streamers of mass toward me while solidifying at its center. It showed its intentions in the way it grasped, the way it roiled, the way it *sang*. It prepared to fracture—and it would make sure it took me with it.

The final seconds until detonation flew by. My nightmare and I were too far from the platform. The pressure on my belt increased. The power supply radiated intense heat that blackened the stone under it. *No, no, no!*

A cannonball flashed between us, shredding the nightmare's tentacles. No, not a cannonball. *Soot-ball.* It spiraled up and raced down again, ripping loose a gauzy mass of cloud at the outer edge of my abomination.

The big, ugly nightmare drew itself together, the dark center tracking the direction the high-flying soot-ball had gone. It lunged, every bit as fast as my little tyke. They engaged and tumbled back toward the platform, the nasty bully engulfing little soot-ball. The power supply gave off a high-pitched whine.

"Fracture now, please, River Madden," Dodo said in a strained voice.

Smokey roared as he lunged past me. The struggling nightmares slammed into the invisible dimensional barrier. An enormous fissure ripped open. The nightmares and Smokey vanished. The platform did, too.

Tidal force grabbed me. I shot toward the fracture. If I died in D-space, would I know?

A curtain of flame rose before me. My hands and face *burned*. It hurt like hell, but the drag of the fracture cut out. Claws pricked my arm, and I toppled back onto the bed of a supply platform. The vehicle angled away from the fracture at its top speed.

Wind blew over me, cooling my overheated skin. I propped up on my elbows and looked back at the giant sparkling fracture. The priests poured their energy into it, and in moments, it closed. The mountain dwindled in the distance.

"Sammie?" I asked.

"Well," Dodo's eyes stayed on her device.

"Take us back. I want to see her." I wanted to witness her safety with my own eyes.

"We must leave this dimension immediately," Dodo said. "If First— If Flash is apprehended here, he will face Neanderthal judgment."

Flash stood over me. He stared down with narrowed eyes, his arms crossed and his posture full of belligerence.

"Oh, yeah, I knew that." I cleared my throat and nodded to the kid. "Thanks for saving me from falling into the fracture."

He jerked a thumb at Dodo. "It was her idea."

I turned my attention to Dodo. Dodo, who was on the bed of the transport with us. Who the heck was flying this thing?

I twisted around. The cab was empty. I stared at the Rap, mouth open, panic rising.

Dodo clacked her teeth and waggled her device. "*Chirp-caw*, or as you say, universal remote control."

I collapsed onto the bed for the much slower return trip to the fracture.

35

When Dodo tapped my arm to waken me, the sun was noticeably higher. We'd landed at the main N-Prime fracture. The previously unconscious Raps and humans were sitting up. None of them stood to greet us. I wouldn't have either if I'd looked that green.

Dodo had a quiet warble with her fellow navigators while Flash lugged me to our stolen platform—which I recognized only because it wasn't parked with the others. How *did* everyone tell them apart?

In a moment, Dodo joined us. She pointed to the sky. A speck drifted towards us. The priests were coming. Flash's mouth turned down.

Dodo lifted off and waited for Flash to bring on the inferno. To my relief, the kid managed to keep the flames at a sweltering medium high that didn't quite gobble all the oxygen from the air or curl the flesh from my bones.

We made a speedy and survivable trip back to the E-Prime fracture chamber, where Capt. Samuels was in the midst of redecorating. Jackhammers bit into the chamber walls, creating nooks large enough to comfortably shelter a human or two. A fog of rock dust hung in the air. Stacks of sandbags rose near the new guard positions, waiting to be formed into blast walls.

Dodo steered the platform to the side of the chamber. Sirens wailed. Two dozen soldiers pointed their weapons at us. It was great to be home.

"Lay down your arms! Hands on your heads!" a stout soldier shouted. He ran closer, his rifle pointed at my chest.

I complied. Crazy, not stupid. Besides, I didn't have any weapons. The Rap and the Nean exchanged glances. *Uh-oh.*

"Your request is irrational, and beyond the laws of the multiverse," Dodo whistled. "The arms cannot be detached from the body, and if they were, it would then be impossible for the hands to reach the head. Therefore, I cannot comply."

She batted her baby blues. The soldier frowned.

"I kidnapped them and forced them to help me steal the platform," I blurted. "You can let them go. Just take me."

Flash crossed his arms and snorted. "The demon spawn hasn't the strength to stand. He could never take a Neanderthal warrior *by force.*"

Oh, boy. What a team! I longed for the days when Sammie and I were guests of the feds at E-4. Would Sammie visit me in prison, assuming I wasn't gassed, electrocuted, injected, hung, or shot first?

Capt. Samuels crashed through the door, pistol drawn.

My insides went all squishy, and my knees shook. *Yep, shot first.*

Samuels marched down the floor, its surface trembling away at every step. Waves of energy rolled to the walls and raced up them in ripples. The roof rocked and rattled. The earthquake had come to the madman.

"It's not their fault," I said. *No, wait. Forthright evasion, not lies and blathering.* I sighed. I'd never get it right. "It's my fault. But Sammie's okay. Or... she's going to be okay. And the Nean dimension, too."

A tiny tremor of fear skipped across Samuels' face and was gone. "Explain."

"Well—"

"Capt. Samuels, the Nean's bleeding." A soldier gestured to Flash's leg.

"A warrior's wound of little consequence." The kid glared first at the soldier and then at Samuels.

"You two, take this man to the infirmary for treatment and remain with him until you're relieved," Samuels said.

Flash limped across the chamber in the company of two burly soldiers.

Dodo dipped her muzzle. "A wise decision. His Highest Eminence Sacred Leader Schlauzauber Frommanisch will join us momentarily and should not be in the same room with his outcast son."

He would? How'd she know that?

"Your Col. Juarez will wish to attend, also." Dodo stepped off the platform. "Perhaps we can adjourn to the conference room?"

As the Rap predicted, a platform coasted through the fracture. The Rap navigator steered the vehicle over to park beside ours. His High Muckymuck stood tall near the control console. Sammie waited at parade rest beside him, her face pale. Three senior priests created a dazzling shield at the edge of the stone. They dropped the light when the platform touched down.

Samuels' sharp eyes raked Sammie up and down. She gave him a snappy salute. Tension lines eased in his face. He stepped forward to greet the approaching Nean.

"Sacred Leader, we didn't expect you to return so soon."

His High Muckymuck extended a hand. "Talent Samuels informs

me that unbiased verification of events in my dimension will be required. And I felt I must come personally to thank our human and Rap partners for averting... a disaster?"

The old priest leaned closer and lowered his voice. "I want to understand what happened as much as you do."

"Of course." Samuels gave a little nod that stopped just short of a heel clicking salute. "May I suggest we use the conference room? I'll notify Col. Juarez of your arrival."

Samuels and His High Muckymuck took the lead. Dodo produced her frisbee, slightly warped and scorched, for me to use. Sammie smiled and squeezed my arm, but her gaze circled the chamber as we marched out.

"He's okay, just a little nick in the leg," I murmured. "Your dad sent him to the infirmary."

Relief washed over her. She looked tired and disheveled.

I swallowed, uncertain about whether she wanted to be in my company. "Maybe you should go there, too, just to get checked out."

Her beautiful eyes opened wide. "If anyone ought to be in the infirmary, it's you. Doc said you weren't to be out of bed for a week. Instead you're galloping around saving the multiverse—again. I'm staying right here with you."

I thought my heart might burst from the joy I felt. "Um... I kind of have to explain why we stole a platform right now."

Sammie stifled a grin. It looked great on her.

Minutes later, after a short argument about whether I'd take elevators or the stairs to our destination, we assembled in the conference room. Col. Juarez looked another ten years older. I felt bad about that and reminded myself that I still had to get Doc out of the feds' clutches and make up for spying on him. A hero's work is never done—which is another reason I never wanted to be a hero.

Dodo did a coherent job of explaining our actions and mostly lied by omission, which isn't technically lying, is it? I could tell by the look on Samuels face that there'd be a private grilling later about how we got the information off the computer thingy. Since I hadn't a clue, he wouldn't be happy with my explanation.

Dodo apologized profusely for stunning numerous guards and taking a platform without permission. And failing to return the one she borrowed in N-Prime. She assured Juarez and Samuels that if we'd been one minute later, hundreds of thousands of Neans would have died. As the seriousness of Hothead's plan sunk in, His High Muckymuck's face paled.

"You're convinced that Sekunde Selig Deputy Bischoffs Oswin knocked Smith from the platform in D-space in order to prevent anyone from learning that he and his cohorts intended to cause the split at M-Prime?" Juarez asked Dodo. "And you think he had the priests drug the humans and Raptors there so they could get away to place the power supply near the volcano?

"According to my numerical assessment, M-Prime was a test to determine whether it was possible to trigger a split. It was critical for the plan to remain undiscovered if it was to be replicated in N-Prime. I believe that Smith was observed taking the pictures of the Raptor device that also captured the Neanderthal prayer. When Sekunde Selig Deputy Bischoffs Oswin arrived on the next platform run, he was told of the incident. He acted to prevent Smith from relaying the information. The priests at M-Prime, under his direction, carried out the plan.

"Once River Madden went to M-Prime and reported the missing staff members and the indications of a search—his comments about Smith's messy habits, which Sekunde Selig Deputy Bischoffs Oswin feared would eventually be correctly interpreted—then River Madden also became a target, both to prevent more questions and to distract everyone until he could enact his plan at N-Prime."

My exhausted brain flashed back to the horrific moment when Smokey pulled the demon from Hothead's chest, and then to my hallucination of the mole in the cowboy hat at Black's lair. The rodent wore the trappings of a human. The demon wore the trappings of a Nean.

I thought about Smokey's anger as he dislodged the creature in Hothead, and the insanity of positioning the power supply so close to the temple. What really happened at N-Prime?

"You disagree, Talent Madden?" His High Muckymuck studied me.

"Just... tired." I squirmed. I hadn't apologized to him yet, and I should.

The old priest leaned forward, worry in his eyes. "What can you tell us of the..."

"That thing that Smokey dragged out of Hot—er, Second-whatever?"

He nodded and leaned back, apparently grateful he hadn't had to say the 'D' word.

"I've never seen one like it. But I'll ask Smokey and let you know. If I see Smokey again."

His High Muckymuck nodded, dissatisfied, but unwilling to press the issue. He turned his attention to Juarez.

"I understand that the actions that saved the lives of so many Neanderthals also broke many E-Prime laws. What will you do?"

Juarez frowned. "We'll have to give it some thought first, but in light of the end result—"

"We'll throw the book at them." Samuels slapped a hand on the table. "They staged an attack on a facility of the United States

Government. Lengthy penalties are in order. If, after the sentences have been served, you wish to petition for the extradition of the Neanderthal involved, you are free to do so. However, our extradition process tends to be thorough and therefore slow. Is that acceptable to the Holy Order?"

Wow, had I heard Samuels right? You'd think we'd flattened the facility and killed a bunch of soldiers in the process. And what would the Raps say about the humans incarcerating one of their own?

The old priest's eyes glistened, and he fought to keep a smile from his lips. "The Holy Order has no alternative but to agree. You will keep us apprised of the legal process?"

Juarez looked a little confused. "Absolutely."

I'm sure my face mirrored the colonel's. Then I got it. Of course His High Muckymuck didn't want his kid to go free. If Flash did, he'd be headed back to N-Prime and punishment.

Everyone rose and shuffled for the door, except me.

"Um, excuse me," I said. "Can I speak with you for a minute, sir?"

His High Muckymuck stepped out of the way while the others filed out. He stood quietly, watching me.

"I'm sorry about what happened to your son. I was jealous and stupid and—" I lurched to a halt. "If I could trade places with him, I would."

The old priest smiled, just a little. "Neanderthals believe in paying their debts. By your honorable behavior, you have saved my son's life. By including him today, you gave him a chance to regain his sense of self-worth and purpose—and ensured that he will likely never be returned to N-Prime. I owe you a great debt."

"The shoe's on the other foot," I said. He looked puzzled. "You saved Sammie. Doc explained how there aren't enough healers to go around, and this was the day of your big ceremony when you needed all your... juice. But you saved Sammie."

His High Muckymuck's smile broadened. "Then perhaps we're even and our debts erased."

He turned to go.

"Not really," I said.

He turned back, perplexed.

"See, I figure that saving hundreds of thousands of Neans ought to be worth *something*. And I want a favor."

The room got chilly fast. The old man waited.

"I've seen what your best priests can do, and I've seen the yokels you send to us to man the shields. Those youngsters are crap. You aren't missing them, you're giving them a dignified refuge so you don't have to kick them out of your Holy Order."

His eyebrows crept up his forehead. "What is the payment you demand?"

"I want a visiting priest, a decent one, to help Doc with the mad super-talents. Once a week. Or whatever Doc and the priest think is best. You'll also send two of your smartest but weakest acolytes here to train with Doc. He'll teach them healing the way humans do it. Without magic. If what they learn helps your people, you and Doc can figure out what comes next. Is it a deal?"

The old priest gave a sage nod. "You drive a hard bargain."

I grinned, the image of Smokey swirling in my head. "I learned from a master."

36

Dodo, Flash, and I had all been given time-outs in our rooms while Juarez and Samuels figured out what to do with us and dealt with the feds. I kept glimpsing a hooded, ax-wielding executioner standing in the corner or following me while I paced. Overhead, the light bulbs displayed their vast knowledge of depressing dirges.

I hoped my deal with His High Muckymuck would mend fences with Doc, but that didn't clear him of charges. Despite Juarez trooping off to the federal building in Spokane, he and Samuels hadn't freed Doc from FBI custody—especially when they'd been forced to rush back to deal with my latest escapades.

It was my fault that Doc got arrested. There had to be something else I could do. The only sure way to get him released was to find the real spy, which had to be either Natasha or Higgins, according to the FBI timeline.

I knew darn little about either suspect. Where could I learn more? I stared at the wall, thinking. The wall developed eyes and stared back. I blinked first.

Ah ha! Images on the wall. Dodo had cracked the DPS computer system and stolen everything. I bet those files could tell me a lot about Higgins and Natasha. Reading through them beat losing stare-downs with walls. I ought to get to it—before Samuels asked for them back.

The executioner and I strolled up to the third floor. Dodo had the room next to Flash. No guard waited in the hall, a tacit admission by Samuels that he couldn't stop the Rap if she decided to leave.

I was just about to knock when I heard a loud thump, curses, and a tweet from inside. Had I come at a bad time? A strangled squawk and more curses followed.

What the heck was Dodo up to, and did I want to know? We hadn't gotten to Rap love-making in Prof. Higgins insufferable class. I didn't want to walk in at a key moment, although curiosity had me rocking where I stood.

Something broke. Something tore. A muffled whistle sounded, then silence fell.

When I'd just about decided to turn away, the door jerked open. I stood face-to-face with Prof. Higgins. He dragged a wheeled suitcase. Behind him, the room was a shambles, with bits and bobs and blankets strewn everywhere. Maybe Raps didn't have high housekeeping standards. I didn't see Dodo, though.

Then I noticed Dodo's vest and belt on the floor amongst the wreckage. Had she disrobed to shower? While Higgins visited? It seemed unlikely. The bathroom door was open, and I didn't hear water running. Or splashing.

Higgins glanced over his shoulder to the Rap's garments. His hand disappeared under his suit jacket and reappeared with a snub-nosed revolver, which he pointed at my chest. A moment of indecision passed over his face. Then the shine of pure craziness lit his eyes.

"You're coming with me, Madden. It's discount week, two freaks for the price of one."

Higgins gestured down the hallway. The suitcase wiggled.

He'd stuffed Dodo in the suitcase, and now he was making his getaway.

"Can't." I held my ground and blocked the doorway while I fervently hoped someone would come along the hall, someone tall and strong and fast on the draw. "I'm on report. The guards won't let me past the gate."

Higgins ground his teeth, hatred fueling his glare. He stepped back and used the gun to flag me into the room.

I walked through and pointed at his pistol. "You don't want to use that. This is a military facility. Everyone knows what a gunshot sounds like. You wouldn't make it out of the building, never mind getting off the base."

"This is your fault, you mentally deficient piece of—"

Higgins kicked the door shut and dropped the handle of the suitcase. It crashed to the floor. A muffled 'oof' came from it.

"You just had to invite the FBI in, had to go to M-Prime to find out what happened to Smith. Had to be the hero. Well, you screwed up when you fingered Dr. Polaski, but if you hadn't, I wouldn't have known how close the feds were getting. Thanks to you, I'll be long gone before they figure out they have the wrong man."

He looked around the room with wild eyes. His focus fell on a roll of yellow duct tape on the desk. He waved the gun.

"Get down on the floor and put your hands behind your back."

I lowered myself to the carpet. He put a knee in my back and wrapped tape around my wrists. I wasn't overly worried. I'd mastered escaping from restraints as part of my looney bin curriculum during my six-month stay in the mental hospital. I'd be free five seconds after Higgins left.

The nutsy professor tore off more tape. "We have the greatest opportunity that humankind has ever seen to work with other intelligent beings, and what do we do?"

He moved down to bind my ankles. "We squander the opportunity for cooperation and exchange on people like you who have no training, no education, who can't be bothered to better themselves."

I'd worked darn hard to better myself and resented his implication that I was lazy. I'd like to see him survive fifteen years as a crazy homeless person. He wouldn't make it fifteen minutes in my world.

"At least *I'm* not selling DPS secrets for cash." I squirmed to test the strength of my bonds.

Higgins rolled me to my back and tore off another piece of tape. For one very scary moment, I thought he might plaster it over both my mouth and nose, but in the end, he didn't have killer instincts and only taped my mouth.

"I gave up my career and any chance to have my name recorded in the annals of anthropology to work with DPS. And how have I been repaid? I'm not allowed to conduct research in our partners' dimensions. I waste my time teaching a bunch of imbeciles about the intricacies of cultures so complex that they can be understood by only the best minds."

Now that Higgins had turned me into a veritable duct-tape mummy, he climbed to his feet and rolled the suitcase to the door. "But I'll have my recognition. There will be a chair in my name at Harvard, financed through an untraceable foundation set up by the Chinese. When I'm out of the US, I'll publish everything I've learned while I've been here. Goodbye, Mr. Madden. And don't get any ideas about being a hero, or I'll shoot the Rap."

With that, he stepped out, dragging the suitcase behind him.

The door closed. I wiggled. Duct tape proved to be a lot harder to escape than straitjackets or bed restraints. While I struggled, Higgins made off with Dodo.

What would the Raps say if they learned about Dodo's kidnapping? What if we didn't get her back? All my fears would come true. No cuffs, no life with Sammie. Scratch that. I had to get Dodo back because I was her friend, and that's what friends did for friends. My previous confidence washed away, and panic ensued.

This time of day, not much of anyone was in their quarters. My only hope lay with the Nean in the room next door. I rolled to the wall, bunched my legs, and kicked as hard as I could.

I kept kicking until the plaster cracked. I added ineffective cries for help. Where the hell was the kid?

Haughty laughter came from the doorway. Flash leaned against the jamb, his arms folded on his chest and that annoying smirk on his face.

I rolled and thrashed harder, trying in vain to communicate the urgency of the situation. After an age, he sashayed over and mercilessly ripped the tape from my mouth.

"Untie me! Higgins kidnapped Dodo. He's getting away."

Flash rocked back. For the first time since he'd entered the room, he registered the surrounding devastation. His hands flew to release me.

I jumped to my feet and rushed to the window. Flash joined me. In the distant parking lot, Higgins strapped the suitcase into the front passenger seat of his expensive sedan.

"We have to stop him," I said.

"Tell Capt. Samuels. He has superior forces."

"Rushing after Higgins with sirens wailing is a good way to get Dodo killed. We need a stealth approach to take him by surprise."

I looked around the room. There was Dodo's belt, and one of the dozen silver rods attached to it was the tinfoil frisbee. I'd seen how fast it could go when she'd dropped into the ravine to retrieve the power supply. If I used the frisbee and the cloak of invisibility, I could follow Higgins and pick my moment to recover Dodo. He'd never see me coming.

I scooped the belt from the floor and detached a likely looking rod. No amount of shaking or snapping made it fan open. Flash watched with interest.

I grabbed another rod. Three balls of lightning leaped from the end, shattered the window, and zoomed over the quad. I dropped the rod on the carpet and jumped back, my heart pounding. A second later, alarms screamed across the base.

Flash narrowed his eyes. "This is your stealth approach, demon spawn?"

I gingerly picked up the rod with my thumb and forefinger and reattached it to the belt. "We need the frisbee."

"The what?" the teen asked.

"The round flying tinfoil gizmo." I looked over the other rods without touching them.

"Here." Flash jerked the belt from my hands, pulled a rod free, and gave it a snap. The frisbee popped open and hovered at chair height. "Now what?"

Soldiers ran across the quad toward our building. Higgins' car rolled out the front gate. By the time I explained, he'd be long gone.

I grabbed the belt from Flash and hung it around my neck. Then I gathered the vest from the floor and sat on the frisbee.

I bounced up and down.

It hovered in place.

Flash threw up his hands. He wrenched me off the frisbee, sat on it, and then slammed me in his lap. He leaned back, dragging me with him, and we shot out the broken window. I screamed for the entire three floors down.

The frisbee stopped its plummet four feet off the ground and raced across the quad headed for the parking lot. Higgins' car was a quarter mile beyond the gate and accelerating.

Behind us, the alarm system drowned out the surprised shouts of soldiers. Ahead, guards swung the gate barricades closed and pointed their rifles at us.

"We'll ram it," Flash's malicious voice said in my ear.

"Don't even think about it! And no fire, either."

The frisbee jigged left, avoiding the main entrance. It climbed into the sky, skimming over the chain-link and swooped down again on the opposite side. I thanked my lucky stars that the soldiers didn't shoot and reminded my lungs that breathing was a good thing.

"When we're closer, I will disable the car with a fireball," Flash said.

"Are you kidding? You could blow the gas tank and fry Dodo."

Contempt filled the Nean's voice. "Tell me *your* plan so I may laugh."

"We'll hide under the invisibility cloak, make Higgins think he lost us. When he gets where he's going, we'll move on him."

Flash laughed. He squiggled under me. The next thing I knew, we were flying backwards. Fifty yards behind, a black SUV bore down on us. Agent Lloyd drove, and Agent Black rode shotgun, face triumphant. A twin to Black's SUV drafted off his bumper. Much farther back, blue flashes strobed across the light bars of three white DPS security vehicles.

Crap. I attributed the heat in my face to wind burn. How would we rescue Dodo now?

Flash spun us to face forward again. I had no idea how he did it or how he'd learned to control the contraption. I just hoped he didn't drive as crazy as Dodo, although his stunt jumping the fence indicated a certain risk-taking that made me uncomfortable—especially since I didn't have a seatbelt.

Higgins sped through the stop sign at a crossroads, and we did, too. At the next crossroad, Higgins braked hard and yawed into the road on the right. From the left, a sleek black motorcycle zoomed through the intersection. Another black SUV chased the motorcycle, and a DPS jeep chased the SUV. We dropped in behind the jeep. Where the hell had all these guys come from?

The two-lane blacktop wound up into the foothills away from Lake Point. On each side of the road, stretches of heavy pine forest alternated with open pasture and meadow. My stomach churned with worry for

Dodo. Did she have enough air inside the suitcase?

I tapped Flash's arm and turned my head to shout into the wind. "We have to warn everyone not to shoot. They could hit Dodo. Pull up beside the jeep."

Flash maneuvered to the left and zipped forward until we were even with the driver's window. The driver lowered the glass and pointed a pistol at me. I gulped and raised my hands in the air. The vest flapped madly.

"Higgins kidnapped Dodo, the white Rap!" I pointed ahead with one finger while keeping my hands elevated. "Tell everyone not to shoot."

The MP frowned, raised his window, and reached to activate his microphone. His lips moved, and then we lurched forward and left, shoved hard from behind. A metallic bang sounded, and the jeep spun toward the right shoulder.

Flash and I wove across the road, the ditch, and a barbed wire fence before we recovered some semblance of controlled flight. I took pine branches in the face while Flash growled in my ear.

By the time we were racing over the road again, Black's SUV had replaced the jeep in front of us. The bastard had rammed us! Over my shoulder, I saw the jeep, mired a hundred feet off the road in a cow pasture.

Flash muttered. His grip loosened, his hands opened in front of me, and heat washed over us.

"No fire!" I shouted. "They're on our side... sort of."

"Then why do they attack us?"

Flash twisted. We skittered to the right side of the road. The nose of the second FBI vehicle appeared off Flash's left arm. The jerk at the wheel had tried the same maneuver Lloyd used.

We needed a way to derail the pursuit without killing anyone. I patted the pockets of Dodo's vest. The little Rap had to have *something* that would be useful—and non-lethal.

Marbles rolled under my fingers. Were they the kind she'd used to blow up zombies? Or the flash-bang kind she'd used on the soldiers in the fracture chamber? I had no idea. But I had a plan to find out.

I dug one of the marbles out and pitched it to the side of the road, just to see what it would do. It clipped a power pole and exploded, taking the pole out three feet above the ground. The upper section of wooden pole fell in slow motion, snapping the power lines as it dropped across the road.

Oops. Would they make me pay for that?

37

The toppling pole came down behind the FBI car. The first DPS vehicle skidded until it collided with the pole, and then it went airborne. It landed on its wheels, swerved from one shoulder to the other, and finally ran off the road. But it had moved the splintered pole enough that the other two DPS vehicles swept past unimpeded.

Two down on our side, none down for our enemies. We needed a score of our own.

I gritted my teeth and tried another pocket. Flash chose that moment for more evasive maneuvers. Marbles slipped through my fingers and dribbled across my lap, then down, down to the road. I closed my eyes and held my breath.

When nothing exploded, I opened my eyes and looked back.

Four lighted, egg-shaped balls three feet tall were plastered across the windshield of the second FBI car. They bounced and rocked while they peeped and tweeted a bizarre song.

I blinked, but the egg quartet still sang along on the windshield. *Real? Really?*

A hand reached out the passenger side window and tried to swat the eggs away. They stuck like glue. A second later, a gunshot rang out, and one of the balls disintegrated—along with a big chunk of shattered windshield. The shooter was a few seconds too late. Blinded by the balls, the driver plowed through a guardrail and slid down a shallow embankment.

I pumped my fist in the air. "Woohoo!"

"Hmpf. Fire would have been faster," Flash said.

I tightened my grip on the vest. "Can you get us in front of those guys?"

Before Flash could react, Black had jerked into the left lane, raced ahead to align his front tires with the leading SUV's rear axle, and then sideswiped into it.

I thought I was seeing things. I'd assumed the motorcycle and SUV from the crossroads were part of the FBI contingent. But Black wouldn't attack his own people. Who the hell were *they*?

The driver of the SUV fought the attack, but he had no chance of recovery. I caught a glimpse of his face before he spun once and ended up in the left ditch. It was the latecomer at the bar, the one Samuels showed me the picture of.

I looked hard at the motorcycle now less than two hundred yards behind Higgins. Something about the trim figure on the bike seemed familiar.

Natasha! But why was she chasing Higgins? More important, whose side was she on?

Higgins took another right into a narrow private drive that wound through thick trees. There'd be no bumper-car games here. Even Flash and I would be hard pressed to squeeze between the side of a car and the stands of pine. The motorcycle and the SUVs had the advantage in the rutted dirt and gained on Higgins while he jounced along in his sedan.

"Where is he going?" Flash asked.

"No idea. He's supposed to meet someone to hand over Dodo in exchange for what he needs to flee the country. Unless he intends to head for the Canadian border via pack mule, this is a strange place for the handoff. Stick close so he doesn't lose us."

I didn't think it was possible to drive in a manner more terrifying than Dodo had demonstrated in the fracture chamber, but Flash proved me wrong. He leaned back. We climbed. I fought to keep from puking. Or screaming. When he brought us down again, we were beside Natasha, and I was a babbling wreck.

The crazy Russian scientist turned her visor toward us, tipping her head up and down as she took in our mode of transportation. A hand holding an effing huge pistol flipped up her visor.

"What are you doing?" she screamed over the whine of the engine and the road noise of her tires.

"Don't shoot! Dodo's in the car!"

Natasha's eyes lit up like a Roman candle. "You hand over ze vest and belt, and I will ensure ze Rap's safety."

"What?!" I couldn't believe she'd bargain for Dodo's life.

She shrugged, flipped her visor down, and gunned the motorcycle. *Definitely not on our side.*

Higgins laid on his horn. Was he warning the local deer and elk to stay out of his way? Maybe he had a soft spot for slow-moving porcupines? With the wailing of the DPS vehicles' sirens, I doubted there was any wildlife within a mile of us by now.

We burst out of the trees and accelerated across a flat toward a farmhouse. The house hunkered in the middle of a large clear area dotted with a chicken coop, old weathered barn, and lots of post-and-rail livestock fences. Far to the right of the outbuildings, a long, level, recently mown pasture stretched for a mile.

Two figures ran out of the house. Both carried fancy rifles that they pointed our direction. They braced themselves, ready for us to draw closer.

Natasha bent low over her handlebars and veered toward the barn, using the angles to keep Higgins' car between her and the rifles. In the corner of my eye, I glimpsed Black peeling off hard right. He was headed for the wire enclosure that encircled the chicken coop.

I pointed left. "That way! Now!"

Flash leaned right, which seemed all wrong to me. The frisbee speared left, headed toward the back side of the house. The shooters opened fire. I yelped and ducked.

Higgins continued past the men with rifles, who covered his escape by pinning the DPS vehicles at the edge of the woods before they took cover at the corner of the house. The professor raced by the barn and the animal pens, and headed toward the open pasture.

"They are enemies?" Flash pointed to the riflemen while he zigzagged closer to the back of the house. Heat rose around us.

"Probably. But there might be innocent bystanders inside the house, so no torching it."

Anger rumbled in the Nean's chest. We whooshed through the back yard. I let out a breath now that we had the bulk of the house between us and the shooters. Flash leaned left. We curled right around the corner of the house and charged into a clothes line loaded with sheets and underwear.

Impact with the line nearly tore us from the frisbee. We boomeranged into the woods at an extreme speed. I clawed a pillowcase off my face just in time to be raked by branches that tore my shirt and pants in half a dozen places. *Crap!* There went another uniform.

Flash muttered what I took to be Nean curses and leaned hard left. We emerged from the woods in time to see Black's SUV ram the chicken coop. Squawking white birds flew every direction. I was glad Dodo couldn't see the disrespect with which the feds treated her avian relatives.

The demolished back wall of the structure got stuck on the hood, blocking Lloyd's vision. He banged through another fence and slued sideways on the open pasture. Wow, there went his insurance rates.

Natasha plunged out of the barn, trailing a flurry of straw behind her bike. She roared after Black and Lloyd.

I glanced over to see how our guys fared. A lot of bullets flew between the DPS vehicles and the house. Both sides had found good cover and would be at it until someone ran out of ammo or surrendered.

Flash and I had the advantage now. The pasture didn't slow us down like it did the vehicles. We closed quickly on the fleeing professor. But Natasha and Black would catch Higgins at the end of the open field where the trees closed in again.

"We have to stop them from getting to Higgins. Can you lay down a strip of fire behind us?"

"Of course, but your presence impedes my ability." Flash shoved me off his lap.

I landed hard on my hip and rolled and bounced across the muddy ground, cursing all the way. Natasha and Black shot past. Dirt, gravel, and pulverized plants splattered my filthy ripped uniform. It was a wonder neither of them ran over me.

How dare the brat dump me, and for such a flimsy excuse! I rose as far as my knees and shouted, "I call BS!"

From behind me, a buzzing noise spread over the pasture. A small plane cruised over the trees on the opposite side of the grass strip. I caught the silhouette of a rifle in a window.

So that was the plan! Higgins would make his getaway in the plane. Once they got Dodo onboard, we'd never see her again. And the damn kid had dumped me, just when I needed him most.

I patted vest pockets until I found the one where Dodo kept the invisibility cloak. I drew it out and draped it over myself while I ran for all I was worth down the center of the mown stripe.

Ahead, a curtain of fire leaped from the ground, separating Higgins from his pursuers. Dense smoke rose from the wet vegetation. Natasha dumped the bike over in a panic stop and rode it across the slick ground. It stopped a few feet from the conflagration.

Agent Lloyd avoided Natasha and the flames by turning into the trees. The SUV rammed into the pines. A billowing cloud of steam rose from under the hood.

Black and Lloyd abandoned their vehicle, made an end run around Flash's fire line, and sprinted down the field. Natasha struggled to her feet and pelted behind, tossing away her helmet.

I blew past them like they were standing still. Too bad Pete wasn't here. I could have cleaned up betting against my co-pursuers. Overhead, the plane looped around and headed back the way it had come.

At the end of the pasture, Higgins climbed from his car and hurried around to the passenger side, pistol in hand. He paused, gun braced on the top of the car, and fired at the crowd racing to stop him. The other three dove for the dirt. My feet flew faster over the grass. *Neener, neener!*

Higgins stopped shooting and reached inside the sedan. In a

moment, he had the suitcase unbuckled and dragged it to the rear of the car. He snapped off two more shots.

Booms echoed behind me, and lead plinked against the car bumper. I glanced back. Natasha, Black, and Lloyd stood in firing stances, guns aimed at Higgins' car. And more or less at where I intended to be in another ten seconds.

The hum of the plane's engine drew my eyes to the sky. It bore down on us with unmistakable menace. A rifle protruded from a side window. A second later, the rat-a-tat of an automatic weapon punctuated the air. Dirt kicked up around the agents' feet.

Lloyd grunted and went down, hand on his thigh. Natasha and Black rolled left and right, and took aim at the plane, firing round after round for a good five seconds. I clenched my teeth and hoped the lunatic in the plane didn't want to waste ammo by shooting at things he couldn't see.

Higgins made a break for the trees, dragging the wheeled suitcase. He had the good sense to keep his car between himself and his pursuers. The revolver gleamed in his hand, sending a chill up my spine. Maybe he couldn't hit the agents or Natasha, but from so close a distance, even I could hit a Rap in a suitcase.

Maybe he'd run out of bullets. Did he fire six shots, or only five? With all the running, I'd lost track. I poured on more speed.

The plane climbed to treetop level over our heads and banked around for another run. Natasha and Black took the opportunity to rush forward again. Lloyd hobbled toward cover at the side of the field.

Flash lurked in the trees nearby, scanning the battlefield. Heat waves warped the air around him. *Class A pyromaniac,* I reminded myself, *with anger management issues.*

The plane came into sight over the trees, making another strafing run down the pasture. We were all getting too bunched up now, and much too close to Dodo.

My pacifism warred with my need to get Dodo back safe and sound. Even if I reached her and got her under the invisibility cloak with me, it wouldn't protect either of us from all the bullets flying around. I had to save her, or the Raps would never work with humans again.

No, I had to save her because she was my friend, and she'd do the same for me.

I pushed an arm free of the cloak, pointed to the plane and shouted, "Flash! Enemy! Fire!"

The kid gazed around to locate me, smiled, and raised his hands. Surrounding branches popped, hissed, and smoked. An enormous fireball formed in front of him, and then it streaked at the plane.

One minute the plane flew straight and level. The next, it had disintegrated into a thousand pieces. Flaming bits rained down over a long stretch of pasture.

A gunshot rang over the battlefield. Black had his gun pointed in Higgins' direction, oblivious to the destruction overhead. Higgins, no more than thirty feet from me now, lay sprawled on the ground, a dark hole in his head.

I stumbled and skidded to a halt. When I looked behind me, Black had his pistol trained on Natasha. Natasha had her pistol pointed at Black.

"FBI!" Black snapped. "Drop your weapon!"

"DHS!" Natasha snapped back. "Drop *your* weapon!"

"I'm taking these suspects into federal custody," Black said.

"No, *I'm* taking zese suspects into federal custody," Natasha replied.

Uh-oh. We were already having trouble getting Doc back from the damn feds. No way were they getting the three of us, too. I broke for the suitcase, moving quietly. I looked for Flash, but he'd disappeared already, leaving fire creeping up the side of the tree he'd accidentally ignited.

I crouched next to the suitcase, slid the zipper open a few inches, and spread the invisibility cloak over it and me.

"Dodo, it's River. Don't make any noise."

I hoped she could hear me and hadn't suffocated. I crawled away towing the suitcase.

Seconds later, Natasha and Black were beside Higgins' body. I froze.

"Where is it?" Black said. "Where's the suitcase with the Rap? And where's the guy with the rocket launcher?"

Engines rumbled. Natasha and Black wheeled toward the sound. Two white DPS security vehicles rolled to a halt fifteen feet away. Four soldiers scrambled out and pointed rifles at Natasha and Black.

Capt. Samuels marched over to the two federal agents. He had a grim smile on his face and a gleam in his eye.

"You've both been invited to a conference call with the President. We'll be happy to ensure you aren't late." Samuels stepped back and nodded to his men. "Take them away."

Natasha and Black were loaded in one of the vehicles. It made a stop for Lloyd, and then it disappeared into the woods.

"Mr. Madden!" Samuels scanned the field.

I dropped the cloak and unzipped the suitcase, worried sick about Dodo. Samuels strode over. Together we peered in.

Dodo lay on her side, front and back paws bound by duct tape. Another strip looped around her muzzle. Her big blue eyes blinked up at us, and she gave a happy little warble.

Samuels drew a pocket knife and cut the tape that held her paws. She sprang out of the suitcase and pulled the remaining tape free, losing a goodly amount of scorched feathers in the process. The piece on her muzzle proved especially problematic and left her with a plucked strip of bare flesh. Ouch, that had to hurt.

Flash walked out of the trees, drawing a raised eyebrow from Samuels, who looked from the kid to the bits of airplane and back. The kid handed the frisbee—now just a plain silver rod—to Dodo.

"It wasn't our fault," I blurted. *Damn!* "I mean, Higgins kidnapped Dodo. We couldn't let him get away."

Samuels looked neither convinced nor appeased.

"Natasha told Black she worked for the Department of Homeland Security. And Black shot Higgins. They both wanted Dodo." I pushed Dodo's vest and belt at her. "Well... technically Natasha said she'd rescue Dodo, but only if she got to keep Dodo's clothes."

Samuels nodded. "I've been watching her for months, but I couldn't crack her background cover. Only our own government could embed an agent that well. They made a mistake sending someone with only a cursory scientific background. She knew too much about military strategies and spy craft and not enough about physics."

I remembered those looks he'd shot down the table to her while we'd discussed what to do about the zombies and realized he was right.

"Once you gave us Smith's alias, we were able to trace payments from both the FBI *and* DHS to him."

I stared in surprise. "Smith sold secrets to both of them?"

"And to Higgins, who passed the information along to the Chinese, although we haven't found the money trail from them to him yet."

"It went through a trust fund for something-or-other at Harvard. In Higgins' name."

Samuels glanced at Dodo, whose ears were cocked in a way that indicated avid interest. He shifted his feet.

"For all their efforts, none of them got anything of value. Smith wanted money but couldn't stomach being a traitor. What he passed along was useless. His contacts didn't know enough about the subject matter to realize it. We think the Chinese were fed up with what they received and insisted on something better."

Samuels turned to face the Rap. "With Smith gone and Doc arrested by the FBI, Higgins had a dilemma. He had to give the Chinese a final payoff to ensure their assistance with his escape, but he didn't have the science background to know what to trade. Hence his decision to kidnap you as his last act before he fled. I hope the Raptors will understand that this was the reprehensible act of a single individual and not—"

Dodo raised a paw. "Perhaps, Capt. Samuels, it would be best if my kind were not informed of this latest incident. As you have witnessed, many of them already hold the belief that humans are too dangerous and unpredictable to work with. Let's not stone the boat."

Samuels' puzzled over her mangled aphorism for a moment. Then relief flickered in his face. "But you don't agree?"

Dodo clacked her jaws in an off-putting Rap laugh, donned her vest and belt, and padded away to the remaining security vehicle.

38

A white-haired judge glowered at Flash and me. He wore thick-rimmed black glasses that matched his black robe. His little wooden gavel lay on the Administration conference room table, along with a sheaf of papers from which he'd read charges.

Capt. Samuels stood against the wall, a silent observer. A jury and executioner were conspicuously absent.

"Is the description of the altercation I just read accurate, Mr. Madden?"

I swallowed and nodded, and then remembered that I was required to make verbal responses. "Yes, sir."

Flash shifted in his chair. The charge sheet referred to his staff as a wooden club, and that hadn't gone down well, but he'd kept his protests to himself—so far.

"And you, Mr. Flash, how do you plead?"

After an angry glance at me, Flash said, "Guilty."

"I hope you understand that you've committed a serious crime, young man." The judge scribbled his signature at the bottom of a sheet of paper. "Because of your age, the court has decided to show leniency. You will be released to the custody of Capt. Samuels. He will monitor you while you complete the required sentence of 100,000 hours of community service, to be served at this facility."

My mouth fell open. It would take the kid fifty years to complete his sentence. Then I remembered where I was and snapped my gaping jaw shut.

Flash didn't move. The judge rapped his gavel on the table, gathered his papers, and left.

I hopped up, anxious to be gone, too. Samuels was still the scariest man on the planet, and we'd yet to discuss Dodo's rescue the previous day. Or have that private chat about how Dodo cracked the DPS computer system. I'd hoped I could avoid him until he forgot about me—

or retired, whichever came first.

Samuels waved me back into my chair. A minute later, Juarez joined us. The invisible chorus formed behind me. Their whispering was punctuated by the sound of rifle bolts slamming home.

Juarez took the seat vacated by the judge. Samuels continued to loom by the wall. Flash gave me a slit-eyed look. I rocked, just a little.

"Gentlemen," Juarez said, "it's come to my attention that neither of you are suitable as members of a platform crew."

My heart sank. This was it. They'd fire me.

"Flash, to placate the Holy Order, your punishment here will mirror to some extent the punishment you would have received in your home dimension. You will not interact with other Neanderthals. You will spend your community service time cleaning the DPS facility."

The kid's expression darkened. He stared at the tabletop.

"Since you will be here for a very long time, you will also be required to integrate into our culture. Your current level of education will be evaluated, and then a curriculum plan will be instituted to raise your level to that equivalent to humans your age. Should you find a particular area of study to be to your liking, you will be encouraged to pursue further education in that area."

Flash didn't look up. It didn't mask his confusion.

Juarez folded his hands on the table. "Dr. Polaski has advised that you would benefit from anger management training. You'll meet with him for one hour twice a week until he determines that therapy should end."

The kid's curiosity got the better of him. "What is therapy?"

I stifled a laugh. "He talks, you talk, he talks, you talk. Abracadabra, your problems are over."

Flash looked thunderstruck. "Talking with others is permitted?"

"As long as they aren't Neanderthals," Juarez said. "By their own rules, they are forbidden to interact with you."

Flash's shoulders loosened. A genuine smile curled his lips for just a moment before he remembered to be a sullen teen. Moisture collected in my eyes. They would see to it that Flash had a normal life, even if he didn't have a family anymore. And maybe someday, he would.

"Mr. Madden," Juarez said.

All the joy went out of me. If I were unlucky, I'd be looking at a long stretch in the state pen. If I were lucky, they'd only fire me. I'd never stand on my own two feet and make Sammie proud. I had a mental illness. I wasn't employable or anything close to normal. Marrying Sammie was a crazy dream, one I had to give up, for her sake.

"Yes, sir?"

"You've indicated that you don't want to be a talent and create fractures. Is that correct?"

I thought about the unholy abomination I'd created at N-Prime and shivered. "Yes, sir."

"Dr. Polaski also stated that because of your recent brain bleed, you could die if you were to use the Rap robe technology to cross D-space."

My voice dropped to a whisper. "Yes, sir."

Juarez leaned back in his chair. "As it happens, I have an open position here on the base. Would you be interested in continuing your employment with DPS?"

My heart raced. Blood thumped in my ears. I forgot to breathe. I wanted a job like nothing else. My moment of hope snuffed out. I'd been desperate when I accepted Black's offer, and it had cost me more than I was willing to pay.

"Um... I don't have many skills... except drawing. And fracturing. No skills, actually."

A twinkle lit Juarez's eye. "The job doesn't require either drawing or fracturing. We'll provide the necessary training. But first, we'll need Doc to approve you as fit for duty. When you've seen to that, we'll talk further."

Juarez rose and both men left.

What?? They couldn't leave me in suspense. Besides, I wasn't sure I wanted to see Doc. He'd looked pretty steamed at me when Agent Lloyd dragged him out of the hospital ward. But I owed him an apology, and there was no point putting it off any longer. I trailed Flash out.

Sammie waited in the hall. My heart swelled, but I stamped it down. I had no idea what job Juarez had on offer. Life was too uncertain to make any promises to Sammie.

She stepped up to Flash, who smiled so big I thought his face might shatter. Sammie handed him a long package wrapped in soft yellow cloth, skinny along its length, with a lump at the bottom.

She'd brought him a present. I sagged and reminded myself that she had every right to give Flash her attention. I wanted to go, before something dumb and nasty spilled out of my mouth by mistake. I would have bolted, but her hand snaked out to hold my arm.

Flash took the package. His eyes went wide, and his hands hurried to remove the cloth. It dropped away to reveal... a mop. The wooden handle was extra heavy, a good fit in the kid's huge hands, and polished to a satiny sheen. The mop head was made from braided white cotton string threaded with more of the yellow fabric.

Tears welled in Flash's eyes while his hands stroked the gift. He tried to speak to Sammie, but the words wouldn't come. He spun and ran off down the hall carrying his present.

"What the heck was that about?" I asked.

Sammie turned to me, her own eyes glistening. "It's from his dad."

A sigh of relief whispered through me. She hadn't brought a present for the kid. A split second later, jaws of guilt clamped around me. *Let it go, River.*

"Kind of harsh, isn't it? Giving him a mop to remind him of how he screwed up?" I hadn't thought the old man was that cruel.

Sammie's hand went up in a stop motion. "You don't understand. The wood of the handle is from their holy grove, the source of all their staffs. The Sacred Leader shaped it with his own hands. The mop head represents life-sustaining water to balance his fire."

The light bulb came on in my brain. "It's the old guy's way of giving Flash a staff. He's telling Flash he'll always have his Nean family."

Sammie beamed at me. She linked her arm in mine and strolled with me along the hall. Her touch sent warmth surging through me. We walked down the stairs to the building entrance.

"Flash will need your help," Sammie said at last. "He's alone here and doesn't make friends easily."

I stared at her. "He hates my guts! And I'm crap at making friends."

She lifted her brows in amusement. "Yeah? That's not what the other recruits say."

I squirmed. Was that true? Maybe it was, and I'd been too dense to see it. Crazy *and* stupid, that was me.

"I'm sorry," I said. "I shouldn't have been jealous of Flash or your work with the Neans. I wanted to be worthy of having a beautiful and special woman at my side. I wanted to look normal so you'd be proud of me. But Sammie, as hard as I try, I can't fake it. I'll never be normal. I don't want to embarrass you because I'm crazy."

Sammie dabbed a finger at the corner of her eye. "Oh, River, I'm so proud of you. You made a mistake, and you moved Heaven and Earth to fix it. That's what matters. You don't need to be normal to earn my love. You have it just as you are."

My eyes watered. My lips trembled. "How long are you here?"

"Just a few hours. The Sacred Leader dropped off some acolytes to work with Doc. He's trying to help the super-talents. We're finally becoming friends with the Neans. Isn't it exciting?"

I blinked a couple of times and thought about what she'd said. I'd earned her love by being exactly who I was. If I was going to marry Sammie, I had to be proud of what she did, too. I had to let her go away to do important things in order to keep her.

I smiled and nodded. "You'll be the best human ambassador to the Neans ever. And their best friend, too."

She beamed. "I have to go. I have some things to pack and reports to file. I'll be back in two weeks. I'll see you then."

Sammie gave me a peck on the cheek and a long, warm hug. Then she hurried away along the hall.

I watched until she disappeared into an office, my fingers on the tingly spot where she'd kissed me. Two weeks would feel like a lifetime, but she'd be back. I'd be waiting.

I stepped through the doors and strolled across the quad to the hospital ward, mindless of the drizzle. My inner warmth gradually faded. It was time to come out of hiding and make my apologies to Doc.

I slipped upstairs and inside the ward but went no farther. Half way down the right wall, Doc and Hannah watched while His High Muckymuck glowed like the sun near Hannah's mother. A weathered priest and two young acolytes looked on from the side of the bed, joining their voices and their power with their leader's.

Tears streamed down Hannah's cheeks. Her hands covered her mouth, and her whole body shook with relief as her mother changed before her eyes. The woman's improved color and stronger respiration were obvious even from my position far across the room.

Hope had erased the fatigue from Doc's face. Warmth and love and happiness filled the entire ward. The other mad super-talents lay at peace, no nightmares drifting over their beds. Tears pricked at my eyes, and I eased out the door.

In the hallway, I rocked, my courage to face Doc ebbing. He was having a great moment. This wasn't the time to remind him of my betrayal. Maybe tomorrow... or the next day.

I'd taken two steps when the door squeaked behind me.

"River," Doc said in a low voice. "I thought that was you. The Sacred Leader is coming out after he rests a moment. Best if you're not around. Let's go to my office."

He walked to the stairs and started to climb. I followed like a condemned man on the way to the gallows. When we reached his office, he motioned me to take one of his comfortable chairs while he sat behind his desk. His warm brown eyes saw all the way to my terrible, tainted soul.

"I'm sorry," I burbled. "I never believed you were a spy. I needed to find the real one, and I didn't know how to do it, so I agreed to take a job with the feds. If I'd known the trouble I'd get you in—"

Doc rubbed a finger on the edge of his desk and let the silence stretch. I squirmed in my chair and wiped my palms on my pants.

"The Sacred Leader admitted that you convinced him to provide aid for the super-talents in exchange for training his acolytes."

"Sammie said we needed to be friends with the Neans, not just partners. Friends help one another. They need our kind of medicine, and the super-talents need theirs. It seemed like a win for everyone." I studied my hands. "And I thought if I got help for the super-talents, you'd know I was really sorry."

"You're asking for me to forgive you in exchange for helping those I couldn't?"

I sank lower. "Yes, sir."

Doc eased back in his chair. "The recruits who went to the zombie dimension have all asked for counseling, although none of them want to talk when we meet, at least not yet. They say they're your friends, and that they did what you asked. What did you ask from them?"

I hadn't expected his question and struggled to answer. "I told them to find their worst nightmares, and they did."

Doc nodded, thoughtful. "You ask a lot of your friends, River."

I wanted to say I hadn't realized they were my friends, that none of us, least of all me, had any choice. It simply had to be done. Then I wondered whether he meant the recruits or himself. Were he and I still friends?

"If you're really their friend, you'll talk to them about it. You've shared an experience that they're struggling with. They need to process it to heal."

Just the thought of what he asked made me short of breath. But I'd learned that friends helped friends, no matter the cost. I nodded.

"Now it's my turn to apologize," Doc said. "I've been so busy with the super-talents that I've neglected my responsibilities to you. If you're interested, we can try medications that may alleviate some of your schizophrenia symptoms and make your daily life easier. It's completely up to you whether you choose treatment."

I didn't know what to say. I'd read everything I could about my condition. Treatment wasn't always successful, and the drugs had side effects. But maybe it was worth a shot.

"Okay, let's try."

39

"River Madden!"

I jerked in my sneakers and drew my attention away from the patterns the soap bubbles made as they popped in the bucket at my feet. The overhead light sang *Sixteen Tons*, off-key. The air in the basement maintenance room reeked of chemicals.

The latest treatment regime wasn't doing much to tamp down my schizophrenia symptoms. Doc said we needed to give it more time, maybe adjust the dose. I wasn't worried. My new job didn't depend on me being completely sane. As long as I got the work done, no one would fire me.

My thrift-shop jeans were uncomfortably damp from filling the bucket at the too-tall sink in the corner. I hoped the cleaning agent I'd spilled wouldn't cause bleached spots on my second-hand flannel shirt. I would have worn my official DPS coveralls, but the supply clerk cut me off after I ruined my third pair in a week. I hadn't worked up the courage to ask Col. Juarez for more.

Beside me, Flash stifled a snigger. It wasn't him shouting my name.

The grizzled old janitor glowered at me, hands on hips. "How Col. Juarez thinks a young whippersnapper like you can look after this whole facility with just this delinquent for help is beyond me."

He shuffled closer and snatched the mop from my hand. The smell of stale cigarettes washed over me. I coughed and held my breath.

"Now pay attention while I show you the proper way to change a mop head. After all, I retire in a few days, and then who's goin' to bail you out when you mess things up?"

The faces of my friends sprang to mind. Doc and Sammie. Pete, JR, Veronica, Hannah, and Mr. Lee. Even Dodo. If I needed help, I knew exactly who to ask.

And tonight, I'd go on a *real* first date with Sammie. She knew a cozy place with candles on the tables. We'd celebrate my new job. I'd be the best darn DPS janitor. *Ever.*

Calculated Risk

K S Ferguson

Rafe McTavish, charming self-made businessman, owns the most successful private security firm in the galaxy. Estranged from his family since his wife's bloody suicide fourteen years earlier, he's nevertheless honor-bound to find out why his brother-in-law, CEO of the mega-corporation EcoMech, has placed his reputation and the company's future in jeopardy by purchasing a dilapidated deep-space mining station.

Kama Bhatia, outlaw computer hacker and corporate spy, works for socialistic non-profit corporation Oasis, in opposition to the ruthless mega-corporations that control society. She has a mission of her own at the mining station: retrieve a secret document accidentally leaked to the station manager—before he can sell it to Oasis' rivals. If she fails, Oasis loses its best hope to rescue the masses from under the iron boot of the mega-corporations.

But at the station, the crooked manager is missing, and the locals are far from friendly. Rafe takes a savage beating from miners who blame him and his corporate employers for fraud perpetrated against them. His safety relies on Kama, an ally no fonder of corporate executives than he is of criminals. With their own lives and the welfare of millions at stake, can they put aside their mutual attraction and distrust to unravel fraud, blackmail, and murder before the tide of violence overtakes them?

For more information, visit http://www.ksferguson.net/calculated-risk.html.

No Place Like Hell

K S Ferguson

California, 1968. Nicky Demasi, the first woman patrol officer on the Solaris City Police Department, is desperate to prove to her hidebound superiors that a woman can do the job. Shut out of the investigation of a gruesome ritualistic murder, Nicky is obsessed with catching Kasker Sleeth, the charismatic hippie she found standing over the body.

But Sleeth isn't what he seems. He's the hellhound, an ancient creature of the Underworld temporarily clothed in human flesh. His mission is to retrieve an escaped damned soul in any way and at any cost—and Nicky is an impediment to his hunt.

As more victims fall, Nicky must decide what she believes, and whether she can risk going outside the law to stop a killer bent on unleashing Hell.

For more information, visit http://www.ksferguson.net/no-place-like-hell.html.